# HIS END GAME

## RB HILLIARD

Copyright © RB Hilliard, 2017

Edited by Christian Brose

Proofread by Joanne Thompson

Formatted by CP Smith

Cover design by Tania Marinaro – Libros Evolution

Cover model – Lisa Capps

# DEDICATION

This book is for Christian - my end game.

# HIS END GAME

# CHAPTER ONE

Max McLellan appeared on my radar the very first day of my freshman year in high school. I was standing at my locker wondering how I was going to get all of my homework done and cook dinner for my aunt later that night, when I felt an elbow in my ribs.

"I'm ignoring you," I told my best friend, Piper. She'd been blatantly trolling the halls for cute boys for the past thirty minutes, and I was having trouble organizing my locker while listening to her never-ending commentary. Piper O'Connell and I had been best friends since fourth grade, when she moved to Charlotte from Texas. With a head full of strawberry blonde hair and a smattering of freckles across her nose and cheeks, she was extremely loud, very direct, and the polar opposite of me. I loved her with all of my heart, but sometimes she was exhausting.

*Like right now.*

"Oh my," I heard her say. "Ellie, you're so gonna want to see this."

Pulling my head out of my locker, I glanced at what held her attention. A group of guys was sauntering down the hall toward us. I rolled my eyes and was about to resume organizing when I spotted him. He had on black biker boots that were partially concealed under his faded denim jeans. A black T-shirt hugged him in all the right places. From what I could see, he had collar-length black hair, but since it was peeking out from under a baseball cap turned backwards, I wasn't able to get the complete picture. Naturally tan, his slightly bearded face was flawless. I stood there drinking in all six plus feet of this man-looking boy and was disappointed I couldn't see his eyes behind his reflective sunglasses.

*What color are your eyes, beautiful boy? I really want to know…*

He was flanked on all sides by crazy hot guys.

"It's raining men" popped into my head, and I tried not to laugh. Before breaking out into song and dance, which was way more Piper's style than mine, the girl standing next to us chimed in.

"Beautiful, aren't they? It's a shame they're off limits."

"Nothing is off limits," Piper replied in a challenging tone.

"Those boys are," the girl insisted. "They go for hot older girls who put out."

"I put out," Piper declared, clearly offended. This made me laugh.

"Trust me, you do not qualify. Those boys would eat you up and spit you out."

*Wow, she's really serious. Maybe Piper should back off.*

Not at all interested in sharing my sexual status, or lack thereof, I nodded my head in biker boy's direction and asked, "Who's the one in the middle?"

"*That-*" she stressed- "is Max McLellan. He's tough, but fun to look at."

I was about to ask what she meant when the first bell rang.

*Crap!* I hadn't finished organizing my locker.

"I'll call RJ tonight and get the scoop," Piper said.

Richard James, better known as RJ, was one of Piper's big brothers. He was now a freshman in college. Even though he'd spent his last two years of high school away at boarding school, he still knew everyone, and was our official go-to guy for information.

As it turned out, the only thing RJ knew about Max was that he could kick some serious ass, was a chick magnet, and liked older girls.

*Thanks for nothing, RJ.*

Throughout ninth and tenth grade, I would see Max and his friends in the halls. They were enjoyable to watch and provided hours of fodder for my daydreams. Day in and day out I watched him. He was always either surrounded by his friends or a mass of girls. Every now and then I would catch him looking my way, at least that's what I told myself and, each time it happened, it made my day. Yes, I was pathetic.

The summer before my junior year, my life took a turn for the worse. It was a Thursday and I had the day off from Providence, the café where I waited tables. I had my black, polka-dotted, skimpy bikini on as I was going to lie out in my backyard. Carrying my iPod in one hand and my iced tea in the other, I was headed out the door when my phone rang. Seeing Piper's name on the Caller ID, I hit the Talk button, and said, "Put on your skimpiest bikini and come lay out with me." I heard her sniffle and instantly knew something was wrong.

"Honey, what's wrong?"

"Mom and Dad are making me go away to school next year,"

she tearfully responded. "They just told me we are leaving in a few days to visit schools and I'll be going off this coming year. They won't listen to me, El. They don't care that I don't want to leave. They just want me out of the house so they can travel and party without the hassle of having to deal with me."

*Travel and party? Really?*

Richard and Marie O'Connell were two of the nicest people on the planet. They treated me like their own child, and I dearly loved them. Coming from old money, they'd both been raised in boarding school families, where all of the kids went off to school in ninth grade. I was surprised they'd let RJ, Rex, and Piper stay at home through their sophomore year. I did not, however, voice this out loud. I was heartbroken. I was losing my best friend for our last two years of high school.

Three days later, I said goodbye to a depressed Piper and a morose-looking Richard and Marie. By the time Piper returned a week later, she'd chosen a school in Virginia and it was a done deal.

Piper leaving weighed heavily on my heart. I didn't want her to go away. I didn't want to be left alone with my aunt. For as long as I could remember, Piper and her family had been my buffer. They were who I ran to when I couldn't take the criticism or negativity from home any longer. Take them away and I was… alone. The only saving grace was my job at Providence.

My aunt demanded that I get a job the summer before my freshman year in high school. She believed working would keep me out of trouble. Piper's mom thought this was silly, but being her awesome motherly self, she introduced me to her friend, Amy, who owned Providence. Not only was Amy laid back and extremely cool, but she let me pick up as many shifts as I wanted, whenever I wanted. Two years later, I held the title of the longest lasting employee.

The week before the start of my junior year, I was working when a girl about my age came strutting into the café drenched from head to toe. The confident way she walked reminded me of Piper, who'd been gone for over a week. It had been a long, lonely, rainy week without her. Shaking off my nostalgia, I sat the wet girl in my section and, since she was my only customer at the time, proceeded to chat with her.

"Looks crazy out there," I said, nodding my head toward the park. "What can I get for you?"

"A beer?" she asked, winking at me. I immediately liked her.

"How about a Coke?" I smiled.

I discovered her name was Josselyn Speilman but she preferred Joss. Like me, Joss was about to turn seventeen and was going to Myers Park High School. Her family had recently moved to Charlotte from Washington DC. I watched her ring out her gorgeous curly, white-blonde hair and felt a stab of envy. I couldn't help but notice the contrast between the two of us. She was the all- American girl with perfect hair and big blue eyes. Next to my long, blondish brown hair and odd shaped golden eyes, she looked like a fairy. We talked for a while about the upcoming year before I had to break away and take other orders.

As I was cashing out a customer, I felt a tap on my shoulder.

"I have to get going but wanted to give you my phone number, in case you ever want to talk or hang out," Joss said.

I walked her to the door, exchanged numbers, and said goodbye. For the first time since hearing that Piper was leaving, I found myself looking forward to something.

Piper decided not to come home for Thanksgiving, which I took personally. I'd filled every second of every day since the first day of school with homework and work. The only enjoyment I allowed myself time for was watching Max in the halls, talking to Piper on the phone, listening to music and reading. I had been counting the days until Thanksgiving break and seeing Piper again. When she told me she was spending the week with a friend from school, it really shook me.

The first few days of break, I moped around. Then, not being able to stand the silence any longer, I picked up the phone and dialed Joss. It wasn't that I didn't have other friends. I did. I just wasn't interested in who was getting cheated on, screwed, or dumped. I liked boys, a lot. I just didn't plan my life around them. I'd seen Joss in the halls at school and, like me, she seemed a little lost. I hadn't made an effort to reach out and felt it was way past time, so I called her up and invited her over.

It turned out Joss was a scary movie addict. In fact, she brought over a few of her favorite horror flicks for us to watch. I greatly disliked scary movies and practically hid under the sofa the whole time.

We'd just finished watching *A Nightmare on Elm Street* and were popping popcorn before watching *Halloween,* when she asked the dreaded question everyone eventually got around to asking me. "Is it too personal or can I ask you why you live with your aunt and not your parents?" It wasn't that I minded talking about it. It was the look of pity I received after telling my story that got to me. "I'm sorry," she said. "That was rude of me to ask."

"No, it's fine. It's just that every time I tell someone, they look at me different, and I really hate that."

"Hey," she said, "trust me when I say that your story can't be much worse than mine."

*Wanna bet?*

Internally sighing, I began to explain, "My parents slept together in high school and...oops-" I pointed to myself - "conceived me." It was hard explaining my mom's slutty tendencies, so I just gave it to her short and sweet. "Supposedly, my mom really got around. When she told my dad she was pregnant, he offered to pay for an abortion, but only because he couldn't deny he'd taken a turn on her merry-go-round and there was a chance I could be his kid. He got really angry when she told him she was having me and, before I was even born, he left town. About a month before my birth, she decided she didn't want to be tied down by a kid after all, so she began adoption procedures. That's when Aunt Elizabeth, my dad's older sister, stepped in and stopped her."

"So, your mom had you and gave you to your aunt?" she asked.

"Yes, but she made my aunt go through regular adoption procedures, because she needed the money." *Something my aunt reminds me of regularly.*

"What about your grandparents?"

"Oh, they're all long gone. My mom's parents were around some when I was little, but I don't remember them. My dad's parents died before I was even born."

"Do you mind me asking what happened to your mom?"

"She took off for California right after I was born."

"Have you ever tried to find her?"

"No, she was killed in a car accident when I was four."

"God, Ellie, I'm sorry."

"Don't be," I shrugged. "It's not like I knew her. It's hard to feel something for someone you've never met."

"And your dad?"

"Who knows?" I shrugged. "I've only seen pictures of him from when he was in high school. He took off and never came back. I'm his daughter, though, that's for sure."

"Oh?"

"I look just like him."

"So your aunt named you Ellie?"

"Ellison Elizabeth Davis."

"I like it," she said, smiling.

Talking to Joss turned out to be just like talking to Piper, easy and comfortable. Changing the subject, I asked about her family. She told me she was the only child of parents who never wanted kids.

*Yes, they actually told her this.*

Primarily having been raised by nannies her whole life, she felt like her parents were more like housemates. They were incredibly wealthy and traveled all the time, leaving her at home alone or with housekeepers. This made my aunt look like freaking Mary Poppins.

I think because neither of us really had a sense of family or a lot of love in our lives, Joss and I related to each other. Regardless of her crappy upbringing, she'd turned out well and I was glad I'd made a new friend.

# CHAPTER TWO

The morning of my seventeenth birthday started like any other day. I woke up and made my way downstairs for my usual Pop-Tarts or frozen waffles. I was floored to find a plate of piping hot eggs and crispy bacon waiting on the table for me. In the middle of looking around to make sure I wasn't in my next door neighbor's house, my aunt came walking out of her office.

"Happy Birthday, Ellison."

I hated when she called me Ellison and instantly wanted to correct her, but didn't want to start a fight. She seemed to be trying, so I let it go. "Thanks," I said.

"Here." She held out her hand. I wondered if I should shake it when she produced a set of keys. "The time has come," she cryptically announced.

My aunt had never been one for words. As a hospital accountant, she was extremely analytical and ultra-critical. I stood there waiting for the rest of her sentence. After a minute or so I finally gave in and asked, "Time fooooooor?"

"You to have more responsibility."

I tried not to flinch. *Really?* From where I was standing, I had plenty of responsibility. In fact, that's all I had. I did all of the grocery shopping, cooking, and cleaning. On top of that, I was expected to maintain a perfect grade point average.

*What more responsibility can the woman possibly give me?*

It turned out that my aunt had gone out and bought herself a brand new Cadillac. My new responsibility was the keys to her crappy, old, beat up diesel Volkswagen Rabbit that looked like it had barely survived the Dark Ages. At this point, however, a car was a car. This meant I would no longer have to bum rides from all of my friends.

*Thank you, Aunt Elizabeth!*

My aunt was a strict believer in tough love, so the fact that she'd given me a birthday present at all was huge. Of course, not feeling the need to overextend herself, she handed it to me with the gas tank empty. On my way to Joss's house for cake, I stopped off at the corner station to fill up. Thank goodness one of the two places in the county that still sold diesel gas was right by my house. I was standing at the pump, thinking about how I could now drive to work instead of walk, when something across the parking lot caught my eye.

*Max McLellan.*

He had on his usual worn, faded jeans, tight fitting tee, and motorcycle boots. He was standing, foot propped up on the runner of his vintage Bronco, talking on his cell phone. Yes, I knew the exact make and model of Max McLellan's vehicle. *Just call me a stalker.*

Not wanting him to see me, I hurried inside to pay the cashier. Still in hurry mode, I flung open the door to leave and smacked right into him. "Shit!" I screamed, and promptly covered my mouth with both hands. *Of course, the first words I ever speak to Max McLellan can't be Hi or How's it going? Nope, it has to be a word used for excrement. Nice.*

"You okay?" he asked, looking down at me. *Wow, he looks good up close and...I knew he was tall, but he's really tall.* Being a whopping five feet eight inches tall, it was rare that I looked up at anyone. So, needless to say, finding that Max was that much taller than me, made me very happy. The corners of his mouth slowly turned up, forming a heart-stopping smile. *His eyes were blue with green flecks in them and, oh my, are those...dimples? How did I not know he had dimples?*

Thinking about all that was Max, I managed to nod and say, "Uh huh."

"Nice ride." His eyes twinkled as he glanced over at my crappy car. "I didn't know they still made those in diesel."

Of course, being shy and at that moment floored that Max McLellan was standing there speaking to me, I blurted, "You know, you really shouldn't talk on the phone while pumping gas, or you could blow the station up, and for goodness sake, whatever you do, do *not* light up a cigarette." The second I said it, I wanted to take it back. I especially wanted to take it back when I saw his lips quirk with obvious amusement. *Yes, Max McLellan is now trying not to laugh at stupid Ellie Davis.*

"I'll keep that in mind when I fill up in the future." He smiled and winked when he said this. I could feel my face flaming at this point and wanted to just get in my crap-heap car and go. "And, just so you know, I don't smoke," he added, his sexy blue eyes taking me in.

"Okay, uh, good to know. Well, guess I'll see you around." I made myself turn away before I said or did something really stupid.

"Hold up." I felt his hand on my arm.

"Yes?" I tried not to gasp at the fact he was touching me.

"I just wanted to say thanks for the advice on...uh... car safety." He was now unabashedly grinning at me.

*I am such an idiot.*

"I'm going now." I squeezed out breathlessly, sure that the color of my face was showing the degree of my embarrassment.

"Okay, Ellison, maybe I'll see you around?" *Oh my God, he actually knows my name.*

The timber of his voice resonated through my body. It was deep and rich and, like a favorite song, was something I wanted to hear over and over again. Bypassing Joss's house, I drove back home thinking about how Max McLellan knew my name. I was so enthralled with the experience that I even forgot to correct him when he called me Ellison. I hated my first name with a passion. Probably because my aunt only used it when she was ordering me to do something or when I was in trouble. I had to admit, I kind of liked it when Max said it, though. That was definitely something to ponder over later.

The moment I got home I headed straight to my bedroom. After tossing the keys on the desk, I flopped down on my bed and immediately called Piper. Piper, of course, didn't care that I'd finally had an actual conversation with my dream guy. No, she was more worried about what she deemed as my debatable 'stalker obsession' with Max. In total Piper-like fashion, she hung up with me and immediately phoned her brother RJ to discuss my obsessive behavior. RJ called his ex-girlfriend, Linda, who was a senior in Max's class, to get the scoop. Piper then called me back to inform me that Max was currently involved with a cheerleader named Jennifer Tilson. Being that I knew pretty much everything there was to know about Max McLellan, I was well aware of his so-called relationship with Jennifer. RJ also strongly suggested I back off. *Back off of what? I haven't done anything.* He said that Jennifer and her senior friends were a bunch of man-eating bitches and could really cause me problems. This, too, was not news to me as I'd already been warned on more than one occasion to keep my eyes to myself, which I found greatly amusing. Max was way out of my league. That they would find me, a mere nobody, remotely threatening…was funny. I found it ironic that a guy like Max was dating a cheerleader- A musician or an artist, maybe, but a rah-rah cheerleader? - *Not so much.*

Piper was worried about me, but instead of criticizing, she just told me to be careful and to make sure I took care of myself and my heart. She was good like that. She would charge in and get her heart shattered into a million pieces, but would do anything and everything to protect mine.

I was well aware of Max before the gas station incident. After all, he was my fantasy guy. I couldn't help but pay attention to what he was wearing or who he was with when he passed by my locker. Watching Max and his trail of girls was fun and helped to pass the time. After running into him that day at the gas station, however, something felt… different. It was as if he was now aware of *me*. He suddenly seemed to be everywhere. Had he always been everywhere and I just didn't realize it, or was this new? Whereas before, I didn't exist, I was now on his radar. I knew this because I could now *feel* his eyes on me. Every now and then I would catch him watching me. Whenever this happened, his eyes would soften and his mouth would quirk, as if we shared a secret. It always happened so fast that it made me wonder if I'd imagined it. Piper said he was probably having gas pains, because everyone knew Max didn't do soft and definitely didn't do innocent.

I wouldn't call myself completely innocent per se, as I'd kissed my fair share of boys. I was, however, still 'intact,' but only because I'd not found the right guy…yet. Yes, I was aware I was probably the only eleventh-grade virgin alive, but because my mom had given it up so easily, which had resulted in such extreme consequences, I was extra careful. Plus, I knew that every time I walked out the door, my aunt held her breath, wondering if this was going to be the moment that, like my dad, I screwed it all up. Piper was no help whatsoever. She had a very liberal view about sex and had been pressuring me to give up my virginity since what seemed like kindergarten. The truth was I was afraid to disappoint or be disappointed. I didn't want to experience the walk of shame or to hear how I rated on a scale of one to ten the day after. I wanted to be loved like the women in my favorite books and movies. I decided the best thing for me to do was to wait and hope the right guy would someday come along.

The beginning of February, Piper called and told me she was coming home for the weekend to celebrate her oldest brother, Rex's, birthday. I couldn't wait. I hadn't seen her since Christmas and, because of school and work, had only talked to her a handful of times. To have her home, even if it was just for two days, was exactly what I needed.

Piper flew in on a Friday afternoon and dropped by school early to surprise me and catch up with her old teachers and friends. Within the first half hour of being home, she'd managed to get us invited to a coveted senior party happening that night. I wondered if Max would be there.

After school, Joss drove us over to Piper's house to get ready. We spent over an hour lying on her bed, comparing high school stories, and talking about boys. Piper was in the middle of telling us about some twenty-two-year-old guy she'd kissed in order to score free tickets to a concert, when I spotted her iPod sticking out of her purse. Grabbing it, I scanned her play list. Once I found the song I wanted, I placed it on her iPod dock and pushed play. As Amy Lee of Evanescence started singing, I let out a huge sigh. "Bring Me to Life" was a hauntingly beautiful song, and I absolutely loved it.

"I want to talk to you about something," Piper said, turning Amy down.

"Hey," I complained.

"Do you hear me?" she asked.

"You're kind of hard to miss," I snapped, causing Joss to snort with humor.

"Don't you think you've taken this whole virginity thing a little too far?"

"What virginity thing?" Joss raised an eyebrow in question.

"Mine," I informed her. "Piper's obsessed with it."

Joss's mouth dropped in shock. "You're still a virgin?"

"Yep, as pure as the driven snow," I sarcastically replied.

"Ellison," Piper said in her most sympathetic voice, one I'd heard a thousand times before and greatly disliked, "I keep telling you to just get it over with. Yes, it hurts the first time, but that sets you up for all of the great times after."

"Gee, Piper, you sound like you're doing a PSA. Try it. It's painful as hell, you'll bleed for a day and won't sit down for a week, but in the end…it's all worth it!" Joss said in a deep voice.

"Good one," I snorted with laughter. Joss held up her hand. As I high-fived her, I shot Piper a dirty look. "You know why I don't sleep around." It took me a year to trust Piper enough to tell her about my family dynamic, or lack thereof. She, of all people, knew why I was still a virgin.

"What exactly are you waiting for?" Joss asked.

"Max," Piper sweetly told her.

*I wish.*

"No, not Max," I hastily clarified. "Plus, we all know that

would *never* happen, because he is way out of my league. He goes for cheerleaders and girls with experience and, since I am neither of those….. Look, you both know what happened between my parents. I simply refuse to end up like my mom."

"Hey," Joss said, squeezing my hand. "You are so much better than that or any of those girls, which, by the way, makes you way too good for the likes of Max McLellan, okay? I say, no matter what, do what's best for you. The right guy will come along."

"When that time comes, I have one word for you," Piper chimed in, "Con-dom."

*Whatever,* I thought.

When we arrived at Matt's house that night, I could tell by the number of cars down the street that the party had been going on for a while. It was unseasonably cool weather for mid-September in Charlotte. I was glad I had on my raspberry jewel-neck velour sweater and my black jeans. I was going to wear a skirt but decided at the last second not to. Piper, who was wearing a short sleeve top and an obscenely short skirt, was already complaining about frostbite.

We could hear Maroon 5's "She Will be Loved" blaring from halfway down the block where we parked the car. A tall, somewhat attractive guy was standing at the front door greeting everyone.

"Hi Matt! Thanks for inviting us. These are my friends, Ellie and Joss," Piper said.

"Come on in." Matt handed us each a beer and then proceeded to show us around the house. It was an amazing spread with six bedrooms and a huge kitchen that opened up into an enormous great room. I noticed there was even a large fire pit blazing out back.

"Holy shit, this house is amazing," Piper whispered after we lost Matt to the doorbell. I didn't disagree. The house was amazing, but I couldn't help but feel a bit claustrophobic. I hated big crowds, and it was wall-to-wall people from one end of the house to the other. Joss, who had come through the door with us, had already disappeared into the sweaty crowd of people.

"I'm going to look for Joss. Want to come with?" Piper asked.

Eyeballing the mass of bodies gyrating to the music, I said, "No, I think I'll hang here in the kitchen and then maybe go look at the fire in a few." There was no way in hell I was going back out into *that*. It was bad enough the first time.

"Okay," she hesitated, looking at me strangely. "You okay? I'll come find you in a bit and you can introduce me to all of the hot guys."

"Sure thing," I assured her, rolling my eyes. "I'll be fine right here."

So, off she went and there I stayed. After saying hello to a few people I recognized, I refilled my beer and headed outside to the pit. I should have known who I'd find there. Standing beside the fire, reflected in the light, stood Max with four of his friends and a flock of girls, *of course.* Dressed in all black, the boy was simply mesmerizing. His head was down and he seemed to be listening intently to something the guy next to him was saying. As if sensing someone watching him, he glanced up. Our eyes met, and I was completely and utterly captured in his stare. A palpable tension surged between us, an instant connection. From the way his eyes roamed over me, I was certain he felt it, too.

Jennifer, who was suctioned to his side, had on a cream colored see-through blouse. This wouldn't have been so bad except for the black push up bra underneath. Her mini skirt was so tight that I was surprised she could move in it and, by the look of the heels on her feet, she was in for a rough night. With his eyes still on me, Max leaned forward and said something in her ear. It must have been really funny because she suddenly threw her head back, dramatically jumped up and down, and made a rather obnoxious noise that sounded like the squeal of a dying pig. The pained expression on Max's face when she did this was priceless. Trying not to laugh, I turned my back to the fire and slowly counted to ten. After gathering myself, I turned back around. Max was still watching me and, by the amused expression on his face, he knew exactly what I was thinking.

*Crap!*

Dropping my eyes to my feet, I tried not to smile. When I looked back up, Jennifer had him by the hand and was steering him toward the house, *probably to have sex in a coat closet.* When they passed by me, I caught his scent and shivered.

*He smells like leather and spice.*

Feeling disappointed, I decided it was time to leave. As I started across the yard toward the back gate Piper appeared.

*Double crap!*

"E, what's wrong?" She grabbed my sleeve to slow me down.

"I think I should leave," I told her.

"Why? What happened?"

"Max was out here at the fire and so was Jennifer and…Oh, never mind." I shook my head. There was no way I could make her understand what I was feeling, so why bother?

"Well, honey, they *are* together," she murmured, as if telling me something I didn't already know.

"I know, but did you *see* her tonight? Why would he want someone like *that*?"

"Probably because all the guys say that even though she's a bitch and dresses like a ho, she's super limber and puts out in a variety of ways. Look-" she pulled me in and gave me a big hug - "he's not worth you being upset over. He's just an incredibly gorgeous asshole, and you are way too beautiful to want someone who would treat you like that. Now, it's high time you forget about Max. You need to have some fun, quit acting like Debbie Downer and stop taking everything so damn seriously. We are juniors, *in high school,* for Pete's sake!"

"I'm pretty much done here, Pi," I told her.

"Don't be, please? Come back inside with me. We'll grab a drink and try and find Joss. After that, if you still want to leave, I promise we'll go." Maybe she was right. Maybe it was time to let my childish fantasy of Max go...*maybe.*

Several beers later, we were standing in the kitchen when Piper pointed to a guy who was standing across the room from us. "That's Carter Andrews," she slurred. I kind of recognized him, but unlike Piper, I wasn't personally acquainted with all of the males in the entire high school. "He's cute and supposedly a wild man in bed," she informed. As soon as the words left her mouth, Carter's head shot up and his eyes landed on both of us.

"Nice Jedi mind trick," I whispered. We both giggled as we watched him approach.

"Piper," he purred, "Where have you been?"

"Away," she nonchalantly replied. "Carter, this is my best friend, Ellie. Ellie, this is Carter," she introduced. Carter was no Max, by all means, but with my beer goggles securely fastened and ready for lift-off, he was looking pretty good. *Fun with no strings, Ellie. You can do this,* I told myself.

Carter toothily smiled. "Ellie, nice to meet you. You are looking hot tonight." His left eye was wildly twitching and I was just about to ask him if he had something in it, when it hit me. *He's winking at me.*

I opened my mouth to thank him when Piper slapped him on the back and said, "And I thought my eye allergies were bad. I just discovered these new over-the-counter drops at the drugstore that work miracles. You might want to check them out." The confused look on Carter's face was beyond hilarious. Piper shot me a conspiratorial wink and I struggled not to spew my beer everywhere. If anyone could make me smile when my heart was hurting, it was definitely Piper. "Well, have fun, you guys. I see Kurt Greenfield over there and I'm so not letting this opportunity pass me by," she announced.

Kurt Greenfield was Max's all-time best friend. I watched Piper make her way across the room to where Kurt and Max were standing and couldn't help but compare the two. Where Max was all bronze skin, black hair, and blue eyes, Kurt was blond and pale with hazel eyes. Max was built like a fighter, whereas Kurt looked more like a distance runner.

Carter's fingers trailing down my arm brought me back to the moment.

"I haven't seen you around before. What year are you?" he asked.

"Oh, uh, I'm a junior, and you?"

"Senior…. So tell me sugar, where have you been? You are way too gorgeous to go unnoticed."

"Well, I haven't been to many parties this year," I shyly admitted.

"I guess tonight's my lucky night then," he hummed. I shivered when I felt his fingers trail down my back, and it wasn't in a good way. Even with a serious buzz I knew this guy was a bit of a tool, cute, but nevertheless a tool. It certainly didn't hurt that I was seeing two of him at the moment. When he asked if I wanted to check out the upstairs with him, the earlier conversation I'd had with Piper flashed through my mind. Not wanting to be a Debbie Downer anymore, I said, "Sure."

# CHAPTER THREE

We were standing at the bottom of the stairs waiting for people to pass by when I felt a chill run down my spine. I suddenly had the feeling I was being watched. Halfway up the stairs, I glanced back over my shoulder and around the room. *Huh…Nothing there*….Shrugging it off, I headed the rest of the way up.

Carter directed me to a large bedroom at the top of the stairs. By the time he closed the door, I was beginning to feel nervous. My liquid courage was faltering, and I was starting to second-guess my decision to be alone with a guy who I really didn't know.

He danced his way over to the iPod dock. "How about we turn on some music while we hang out?" he suggested.

"Sure," I answered through my laughter. If anything, this guy was definitely amusing. When "Dirty Little Secret" started playing, I was no longer amused. Don't get me wrong, I liked The All American Rejects, but this song at this moment in time was a complete mood kill. As I stood there trying to figure out how to nicely ask him to change the song, he skipped back across the room and circled around behind me. *Okay, so maybe the guy is a little strange. I can do strange. After all, Piper is my best friend and she's about as strange as it gets.*

"Ellie," he loudly moaned, before pressing his lips to my ear. I nearly jumped out of my skin. As I turned my head to get away from his hot breath, I caught him leering down at my chest. His eyes cut to me and he grinned. "Has anyone ever told you what an incredible rack you have?"

*Nice.*

"Look, uh... Carter, I don't normally do th-this kind of th-thing," I stammered.

"Hmmmm…Innocent. I see how you like to play it. That's cool. I'll play this *any* way you want." His condescending tone shot red flags straight to my beer-soaked brain. *How I like to play it?* As I was busy trying to figure out what he meant by this, he gripped me from behind and inserted his tongue in my ear. *Ewwww.* Shivering in disgust, I took a step forward and disengaged myself from his hold. "You smell gooood," he hummed and pulled me back against his chest. "Like sex on a stick." His breath stunk like sour Fritos. Trying not to gag, I glanced longingly across the room at the door and wondered if I should try to make a run for it. Before I could decide, he spun me around. Caught off guard, I looked up into his eyes, and my stomach lurched when I saw the way he was looking at me. *This guy wants to hurt me.*

"I uh… need to go find Piper," I stammered, trying to pull away from him. "She's probably looking for me by now."

"Shhhh," he whispered, placing his finger across my lips. "I promise I'll be quick. I never planned on hanging out for long anyway." He grabbed my ass and started reeling me in. When I realized what he was doing, I reared back in protest. This made him mad, and he yanked me the rest of the way in. As I opened my mouth to protest, he shoved his tongue down my throat and began dry humping my left thigh.

*Time to leave, Ellie.* Surprised by his strength, grossed out by his breath, and feeling utterly helpless, I mentally scrambled for a way out of the situation I'd not-so-happily landed myself in. "Stop Carter," I wheezed. "You are squishing me and I can't breathe." I pushed at his chest, hoping he would let me go. "I'm not good with this anymore and want to leave, now."

"Not until you pay the piper," he sang and rammed his smelly Fritos-tongue back down my throat.

By this point I was completely sober and officially *done*. This was not what I had in mind for this evening. I'd been rejected by Max, assaulted by Carter, was now scared and pissed off, and needed to get the hell out of here. So doing what any smart girl would do, I bit down on his tongue… hard. This got me a mouth full of blood *and* a backhand to the face. Completely taken off guard, I screamed out in pain. The throbbing in my cheek was excruciating and all I could think was…run.

I was halfway to the door and almost home free when I felt a blinding pain sear across the back of my head. As I was jerked backwards, I shouted out in fear. Somehow I managed to keep from falling. It took me a minute to realize what had happened. Carter, the giant a-hole, had me by my hair. My eyes smarted, but I was determined not to cry. I was completely trapped and wondering how in the world I got myself into this predicament, when I felt his sour breath waft across the back of my neck. My face and head were both pounding like crazy and all I wanted was to go home. I'd take my cranky aunt over this any day.

"Not smart, Ellie," he sang.

*What the hell is with this guy? Hi, my name is Carter. I'm a complete jerk who likes to dance and sing and assault innocent girls.*

Before I could get my next thought out, the door flew open and slammed against the wall with a loud bang. My eyes widened in surprise as a really pissed-off-looking Max stormed in, followed by two of his friends.

*Thank God.*

Carter immediately released my hair. Before I could say anything, Max yanked him away from me and was dragging him across the room.

"Hold him," he commanded. Two sets of arms pinned Carter to the floor.

"You like hitting girls, you sick fuck?" Max growled as he pounded his fist into Carter's face. Blood from Carter's nose shot across the floor. "Tell me," Max ground out through clenched teeth, "Did she say no?" Carter, who was straining to break free, looked defiantly up at Max and smiled.

*Not smart.*

Max went wild. In between each punch, he shouted, "No… Means… No!"

Feeling slightly sick and fully vindicated, I said, "Max, please stop."

His hand froze midair and his eyes shot to mine. The look of concern on his face made my breath catch. "Are you okay?" he asked.

"I think so," I hesitantly replied as I rubbed my stinging cheek.

"Please tell me he didn't do anything else?" His eyes scanned over my body for any other damage.

I pointed to my face. "No, this is the worst of it." I tried to control my shaking voice, but failed miserably.

With that being said, Max slammed a groaning Carter on the floor like a sack of potatoes. "You just seriously fucked up," he growled. He then told his friends to take Carter out and leave him on the street. Slowly, he walked over to where I was standing. I could tell by the way he was clenching his jaw that he was having trouble reining it back in. This version of Max was both scary and…arousing. I wasn't quite sure what to do with the combination of feelings he evoked, so I just stood there staring at him. Scowling down at the bruise that was already forming, he lifted his hand and lightly stroked it across my cheek.

Letting out a sigh of relief, I said, "I don't think Carter will bother me again after that."

"Not if he knows what's good for him. I can't believe he hit you," he murmured. I was staring at the wall behind his head, too embarrassed to look him in the eye. "I think I would have killed him had you not asked me to stop," he continued. I felt his fingers drift from my lip to my chin. "Ellison," he whispered and then paused. I glanced up to see why he'd stopped talking and was trapped in his eyes. They were so beautiful and so troubled… for me. "Why were you in here alone with him?"

What could I say to this? *Nothing I would admit out loud, especially not to Max.* Feeling emotionally and physically drained, I dropped my forehead to his chest, wrapped both of my arms around his waist and burst into tears. He held me and, while stroking his hands soothingly up and down my back, softly whispered in my ear. It felt so right, and for a second, just a second, I pretended he was mine.

"Hey," he said, pulling me in. "You're gonna be okay, I promise." Staring up into his eyes, I believed him. His scent of leather and spice was an intoxicating balm, and his mouth…. *God, it was perfect.* I found my tongue unconsciously touching my swollen lip. His eyes dropped to my mouth, and he moaned. There was no better sound than Max McLellan moaning for me. It was something I would never forget. I fought the urge to lean up and kiss him, to touch my lips to his… just this once. He must have felt the pull, too, because I heard his breath hitch. His eyes devoured me as he leaned in - and I knew that I was about to get my wish - when suddenly Piper burst into the room. Kurt and Jennifer were fast on her heels. *Perfect timing, as usual, Piper.*

"What the hell happened?" she shrieked when she saw me.

"Why are you touching her?" Jennifer snarled at Max. Max and I both froze for a second and then carefully stepped back from each other.

Max narrowed his eyes at Jennifer. Then he leaned toward me and whispered, "Glad you're okay. If Carter so much as blinks in your direction, please find either Kurt or me and I promise we will take care of it, okay?"

Before nodding my consent, I searched his eyes to make sure he was serious. Once I was convinced it wasn't all a sick joke, I whispered, "Thanks for saving me."

His eyes softened as he reached out one more time and rubbed his finger over my swollen cheek. "Anytime," he murmured. Just his touch made me suck in my breath. I fought the urge to grab onto him and never let go.

"Did that pecker head hit you? Where is he? I am going to kill him!" Piper screeched and, like that, the moment was over.

"Later," Max said to the room, as he walked with Jennifer out the door.

I let out a shaky sigh of relief and found myself enveloped in Piper's arms.

"Oh, honey, I'm so sorry I introduced you to him," she said, her voice shaking.

I could tell she was on the verge of tears, so I told her I was all right but wanted to go home. I needed to process the night. It wasn't until much later that I wondered how Max knew I was upstairs with Carter. Had he followed me? I also wondered was it my imagination, or was he about to kiss me right before everyone barged in? It was a long time before sleep found me.

When I showed up to school on Monday, Carter, Max, and I were the topic of discussion in the halls. Carter, thank God, avoided me like the plague. He looked horrible and was being shunned for how he'd treated me. Max? Well, he was just one big disappointment. I didn't expect him to declare his undying love for me, but I also didn't expect him to ignore me and act like that night never happened. I could feel his eyes on me in the halls, but that was about it. I avoided Jennifer and her friends, because every time they saw me, they said or did something horrible. Max rescuing me had evidently tipped his nutso girlfriend right over the edge. After weeks of putting up with this, I was finally fed up.

"It happened weeks ago. It's done," I told Joss during lunch one day. "It happened to me, not her. All Max did was help me out of a jam. She's the one who needs to get over it and just... move the hell on." I threw up my hands in exasperation.

"She probably thinks you're the reason he dumped her."

*What?* "What do you mean, he dumped her?"

"Dumped her, broke up with her, kicked her ass to the curb. You know....dumped her," she repeated as she took a bite of her sandwich.

"Let me get this straight. You're telling me that for the past three weeks they haven't been together?"

She shook her head. "Nope."

"At all?" I squeaked.

"At all," she confirmed.

I narrowed my eyes at her. "Who told you this and why didn't you tell me?"

"Kurt, and because I just found out myself," she answered between chews.

"Greenfield?"

"No, Cobain," she deadpanned.

I snorted in amusement. When she didn't crack a smile, I

whispered, "Wait, he is still dead, isn't he?" For a split second I thought maybe she knew something I didn't about one of the greatest grunge Band lead singers of all time.

She rolled her eyes at me. "Jeez, Ellie, could you be any more gullible? Yes, Kurt Greenfield."

Ignoring her insulting tone, I asked, "Since when do you hang out with Kurt Greenfield?"

"Since last weekend," she nonchalantly replied. "Right before lunch he stopped by my locker and told me Max dumped Jennifer's ass like a bad habit the night of the party and wasn't going back, *ever*, no matter how much she begged him. Look, it's not like Max was exclusive with her or… well… really any girl for that matter."

I had no idea this had happened.

*Where the hell have I been for the past three weeks?*

"What do you mean, they weren't exclusive? They looked pretty exclusive to me."

"Max McLellan is the type of guy who won't do exclusive. Trust me on this."

This was just too much. It was then that it hit me. Max didn't want to kiss me that night. He was just being sweet. It was all in my head. *He isn't with Jennifer anymore. This is good. However, he certainly isn't making a move on me. This is not good. In fact, this is downright depressing.*

Needing to process what Joss had just told me, I cut out before last period and drove straight home to call Piper.

For weeks after my enlightening talk with Joss, I managed to somewhat effectively avoid Max. This, of course, was easier said than done. He was ridiculously hard not to look at. Since the night of Matt's party, he'd kept his distance. Though, strangely enough, he kept popping up everywhere. Every flipping time he caught my eye, which was a lot, he would give me a look. *Whatever.* I figured if I kept my head down, things would blow over and, eventually, everything would go back to normal. My normal, that is, where I would watch Max from afar as he prowled up and down the halls while fending off his bevy of beautiful bubbly bitches.

*Just shoot me.*

A week-to-the-day later, my plan to avoid Max blew up in my face. I was coming out of the gym as he was leaving the wrestling room when he spotted me across the hallway.

"Sorry," I mumbled to the poor person I almost fell over while trying to get away. I'd made it two steps when I felt a hand grab my arm.

"Ellison," Max said in that deep, crotch-tingling voice.

*Crap!*

Closing my eyes, I told myself to keep walking. Did I do this? Noooo. Instead, I stood there frozen in his clutches while waiting for everyone to pass by. When the coast was clear, I opened my mouth to speak, but before I could get the words out, I was being dragged down the hall and into the equipment closet.

"Max," I said, as he shut the door.

"Why are you ignoring me?" he asked.

I could tell by his tone that he was not happy, but was instantly distracted by his beautiful eyes and the yummy minty smell of his breath.

"What?" I asked, pretending not to understand his question.

"You're avoiding me, and I want to know why."

"Seriously?" I wondered if I'd heard him correctly.

"I can always tell what you're feeling by your facial expression." I shot him a skeptical look, and he quickly explained, "When you're having a bad day, you hide your head in a book. When it's a good day, you walk around with a cute little smile on your face. When you're frustrated, you purse your lips and your eyes get all squinty. When you won't even look at me, like you've been doing for the past three weeks, I know that something is wrong. Tell me what it is." I was shocked at how perceptive he was. Not to mention that he'd been watching me, possibly more than I'd been watching him. *Think about this later, Ellie.*

"I'm okay, Max," I told him.

"You're okay," he repeated.

"Yes. I'm good now. You rescued me and Carter hasn't said a word to me since that night, so you don't have to look out for me anymore. You're off the hook."

He dropped his forehead to mine. I tried not to gasp when I heard him say, "But what if I don't want to be?" Not knowing how to respond, I just stood there breathing him in. *Mint mixed with leather and spice. I wish he'd just kiss me.* As if reading my mind, he slowly slid his hand up the back of my neck. Right as I thought he was going in for the plunge, he grabbed my ponytail and, in a non-threatening but crazy hot move, he pulled my head back, using just enough pressure to get my attention and my eyes. "Answer me Ellison," he commanded.

*Oh my.*

"Look," I told him, trying to sound logical. "After what happened with Carter, it's normal to feel responsible. I'm just letting you know that I'm really okay."

"No, you're not," he replied.

"Yes…I…am," I enunciated each word, hoping it would sink in.

"Nope," he said, shaking his head.

This made me mad. I *was* okay. I didn't want him to feel obligated because of what Carter did or didn't do. I wanted him to want me because of....*me*. So, in true Ellie fashion, I blasted him. "You have done nothing but watch me in the halls for months now, Max. Then you come to my rescue, where I know…I know that we connected, and what do you do? You ignore me and act like it never happened. When I find out weeks later that you're no longer with your big, nasty leech of a girlfriend, I don't know what to think, except that you obviously don't want me." I took a deep breath, because I was completely out of air.

"Big nasty leech?" he asked, lips twitching.

"Really nasty," I said, trying not to smile.

His hand, still gripping my ponytail, slid down the back of my neck. "That's the problem, Ellison, I do want you. I probably shouldn't, but I do." Oh so gently, he drew me in and touched his lips to mine. When he stroked his tongue across my bottom lip, I moaned, floored by how good it felt. Taking this as a green light, he slowly dipped his tongue inside my mouth and touched it to mine. I was so caught up in the moment that I didn't even blink when I felt his hand steal under my shirt.

"You taste so sweet," he whispered against my mouth. Pulling me in closer, he turned his head to deepen the kiss when a door slammed down the hall. The sudden noise made me jump and I jerked back to reality.

Without thinking, I pulled away. "I'm so sorry," I said, touching my mouth. Before he could stop me, I slid out the door.

"Ellison!" I heard him call out, but I was already halfway down the hall.

*What in the hell just happened?*

# CHAPTER FOUR

Max's graduation ceremony was bittersweet.

I screwed up the day I ran out on him. What I didn't know was how badly it would affect me. I still saw him in the halls, but now, instead of watching me, he acted as if I wasn't there, like he didn't know me, and it was completely my fault. I knew this, but I didn't know how to make it right. By the time graduation came around, I was a neurotic head case. I had zero appetite and was having trouble sleeping through the night. Piper assured me that what I was feeling was normal.

*Nothing about this is normal,* I thought.

Piper was finally home from Virginia and I had her for the entire summer. She and Joss were standing on the grassy knoll with me watching the ceremony. Yes, they actually named it the grassy knoll. I held in my tears as I watched my beautiful Max and his friends graduate.

"You okay?" Piper asked, sliding her hand into mine.

"No. I keep wondering where I would be right now if I had stayed in the closet with him."

"You do know how that sounds?" she mused.

I threw her a small smile. "For some reason that song by Cinderella keeps running through my head."

"Cinderella, as in the 80's hair band?" Joss asked.

I couldn't help but laugh at the look on her face, so I explained. "When we were in fifth grade, Piper's brother, Rex, was going through a hair band phase."

"He would blast his music through the house and drive us all crazy," Piper added.

"He did this with Country and Rap too," I pointed out.

"He did, didn't he?" she laughed.

"Anyway, Abby Bartolo had just broken up with him and he was a mess about it."

"I'd completely forgotten about her. You were spending the night, and he played that Cinderella song "Don't Know What You Got", like a million times," Piper quietly murmured.

"Till it's Gone," I finished.

"Let's get out of here," Joss suggested. She and Piper slowly started walking down the embankment.

I stood there for a few more minutes watching. As soon as Max tossed his cap into the air, I turned away.

*Goodbye Max.*

Over lunch Joss invited us to her lake house for the weekend. Her parents, of course, were traveling. Assuming that this was a girls' only weekend, there was no need to glam up. This meant that I was wearing my usual cut-offs and tank top. The only reason I still had makeup on was because I'd worn it to graduation that morning.

Piper picked me up in her mom's beat up old Suburban that

we dubbed 'The Beast' and, with the windows down and Fall Out Boy on the radio, we were off. Finally, summer was here.

As we pulled into a driveway full of cars, Piper asked, "Are you sure this is the right place?"

"Yep," I answered after double-checking the address. "I thought Joss said she was expecting three people, four if her cousin showed up and please, tell me that is not a red Bronco with a black stripe down the side?" I pointed my finger in the direction of the truck parked at the front of the house.

"Sure looks like one. Hey," she turned her surprised eyes to me, "doesn't Max drive one of those?"

"Crap," I whispered.

"Okay…before you freak out, Negative Nelly, think about it. This could be a good thing. If Max is here with someone, we'll make an excuse and leave. If he's flying solo, you can finally get some closure or....not." She waggled her eyebrows suggestively.

I dropped my face to my hands and groaned, "Why is he here, Piper? I mean…seriously. I've been a ghost to him for weeks now. Do you think Joss forgot to tell him I was coming?"

"I say we go find out. It might not be what you think, so you should just go with it for now. Whatever you do, do not let him know he still affects you." Throwing both her hands in the air, she made devil horn signs with her fingers, screamed "Summertime baby!" and ran inside the house. Shaking my head, I waited a few extra minutes to catch my breath before following behind her.

*What a nut.*

As I followed the sound of voices through the house, my stomach lurched. I was afraid of what I was going to find. I spotted Joss first. She was standing across the kitchen with a strange look on her face. Next to her stood a guy I'd never seen before. He had shoulder-length, frizzy, blond hair and, for some reason, seemed familiar to me, but I couldn't place where I'd seen him. Tugging on his goatee, he bounced up and down on the tips of his toes. He kind of reminded me of a heavily caffeinated Garth from the movie *Wayne's World*, except with a goatee.

Last summer, Piper and I had to stay with her brother, RJ, after he had his wisdom teeth taken out. He made us watch *Wayne's World* four times in a row. Needless to say, I was now a huge fan of Mike Myers and Dana Carvey.

Slowly, I made my way to the kitchen doorway and immediately understood the look on Joss's face. Piper had cornered Kurt on the other side of the kitchen and was plastered, boobs to crotch, to the front of him. Kurt was staring across the kitchen at Joss with a guilty look on his face.

*I knew something was up with those two!*

I wanted to help Joss, but first I needed to see if Max was really here and, if he was, whether he was alone or with someone. Scanning the room, I found him leaning against the far counter with a beer in his hand. Of course he was staring straight at me.

*Busted.*

Trying to play it cool, I smiled and lifted my hand in a half wave.

He winked and gave me a two finger salute.

I felt my shoulders instantly relax when I saw he was alone.

Trying not to dwell on all that was Max, I announced my arrival. "Hi, guys."

The Garth look-alike jumped as if he had been shocked by a thousand amps of electricity and bolted straight toward me with his hand out.

"Hi, I'm Kurt's cousin, Harry Greenfield," he quickly said.

"Hi, Harry, I'm Ellie." I felt strange shaking his hand. Normally, I just nodded when I met someone new…especially when they were my own age. *Garth sure has nice manners,* I thought.

"Eelllieeee," he cooed. "I know who *you* are."

I glanced over at Max and then quickly back to Harry. "You do?"

"Harry," Max's deep voice warned.

"Whaaaaat? I *have* heard a lot about her," he replied.

"Be cool," Max warned again.

*Hmmmm, interesting…So Max has been talking about me and it seems that 'ole Harry is lacking a filter. I bet that if I stuck Piper on him, she could find out what Max has been saying about me.* I tore my eyes from Max long enough to see if Piper had managed to pry herself off of Kurt, yet. *Nope…still attached.* It was definitely time to intervene. The last thing I wanted was for my two best friends to be at odds with each other, especially over a guy.

"Piper, uh…can I talk to you for a minute, please?" I asked. I was trying not to be too obvious, but by the knowing looks on Max and Kurt's faces, I was clearly unsuccessful.

She rolled her eyes at me. "Sure, go for it."

"In private?" I stressed.

"Fine," she dramatically huffed.

"Third door on your right is an office you can use," Joss offered.

"Thanks." I gave her what I hoped was a sympathetic smile. As I passed by Kurt and Max, I oh-so-maturely stuck my tongue out at them. I could hear them laughing all the way down the hall.

I made sure to close the door behind me before laying into her. "That was not cool. You have got to back off."

"Back off? Moi?" she innocently asked.

Sometimes I really wanted to slap her. "I love you, Piper, but sometimes you are a serious pain in the ass. Kurt is into Joss and you know this. Joss is your friend. Whatever happened between you and Kurt that night at Matt's house was a one-time deal. So, before you ruin important friendships, you need to back off."

She gave me her vintage *screw you* look. When she realized I wasn't going to back down, she huffed. "Oh, all right. It's not like anything happened between us that night anyway. I was just messing with him, and it really pisses me off that Joss is hiding their relationship from her two best friends."

"You know how private Joss is. She'll tell us when she wants us to know, but you need to quit goading her. Did you by chance notice Kurt's cousin, Henry? He's cute in a 'boy next door' kind of way. Why don't you see what he's all about?" I not so subtly suggested. *Wow, I can't believe I actually said that with a straight face and didn't get struck by lightning.*

She made a funny noise. "Boy next door, my ass, he looks like a jacked-up Garth from *Wayne's World* and, thanks, but no thanks. I can get my own guy. By the way, what's up with you and luscious lips? He couldn't take his blue orbs off you in the kitchen."

"Nothing is up. I don't even know why he's here. I'm sure he has a million other places he'd rather be right now. For goodness sakes, he just graduated from high school. Shouldn't he be out partying or something?" My mouth was like a runaway train, and I needed to catch it before it did some serious damage.

Not about to let me off the hook, she said, "It's pretty obvious why he's here, Ellie, don't you think?"

Piper prowled around the room. When she settled behind the huge antique-looking desk, I took a cleansing breath and answered. "Nothing is obvious with Max, Piper. It never has been."

"Well, then you are blind, but I've always known this."

"What is that supposed to mean?"

I could see she was gearing up for a fight. Normally when this happened, I appeased her by agreeing with whatever she had to say, but this was Max we were talking about.

"What that means is that you don't see yourself the way

everyone else does. You never have and because your aunt is a critical old biddy who never told you how out of this world beautiful you are, you never will. Clearly, Max…wants…you," she slowly enunciated. "Believe it."

"*If* Max wanted me, he could have had me years ago. *Years…* Piper," I stressed. "You haven't been around for the past three months." She opened her mouth to interrupt, but I held up my hand to stop her. "More like you haven't been around for the past *year*. You haven't seen how he watches me in the halls, winks at me whenever I catch his eye, or brushes up against me every chance he gets." Placing both hands on the desk, I leaned forward, my face inches away from hers and whispered, "After the best kiss of my whole life, I got scared and bolted. Instead of talking to me about it, he acted like it never happened. Like that -" I snapped - "I stopped existing. No more staring, winking, or brushing. Just. Like. That. What kind of guy does that?"

She gave me a hurt look. "You never told me he kissed you."

*Crap, crapity, crap!* I didn't tell Piper or Joss about the kiss. Not because I didn't want them to know, but because it was special and it was mine. I hated that she was hurt, but that didn't change the way I felt about it. The kiss was mine.

"Let me finish and then I'll explain." I was on a roll now and, by golly, I had a point to make. I was so wrapped up in doing this that I failed to see her eyes bug as she stared at the doorway behind me. "I've been reminded every day since Max kissed me that I will never have what I want. God, why did he have to do that, Piper? All it did was complicate things." I could feel my eyes welling, which pissed me off. My aunt had taught me long ago that tears were weak and pointless. I hated feeling weak. "He got me where he wanted me, tried me out and -" I threw up my hands - "I failed. You told me I wasn't going to be enough for him and you were right. I wasn't." There, I was done. It took about two seconds for me to notice that she was staring at the door behind me.

Dropping my head, I sighed deeply and asked, "Is he standing behind me?"

"Yep," she said and stood up. "I'll just leave you two here to hash this out." As she quickly skirted around the desk, she squeezed my shoulder, and whispered, "Good luck," as she passed by me.

*Traitor.*

I heard the door click shut and slowly turned around to face Max. He had his arms crossed and was leaning against the frame with a scowl on his face. I couldn't decide if I wanted to wipe it off, kiss it away, or run. Running would probably be the smartest of the three, but when it came to Max McLellan, I was far from smart.

"I got you where I wanted you?" he asked. The tone of his voice was intimidating.

I just stood there, frozen.

"You think you weren't enough for me?"

I didn't answer. I couldn't. I was mired in all that was Max and Max was *not* a happy camper. In fact, this version of Max was a little scary.

"You think you failed?"

I managed to nod my head. I could deal with anger and I could deal with hurt, but what Max was at this moment, I didn't know what to do with.

"Fuck me," he muttered, running his hands through his hair. His harsh words made me flinch. I couldn't tell what he was thinking and it bothered me. In a deceptively soft voice, he asked, "So you think I was playing some kind of game, is that it?"

I didn't know what to say. I didn't *know* him. Yes, I'd spent the last three years obsessing over him, but in all reality, I had no clue who he *really* was. We'd had one brief encounter, *in a closet*, which obviously meant less to him than it did to me. He was my fantasy guy…the one by whom all others were judged. I couldn't tell him that it hurt watching him with Jennifer or that it hurt even more knowing he was no longer with her but didn't want me. I had no right. He wasn't mine and never had been.

"You aren't mine," I blurted. "I have no right to feel anything about you."

"*What?*" He was staring at me like I was insane. I felt totally out of my depth. Instead of shutting my mouth, I dug deeper.

"At Matt's party…I thought…I thought that we….connected. But then nothing happened, so I figured it was all in my head. Then Joss told me you'd broken up with Jennifer…." I knew I was making a mess of this but kept on going. "When you pulled me into the closet and kissed me like I've dreamt about a million times over, it scared me - so I ran and you…just let me go, thus proving me right all along. You didn't want me. I was simply a fun distraction."

"You must be shitting me," he whispered, pushing off of the doorframe and taking a step toward me. "You are all I've thought about for the past three months, Ellison."

Completely confused by his confession, I said, "I don't understand."

"Clearly," he snidely replied.

The word asshole came to mind, but I didn't dare say it out loud. "Well, then why don't you explain it to me and, by the way," I snapped, "my name is Ellie, not Ellison." His eyes flashed and his mouth thinned. Angry Max was back.

"No, it's not," he corrected.

"Yes, it is," I shot back.

"Tough," he stated.

*What a horse's ass*. Being that Max didn't know my history, I decided to give him some clarity. "My aunt has raised me since birth. She gave me that name and wields it like a weapon whenever she pleases. So now you can see why I don't like it."

An undecipherable look appeared on his face before he said, "We'll have plenty of time to get all of the details later, but for right now, whoever the hell gave you the name Ellison did a good job, because that name is beautiful and different and so are you. So you'd best get used to hearing it." My eyes widened in surprise. *He thinks my name is beautiful and different, that I'm beautiful and different...* He opened his mouth to say something else when we heard a knock on the door.

"You guys want dinner?" Joss asked. "We have pizza."

Max glanced over at me. "You want to eat or do you want to keep talking?"

Without even having to think about it, I answered, "Keep talking."

"Come," he said and held out his hand. I placed my hand in his and tiny butterflies broke free throughout my body. Max opened the door and informed Joss we had "Things to discuss" and would see them all later. I had no idea where he was heading, but nothing in the world was going to stop me from going with him.....absolutely nothing.

# CHAPTER FIVE

"Where are we going?" I asked, practically running to keep up with him.

"To the boathouse. Watch your step," he cautioned before heading up a narrow flight of stairs. When we reached the top, he pulled me through a doorway and into a large open room that was decorated in blue floral and garish nautical themes. The room was large enough to accommodate a queen bed, a closet and a small kitchen. Before I had the chance to take it all in, Max was herding me across the room toward a sitting area. "It's ugly but it'll do," he mumbled. I had to agree, it was ugly. The loveseat and club chairs were covered in a hideous yellow fabric. Dog vomit immediately came to mind. Sinking down into one of the overstuffed chairs, he pulled me sideways onto his lap. *I can't believe I'm sitting on Max McLellan's lap right now.* The pressure of his hand on the nape of my neck interrupted the mini fantasy playing in my head. I tilted my face so I could get a better look at him and tried not to gasp at the carnal glint in his eyes. It was both raw and intimate, and for a split second, I wondered if I should cut bait and run. "I want to see your face while we talk. I want to see your eyes and know that you understand what I'm saying." His deep voice sent chills down my spine.

"Uh, okay," I replied, not really understanding what he meant by this, but willing to go along.

"I noticed you the first day of your freshman year. I was standing in the hallway, by the lockers, talking to Kurt and Allen. You walked through the door with Piper. I noticed the color of your hair, your unbelievable eyes, and sweet smile. You were so beautiful, but so young." As he spoke, he rubbed his hand up and down my thigh. Not only was it very distracting, but it made it hard for me to concentrate on what he was telling me.

"You are aware that you're only a year older than me?" I laughed.

"Yes, but I have seen more shit in my eighteen years than most people have in their whole lives, Ellison." All kinds of horrible images shot through my head when he said this. Shifting my shoulders so I could see his face better, I gave him a questioning look. "This, like why you don't live with your parents, is a story for another time, another place," he explained.

"Can I ask you something?"

He smiled up at me. "You can ask me anything." I really wanted to kiss him right then. Instead, I asked the question that had been on my mind since we walked through the door, "Why me? I mean, you don't really....know me."

"No? I bet I know you better than you think. For years now I've watched you. The look on your face - you know - the one you wear when you think no one's watching? That lost look is how I feel most of the time. So I'm thinking I do know a little bit about you."

His words made my heart ache. "But...why now?" I blurted.

"You couldn't have handled me two years ago, and I knew

it. I was angry and wild, and you were pure and innocent. Don't get me wrong, I wanted you, but I couldn't do that to you. Not then."

I focused down on my blue toenail polish. "Is that why you chose Jennifer, because she could *handle* you?" The thought of him with her made me want to throw up, but it didn't stop me from wanting to hear his answer.

I felt his fingertips on my chin. When he got my eyes, he explained. "I can't tell you I didn't go there, because I did. I also can't lie and tell you it was all bad, because it wasn't." *Changed my mind, I definitely don't want to know*, I thought, as I tried to pull my head out of his grasp. Of course, he wouldn't let me. "What I will say -" he continued - "is that, like all the others, she was a distraction. It's over and you have nothing to be jealous of." I immediately stiffened. *The nerve.*

"Jealousy is *not* what I felt for your girlfriend," I informed him. *Okay, well it was part of what I felt, but not all of it.*

"No?" he asked, lips twitching.

It infuriated me that he could read me so well. "No, Max. For your information, Jennifer Tilson is a hateful bitch. She and her bubble-headed friends have been horrible to me ever since Matt's party. You would think that if your crazy, sexy hot boyfriend stopped some innocent girl from being raped, you would be nice to that girl, because you felt bad for her. You would also stand tall with your head held high, because your guy was a hero, but noooooo, not Jennifer. She turns into the queen of all bitches, sicks her evil minions on me, and, as if that isn't enough, decides to make my life a living hell." My words wiped away his beautiful smile, and I instantly regretted them.

His hand stilled on my leg. "I didn't know. Please believe me, Ells. Had I known, I would have stopped her," he admitted.

"It's over," I shrugged. Somehow, I didn't think he was going to let it go that easily. Sick of talking about Jennifer, I came right out and asked, "What do you want from me, Max?"

"Hmmmm, let me see. So many things come to mind, but for right now, what I *want* is for you to accept that the past is the past and that starting here tonight, it's just you and me and the future, whatever it may bring. What I *want* to do and have for a very long time is to touch and taste every single inch of you."

Wow. He definitely had my attention now. In fact, just thinking about his mouth on me made me restless. I shifted, hoping to relieve some of the pressure that was beginning to build between my legs. As if sensing my sudden mood change, he lifted me off of his lap, twirled me like a ballerina, and pulled me back down. We were now sitting face-to-face and I was straddling his lap. I couldn't help but notice that certain parts of him felt much larger than others and my heart started racing. *My Lord, he's a big boy.* Crazy thoughts ran through my head. *If we have sex, will it fit inside me? What if it gets stuck? What if I end up in the hospital needing to have an exceptionally large penis removed from my hee-hoo because it's stuck? Can that even happen?* I needed to tell him I was a virgin, but how did I go about doing this without totally and completely humiliating myself?

"What are you thinking, pretty girl?" he asked. His question pulled me out of my head. When I failed to reply he said, "Talk to me, babe, I can't read your mind."

I loved his words of endearment. Nobody had ever called me anything but El or Ellie, except for Piper. It made my heart hurt in a good way. "Before we...uh...take this any further, I think I need to tell you something."

He slowly wound his fingers through my hair and I snuggled against him. "You can tell me anything, anytime," he said in his quiet, sexy voice.

"Max, I....I don't really have much experience with...with any of this." I closed my eyes when I said the last part so that I didn't have to see the disgusted look on his face. It didn't, however, stop me from feeling his body tense beneath me. *Crap! He's going to toss me from his lap now and break into fits of hysterical laughter.*

"What do you mean by *this*?" he asked.

"Ummm, this," I stammered, "You know…I've kissed and messed around some before, but…" I didn't know how to properly define what little sexual experience I'd had, so instead of finishing my sentence and embarrassing myself even more, I lowered my eyes back to my toenails and let the rest hang in the air between us.

"Hey," I felt the pressure of his fingertips on my chin again as he forced me to look at him. "If you're trying to tell me that you're a virgin, I already know."

I inwardly cringed. "Who told you?" Flashes of me stabbing Piper a thousand times flickered through my mind.

"No one had to tell me, and it's absolutely nothing to be ashamed of." *Okay, wow, that's super sweet of him to say, but really?* Cupping my face, he continued. "Here's what you need to know. I want you. I've wanted you for what seems like forever, and I need for you trust me when I say I'll take care of you. However, this is completely your call. If you want to wait, I'm good with that. No matter what, this is yours to give, not mine to take. We will go at your pace, and if you want me to stop, all you have to do is say so. Are you with me?"

I nodded, and then let out a relieved breath. "Ummm, do I need… like a code word or something?" He threw his head back and laughed. On any other occasion, watching Max laugh would have been something to see, but right now, at my expense? Not so much.

"Fuck using code words. No means no. That's all you ever have to say, okay?"

"Okay," I said without hesitation.

"You're good?" he asked.

"Yes," I said looking directly into his eyes. "I'm great, Max, I promise." I wanted him to understand that this was something I wanted with him, right here, right now.

He lifted me off of his lap and patted me on the ass. "God, you're so sweet." Grabbing my hand, he led me across the room to the bed. Before we reached it, he veered over to the door and locked it. Then, hooking his hand around the back of my neck, he reeled me in and kissed me. After a few seconds, I felt him relax into the kiss and realized that he, too, was nervous. I can't say why this made me feel better, but it did. Wrapping both arms around me, he coaxed my mouth open with his tongue. My hands traveled straight to his hair as if they had a mind of their own, and I practically climbed up his body wanting more. I felt his hands on my ass as he lifted me up. Sensing what he wanted without him having to tell me, I wrapped my legs around his waist and he carried me to the bed.

"Thank you for trusting me with this," he said, as he lowered me onto the bed. "Promise you'll tell me to stop if I do anything that makes you uncomfortable. Okay?"

"I will," I breathily replied.

He crawled onto the bed beside me and kissed my forehead. "God, you're so damn beautiful," he murmured, as he gently stroked my hair. *So are you*, I thought, but didn't say out loud. Somehow I didn't think Max McLellan would like me calling him beautiful.

A look stole across his face, and I immediately tensed. "What's wrong?" I asked. *Please tell me he's not changing his mind. We haven't even gotten to the good stuff yet.*

"Nothing is wrong. I just want to do this right," he quietly admitted, and my heart skipped a few beats. *He's worried and wants to make this good for me.*

Taking a huge leap of faith, which was very uncharacteristic of me, I sucked in a deep breath, reached down to the hem of my shirt, and slowly maneuvered it up my torso and over my head. If my aunt had done anything kind for me in my life, she'd drilled into my brain to never leave home without wearing decent underwear. Of course, her reasoning wasn't - in case you find a hot guy to screw six ways to Sunday, *you must wear fresh undergarments*, but was more - in case you find yourself in a wreck and they have to cut off your clothing, *you must have on fresh, clean underwear*. Nevertheless, at this moment in time, I was giving thanks for having on decent undergarments.

"Gotta say, this exceeds every fantasy I've had about you and, trust me, I've had some good ones," Max said. Our eyes locked and I sucked in a sharp breath. He looked as if he wanted to devour me. "I'm going to touch you with my hands and mouth, Ellison. If you're going to stop me, do it now." His voice was filled with a need I couldn't help but respond to. Nodding my consent, I watched as he slid his hand up my stomach. His fingers circled around my bra before lifting it up and spilling my breast out into his hand. I couldn't help but notice that even his hands were attractive. As he lowered his head to my breast, I tensed up. This was more from anticipation than fear. I felt the heat from his breath on my nipple right before he took it into his mouth. *Holy Mother Mary, his mouth feels amazing.* Piper wasn't exaggerating when she told me her nipples were directly linked to her crotch. *I get it.* Max switched to the other breast, and daggers of pleasure shot up my spine. Carefully reaching around my back, he unhooked my bra and pulled it off. Then, focusing back on my nipples, he tenderly pulled and rolled them between his fingers. It felt incredible. The boy had a wicked tongue that set me on fire and had me begging for something I didn't understand.

"I need," I gasped.

"I know and I promise I'm gonna take care of it," he assured me. I was so lost in his mouth on my breast that I barely noticed his hand undoing the button of my shorts. Before I could protest, he had them off and was tossing them on the floor. I tensed, once again, when I felt his hand on my panties. He must have sensed my hesitation, because his hand froze and his head shot up. "You okay?" he gruffly asked.

"I'm okay. You just surprised me. Don't stop," I encouraged.

After giving me a rough kiss, he returned his hand back to my panties. "So wet," he murmured. I didn't know if this was a good or bad thing. As long as he didn't stop what he was doing, I didn't care. "I want to touch you and taste you, now. Are you still with me?"

"Yes," I whimpered. I was so with him.

"Has anyone ever touched or tasted you down here?" He rubbed his fingers from the waistband of my panties down. Up and down. Over and over until I was going crazy with want.

"No," I panted. I was so turned on that I didn't know which end was up. Hell, I didn't even question when he rolled off the side of the bed, snagged my foot, and dragged me all the way down to the bottom. I shifted to my elbows to see what was happening and found him kneeling on the floor between my legs. Two words popped into my head - *sexy and wild.* I tried not to tremble as he slid my panties off but, my gosh, this was about as personal as it got and stratospheres away from my comfort zone. Grabbing both of my legs behind my knees, he lifted them to his shoulders. I gasped when I realized what he was about to do, and quickly started to scoot back up the bed. Sensing my unease, he lowered my legs back down. At the same time he placed his hands on the outside of my thighs to halt my escape. "Hey," he soothingly called out. My eyes shot to his. "I've got you, Ellison, but I need for you to trust me. Can you do that?" Exhaling loudly, I released my elbows and dropped back onto the bed. My knees were about to be on Max McLellan's shoulders, his mouth inches away from the most vulnerable part of my body, and I had a life-altering decision to make.

*Go with your gut, Ellie.*

Lifting my head back up, I stared Max in his beautiful blue eyes and nodded my consent. "Okay, Max, I trust you." I wasn't sure about the experience, but I was sure about the guy. He trailed his fingers from the inside of my calves up to my thighs, and I shivered as if all of my nerve endings were on fire. I jumped when I felt his finger dip inside and braced for the pain that never came. He gently placed a kiss on my inner thigh. At the same time, he slowly moved his finger inside me. A surge of pure ecstasy flowed through me and I wanted more.

"I see you like that," he chuckled. Chills of pleasure were trickling down my spine and an indescribable pressure was building at my core. I wanted release but didn't know how to ask for it. When Max placed my legs on his shoulders again, I didn't pull back. My body felt taut like a rubber band that at any moment could snap and shatter everything in its path. Replacing his finger with his tongue, he dragged it through my center and gently sucked. This time, when he inserted his finger back inside, he pulsed it in and out using the same rhythm as his tongue, and I had my epiphany. *This, right here, right now, is why I waited.* Suddenly, the pleasure was too much. As my back arched up off the bed, I snapped. Waves of pleasure held me captive as I shouted his name over and over again. I was in absolute heaven. No form of self-gratification in the world could ever top this. *I had no idea anything could make me feel this way.*

Max slowly rose from the foot of the bed. Placing a knee on either side of my waist, he hooked his fingers under my armpits and lifted me back to the top of the bed. Now, lying between my legs, the friction from his denim-covered erection rubbed against my bare and extremely sensitive core. It was almost too much. Feeling heady from my first Max-induced orgasm, I threaded my fingers through his thick hair and pulled him in for a kiss. Once our lips touched, I slowly sucked his tongue into my mouth and deepened the kiss.

Breathing heavily, Max pulled back and smiled. "I take it that was good for you?" he rasped. It took me a minute to figure out what was different about him, and suddenly it clicked. This was the first time I'd seen him unguarded. I wondered if he saw the same in me. If not, I wanted him to. I wanted him to see how special he made me feel.

I gently stroked my hand across his face. "Good doesn't even begin to describe what that was."

As he slid off the bed and began unbuttoning his shirt, my eyes drifted down his body to the gloriously large bulge in his jeans. Smiling at my uncertain expression, he continued flicking open the buttons, one...by...one. I couldn't help but blush at the intimacy of this. His shirt dropped to the floor and I gawked. His chest muscles tapered into a twelve pack. Or maybe it was a sixteen pack, if there was such a thing. His jeans dropped to the floor and I did a double take. *Holy Hades, he has no underwear on.* Not only that, but he was huge! I stared open-mouthed at all that was Max McLellan. There were no words to do it justice. He started to crawl back up the bed when I felt a sliver of panic.

"It will never fit," I whispered.

His somewhat smug expression softened, "Sweetheart, I'll make sure it fits and that you enjoy every second, okay?" he assured me.

I knew I was being silly, but was there a proper response to one's first glimpse of an extremely large penis besides shock and awe? If so, I'd be interested to know what it was. "Can I touch it, I mean...you?" I stammered, blushing at my slip.

"I'd be upset if you didn't," he replied. The low, sexy pitch of his voice made my stomach clench. The taut rubber band feeling was back, and this time I knew what it meant. "Hold up," Max said. I paused as he flipped around to his back and placed his hands behind his head. He looked as if he were leisurely lounging. *Smug ass.* In order to get the angle I wanted, I scooted over beside him and shifted up onto my knees. Now, when I relaxed back on my haunches, I didn't have as far to reach. Hesitantly, I lifted my pointer finger and stroked his cock from the tip to the base. I was surprised at how soft the skin was. He let out a hissing noise, which caused me to yank my hand back. "No, don't," he said. Then he took my hand in his, entwined our fingers together, and showed me how he liked to be touched.

"What if I bleed to death?" I asked, as I began to pick up momentum.

He hummed in pleasure. "You'll bleed, but only because that's what you do the first time. I promise it won't kill you."

"So…what… you're an expert on de-virginizing innocent girls?" I felt a prick of jealousy.

"Nope, but I experienced it once and remember what it was like."

"Oh."

He chuckled. "Is de-virginizing even a word?" He was making fun of me again. I gripped him harder, picked up the speed, and tried not to smile when he let out a semi-growl.

He stilled my hand and said, "I need to be inside you, Ellison, but will stop right now if you're not okay."

"I'm okay," I said, and I was. I was more than okay. I wanted this.

"Switch positions with me," he demanded, and before I had the chance to move, I was flat on my back with him resting between my legs. *I love how he handles me.* Having his large body on top of mine was strangely comforting. For the first time in my life, I felt warm and protected. He reached across me, snagged his jeans off the floor, grabbed his wallet, and pulled out a condom. Watching his arm muscles flex as he rolled the condom on made my insides contract and my nipples pebble. He began to slowly rub his condom-clad cock up and down my sex and I thought I was going to lose my mind. "Trust me, this will help us both," he explained.

"Oh, okay," I breathily replied. I was scared yet lost in a myriad of sensations that were new to me.

"Breathe, baby," he whispered, as he placed himself at my entrance. His head dipped and he ran his tongue down my neck, which instantly loosened me up. At the same time, he pushed deeper inside me. "I have never wanted anything more than I want you right now," he half-groaned, half-panted. I could hear the strain in his voice as he fought to stay in control. "Hang on to me and take a deep breath."

Doing as instructed, I took in a deep breath and felt a sharp searing pain shoot through my core. I opened my mouth to scream, and he swallowed it down with a tongue-sucking kiss. When seated all the way inside me, his whole body stilled. "This makes you mine now," he declared, as he stared into my eyes. The look of lust on his face completely erased the pain.

"Yes," I hissed, as I arched my body up to meet his. He pulled back slowly and then pushed back in. Out and in, he rhythmically drove deeper and deeper into me. I don't know what got me there faster, the fact that this was finally happening with my fantasy guy or the reverent look in his eyes, which were glued to mine the entire time. Either way, I was close and, from the sexy noises that were coming from his mouth, so was he.

"Max," I gasped.

"I'm there, babe," he growled, and that was all it took. I shouted his name as I broke apart. One thrust later, he shouted his release and then buried his face in my neck.

After cleaning us both off, he crawled back in bed and pulled me close. I was a total and complete marshmallow, and he knew it. He wrapped his arms around me and trapped my legs under his as if he were afraid I would escape. "Mine," he groggily mumbled. I felt his lips kiss the back of my head right before he fell asleep.

*Was I his?* As I lay there in the dark, I thought about the guy I'd dreamt of for as long as I could remember and relived every second of the day. The reality was so much better than the dream. No matter what the future held, I knew I was forever changed.

# CHAPTER SIX

Waking up next to Max was amazing. His sleepy eyes and untamed hair made him look sexier, *if that was even possible*. We were one steamy hot kiss in when an obnoxiously loud Piper started banging on the door and shouting for us to get up.

"Stay here. I'll get it," he sighed and kissed the top of my head. He had his jeans on and zipped before I could get another peak of his amazing body. *Darn.*

I heard the door open and couldn't help but giggle when Piper shrieked, "Lord almighty, you are so fucking hot!" I heard Joss mumble something and Max laugh. The sound of his laughter made my heart stutter in my chest.

"Ells, I'm going next door to grab some caffeine. Come on over when you're done gossiping, and we'll figure out breakfast!" he shouted from the front door.

"Will do!" I laughed as I shouted back. *He so has me pegged.*

"Wellllll?" Piper asked as both she and Joss settled on the bed with me.

"Well, what?"

"Come on El, Max answers the door with no shirt on – looking like that, and you're lying in bed completely bare-assed. Spill!"

I covered my face and laughed. "I can't," I told them. "There are no words."

"It was that good your *first* time?" Joss skeptically asked. A look of disbelief was plastered on her face.

"I know, right? After Max fell asleep last night, I thought about it, and there's not one person I know who's said their first time was amazing."

Joss, now sporting a shit-eating grin, asked, "But I take it yours was?"

"It was…. it was… beyond my wildest everything." I paused for a second to get my thoughts together. I wanted to explain it in a way they would understand. "It was better than the best love scene I've ever read, and you both know how much I read."

"You and your books," Piper teased.

"Shit, we get it," Joss said, laughing.

"How about you guys? What did you get up to last night?"

"Kurt and I went to bed early," Joss replied, her face red with embarrassment.

I raised my brow at Piper. "And you?"

"Harry and I drank, and before you jump all over it, that's all we did," she directed at me. "He's actually really funny. Ummm, listen, I talked to Joss already this morning, but now that I have you here, I wanted to tell you that I kind of met someone. His name is Thomas Smithfield, but I call him Tom, and he goes to a boarding school near mine in Virginia." Grabbing my hand, she continued. "I wanted to tell you, but didn't want to rub in that I had a boyfriend when you were so sad about Max. In fact," her voice wavered and she nervously bit her lip, "I've been invited to spend the summer with him in Wyoming."

I was shocked. This was the last thing I expected her to say. "But I thought you were in Charlotte for the summer?" I know I sounded desperate, but she just got here and now she was talking about leaving again.

"I know, El, but I *really* like this guy. He's....different. Please don't be mad. He's way smarter than me and comes from a very wealthy family. His people descend from King Henry or someone like that. Anyway, I don't want you to be mad at me."

I was disappointed. We'd made plans for the whole summer. I wanted her to go but also wanted her to stay. "I can't say I'm not disappointed and won't miss you terribly, but I get it."

"You do? Promise you're not mad?"

"Of course I'm not mad. Now, tell us all about him. What's he like?"

The rest of that day was filled with fun and laughter. We swam, tubed, sunned, and Max and I kissed *a lot.* Harry buzzed spasmodically around us, purposefully trying to annoy Piper, while Joss and Kurt pretended not to be crazy about each other. Every time Max and I tried to sneak away we got busted. By the end of the day, we were desperate for alone time.

Max convinced me to move into the boathouse with him for the remainder of the weekend. The second we finished dinner, we were out the door. We had each other's clothes halfway off before even making it across the back lawn. As soon as we entered the boathouse Max lifted me up, threw me on the bed, and jumped on top of me.

"I had fun with you today," he said, kissing my shoulder.

"Did you think you wouldn't?" I teased.

"Hmmmm," he hummed, as he ran his tongue up my neck. "Let's just say that I don't normally do this kind of thing and am really glad I did."

"What kind of thing don't you do?" I asked, trying not to moan at his erotic assault on my senses.

"I don't normally... hang out with the girls I sleep with."

I froze at his declaration. "Please tell me you are joking. I mean, how do you date someone without hanging out?"

"I don't." I could feel my heart start to race.

"You don't," I repeated.

"Not until today," he said, and ran his lips down my arm.

"Uh, what did you do before today, then?" *Do I really want to know the answer to this?*

"Sex."

"That's it?" I squeaked. Pulling my arm away from his lusciously distracting lips, I reared back so I could see his face. "You're telling me you've never actually *dated* anyone before, just screwed them? But…I *saw* you with Jennifer all year and… outside at Matt's party that night."

"You saw me with her at school because we both had to be there, but we never hung out after…unless…," he didn't need to finish the sentence. I got it. "And," he continued, "I was at Matt's party and Jennifer was at Matt's party, but we didn't ride there together, nor did we go home together. In fact, after she gave me shit for helping you out, I was done and told her so before I took off."

"So you broke up?"

"No, no break up, just done. In order to break up, we would've had to have been together in the first place. All we did was hook up whenever we were both available." *Oh my God. I don't know what to say to this.* My heart lurched.

"So, this here with me" - I waved my hand across the bed - "is just a hook-up?" I felt sick inside, but I had to know.

"Babe, have you heard anything I've said in the past fifteen hours? Did last night feel like just sex to you? Did you hear me when I said you're mine?" I could see he was frustrated. Dragging his fingers through my hair, he tugged hard enough to get my attention and said, "You are a game changer, Ellison. This -" he mocked me by waving his hand across the bed - "is a game changer. Do you understand?"

"Yes," I breathed, and I did, because he also was a game changer for me. I can't say his past didn't bother me or that I didn't worry about my place in his future, but I understood that if there was any *hope* of a future with Max, I was going to have to let it go and learn to play by his rules.

It took him all of five seconds and a soul-scorching kiss to get me over our conversation and on to better things. "Are you too sore for me after last night?" he asked, running his finger over my bottom lip.

"No," I replied and sucked his wandering finger deep into my mouth. I watched his eyes darken with lust. *For me.* Seconds later, he had one hand on my breast and the other between my legs, when his cell phone rang. "Don't stop," I panted.

"Hang on," he growled and answered it. "Sarah, talk to me," he said, followed by, "Okay, honey, just calm down and then tell me from the beginning." *Sarah? Honey? Who the hell is Sarah?* "It'll be okay," he said in a tone I'd never heard him use before. "I'll be home in twenty minutes, I promise." He hung up and stared out the window. His mind was obviously a million miles away.

My heart dropped. "Is everything okay?"

"No, not really," he sighed.

Trying not to sound jealous, I asked, "Who is Sarah?"

He paused for a second before answering. "Sarah is my thirteen-year-old sister." *Max has a sister? How did I not know this?*

"Oh my God, is she okay? What time is it?" I searched the room for a clock.

"It's almost two in the morning. Ells, I'm sorry, but I need to get home." He hopped off the bed, pulled on his jeans and shirt, and began packing. "Get some sleep. I'll try and come back tomorrow if I can." *He's leaving? Just like that?*

"So, you're just going to leave and... maybe you'll come

back?" I tried not to wince at the pathetic sound of my own voice. "What if you can't? Come back, I mean. Will I talk to you ever again?" *Please say yes, please tell me you meant everything you told me earlier.* I couldn't help but feel insecure. I'd never done this before, so I didn't know the rules. I just knew he didn't do relationships or date or... whatever.

He stopped packing his bag and paced over to the bed. When he got to me, he cupped my face in his hands and said, "My little sister had a nightmare. She woke up and, as usual, my deadbeat dad wasn't there. She's scared and alone, and I need to get home to her. If my dad shows back up, whether he's sober or not will determine if I can come back. If it was anything other than this, trust me, I wouldn't be leaving, okay?"

"Let me come with you," I blurted. *Where did that come from?*

His eyebrows shot up in surprise. "You want to come with me?" I nodded. "You really want to come to my house to help me take care of my little sister?" he skeptically asked. I nodded again. Both of his eyebrows shot up. "Seriously?"

"Seriously," I said. "I know nothing about you really. I didn't even know you had a sister."

"My life is really messed up, Ellison. Nobody but Kurt and my boss, Benny, know anything about me, and even they don't know the half of it."

"Whose life isn't a mess, Max?" *I mean, really...Mine sure is.*

After staring at me for a minute, he said, "Okay, pack up quickly and let's go." I promptly leapt off the bed, got dressed, packed up my things, wrote a note to everyone, and ran out the door to catch up with him.

I found out on the ride to his house that Max liked really loud music... especially classic rock. Every time I tried to turn down the radio to ask a question, he just smiled and cranked it back up.

I liked loud music, too, but not when I was attempting to carry on a conversation with someone.

*Why is he shutting me out? Maybe he didn't want me to come with him?* Maybe this wasn't such a good idea.

Max lived in a small one-story house on the south side of Charlotte. In fact, he only lived about a mile away from me. It seemed there was quite a lot about Max McLellan I didn't know. Shifting into park, he jumped out of the truck and rushed into the house. Grabbing both of our bags, I hesitantly followed behind.

Sarah McLellan was the spitting image of Max. She, too, had black hair and greenish-blue eyes. *Wow, if she's this lovely now, she's going to blow minds later*. While Max was busy with Sarah, I glanced around their house. I couldn't help but notice the sparsely worn furniture, the lack of any photographs, and the clutter. The décor was very dark, very masculine, and was seriously lacking a woman's touch. This made me think back to my earlier conversations with him. He'd mentioned his dad and sister, but never his mother. I wasn't surprised in the least that Max was great with Sarah. I watched as he gently pulled her onto his lap. As he stroked her hair and spoke in a low, soothing voice, my heart completely melted. I knew I was getting a view of him no one else had. Gone was the dominant, controlling Max. In its place was the sweet, loving brother. I liked this side of him and liked even more that he trusted me enough to let me see it.

"Ellison, this is my little sister, Sarah. Sarah, meet Ellison."

"I'm thirteen, Max," she said, glaring over her shoulder at him.

"Sorry," he said. "Ellison, this is my very mature younger sister, Sarah," he straight-faced. She smiled at him before settling her eyes on me.

"Hi, Sarah, nice to meet you," I told her.

Her eyes widened and she turned to Max. "Is she your

girlfriend?"

"Something like that," Max mumbled.

"Really?" she skeptically asked, as if she didn't believe he could land a girlfriend.

"Yes, really." He smiled. "We're here now, honey, so it's time for you to go to bed."

"My room is the first on the left, Ells. You can crash out if you want. I'm going to make sure Sarah is okay, and I'll be right in."

I loved when he called me Ells. Feeling like I needed to say something, I lamely asked, "Do you need any help? Ummm… and will your parents mind that I am here and… in your bed?" I whispered the last part and hoped Sarah wouldn't hear.

His lip quirked with humor. "Thanks, gorgeous, I think I've got it handled, and no, my dad won't care. He probably won't be back before we leave tomorrow."

"Oh, okay." I wanted to ask about his dad not coming home and where his mom was but didn't think this was the right time. "Night, Sarah," I said, smiling at her pretty face. She really did look just like Max.

"Night, Ellison," she replied.

"Oh, please call me Ellie. All my friends do, and I can tell that you and I are going to be great friends."

She cut her eyes up at Max. "Why don't you call her Ellie?"

"Because I don't want to," he replied.

I left them in the living room debating about my name, grabbed my bag, and made my way to Max's bedroom. While I waited on him to appear, I brushed my teeth, washed my face and scoped out his bedroom. He had an iPod dock, an old television and a picture of Sarah and him with a woman who looked exactly like them. I assumed this was their mother. When I got tired of snooping, I threw on a T-shirt and crawled into his bed. I fell asleep thinking about how the bed smelled deliciously of leather and spice.

Sometime later, I woke with something hard pressing against my back.

"Shhhhh," I heard Max whisper behind me. "It's just me. Raise your arms," he ordered, and I lifted my arms. He quickly pulled off my shirt. His fingers brushed across the band of my panties as he slid them down my legs. I heard the foil tear right before he rolled on a condom. I'd barely had time to register what was happening, when he lifted my leg, cocked it over his hip, and slowly pushed inside me from behind. *How will this work with him behind me?* I silently wondered. Placing his hands on my hips for leverage, he pulled himself in deeper. I had my answer. It felt so crazy good that I couldn't help but moan loudly.

"Shhh," he warned, "my sister is in the room across the hall."

Nodding, I let him know I understood. He cocked my leg higher and began gliding back and forth. Wanting more, I tilted my hips and pumped back into him as he pushed forward. Growling, he dug one hand into my hip while sliding the other between my legs.

"Max," I gasped.

"Fuck," he whispered and let go of his control. His hips clashed with mine. Each stroke drove us higher and higher until we both blew apart. "So fucking good," he whispered. Then he pulled out, rolled me over onto my back and kissed me, never once taking his eyes from my face.

As I wrapped my arms around him, I buried my face in his neck and held on tight. I was afraid for him to see how deeply he affected me. At that moment, nothing in the world could make me let him go…ever.

The next morning, we heard Sarah get up. I wanted to laze around in bed all morning. There were so many questions and so many things to learn about each other. I wanted to know what all of this meant, but Max quickly got dressed and suggested we take Sarah to breakfast to help distract her from the fact their dad had stayed out all night, again. *How long has this been happening and where is their mother? Something tells me I'm not going to like the answer.*

Watching Max and Sarah together was fascinating. The closest I'd come to having siblings was Piper and her brothers. They loved each other, but it was a different kind of love than Max demonstrated with Sarah. Piper's brothers were playful, fun, and sometimes mean, whereas Max was more protective and fatherly.

During breakfast, Sarah mentioned their mother's pancakes.

I finally had my opening and went for it. "I take it your parents are divorced?" I asked.

Max and Sarah glanced at each other for a second, and then he said, "Our mom died five years ago."

"Oh my gosh, I'm so sorry." I felt horrible.

He squeezed my hand. "That's okay. You didn't know." *That would have made Sarah seven and Max thirteen when their mother died.*

"How? I mean…"

"She had a brain aneurysm and died in her sleep."

*Shit.*

"Max," I whispered, squeezing his hand back.

"My dad has had a hard time of it since Mom's death, so basically it has been just the two of us. Dad pays for our food and Sarah's sitters, and I take care of pretty much everything else. We get by." *We get by?*

And here I thought I'd had it tough. For the first time in my life, I was thankful I'd never known my parents. This way I wouldn't know the pain of losing them. I could see the loss etched across Max and Sarah's faces and wished I could take it away.

# CHAPTER SEVEN

From that weekend on, Max and I spent every possible second with each other. He took me over to the garage where he worked and introduced me to his boss and good friend, Leroy Benny, otherwise known as Benny, as well as to all of his co-workers. It was apparent that Benny loved Max like a son. As a result, I couldn't help but love Benny.

I missed having Piper around but talked to her regularly on the phone. Joss and I grew closer. She was a wonderful person with a big heart, and I needed that in my life. The fact that Max and Kurt were best friends was simply icing on the cake.

I learned that Max's favorite color was blue, he loved his sister to pieces, was crazy loyal to his friends, incredibly dominating, and he considered me his girlfriend. *Yes, I, Ellie Davis, was finally Max McLellan's girlfriend.*

I told Max pretty much everything there was to know about me other than the gory details about my childhood. I wanted him to get to know me for me. There was plenty of time to learn the rest…later.

We'd been together for three weeks when we had our first big fight. I know couples fight. Hell, Piper fought with every guy she'd ever dated. I, however, had never had the pleasure of this experience. So to say I handled it poorly was putting it mildly.

We were leaving Max's house to take Sarah to the movies one evening when we ran across his dad. He was pulling into the driveway as we were walking out of the house. Up to this point, Max had shared very little about his dad with me. I knew he drank a lot and was rarely at home. When he was around, all he did was sleep. I also knew he could be kind of mean. Max's aversion to talking about his dad bothered me. So, seeing the man up close for the first time made me pause - as in - I stopped dead in my tracks in the middle of the pathway leading to the driveway. The least Max could do was introduce us. For some reason, this made Max angry. The next thing I knew he had me by the arm. With a sharp tug, he practically frog marched me the rest of the way to the car. As we pulled out of the driveway, he gave his father a nod of recognition. I was both confused and hurt by this. *Why didn't he introduce me? Is he ashamed of me? Does his dad even know he has a girlfriend? Maybe he has more than one girlfriend and is afraid his dad will call me by the wrong name…Oh God, maybe his dad thought I was Jennifer.*

We were halfway down the street before I finally gathered enough nerve to say something. "What *was* that, Max?" I asked, trying to get myself under control.

"*That* was my jerk of a dad."

"Why didn't you introduce me?"

"Because."

"Because?" I questioned.

"Yeah, Ellison, because," he firmly stated.

"Really? That's all you're going to say?"

"Yep."

Now, I was angry. I turned to the back seat and asked Sarah,

"Do *you* know what that was about, because I sure don't." She shrugged her shoulders before dropping her eyes to the floorboard.

Evidently my asking Sarah was not cool in Max's book, because he growled, "Ellison," in warning.

"What?" I shot back. His jaw ticked with anger. I no longer cared if he was mad or not, because I was mad enough for the both of us.

"Don't pull Sarah into our shit," he hissed. *Is he for real?*

"Into what...*shit,* Max? Me wanting to know why you won't introduce me to your dad, me thinking that you won't introduce me because I embarrass you, or me asking your sister to explain because you won't?" I barely got the last one out. I waited for his reply, but he gave me nothing – nope – not a single word. Normally, it took a lot to rile me up, but his silent treatment infuriated me. My imagination was on hyper drive and I was seriously scaring myself. When he just sat there ignoring me, I was done. "Take me home," I demanded.

His head jerked and his eyes landed on me. "What?" he asked.

"I want to go home... *now.*"

"You have got to be shitting me!" he snapped.

I was about to completely lose control and didn't want his sister to see my meltdown. I didn't understand what had just happened and wasn't really sure I wanted to. Whatever was going on made me sick inside and I wanted away from it. "Take me home, please?" I pleaded. Max must have heard the tears in my voice, because he suddenly slammed on the brakes, turned the car around, and headed back in the direction of my house.

"Is this what you really want?" he asked as he pulled in front of my house. *Yes, no...I don't know.* Instead of answering, I just stared out my window. My silence evidently did not sit well with Max. "I don't owe you shit, Ellison," he gritted out. "I tell you things about me on *my* terms, not because *you* decide you need to know. My family is *my* business, and I'll introduce you if and when *I* choose, not you. Are we clear?"

"Crystal," I said. Before he could say another word, I opened my door, slammed it behind me, and took off for my house.

I was determined not to cry in front of Max and was almost to my front door when I felt his hand on my arm. "What the fuck?" he growled.

"Let me go," I tearfully said. "I can't do this with you, Max, not right now, maybe not at all." I ripped my arm away from his hand, charged through the door, and slammed it in his face. I watched through the curtains as he drove away. Ignoring my aunt's questions, I stormed straight to my bedroom and turned off my phone. I lay on my bed, a sobbing pile of hurt and confusion.

Half an hour later I was washing my face when I heard a knock on my door.

"Come in," I called out.

Aunt Elizabeth poked her head in and asked, "You okay?"

"No."

"Do you want to talk about it?"

"Not really," I answered, and then proceeded to spew my Max issues all over her…minus the sex, of course.

She sat on the edge of my bed and patiently listened to me rant for a while. When I was done, she proceeded to say, "I know I am a poor example for you, because I am not your mom or dad, but I do love you like you're my own child. Lord knows I don't tell you this hardly ever, but… I do and I want you to lean on me if you need to." It was hard to tell her what I was feeling when I didn't know or understand it myself. I was shocked we were even having this discussion. *Yes, there's a first for everything.* "Have we ever had the talk about the birds and the bees?" she asked.

Physically cringing at the thought of this, I told her I'd found out about the birds and the bees from Piper when we were in second grade.

"Well, hell, I should have known that," she mumbled, and I couldn't help but laugh. "Some people are lucky in love, Ellison. They find it once and know that's it for them. If you find yourself to be one of these people, then grab it tight and don't ever let it slip through your fingers. Remember not to let life get in the way. I wasn't lucky in love, but I sure have been lucky in life. After all, I got to raise you." This made me cry all over again. It was the first time in my whole life I truly felt her love for me. She stayed with me for a while and then headed down to bed. It took a long time for me to fall asleep. I was confused by how Max had acted and ashamed by my reaction.

*What a mess.*

I jerked awake when I felt a hand on my mouth.

"It's just me," Max whispered. Inhaling sharply through my nose, I shook my head at him. "I've been trying to call you for the past four hours. I'm going crazy here. Talk to me." My eyes instantly filled with tears. I nodded my head, and he took his hand off of my mouth.

"How in the world did you get in here?" I whispered.

"You have a huge Magnolia tree right outside your window. It's perfect for sneaking in and out," he explained.

"Oh," I thoughtfully replied.

He chuckled at this. "I see you never thought of sneaking out before, huh?" I didn't answer him. I wasn't over my hurt and anger, yet. "Is your aunt's room close by?"

I narrowed my eyes at him. "Downstairs on the opposite end of the house, why?"

"Just wanted to know how loud we could be," he said with

a grin.

"There will be *none* of that," I stressed.

Picking me up off of the bed, he sat back down with me in his lap. After he had us positioned to his liking, he started talking. "Don't be mad at me, Ells. I couldn't talk to you about my dad in front of my sister. I let my temper take over and said a bunch of shit I didn't mean. There are so many messed-up things in my life right now. It's hard to know where to start. I'm trying to keep Sarah from seeing how bad it really is. The hell if I'm subjecting you to it." Sweet Max was hard to stay mad at. He pulled us back against the headboard, and slowly began talking to me about his dad. He explained that he wasn't the best father or husband to begin with, but after his mother's death, he was practically nonexistent. When he was sixteen, he overheard his dad talking on the phone to someone about how he was cheating on Max's mom. The guilt from cheating made his dad unbearable to be around, therefore killing any love Max had for him. He also told me he hated his dad, because now, whenever he was at the house, all he did was drink. This only led to fits of rage and abuse toward Max and Sarah. Just thinking about someone hurting Max or Sarah made me sick to my stomach.

Shifting, so I could see his eyes, I asked, "He doesn't... hurt you, does he?"

"No, Ellison, he doesn't. I'm stronger, which pisses him off but also keeps him in check. He knows better than to lay a hand on either of us." *What a relief, but still...* Max told me he wasn't sure what his dad was doing for money and was worried about the strange men who were in and out of their house all the time. This made him nervous, especially for Sarah, so he found her some after-school care for when he had to work. His mom had some family money, which went into a trust for both kids when she died. He planned on using the trust to support both him and Sarah through college but was worried because the lawyer who set up the trust had called him last week to inform him that his dad was trying to break the trust in order to get to the money.

"Can he do that?" I was shocked that anyone's parent would act this way toward their children. *But what did I know? Both of my parents abandoned me.*

"No. I took over as trustee when I turned eighteen. Those were my mother's legal wishes. The lawyer said my dad was furious that my mom appointed the lawyer as trustee until I came of age, and not him."

"What are you going to do?"

"The only thing I can do. I'm going to go to college and do my best to protect my sister."

This made me want to cry. I also felt incredibly silly. "I thought you were embarrassed to be with me and that's why you wouldn't introduce me to your dad."

He laughed, and I made sure he saw my eyes when I glared at him. "I can see you're serious," he muttered. He smiled, stroking his fingers across my cheek. "I'm gonna tell you something, but I don't want it going to your head, okay?"

"Okay."

"There's not a guy in the world who wouldn't be proud to call you his, Ellison."

My eyes filled with tears when he said this. "Thank you," I whispered. I lifted my mouth to his and slowly ran my tongue over his bottom lip. "Has anyone ever told you that you can be really, really sweet?" He shook his head from side to side. "I'm glad I'm the first then, and I'm sorry for earlier. I overreacted."

"Me, too," he replied and gently pressed his lips to mine. "I don't mean to shut you out. I'm just not used to sharing personal stuff with anyone. Other than Benny and Kurt, you're the only person I talk to about all of this. I'm sorry I was harsh with you earlier, babe. Just know that I never *want* to hurt you." As he said this, he sifted his hands through my hair. This sent a tingle down my spine. "You know, I've heard make-up sex can be a lot of fun." He gave me a wolfish smile.

"Good thing because I really want you right now," I whispered.

"You've got me," he whispered back.

As I slowly lifted his shirt up and over his head, I felt the power of my newfound sexuality. I ran my tongue down his neck and over his yummy muscular chest. I couldn't help but wonder what crazy workout regimen he did to look this good. I slowly slid down his legs. When I reached his calves, I unbuttoned his shorts and pulled them off. *No underwear, of course*. I knelt on my knees between his legs and lowered my mouth to his very impressive erection. As I took him into my mouth, he groaned loudly. I'd never done this before and was going off of pure instinct. I felt his hands in my hair. Then his hips pressed forward and he drove deeper inside my mouth. His breath accelerated with each suck. I wanted to give him what he'd given me. I wanted it all.

"I want inside you," he panted. Before I could protest, he pulled out of my mouth. I tried to grab him back, but he was already putting on a condom. In one swift move, he flipped me onto my back, and positioned himself at my entrance. When he thrust deep inside, I gasped at how good it felt. Then again, it always felt this good with Max. He pulled out and thrust back in. By the third time he did this, I caught on and with my thighs and knees helped to set the tempo. What an amazing dance it turned out to be. Using our lips, tongues and hands, we, kissed, licked and touched, until, totally embedded in one another, we tumbled over the edge. I was completely and utterly in love.

The quarry was senior territory. You only went there if you were a senior or a senior had invited you. It was located about twenty miles out of Charlotte and was surrounded by national forest. Max took me there for the first time on July 4th. The night was warm and clear. There were a million stars in the sky; a perfect night to watch fireworks.

When we arrived, a group of seniors was setting up the bottle rockets down by the water. There was a bonfire going and a keg already tapped. A truck parked near the fire had its doors wide open with Led Zeppelin's "Kashmir" pouring out.

This was our first outing as a couple, and I was a little nervous. I knew Max had been with a lot of girls before me. After all, I *had* been sitting in a front row seat to the Max McLellan show for the past three years. I wasn't jealous, just uncomfortable and a little insecure as to where our relationship was going. I was looking around, hoping Jennifer wasn't going to show up and ruin our night, when Joss and Kurt pulled up. They'd finally admitted they were dating, which made me really happy, as they were two really good people who deserved each other. Joss and I drank a beer and played catch up, while the boys wandered off to look at the assortment of fireworks.

I was staring into the fire thinking about how happy I was when I felt Max behind me. My senses were so attuned to him that I could feel whenever he was near. Leaning back into him, I pulled his arms tightly around my stomach and sighed. *Life is great.*

"Hey, pretty girl, I want to show you something," his deep voice rasped in my ear. Grabbing my hand, he led me over to his car, reached inside, and snagged a blanket from the back.

"Where are we going?"

"You'll see."

We walked through the woods for about ten minutes until the trees opened up to a clearing. Standing directly in front of us was a gigantic rock wall. To our left were some steps. Max led me up to a large flat rock surface. When we reached the top, he dropped my hand in order to sort the blanket. Then he sat down and patted the surface between his legs. It took me a minute to get settled. Once I nestled back against him, I looked up, and gasped. We could see the entire quarry down below us.

"It's breathtaking," I whispered

"Yes, it is," he said, staring sideways at me.

"I meant the view, silly."

"My mom used to bring me and Sarah here before she died. She and my dad started coming here together their senior year in high school, and she wanted to share it with us. After she died, I would ride my bike out here when I needed to think or just to feel close to her."

"I'm sorry you lost her."

"Me, too. Speaking of moms, are you ever going to tell me what happened to yours?"

It was inevitable that this moment would come and, after hearing all about his parents, it was more than my turn to talk. So I did. I told him about my mom and dad and how lonely my childhood had been before Piper appeared. When I talked about my aunt and her crazy expectations, he tensed up. I explained how this was all I knew and I was used to it.

"So, this is why you waited," he stated.

I shrugged. "Part of it, I guess."

"This is also why you spend so much time with your face in a book." *He gets it.*

"Probably. I've always had the feeling there was someone out there just for me and if I waited long enough, he would come along."

"I'm a lucky guy," he said as he stroked his hand through my hair. "Don't think for one second I don't know this."

Settling deep into him, I asked the question that had been on my mind. "What happens after this summer, Max?"

"Hmmm, I guess we've been so busy getting to know each other that we haven't really talked about the future. I don't think I've even told you what my plans are for next year have I?"

Shaking my head, I admitted, "The future scares me."

"Why?"

"Because I can't control what happens."

"Appalachian State offers the type of degree I need and is only two hours away from here. I made sure I picked a college close enough that I could come home and check in on Sarah and…now, you." He lightly kissed the side of my head and I instantly felt better. This sounded like a good plan.

"What are you going to study?"

"Business. Benny has been bugging me about coming home after college and taking over the garage."

"As in run it?"

"For the most part. I'd like to eventually own a chain of garages that cater to all types of vehicles."

"You and Benny seem really close."

"After my mom died and my dad fell apart, I was a mess. Benny and his wife had been friends with my parents for a long time and knew my situation. They stepped up when I had no one."

"Benny's married?" Max had never mentioned a Mrs. Benny.

Max pulled me in closer and sighed. "Benny's grandfather built the garage and passed it to his dad. Benny and Rachelle dated all through high school. They were crazy about each other and got married the second they graduated. His dad paid for him to go to UNC Charlotte and get a degree in sports medicine. He had always wanted to work on sports injuries. Back then, he worked out once or twice a day. The man was a machine, and I completely idolized him. I still do. Anyway, Benny and Rachelle had a son shortly after Benny graduated from the sports med. program. They called him little Ben. The three of them settled near Benny's dad in the foothills near Morganton. When little Ben was three, Benny was out of town on a business trip. His dad had taken Rachelle and little Ben to dinner and a deer ran out in front of the car on the drive home. Benny's dad swerved, the car jumped the guard rail, and they were all three killed instantly. I was ten years old when it happened."

"Oh my God, Max!" I gasped. "That's horrible! Poor Benny." My heart hurt for the man and the family he'd lost.

"It was beyond horrible. There was no one to blame. It was just a freak accident. Benny went off the deep end for a while but somehow managed to pull himself together. He gave up on sports medicine and took over the garage. When my mom died, he was the one who got me to steer my anger toward something healthy instead of harmful."

"You're lucky you have each other."

"Benny started working out again, something he hadn't done since the wreck, for me. He wanted to give me direction and purpose. I was really angry and hurt, and since he'd already been there, he could relate." I didn't know what to say to this. It was all so terribly sad. "I can only hope to have a marriage like Benny and Rachelle's one day. They loved each other like crazy. I want a family, stability…a place to call home. What do you want?"

I glanced over my shoulder and into his eyes. *I want you for the rest of my life,* I thought. "I want it all," I said out loud.

"If Sarah didn't need me, I would have left this place a long time ago. I'm glad that didn't happen, because I wouldn't have met you. Now that I have you, you're stuck with me, 'cause nothing in this world will ever make me leave you."

I pressed my lips to his. Right as he deepened the kiss, the fireworks started. We held each other close and watched them. Then we slowly made our way back to Joss and Kurt, and the bonfire.

# CHAPTER EIGHT

Our talk at the quarry stayed with me for a long time. Max made me think about the future, something I'd gotten good at avoiding. He made me wonder how different my life would be now if I'd been part of an actual family. He'd been blessed with nine years of that type of foundation and wanted it for his future. I had no clue what that felt like, but listening to Max talk so fondly about it made me want it more than I thought was possible. I was totally and completely in love with him. I had been since the first night at the lake house. He filled up the empty places inside of me that I didn't know existed, and for the first time in seventeen years, I felt like I mattered to someone.

A few weeks after the quarry, Piper called. I was pleasantly surprised when she told me she was flying home that Saturday and was dying for a girls' night. Apparently, she had some things to talk about. She wasn't the only one with tales to tell. I'd just taken my first birth control pill that morning. I had a month to go before surprising Max and couldn't wait to spill my news.

After I hung up with Piper, I called and switched around my

work schedule to get the weekend off. Piper would be arriving sometime after lunch on Saturday. RJ was picking her up at the airport, and they had family plans until five or so. She was going to meet us at Joss's house after that. Joss informed me there was a party that night so if we got bored, we had a back-up plan.

When Friday night finally rolled around, Max, Kurt, Joss, and I hung out at Kurt's house. I was worried that Max would be upset when I told him I would be spending Saturday with the girls. This would be our first weekend night apart, and even though it was my idea, I was hesitant. For some reason the thought of spending a night away from him made my stomach ache. I knew how much guys hated crazy possessive girls, and I vowed I wasn't going to be like that. When I finally managed to pull Max aside to talk to him, he shrugged it off as no big deal. I can't deny I was kind of hurt by this. It had taken me three days to muster up the nerve to tell him, so for him to act like he didn't care, bothered me. Now, I had all kinds of messed-up things trampling through my head.

Max and I fooled around in his truck that night after we left Kurt's house. I didn't want to leave him since I knew I wouldn't see him until Sunday or Monday, but I was beyond exhausted and had to get some sleep.

The next day, I kept myself busy. At four-thirty on the dot, I was out the door and headed to Joss's house for the night. I couldn't wait to see Piper.

As planned, Piper showed up around five, only she wasn't alone. She had her boyfriend, Tom, with her. From the second I laid eyes on her, I could tell something was off.

After all of the squealing and hugging, she sheepishly introduced us. "Tom really wanted to come home with me and meet my family and friends," she explained in this pitchy fake, so-not- Piper, voice. She introduced me as Ellison and Joss as Josselyn. *What the hell?*

Joss and I stood there, dumbfounded. "Hi," we both awkwardly said.

Tom was not someone I'd envisioned Piper dating. He was about six feet tall and super skinny with beet red hair, bright blue eyes, lackluster skin, and a face like a really pretty girl. I couldn't believe that out of the hundreds of times that I'd talked with her this summer, she'd never physically described Tom to me, other than the one time she referred to him as 'different.' *I'll say...*

Eyeing us up and down and obviously finding us lacking, Tom said, "So sorry to intrude upon your girly get-together this weekend." Joss's eyes bugged, and I had to turn my head away to keep from laughing. *Girly get-together? Who is this guy?*

From the looks of it, Piper was clearly enthralled by him. I'd never seen her act this way before, and it was disturbing... to say the least. After watching her gaze adoringly at him, I cut my eyes back to Joss. She was staring at the two of them with a strange look on her face.

"You guys make yourselves comfortable," she told them. Then she mumbled something about phone calls and changing clothes as she grabbed me by the hand, and shot out the door, while pulling me behind her.

"What in hell was that?" I asked.

"You'd be amazed how people change when they think they're in love."

*Was she referring to me?* "Have I changed?" I asked.

"I wasn't talking about you, Ellie," she assured, "I was just speaking in general terms. It's normal to want to please the person you love, but sometimes people will bend over backwards and completely change for someone else. If I ever do that, tell me."

"Only if you do the same for me."

"Deal," we both agreed.

We spent the next half hour frantically trying to call Kurt and

Max with hopes they would let us tag along with them for the evening.

"What am I not getting?" I asked.

"Huh? Damn it, Kurt is not answering his phone." She started dialing another number.

"Who are you calling now?"

"Harry. Why don't you try Max?"

"I already got his voicemail and left him a message. I still don't get it," I repeated.

"What? That Piper is clearly in love with a guy who looks like a Chucky doll?"

My breath hitched when she said this. We'd spent a long weekend back in March watching the Child's Play series. It took me weeks to stop having Chucky nightmares. *Holy shit, Piper is dating a life-size Chucky.* I tried to hold back my full body shudder. "This is bad."

She threw me a sarcastic eyebrow raise. "You think? Okay, I'm making an executive decision here. Get changed. We're going to that party. There's no way in hell I'm staying here with those two all night."

I hadn't properly planned for this, so the only thing I had to wear was a pair of old jeans. I was going to have to raid Joss's closet for a top, and not only was she shorter than me, but her cup size was miniscule compared to mine. *Nice.* After spending what seemed like forever trying to find something that didn't look obscene, I finally settled on a white V-neck sweater that had a little stretch to it. *If I don't get cold or bend over, this should work.* I knew Max would be seriously unhappy if he saw me in this top, but what choice did I have? Plus, he was out with his friends. My gut told me to get in my car and go home. Did I listen? *No.*

We pulled up to the party and I cringed. Of course, it had to be at someone's house who'd just graduated with Max. We got out of the car and started for the house. *Please don't let Max be here.* My heart was thumping out of my skimpily clad chest. "Joss," I said through gritted teeth, "does Kurt know about this party?"

Her face broke into a grin. "How do you think I heard about it?"

I jerked to a stop and Piper bumped into me from behind.

"Hey, watch your step," she complained.

"Max is going to kill me," I announced. "I told him we weren't going out, and if he's here, he's going to think I either lied to him or I'm stalking him."

"Yeah, but once he sees you in that get-up, Chesty La Rue, he'll forgive you anything." Joss winked, and I just stared at her. "Come on, Ellie. Where's your sense of adventure?" I shot her the bird and she laughed.

"Don't worry about it, Elsie, just follow Pips and me. We'll protect you," Tom said, patting me on the back.

"Ellie," Piper corrected.

Joss let out a loud snort. "Elsie and Pips?" she mouthed at me, and I couldn't help but laugh. This scene was beyond comical. As we watched Piper and Tom disappear through the door, Joss elbowed me. "Chucky doesn't protect people. He humps them and then kills them," she whispered in my ear. Then, grabbing my hand, she dragged me through the door and into a room full of sweaty, dancing bodies. While I was taller than most, I couldn't see a thing in front of me except for wall-to-wall bodies. It reminded me of the last party I'd been to. *And we all knew how that night turned out.*

Blink 182's "Violence" blared throughout the house, and I marginally relaxed. If Max was here, there was about a three percent chance he would run across me in this crowd. We mulled our way through the mass of people and into the kitchen.

"Do you want a beer?" Joss asked, handing me a cup.

"Is it imported?" Tom asked. His whiney voice seriously grated on my nerves. We both looked over at Piper, waiting for her to answer in her sarcastically funny way, but she just stood there acting like a doorknob.

"Uh, it's just regular old Bud Light, Tom," Joss sighed, clearly disappointed.

After thirty minutes of standing around in the kitchen staring at each other, Piper started telling us about some play Tom had taken her to recently. Joss kept making funny faces behind Tom's back, and all I could think was *what has happened to my best friend?*

The kitchen window looked out onto a large deck. In between listening to Piper ramble, I watched the people outside, and formulated my escape plan. When I saw what looked like Bobby McManis walk by, I froze. *Max said he would be with Kurt, Harry, Tyler and Bobby tonight. Shit, this means Max is here.* Right as I turned to tell Joss, Kurt and Tyler appeared, and Tyler was holding hands with none other than Missy Landry, one of Jennifer's evil minions. Snapping my finger at Joss, I nodded my head at the window.

"No way," she moaned when she saw what I was staring at. "Can this get any worse?" *My thoughts exactly.* We watched Tyler lean down and plunge his tongue into Missy's mouth. Kurt and Bobby were shaking their heads and laughing at him.

"Yep, it just did," I said. "Shit. Do you think that-"

"Yep," Joss answered, before I could finish. *Max is here somewhere, and so is Jennifer.*

Turning to Piper and Tom, I announced, "I'm feeling a bit claustrophobic and need some air. I'm going outside for a minute."

"I'm going with her," Joss told them, and we both bolted for the door.

As I followed Joss across the crowded deck, all I could think about was Max. When she jerked to a stop, I barely avoided running over her.

"What's wrong?" I asked.

Joss stood there staring open-mouthed at something. When she reached between us and grabbed my hand in a tight squeeze, I knew. Still, seeing it with my own eyes was a shock. Sitting, all relaxed back in a deck chair, was none other than Max. That wouldn't have been so bad if Jennifer Tilson hadn't been sitting on his lap with her fingers in his hair and her lips on his neck. I was absolutely floored. The pain I felt as I stood there staring at my guy, with *her,* was indescribable. Max knew how much I despised Jennifer, yet there he sat. His words ran through my head. *She was a distraction. I need for you to trust me when I say I will take care of you. ...you're a game changer.*

It was all a lie, every last word of it, and I was...such a fool.

"Ellie," Joss whispered, her voice filled with pain. "Come on, we're leaving."

I couldn't take my eyes off of Max. All I kept thinking was *why would he do this to me?*

"Joss?" I heard Kurt shout from across the deck. *Was this all one big joke and I'm just the punch line?*

"I'll catch up with you later!" she shouted back.

When he heard Kurt call out Joss's name, Max's head shot up. His beautifully traitorous eyes connected with mine and flared in surprise. *Surprise, asshole, you're busted.* Heartsick and desperate to get away from him, I bolted off the deck.

"Fuck!" I heard someone shout and then, "Ellie, wait!" But I was already halfway across the front lawn and not stopping for anyone.

*I can't believe it, I can't believe it,* I chanted in my head as I sprinted down the street. *How could he do this to me? Why would he do this to me? I gave him all of me. Everything...I... had.* My heavy panting and internal dialogue were taking up so much space in my head that I wasn't aware Max was right on my heels until I felt his hand yanking me backwards.

"Ellison, stop," he said. I heard a gut-wrenching sound, somewhere between a wail and a keen, and realized it was coming from my mouth. He wrapped his arms around me, and for the first time, the smell of leather and spice didn't comfort me. They made me want to vomit. "Ells, baby, it's not what you think. Let me explain."

I reared back and yelled, "No!" I couldn't stop the tears. I was heartbroken and having a hard time catching my breath. "I saw y-y-you."

"You need to let me explain," he repeated, also breathing heavily.

"I saw her hands and m-mouth on you, Max." I was having trouble voicing the jumbled-up thoughts in my head.

"It's not what you think," he whispered, pulling me in closer.

I wanted to believe him, but I couldn't get the visual of them together out of my head. "She was sitting in your lap! I…Saw… Her…Lips…On…You. It's seared into my brain now," I said, slapping the front of my head. "And you were just…sitting there, letting her touch you! Why?" I cried. "Why?"

By this time, Joss, Kurt, Bobby, Tyler, Piper and Tom had all caught up with us.

"I think you've done enough damage here, Max," said Piper, who'd managed to grow her spine back for the moment.

"You don't know the half of it," I heard Joss mumble. If it had been any other situation but the one I was in, I would have laughed.

"Fuck you, Piper! You weren't even there," Max said.

"Now, now, no need for vulgar language here," Tom calmly said with his hands in the air as if he were talking down a fugitive.

"Who… the fuck…are you?" Max growled.

Before Tom could answer, Joss cut in. "Well, I was *there*,

Max, and from where I was standing, it looked pretty bad."

"Joss," Kurt warned.

"Please don't *tell me* you agree with him?" she hissed.

"I want to go home," I said, trying to get myself together.

"Baby, let me take you home and we can talk," Max said. His eyes flicked down and narrowed when he noticed what I was wearing.

"Don't call me that," I said, ignoring his scowl. "You don't get to call me that or anything else ever again."

I turned to Joss, the one person I knew I could count on. "I need to be alone. I need to get out of here. Please get me out of here," I implored.

"I'm asking you...please," Max begged, "don't do this." *Don't look at him....Don't give in.* Hearing the pain in his voice made me want to give in, but that would be weak and stupid, *wouldn't it?*

I leaned in and whispered, "You told me to trust you. So like a stupid, naïve little girl, I trusted you... *with everything*. You know what I'm talking about. You could have stayed with her doing - whatever you were doing, Max. Why couldn't you just let me be?"

"I've heard enough," Joss said. "Let's go." She put her arms around me and led me back to the car. Joss wanted to take me back to her house, but I just wanted to be alone. I needed to figure myself out, and the only way I could do this was alone. Piper was stuck so far up Tom's ass that she didn't even offer to ride back with us. I would never abandon her in a time of need and thought she felt the same way. It hurt to know I was wrong.

"I can stay here with you, if you want," Joss offered as we reached my driveway.

"No. I need to be alone right now."

"Okay, but I'm calling you first thing in the morning. We need to say goodbye to Pips and Chucky before they leave tomorrow afternoon, and I need to get your stuff back to you."

I gave her hand a squeeze and told her how much I appreciated her friendship. Then, I confessed what had been running through my head the whole way home. "He played me and got my virginity out of it, Joss. I am such an idiot."

"Ellie, look at me." I gave her my eyes and she cupped my face between her hands. "I know what it looked like tonight. I know you're hurting and, God knows, if Kurt did this to me, I would be, too. But...I heard Max's voice and saw his face when he was trying to explain it to you, and I gotta give it to him, either he's the best actor on the face of the planet, or we're missing something. Either way, take your space and get some sleep. I can't help but think that things will look better in the morning." With a nod of acknowledgement, I got out of the car. I was beyond emotionally exhausted. All I wanted was a hot shower and a good long cry. "Love you, girl," she said from her window as she drove off.

I could hear the phone ringing from my driveway and my aunt's voice as she answered it. "Hang on just a minute, Max," I heard her say as she set the phone on the counter.

I opened the screen door, shook my head, and mouthed, "No," to her.

Narrowing her eyes at me, she picked it back up. "Uh...she's not back from Joss's house yet. In fact, I don't expect her back until sometime tomorrow. I'll be sure and tell her you phoned, though," she told him. As soon as the phone hit the cradle, she asked, "What has that boy done to you now? Your eyes look like you've been stung by a swarm of bees and you sound like you've just smoked a carton of cigarettes. I don't like it, Ellison, not one bit."

"I can't talk about it right now. Can we talk tomorrow? Please? I just really need to be alone right now, okay?"

"Okay, sweetie, but I'm here for you if you want to talk," I heard her say as I hit the stairs.

I opened my bedroom door, walked directly to my window, and locked it. No surprise visits tonight. My heart couldn't take it. Grabbing my pillow and favorite blanket, I turned off my light, shut my door, and walked across the hall to the guest room. After a scorching hot shower, I crawled onto the bed and cried myself to sleep.

# CHAPTER NINE

The next morning, I woke to someone crawling into bed with me.

*What in the world?*

"Ellie, it's me, Joss," she crooned, rubbing my back.

Mentally chiding myself for being such a wuss, I flipped over and faced her. "God, Joss, you scared the hell out of me," I croaked. After screaming at Max and crying most of the night, I had very little voice left.

"Thought it was Chucky, didn't ya?" she giggled. When I failed to see the humor, she let out a deep sigh. "Honey, I am so sorry I got you to go to that party."

"Just think, if I hadn't caught him with her, he would have kept pretending he wanted to be with me. I am so dumb, Joss."

"Oh, El, has it occurred to you that maybe things didn't happen the way we think? Maybe what we thought we saw wasn't what was really happening?"

"No. You were there. You know what I saw."

"I talked to Kurt after I left you here last night. He said Max was completely destroyed."

"Let me guess, Max was destroyed because he got caught and lost his booty call for the night?"

"*No*. He said Max was destroyed by the thought of causing *you* pain. He also said Max tore into Jennifer the second he got back to the party."

This got my attention, and I couldn't help but ask, "Why?"

"Maybe because things weren't as they seemed?"

I rolled my eyes at this. "What exactly did he say to her, Joss?"

"Something to the effect of how his life is good, for once, and that if he loses you because of the shit she just pulled, he'll make it his personal mission to make her life a living hell."

"Wow." I was surprised, but far from being convinced.

"Yeah, I thought you would want to know that."

"Still, it doesn't excuse that he allowed her to sit in his lap and put her lips on him. If it were me, she would have been kissing the deck the second her nasty ass sat on my lap. I would never do that to him, Joss, ever. So why did he do it to me?" Just thinking about it made my eyes smart.

"I know and agree. But what we *didn't* see was him reciprocating. We were so caught up in what Jennifer was doing we failed to pay attention to what Max was doing. Kurt said Jennifer started chasing Max around the party the second they showed up. He told me that in no way did Max invite that from her. In fact, he said Max had managed to completely avoid her until five minutes before we saw them on the deck. Don't you find it odd she chose that moment to pounce? What do you want to bet she saw us walk through that door? She's wanted to get back at you for ages now, Ellie. What a perfect way to do it, don't you think?"

"I just don't know anymore, Joss. Nothing makes sense right now. This guy has made me lose all of my bearings."

"Like how?"

"My life wasn't great before, but I was dealing with it. Now, I just feel broken inside. I've never felt like this about anyone, so I have nothing to compare it to." I frantically wiped the tears, but they just kept coming.

"Sugar, it's called love. I see it in both of you. You're totally in love with each other."

"It hurts, Joss. Please make it stop." I wiped my face on my pillow. Finally, I just gave up and let them flow.

"You have to talk to him, Ellie. You need to hear what he has to say and decide whether you believe him or not."

"Okay," I whispered.

"Great!" She clapped her hands, jumped off the bed, and opened the door. "The floor is all yours. Don't make me regret this," she warned.

My heart skipped a couple hundred beats when a tired-looking Max entered the room. He walked to my desk, picked up the chair, carried it over to the bed, and set it down next to me. Then he plopped himself down and stared at me. *Joss just totally played me.*

"You were right," were the first words out of his mouth.

"About?" I rasped.

"Baby," he winced, hearing my ruined voice. So I was getting sweet Max this morning. I was okay with bossy Max, really didn't care for harsh Max, but I absolutely adored sweet Max.

Stiffening my spine, I repeated, "What was I right about, Max?"

"The second Jennifer planted her nasty ass on my lap I should have made her kiss the deck." *Oh God, he heard our conversation.* "But I didn't, and because of that, I hurt you and now I'm sitting here asking you to let me explain, instead of lying next to you in that bed." I didn't know how to respond to this. He looked out the window as if gathering his thoughts.

When his eyes drifted back to mine, he said, "I've had the best two months of my life with you and need you to know that I would never, in a million years, throw that away for something as cheap and meaningless as Jennifer Tilson." He took my hand and laced our fingers together. "Hell, I wouldn't throw this away for anything."

"I know what I saw, Max," I protested.

"You saw her making her move and me calmly explaining to her that hell would freeze over before she ever got me again."

"Her lips were on you."

"They weren't until she saw you walk across that deck." *Joss was right.* "I'd convinced myself that I needed to take things slow and give you time before blasting you with shit about my fucked-up family or my feelings. I'm thinking that was a mistake. If I'd simply told you what I was feeling, last night wouldn't have happened. At least it wouldn't have had such a shitty ending. I know it looked bad, and I know I would have done the same if the tables were turned. Hell, who am I kidding? I would have done much worse." He tightened his hold on my hand, as if afraid I would run away if he let go. I was contemplating what to say, when he suddenly stood up. My heart thumped heavily in my chest. *Is he leaving?* His knee hit the side of the bed as he leaned in and physically scooted me over. Then he crawled in beside me. Facing me, with his head on my pillow, he reached up and wiped away my tears. "I love you," he whispered. "I have never felt this way about anyone in my whole life. Before you, those words weren't even in my vocabulary."

"You love me?" I squeaked. I don't know what I expected, but it wasn't this.

"Beautiful girl, I love you so much that I spent the night in a fucking Magnolia tree waiting for the opportunity to crawl through your window."

"You did not!" I both sobbed and laughed at the same time.

"I did. Thanks for locking it, by the way."

"You love me?" I asked, again, through my laughter.

"Absolutely."

"You really don't want Jennifer?"

"Hell. No."

"I was so hurt and mad and…hurt…"

He placed a finger on my lips and my words trailed off into silence. "That's on me, and, if it's the last thing I do, I will make sure you believe how sorry I am."

"I love you, too. I have for a long time," I declared.

His brow wrinkled. "You're not just saying that because I did, are you?"

I shook my head. "When I saw you with her, I felt as if something inside of me had broken."

"I know, baby." He kissed my forehead. "I need you to believe in us and this -" he circled his fingers over the two of us -"I need to know you trust in me and that you believe I will never betray that trust. I will run into Jennifer again, and I need you to know I want nothing to do with her."

"I *really* don't like her, Max," I stressed.

"I get that," he smiled.

"I'm serious. I wanted to rip her off of you and then beat her with the deck chair."

"That would have been really hot, but I'm glad you didn't. She's not worth your time, your tears, or a hefty jail sentence."

I smiled through my tears. "No, but you are."

He was so close that the front of his body was touching the front of mine. His lips were less than an inch away. "I am desperate to kiss you, Ellison, to touch you, but I'm the one who hurt you. I don't want to force your forgiveness before you're ready. You have to be the one to reach out, and I need you to make sure it's what you want, because once you do, I won't let you take it back." Slowly, I leaned forward and touched my lips to his. As soon as he opened up, I slid in. He let out a sound of pure anguish as if it was wrenched from his soul. Flipping me onto my back, he cupped my face with both hands and stared into my eyes. "You forgive me?" I nodded. "I need to hear you say it."

"Yes, Max, I forgive you."

"I love you, Ells."

"I love you, too, Max."

The moment his lips hit mine the pain and hurt washed away.

"I want you," I breathed. I needed proof this was real. I wanted to feel him on me, over me, inside me.

"I want that, too, but your aunt, Joss, Kurt, Piper and that tool, Tom, are downstairs waiting to see how this turns out."

"Tom is *such* a tool, isn't he?" I giggled.

"Where in the hell did she find him?"

"At a Chucky doll convention," I joked.

"No shit?" he asked with raised eyebrows. I could see he was trying to work this out in his head. My fit of laughter made him smile. "Get cleaned up and meet me downstairs, funny girl." With a smile on his face, he kissed the laughter from my lips. "Let's hurry and get this shit over with."

I made myself presentable, we assured my aunt and my friends that I was okay, and life was good again. Later that night, we spent hours making up for lost time.

Max and I were inseparable after the Jennifer incident. His dad was never around, so I got the chance to spend a lot of time with Sarah as well. She was everything I would want in a little sister, and I was excited about spending time with her while Max was away at school.

"I have something for you," Max said one afternoon. We were lounging on a blanket in my backyard, while listening to the radio. He was absently twirling a piece of my hair around his finger.

"Funny you should say that. I have something for you also. In fact, I have two somethings for you." I rose up on my elbow and smiled down at him.

He smirked and waggled his eyebrows. "I'll show you mine if you show me yours."

Shaking my head, I informed him mine wasn't wrapped yet.

On one of our numerous double dates with Joss and Kurt that summer, Joss managed to get a great picture of us. We were at The Alley Cat, a little neighborhood bar and grill, and I'd just come back from the bathroom when Max pulled me down onto his lap. He had me in a backwards bear hug and we were laughing into the camera. That picture captured what we felt for each other better than any words ever could. I'd made two copies, bought two frames, and was planning on giving one to him right before he left for college as a going away present. The other would sit on my nightstand.

"How about we do something special tonight? We can spend the whole night together and give each other our gifts," he suggested.

"Your place or mine?" I asked. We'd been sneaking in and out of each other's houses all summer and had it mastered.

"How about you tell your aunt you're staying over at Joss's, and I'll make sure Sarah has some place to crash for the night."

I looked down into his beautiful face and couldn't believe he was finally mine after all these years. "Can't wait for tonight," I said, pressing my lips to his. He answered me with a knowing smile.

Wearing a short skirt and a fitted tank, I was ready. I made sure I put on sexy, *clean* underwear and my new strappy sandals that showed off my long, tan legs. Max loved my long legs. I grabbed my overnight bag, waved goodbye to my aunt, hopped in my car, and turned on the stereo. "Somebody Told Me" blasted from the speakers. The Killers were just what the doctor ordered. They were loud, had a good-looking lead singer and awesome song lyrics. *Life can't possibly get any better than this.* I was driving to see my guy and was the happiest I'd ever been. My first month on the pill was up, and I couldn't wait to see Max's face when I told him about it.

I pulled up to Max's house and smiled when I saw him waiting for me. In his worn jeans, a tight-fitting Harley tee, his feet bare and a heart-stopping smile on his face, he sure was something to see.

"What's that smile for?" I asked, as I reached the porch.

"You," he answered, with his eyes glued to my skirt.

I gave him a quick kiss. "Thanks, baby. Is Sarah here?"

"I like it when you call me baby and no, Sarah's not here. She's staying with a friend tonight."

"What about your dad?"

"Probably out getting drunk and causing trouble. Who knows?"

Suddenly, feeling a little shy, I asked, "Sooo, whatcha want to do tonight?"

"Come inside, and I'll show you." He threaded his fingers through mine and pulled me into the house. "How about we eat and talk first. We'll get to my other plans later."

As soon as dinner was over, he started in. "We need to talk about me leaving."

"I know, I sighed." Max and I hadn't talked about him leaving for college yet. He'd tried, but I kept putting him off. It made me sad. I was worried that the second he saw what great things were out there in the world, I would lose him.

"I want to put all of your worries to rest, Ells, but can't if you don't tell me what you're thinking."

"What do you want me to say? You're leaving. I'm staying. There will be girls and parties and new experiences for you. I'll be here doing the same things I've been doing for the past three years," I shrugged.

"You're right. I am leaving. I'm going to a new place with new experiences, but my heart is here in Charlotte. I have responsibilities here that I do not take lightly."

"Like Sarah," I said looking down at my lap.

"Yes, like Sarah," he said. I felt the pressure of his fingers on my chin. When he got my eyes, he continued. "I also have a beautiful girlfriend who I'm crazy about, not to mention a job where I make really good money. Benny wants me to work on the weekends, so it looks like I'll be home every Friday through Sunday."

My eyes shot to his face, and I gasped, "Really?"

"Sarah and my job are important, but I also worry about a sweet, beautiful girl, who I'm crazy in love with, falling for someone else while I'm away. I simply can't have that, so I figure I'll need to be here as much as possible to make sure that doesn't happen."

I squealed and launched myself into his lap. "Wait, I have something for you!" I all but shouted as I ran to my bag and pulled out the wrapped frame. "I wanted you to have something that would remind you of me, something that you can travel with," I said, handing him the frame.

He ripped the paper off and froze. "Wow," he whispered, reverently running his fingers over our faces. "This is awesome. Where did you get it? Who took it?"

"Remember that night we went to dinner with Joss and Kurt, and Joss kept taking pictures of everyone? Well, this was one that she took of us."

He stood and deposited me on my feet. Then, he took my hand and walked me to his bedroom. He placed the frame next to the picture of his sister and mother. "Thank you, baby, I have something for you as well. This will hopefully remind you of me, will keep you safe, and will bide the time until I see you on the weekends." I watched him reach into his pocket and pull something out. "Hold out your hand," he ordered. I did as he asked, and the object from his pocket landed in my hand with a jingle.

"A set of keys?" I asked, somewhat confused. I wasn't comfortable being in his house alone, especially with his messed-up dad.

"Come here, gorgeous girl," he said, laughing at my expression. He pulled me to him and wrapped his arms around me like a vise. "We have been together now for three months." I wasn't sure where he was going with this, so I just nodded. "And, in three months, I have fixed your beat-up piece of shit car three times." *Oh God.* I was catching on.

"Max—" I whispered.

"That averages out to a breakdown a month," he continued. "Now, I've asked you to help with my sister and you agreed, right?"

"Max—" I repeated.

"I need to protect the two most important people to me, in any way I can."

"But you love your truck," I managed to get out before he cut me off again.

"Yes. But I love you more, and I want to know that you're safe, especially when I can't be with you."

"But what will you drive?"

"I've been working on a 1970 Chevy Shortbed for Benny. When I told him my idea, he agreed with me and told me to take the Chevy. It's not like I'm never coming back, babe," he whispered in my ear. "Please say you'll do this for me."

"I would do anything for you, Max, but your truck?"

"I want you to be safe. How about this, I'll park it over at Benny's and will explain to him that you'll be coming by to use it… often. That way, you can check on Benny for me *and* use the truck whenever you need. Sound good?"

"Yes," I sighed. "In case you didn't already know it, you're the best, Max McLellan."

"And there is nothing I wouldn't do for you, Ellison Davis." He kissed my neck and gave me a tight squeeze before letting go. I watched him walk across the room toward his window.

"Where are you going?"

"You'll see."

Suddenly, Bono's sultry voice filled the room, and my heart completely melted.

"All I Want Is You."

"How did you know?" I asked. I loved this band and especially this song. It reminded me of Max.

"We like the same music. If I wrote a song for you, this would be it. He held out his hand. Dance with me?" I wanted to cry. I didn't want him to go. I wanted forever. He was sunshine and moonlight, sandy beaches and salty air. He was happy laughter and sexy smiles. He was my best friend, my lover, my heart… He was everything good in this world, and believe me, few things were ever good in my world. I didn't want to lose him, but would never begrudge him this experience.

I took his hand. "We've never danced together, have we?"

"This is just the first of many, Ellison Davis," he murmured, pressing his lips to mine.

"I like the sound of that," I said against his mouth. We danced for the remainder of the song and just when I thought it was over, it began again.

Max walked us backwards until the backs of my knees hit the bed. His mouth moved from my lips down to my neck as one hand traveled to the middle of my back and the other to the side of my breast. The hand on my back slid down and under the waist of my skirt, while the other worked its way under my tank and bra, right to my nipple.

*Two can play this game,* I thought. Reaching my hand down between us, I cupped him and lightly squeezed. Hearing the hitch of his breath made me smile. *Game on.*

With a growl, he yanked my tank off and, with a flick of his fingers, unclasped my bra. His lips were on my breast, his hands on my ass, Bono was singing about promises, and I was in love. Somehow, I managed to get his jeans unbuttoned and off. At the same time, he had me stepping out of my panties. Before I knew what was happening, he had me turned around and bent over, both hands flat on the bed, and was reaching for a condom. Excitement shot up my spine.

"No condom, I'm on the pill," I panted.

"What?"

"No condom. I'm safe, I…" Before I could say any more, he tilted my hips up and was plunging inside me.

"I love you," he ground out. He had a hand on my hip, the other between my legs, and I was shaking with pleasure. I could feel every bare inch of him deep inside. In a total of two seconds, we went from restrained to completely wild. He was pounding me from behind while grinding his fingers between my legs. I was screaming in pure ecstasy. Loving. Every. Second. Of. It.

"Come," he commanded, and I exploded.

Minutes later, I lay face down on the bed with my skirt thrown over my hips and my bare ass hanging in the breeze. Max lay next to me and was running his fingers up and down my naked spine.

"Have I ever told you that I love the way you smell?" I

sleepily mumbled.

"No." I could hear the smile in his voice.

"You smell like leather, exotic spices and everything that's good in the world." I felt his hand still. When it started back up, I continued. "I haven't had much good in my life. I was convinced it didn't exist for me... until you."

I must have fallen asleep, because when I opened my eyes, I was snugly tucked into Max's side with his arms tightly wrapped around me. Apparently, he'd taken off my skirt and sandals while I slept, because they were no longer on my body. I breathed deeply in, wanting to memorize the smells that made up my Max. I knew he wasn't going far or forever, but he was going. Things were going to change, and whether he admitted it or not, so would our relationship. I felt a wave of sadness roll over me. I'd never had anything worth keeping before, so I wasn't familiar with the feelings that came with having to let go. I could feel the tears welling, and thinking Max was asleep, I let them spill over.

"Hey, you okay?" His voice was sexy with sleep.

I buried my head in his pillow and hoped he wouldn't see me crying.

"Look at me, Ellison," he commanded.

Slowly, I lifted my head and looked into his beautifully perceptive eyes.

"Why are you crying? Did I hurt you earlier? Was I too rough?"

"No, it was absolutely perfect. You are perfect. This whole summer has been perfect. I'm just sad to see it go."

"It's not going anywhere. I'm not going anywhere," he huskily replied, wiping a tear away.

"I don't want things to change," I whispered.

Cradling my face between his hands, he tenderly kissed my lips. More tears fell and he deepened the kiss. Sensing his need,

I opened my legs. Slowly, he slid into me and rocked, in and out, until we were both breathing heavily.

"Deeper," I told him.

Sliding both of his hands underneath me, he pulled himself in deeper. Shivering with desire, I wrapped both of my legs around him so that my heels were touching his lower back. I stared into his eyes, wanting him to see everything I felt but couldn't say. Thrusting deeply, he whispered, "You. Are. Mine." Those three words were all it took. Moaning out his name, I came and took him over with me.

"I love you, Max. I always will."

"Always," he replied.

He woke me a few hours later and was already showered and ready for work. He walked me to my car and left me with a kiss and a promise to come by the café when he got off work. I waved as I drove away.

That was the last time I saw him.

# CHAPTER TEN

*Five Years Later*

*I hate graduations.*

This time of year dredged up all kinds of painful memories for me. The best decision I'd ever made was to get the hell out of Charlotte. The past four years at UNC Greensboro had flown by. I'd gone home for holidays to see Joss, Kurt, Benny, and my aunt, but I never stayed for long. It was too painful. School had been my primary excuse to stay away, but I made sure I had a job lined up in Greensboro for the summer. Piper had been my savior, especially during the first two years of college. She could've gone anywhere, but because of me she chose a smaller private college less than a mile away. We saw each other every chance we could.

I almost didn't make it to my high school graduation on account of my failing grades. Thank goodness my teachers took pity on me during that time. Through forgiveness, plus a lot of extra credit, I managed to graduate from high school. Now, I was a college graduate.

*Max would be proud.*

Joss ended up following Kurt to UNC Charlotte. They visited Greensboro every now and then, alternating stays between my fold-out sofa and Piper's guest bedroom. Kurt graduated last May and was, as of a month ago, the proud owner of a bar named Dragonfly. I'd gone home for Joss's graduation. While I was there, Kurt gave me the grand tour. I had to admit I was impressed. With a little bit of TLC, Dragonfly was going to be an awesome place to hang out.

A month into our senior year, Piper's family moved back to Texas. She was heading there for who knew how long after graduation. I was going to miss her terribly. She'd helped me get through one of the toughest times in my life and I dreaded saying goodbye.

This past weekend, my aunt, Joss, Kurt and Piper all came to see me graduate. We went out after the ceremony and lit up the town. Even Aunt Elizabeth cut loose, something I'd never seen before, and didn't think would ever happen in my lifetime. With a brand new degree in Business Administration, I had one week to go before my job at Trace Advertising started. Instead of taking a much-needed vacation, I decided I was going to clean out my apartment and redecorate. I was done dwelling on the past. It was time to focus on the future, to move forward, and I was ready to embrace new adventures. At least, that's what I kept telling myself.

*Five years earlier*

"Max, I've been calling your cell since five this afternoon and am starting to worry. Benny said you left the garage around eleven this morning. I hope everything is okay. I'm trying not to worry here, so… call me. Love you." I pressed the end button and tossed the phone on the bed. *Where are you?*

Max hadn't shown up at Providence that afternoon, which was unlike him. At first, I didn't think anything about it. I figured he got caught at work and would call as soon as he was free. That was then. Now, it was going on midnight and I still hadn't heard from him. Worry had set in and I was calling Joss.

"God, Ellie, do you know what time it is?" a groggy sounding Joss asked, as she answered the phone.

"Joss, have you seen Kurt today?" *Please say yes.*

"He's here with me. Why?" *Thank God!*

"Is Max there, too?" *Please say yes.*

"No. Why? Should he be?" My heart stuttered painfully in my chest.

"Will you ask Kurt if he's seen or heard from Max today?" Something wasn't right. I could feel it in my bones.

"Sure, hang on." I heard her talking to Kurt, but couldn't make out the words. "He says he hasn't heard from Max since yesterday afternoon. Is everything okay? You sound worried."

"I'm sure it's fine," I lied. I wasn't sure about anything. "Max was supposed to come by after work today and didn't. Every time I call his phone it goes straight to voicemail. I already called Benny, and he said Max got a phone call at the garage around eleven this morning and took off right after. Would you please have Kurt see if he can reach him? I just want to make sure he's okay."

"Sure. We'll call you right back." *Kurt will figure it out and everything will be fine*, I told myself.

Not only did Kurt not figure it out, but Max didn't call or answer his phone that night. By the next morning, I knew something bad had happened.

Joss stopped by before lunch the next day to check up on me. We drove by Max's house. I'd had next-to-no sleep the night before and was running on pure adrenaline. Both Max's Bronco and his father's car were sitting in the driveway when we pulled up to his house. The second I saw them, I felt physically sick. *Why are both cars here? Why hasn't Max returned any of my calls?* A million scenarios traipsed through my head and none of them were good.

"Do you want to stop and knock?" Joss asked. *If it weren't for his dad, I would be in there right now.* I didn't know whether to cry or scream. *Why would he do this to me?*

"No. Apparently, he's busy." *At least he's too busy to talk to me.*

"I'm sure there's a logical explanation for this, Ells. Sarah probably needed him, or his dad went on a bender. Stop worrying."

I took in a deep breath and slowly let it out. "You're probably right."

Joss drove me back to my house, told me to take a nap, and she would call as soon as Kurt heard from Max.

My doorbell rang around six that night. I flung the door open thinking it was Max, but it was only Kurt. By that point I didn't care where Max had been or what he was doing. I just wanted him to be okay. "Did you find him?" I asked. I held my breath and prayed his answer would be yes.

"His truck was there and so was his dad's car. I rang the doorbell like a hundred times, Ellie, but no one answered."

Seized by an overwhelming sense of disappointment, I asked, "What if something bad happened to them, Kurt, and we're just sitting here doing nothing?" In my head I pictured horrible things. One of which was Max lying on his floor, bleeding to death. "We need to do something, like go over there and break in or call the police...something," I stressed.

"No police. At least, not yet," Kurt said. "Max would never forgive us if we got Sarah taken away because of some stupid knee-jerk reaction." Kurt was right. Max would hate me if I contacted the police and got his sister put in foster care. Still, why hadn't he called me? What if Kurt was wrong? This was so out of character for Max, and I knew ...I knew... deep in my gut I was missing something important. Kurt wanted to wait a few more days, but I couldn't help but wonder if we were making a huge mistake.

After Kurt left, I went to talk to my aunt. *Desperate times call for desperate measures.*

"Did you call the police?" she asked, after I explained the situation.

"We don't want to involve them unless we have to."

"How about the hospitals? And, why may I ask, no police?"

"First of all, we're not sure Max is even missing. Joss and I called the hospitals already and he wasn't there. Second, Max is barely eighteen and is too young to take care of Sarah. His dad is a loser, an alcoholic, and a possible drug addict. If we get the police involved and they take her away -"

She held up her hand to stop me. "I see. Thank goodness that boy found you when he did. He will call, honey." She patted my hand. "He's probably tied up with something, but I know when he gets the chance, he'll reach out to you. That boy loves you. I can't imagine anything that would keep him away from you for long." That was just the problem, I couldn't either.

After the visit with my aunt, I forced myself to go back up to my room. I was afraid to sleep downstairs. What if Max tried to get into my room and I wasn't there? Pausing outside my bedroom door, I closed my eyes and made a wish. *Please, let Max be sitting on my bed when I open this door.* I flung open the door and...nothing, except my phone that I'd left sitting on my bed. *What if Max tried to reach me?* I raced over to check my messages. As I passed by my desk, I accidentally rammed into the chair and knocked my purse onto the floor. The contents flew everywhere.

"Shit!" I exclaimed, as I snagged my phone and searched my messages. No new messages. *Damn!* Sighing, I bent down to pick up the mess, and there, smack in the middle of it all, sat the keys to Max's Bronco. I thought back on our conversation that night.

*I need to protect the two most important people to me in any way that I can.*

*But Max, you love your truck.*

*Yes, but I love you more, and I want to know you are safe, especially when I can't be with you.*

*If he loves me so much, then why hasn't he called to let me know he's okay?* Something was wrong, I just knew it. Tomorrow, I was going to his house. I was searching his car. Even if I had to break a window to get into the house, I would. It felt good to finally have a plan.

The next morning, I called Providence and told Amy about Max. She told me to take as much time off as I needed. School was starting next week, so my work schedule would be changing anyway. After checking that off my list, I called Kurt to tell him my plan. He convinced me that felonious acts like breaking and entering should only be attempted after dark, and since he had to work tonight, he would be by to pick me up at eight tomorrow evening. I didn't really want to wait, but didn't want to face it on my own either. I was about to call Piper and fill her in on what had been happening when my doorbell rang. My heart skipped a thousand beats. *Maybe it's Max!* I rushed to the door and flung it open.

"Have you seen him?" Benny asked, and my shoulder's slumped in disappointment.

"Hi, Benny. No, I haven't seen or heard from him. You were fourth on my list to call today." Benny and I had been in constant contact since the afternoon of Max's disappearance.

"Wherever the hell that boy is, he should have checked in by now. In all the years I've known him, he's never gone this long without checking in." I gnawed my lip, and wondered if I should tell him my plan. "I drove by the house before heading over here," he continued. "I swear this has his dad written all over it. That man has been up to no good for a long time." I didn't know what to say to this. I wanted to know more about Max's dad but wanted Max to be the one to tell me, not Benny.

"Are both cars still there?" I asked.

He nodded his head. "Yep, I rang the bell and looked in all the windows, but I couldn't see a damn thing." I told him what Kurt said about the police, and not being able to stand it any longer, told him about our plans. "I'm coming with you," he said. *I had a feeling he was going to say that.*

Kurt and Joss showed up at my house right at eight the next night. Benny and three guys who also worked at the garage with Max pulled up behind them.

Benny introduced us. "Ellie, this is Twon, Marcus and Tut. Boys, this is Max's Ellison." Tears sprang to my eyes. *Max's Ellison.* I loved that he called me that.

"Nice to meet you," I barely managed to get out.

Benny's boys were far from boys. Max had told me all about them. They were three extremely large, fit black men. Antwon, or Twon, was Benny's nephew. He was a few years older than Max. Marcus had been in and out of foster homes until he found Benny. Now he was old enough to stay with Benny full time and work at the garage. Tut should have been named Tat. From what I could see, he had them all over, including on his shaved skull. Max hadn't said much about Tut. *I can see why, yikes!* Kurt hugged Benny and slapped the other three on their backs before introducing Joss. Since Max was close to Kurt, and Benny was close to Max, it made sense that Kurt would be close to Benny and the boys.

We parked about half a mile away from Max's house, because Benny was worried about people seeing our cars. *What people?* I wanted to ask, but didn't dare. He then sent Marcus, Tut and Twon to check around and make sure we weren't being watched.

"This is creepy," Joss whispered. "Who do you suppose is watching us?"

"I'm afraid to ask. I'm also surprised Kurt let you come."

"I told him I would cut him off if he didn't."

"Ouch."

When we reached the house, both cars were still there, but no lights were on. My stomach lurched. Benny led us to the furthest window from the living room and pulled out what looked like a chisel. Sliding it under the sill, he wiggled it until we heard a click. Slowly, he pushed the window up.

"We can take it from here, Ben," Kurt quietly said.

"You can, but you're not," he replied. "That boy saved me when nothing else could. I intend to repay the favor. You three stay here. I'm going in to check it out. I'll let you in when the coast is clear, and for shit's sake, be quiet," he whispered. We stood there for what felt like a century before we heard him come back. "Coast is clear. Come around to the back door, and I'll let you in."

We spent the next hour searching through every room and closet in Max's house. Nothing was out of place or looked different, except for the big coffee stain on the hardwood floor between the kitchen and living room.

"His things are still here," I said. We were standing in the middle of Max's bedroom. I toed the bag at my feet. "This is one of the bags he was packing to take to ASU. I was here the day he pulled it out."

"It looks like he was packing winter clothes but didn't get very far," Joss said.

"Shit!" Kurt exclaimed from across the room.

"What?" We turned to look at him.

"Hang on." We watched as he perused the room, obviously searching for something. Finally, he answered, "His duffle is gone."

"What duffle?" Benny asked.

"The duffle he takes whenever he's traveling anywhere. It's gone. Ellie, look real close. Do you notice if anything else is missing?"

I'd been four days without Max, now, and didn't realize how deprived I was feeling. That is, until I sat on his bed and his scent wafted up from his sheets and comforter. I felt as if I was being held together by tiny fragile strings, and one by one, they were starting to snap and break apart. The smell of him sucked me back to the last night I'd spent in this bed. It smelled of us. *We danced…and the room still smells of our love. He promised we would always be together.* The squeeze of Joss's hand brought me back to the moment.

"Ellie, honey, we need you to focus."

*I can do this.* I walked over to his chest of drawers and opened each one. His favorite jeans and T-shirts were gone. "Some of his clothes are missing," I thickly said. It was then that I noticed what else was missing. Closing my eyes, I let the pain wash over me. "And he took the pictures."

"Fuck!" Kurt shouted, causing us to jump. "This is not fucking happening. He wouldn't just leave without telling someone. He would know we would worry. He's crazy in love with you." He stared at me with such intensity it made me squirm. "He would not walk away from that. Not even two weeks ago, he was telling me how you were it for him. He was in this forever. There's no way in hell he would walk away from that!" He gave an angry kick to the bag on the floor.

"He told me the same," Benny stated. "I'm telling you, this has his father written all over it."

"You keep saying that. Why?" I asked.

"Whatever this is -" he swept his arm across the room - "is because of his dad. I don't know if he owes someone money or if he's done something bad. Neither would surprise me, but whatever it is, I can guaran-damn-tee it concerns that fucked-up man."

"Ellie, did you get a chance to look in Sarah's room?" Joss asked before Benny could say anything else. She could tell I was barely hanging on.

I hesitantly walked across the hall to Sarah's room. My eyes went directly to her bed, and the pain washed over me again. "Her blanky and pillow are gone. She never goes anywhere without them," I told them.

"Why did they leave everything else here?" Joss asked.

"Because they plan on coming back? Maybe Max took off early for school? Maybe he took Sarah with him?" Kurt suggested.

*Or maybe, like Benny said, he was running from something his dad did.* I didn't say it out loud, but I knew we were all thinking it.

"I'll drive up to Boone tomorrow and check if Max showed up at ASU," Kurt said.

"Not without me, you won't," I told him. There was no way he was leaving me here.

"Or me," Joss added.

"Damn it, I can't go. I've got two new cars to work on at the garage."

"We'll come by and fill you in when we get back," Kurt assured him.

The last thing I did that night before going home was search Max's truck. I was about to close it up when I remembered the glove compartment. Unlocking it, I reached in and found his iPod. His ear buds were still connected to it. I couldn't imagine him going anywhere without his iPod. Like my books, Max's music was an extension of him. He worked out with it, listened to it while he fixed cars, and when I wasn't around, used it to get to sleep. This scared me more than anything else. Deep down, I knew there was no way Max would have intentionally left his music behind.

*No… way…in…hell.*

# CHAPTER ELEVEN

*Five Years Later*

*One more day of freedom before my marketing job at Trace starts.* I was kicking myself for not taking more than a week off after graduation. *Oh, well.* As my aunt would say, I was now a gainfully employed adult. *I can't believe I graduated from college two weeks ago.*

I'd spent this past week cleaning out my apartment. Throwing away four years of crap was cathartic. So far, my decorating skills went as far as to purchase all new sheets and towels. I had plans of becoming more sophisticated. This, however, was going to take me a lot longer than a week. I was making a list of how to go about doing this when my phone rang. "Hello?"

"Is this Miss Davis?"

"Speaking."

"Miss Davis, this is Dr. Glazer at Presbyterian Hospital in Charlotte. I have you down as the emergency contact for a Ms. Elizabeth Davis. Is this correct?" My heart dropped.

"Um, yes, Elizabeth is my aunt. Why? Is she okay?"

"I'm very sorry to inform you that your aunt passed away at 11:22 this morning."

"What?" I whispered. I closed my eyes and prayed I'd heard her wrong.

"I'm very sorry," she repeated.

"B-b-but…how?"

"It appears she went into cardiac arrest, and our team couldn't revive her. Again, I'm so sorry for your loss. Is there anyone we can call for you?"

"Please tell me this is some kind of joke," I pleaded.

"I'm so sorry for your loss, ma'am, I really am." After she gave me her contact information, I hung up and immediately dialed Joss.

"Hello?" she answered.

"Joss?" I barely got her name out.

"Ellie, what's wrong?"

"My aunt," I sobbed. I heard the phone rustle and then Joss shouting something in the background.

"Hey, El, it's Kurt, what's wrong?" Ever since Max's disappearance, Kurt had been my confidant, brother, and protector. Sometimes I felt as if he was watching over me for Max. Of course, I knew this wasn't the case. After all, Max left Kurt too, but… just hearing his voice made the tears break free.

"The hospital called a few minutes ago. My aunt died of heart failure at eleven this morning."

"Jesus, Ellie. I'm so damn sorry. What can we do to help? Do you want us to come get you?" *I need you to bring her back.*

"Kurt, I need to go. I feel sick." My chest was tight, and I suddenly felt sick to my stomach.

"Okay, but promise you'll call us later today, okay?"

I agreed to call him later and then quickly got off the phone right as a wave of nausea slammed into me. I barely made it to the bathroom, before losing my breakfast. *First Max and now my aunt.*

I didn't call Kurt and Joss back that day. I couldn't. I was too raw. Instead, I turned off my phone and crawled in my bed, where I relived a lifetime of memories with the only parent I'd ever known. True, not all of them were good, but they were mine.

Three days later, I heard my front door open and close.

"You're going to have to get out of bed and deal with this, Ellie," Kurt announced from my bedroom door. *Why did I ever give them a key?*

"Go away," I moaned in his direction.

"Ellie sugar," Joss said, crawling into bed beside me. "Plans need to be made, and your aunt's lawyer needs to talk to you. Your aunt arranged everything through her will, but they need you to sign off on it."

"I don't want to sign off. I don't want to bury her."

"I know you don't," Kurt said, sitting down on my other side, "but you have to." They now had me smushed between them, like a very sad sandwich.

"I didn't get to say goodbye," I whispered.

"I know, and I'm so sorry," Joss whispered back.

"I didn't thank her for adopting me or tell her that I loved her enough."

"She knew," Kurt said. "She was so proud of you."

They both consoled me while I cried and reminisced. Then they helped me plan my next steps.

*Five years earlier*

I read somewhere that there are five stages of grief. The first is denial. I couldn't believe Max was gone, especially after everything we'd shared. That he could or would just up and leave me was almost too much to bear. So I didn't. I made like an ostrich and buried my head deep in the sand or, in my case, deep in denial. I believed to the bottom of my soul that he was going to show up at any second with a plausible explanation. We would all sigh in relief and life would go on. Hope, however, is a tricky thing. Kurt, Joss and I knew deep down that Max wasn't going to be at ASU, but we were drowning, so we grabbed on to anything we could think of. Hope kept me focused and moving forward. It fed my denial and, for a while, I let it.

"Well that was pointless," I huffed. "What's the point of a registrar's office if they won't tell you anything?"

Kurt managed to get the name of Max's dorm and his room number, but that was it. We visited Max's roommate, only to discover what we already knew. Max hadn't shown up.

We were all quiet on the ride back down the mountain.

Finally, Joss broke the ice, and asked, "So, what now?"

"Listen, Ellie, even if Max wanted to leave you, which he didn't, he wouldn't have left without talking to me first. He wouldn't have left Benny without a word. Damn, I really wanted him to be there," he sighed. "I wanted to see his face and then chew his ass. More than that, I just wanted to know he was okay." He ran his hand through his hair. I had no words. I was slowly giving up hope. I stared hopelessly out the window and let the tears fall. We were all disappointed, but I was devastated.

We stopped off at the garage to talk to Benny before heading home. He told us he'd been searching out places where Max's dad liked to drink. "Ailene at the Crispy Catch said she hasn't seen Malcolm in well over a week. He's in the wind, gone to ground, or dead." I wasn't sure the meaning of the first two, but I certainly knew what the last meant. If Malcolm McLellan was dead, then what did that mean for Max and Sarah?

I waited three more agonizing days before breaking down and calling Piper.

"Ellie, you do realize that something is wrong here, don't you?" she asked after I explained all that had happened over the past two weeks.

"I'm sure he'll call when he can," I defensively replied. *Yep, I'm still knee-deep in denial.*

"Has Kurt heard from him?"

"No one has."

"Did you search through his iPod? Maybe he left a clue or something?"

She wasn't telling me anything I hadn't already thought of. "I looked, Piper."

"Are you sure?"

The night we got back from ASU, I couldn't fall asleep. This was nothing new, but that night was particularly bad. I was beyond tired and imagining all kinds of messed-up things in my head. I pulled out Max's iPod, thinking that music, *his* music, would help. One of his playlists was titled *Songs For Ellison*. I cried through twenty-five songs that made him think of me. I explained all of this to Piper.

"Wow," she said, "were any of them good?"

A dry, humorless laugh slipped out. "Let's see, I started crying at Bruce Springsteen's "Secret Garden", thought I was going to throw up by Maroon 5's "She Will be Loved", and had to turn it off at "All I Want is You".

"What about the police? What did they have to say when you reported him missing?" she asked.

"Kurt doesn't want me to go to the police because of Sarah."

"What? That's crazy!"

"What if it's not what we think? We could get Sarah taken away from them, Piper."

"How long are you going to hold out?"

"Not much longer."

"Promise you'll keep me informed from here on out?"

"I promise."

"Ummm, not to change the subject or anything, but I broke up with Tom a couple of days ago." *Thank you, Jesus.*

"Oh, Piper, I'm so sorry. We really liked Tom. Are you doing okay?" *I'm such a crappy friend, and most likely going to hell for lying.*

"Yeah, he was getting to be a bit pretentious." *Getting to be?*

"Well, I'm just glad you're okay." *Sayonara, Chucky, or, as Joss would say, don't let the door hit ya where the good Lord split ya!*

"I'm worried about you, Ellie. This is your senior year. Everything counts now. Remember how we used to sit on my bed and dream about being seniors?"

"I know. It's just..." I tried not to cry, but I seemed to have zero control over my emotions anymore.

"Juuuuust what?"

Clearing the tears from my throat, I continued, "We made plans. He gave me the keys to his truck. We talked of future dreams together. I was his end game and he was my...everything. How am I supposed to go on... without him...not knowing?"

"I can't answer that. I wish I could, and I wish I was there," she quietly replied.

"Me, too."

Before bed that night, I called Max's phone and poured everything I was feeling into my message. I couldn't help but think he was out there somewhere, listening. *Max, where are you? Please come back.*

By mid-September, I was no longer in denial. Max hadn't returned, and I knew now that he probably wasn't going to. I went to school during the day then to work directly after. After work, I went home, ate dinner with my aunt and studied. She was worried about me but I didn't have enough energy to pacify her.

Around ten every night, I snuck out my window and walked to Max's house. I crawled through his bedroom window and into his bed, where I lay surrounded by his things. I had a part of him back when I was in his house and in his bed. His smell comforted me. This was the time when I allowed the pain and darkness to swallow me. Night after night I cried myself to sleep. Max made me feel beautiful and loved for the first time in my life. He filled me up. I was now empty and questioning everything. Did he choose the songs on my playlist knowing he was leaving? Did he leave the iPod in his car because he wanted me to discover it? I couldn't even drive his truck without breaking down, so I gave the keys to Benny and asked him to keep it safe. One thing I knew without a doubt was that, heart and soul, I belonged to Max McLellan, and I always would.

*Five years later*

After packing enough stuff for a week and calling the advertising agency to delay my start date, Joss and Kurt came to get me.

They drove me back to Charlotte, where we spent most of the week dealing with funeral arrangements. By the day of the funeral, I felt as if I'd cried a lifetime of tears. I hadn't allowed myself to cry like this since...*Max. Who was I kidding? I still cried over Max...just not as often as I used to.*

Piper came from Texas with her brothers. I insisted they all stay in the house with me, because I really didn't want to be alone.

My aunt's next-door neighbor, Mrs. Henry, and her niece, Polly, helped organize a reception at the house after the ceremony. Half the town came to the funeral and the other half brought food. I'd never seen so much food. Saying goodbye to my aunt, the only mother I'd ever known, was excruciating. Standing there surrounded by people who knew and cared for her, at least made it bearable.

Piper and I were in the kitchen taking a breather when I glanced into the living room and noticed a man I'd seen earlier at the church.

Nodding in his direction, I asked, "Who is that?"

"Who?"

"The sandy-haired man by the mantle. He keeps staring at me."

She shrugged. "I don't know, but I noticed him earlier."

As I looked around, all I saw were strange faces. "I feel like I should know all of these people, but I don't."

"Earth to Ellie, you've been away for the past four years, and your aunt knew a lot of people. Quit feeling guilty. Do you want me to find out who he is? Maybe he and old Elizabeth had a hot thing going? Maybe they were playing hide the sausage while you were gone." She waggled her eyebrows at me. *Vintage Piper, always trying to make me laugh.*

Just thinking about my aunt and sex made me cringe. "Maybe Mrs. Henry knows him. I'll ask her later." I lost focus of the man when I felt a hand on my arm.

"Ellie, let me formally introduce you to Polly," Joss said. "She works with Kurt at the bar and has become a good friend." Polly Henry was a knock-out. Like Joss, she had long, curly hair but whereas Joss's was natural, Polly's was not. She had big, blue eyes and was about an inch shorter than my five nine.

"Hey there Ellie," Polly said, in a feminine, but very southern accent. "I sure am sorry for your loss."

"Thank you, Polly. I didn't realize you worked for Kurt?"

"I just started."

"Well, thanks for taking care of all of this -" I pointed at the food.

"Shit, darlin,' it's the least we could do. Your aunt was a… kind woman." I almost laughed-out-loud when she said this. If anything, my aunt was a crabby old coot. "I used to stop by my aunt's on the weekend to check up on her," she continued. "She and Elizabeth were always up to something or another. She talked about you and your studies a lot. She sure was proud of you." *Huh, I didn't even know my aunt knew her next-door neighbor.*

"Has your aunt lived here long?" I asked.

"A couple of years now."

"Well, I'm happy to finally meet you, Polly. Good luck with your new job."

"Thanks. Hopefully, I'll see you around now that you're back in Charlotte. Maybe we could hang out sometime?"

"Sure, I'd like that." I didn't bother to disavow her of this notion, because, well, I really didn't know what I was going to do. A part of me wanted to come home. Another part of me was afraid. It had taken most of five years for me to start moving forward. Would coming back to Charlotte with all of its memories be a major setback? *One step at a time, Ellie.*

A little while later, Benny and I were discussing the merits of frozen casseroles when I noticed the sandy-haired stranger from earlier. "Hang on a second," I told Benny, and walked across the room to introduce myself. "Hi, I am Ellie Davis." I held out my hand. "I don't believe we've met before. Were you close to my aunt?"

"A long time ago, I was," said the deep-voiced stranger. I placed him in his early forties, which would be too young to have dated my aunt. *Hmmmm.*

"And your name is?"

"Uh… Samuel. My name is Samuel."

"Well, Samuel, do you have a last name?"

He smiled. "As a matter of fact, I do." I couldn't help but notice his smile seemed oddly familiar.

"Well?"

"My name is Samuel Davis. I'm your aunt's brother, which also makes me your father."

*Oh. My. God.*

Not expecting this in a million years, I choked out, "Excuse me for a minute." Then I turned and bolted from the room.

I found Joss, Piper and Kurt huddled in a corner in the dining room. Latching on to whomever I could get my hands on, I said, "Come, now," and pulled them out of the room and up the stairs while trying not to freak out.

"Ellie, what's wrong?" Kurt asked.

"Shit, shit, shit." I chanted all the way up the stairs and into my bedroom. Closing the door, I blurted, "That man downstairs, the one I was just talking to, claims he's my dad."

"What?" Joss gasped.

"The sausage hider?" Piper asked.

"Yes…uh, no," I corrected.

"What's he doing here? Did he say what he wanted?" Kurt asked.

"No. I went all *Xena; Warrior Princess* on his ass and

practically forced him to give me his name. When he gave it to me, I ran. Why now after all this time?" I threw up my hands in frustration.

"Because, I wanted to say goodbye to my big sister. I also wanted the opportunity to see you and to talk to you," he said from the doorway.

"Shit!" Piper and Joss both screamed.

"Ahhhh!" I shouted at the same time.

"Sorry," he smirked, "I didn't mean to scare you. I just figured that if I didn't get up here and say my piece pretty quickly, you'd be showing me the door."

I was standing in the room with my father. This was hard to take in. "But...why now?"

I repeated.

"Have you got a lot of time, because this might take a while." I just stood there and stared at him. *My father, the man who didn't want me to be born, is standing in front of me.*

"El, maybe you should hear him out?" Kurt said.

I couldn't help but snap when he said this. "Really? I should? Did your father abandon you at birth? Did you grow up with no parents? No, Kurt. That was me."

"That's fair, but I would at least like the chance to tell my side of things," Samuel said.

"Your side...of *things* is irrelevant now. I'm a twenty-two-year-old adult who is well past needing a daddy. Your side of *things* would have been welcomed, oh, let's say twenty years ago," I snapped.

"Look, I get you're angry and have a shitload of pent-up resentment, but there are always two sides to a story. I would like the chance to tell you mine."

"And then?"

"And then nothing... or everything. I'll let you decide."

"I have to think about it," I told him.

"That's fine. I'm staying at the Marriott by the mall, room 405. I leave Thursday. Think about it." After a long pause, he whispered, "You're beautiful." Then he turned and walked out the door.

Three days. I had three flipping days to decide if I wanted to talk to my dad or not.

*Crap...*

# CHAPTER TWELVE

*Five years earlier*

One night, after completing my daily routine of school and work, I was crawling through Max's window, when I thought I heard something. I paused for a second and listened. When nothing happened, I pulled myself over the sill. Out of nowhere, two hands grabbed me and yanked me the rest of the way inside. As I hit the floor with a loud thud, I shrieked.

"I knew it!" Kurt shouted. "What the fuck, Ellie?"

"God, you scared the shit out of me!" I shouted back.

"What are you doing here?"

"The same thing I do every night! What are you doing here?"

"Following your ass."

"Why?"

"Oh, maybe because Joss and I are worried sick about you. Look at you! Have you looked at yourself lately?"

"Sure," I lied. To be honest, I hadn't looked at myself. I was afraid of what I would see.

"You're lying, because if you'd looked at yourself, you would see the dark circles under your eyes and how crazy skinny you are!"

"What do you want me to say?" I shouted. "I'm sorry my boyfriend disappeared. I'm sorry I can't eat. I'm sorry that when I sleep, all I dream about is Max. I'm sorry the only decent sleep I get is when I am here in his bed! I'm sorry I'm so pathetic!"

"God, Ellie. Don't you think I'm sorry, too? Every fucking day I think of something and have my phone in my hand dialing Max's number when I catch myself. I miss him so damn much, but you...you're letting it kill you."

"I know in my head he's gone, Kurt, I do, but I just can't convince my heart. I can't make sense of anything right now."

Kurt let out a sigh of frustration. Then he wrapped his arms around me, and held me while I cried. "I think it's time we go to the police. This is bigger than us and it's killing you."

"Are you sure?" I sniffled.

"I am. How about tomorrow after school? Can you go then?"

"Yes, I'm off work tomorrow."

"Good, meet me at my car after school and I'll drive us."

"Thanks, Kurt."

"I love Joss," he quietly said, "but she doesn't understand, not really. I think you're the only one who gets it."

"I know." I squeezed him tight and stepped back.

He glanced around the room and I knew he saw, because I saw it too. Max was everywhere. "You come here every night and it makes you feel better?" he asked. I nodded my head, yes. "Would you mind company sometime?"

"No, but if you come here, you need to do it for you and not to take care of me."

"How about I do it for the both of us?" We left it at that.

I met Kurt after school the next day as planned. He drove us to the police, where we met with a Detective Mark Copeland.

We told him everything we could think of concerning Max's disappearance. He seemed very interested and asked us to give him a few days to look into it. We wrote down all of our contact information and profusely thanked him for his time. For the first time in over a month, I felt hope.

A week later, he called. Kurt and I had been waiting on eggshells all week, and I just knew, because it took him a week to call us back, he'd found something. Imagine my shock when he explained how he'd looked into Max's disappearance and had discovered no foul play. He suggested we drop it and move on. *Is this some kind of joke?* I wanted to scream.

"Detective, you do realize that Max and his entire family just vanished into thin air - don't you?" I tried sounding reasonable.

"I realize what it looks like, Miss Davis, but things aren't always as they seem." My heart beat in triple-time in my chest.

"So you found him?" I closed my eyes and waited for him to tell me yes.

"Has it ever occurred to you that Max McLellan might not want to be… found? That maybe he needed a clean break and left on his own accord?"

"Are you serious?" I angrily hissed. "Did you actually speak to Max, Detective? Did he tell you this?"

"I'm not at liberty to say, but I highly suggest you and Mr. Greenfield move on with your lives. This case is closed."

"What case? Did you actually open a case?" When he didn't respond, I snarled, "That's what I thought, *Detective"*

"Good day, Miss Davis," he said, and hung up. *He just hung up on me!* What the hell was I supposed to do now? I never imagined the police wouldn't help us.

Kurt showed up at Max's that night and we talked about my infuriating conversation with Detective Copeland. Kurt suggested that maybe they'd hit a dead end and were covering their asses. I disagreed. I felt as if they'd definitely found something. Why hide it from us? Either way, it didn't matter. Max was still missing, the case was closed, and we still knew nothing.

Later that night, while lying in Max's bed, I called his cell phone. I'd been doing this more and more lately. I wanted to hear his voice. I wanted to believe he was somewhere out there, listening to my messages. At the sound of the beep, I said, "Hi, there. I'm lying in your bed right now. Kurt is sleeping in Sarah's room. We both wanted to be closer to you tonight. We went to the police, Max. Please don't be mad. We just couldn't take it any longer. Anyway, it's not like it did us any good. The Detective told us to give up. He thinks you wanted to leave. I don't believe him. I don't believe for one second that you would walk away from me or your friendship with Kurt and Benny. I just… can't."

"The Detective was wrong," Kurt said from the doorway.

I ended the call, before addressing him. "You didn't hear him, Kurt. It was like he knew something we didn't."

"I know you don't want to hear this, but either something bad happened to Max and Sarah, or they were forced to leave. I'll never believe he would desert us for any other reason, and you shouldn't either."

"I don't know what to think anymore," I sighed.

"What's that?" he asked, pointing at the iPod.

"It's Max's iPod from his truck."

"I forgot about that." He smiled, but it didn't reach his eyes. It rarely did these days. "He carried it with him everywhere. Where did you find it?"

"The glove compartment of his truck. Can I ask a favor?"

"Shoot."

"Would you lie here with me? Joss will understand, and so would Max. I don't want to be alone, not tonight."

"He loved you, Ellie. I've known him for a long time and

128

have never seen him act this way about anyone." He crawled into bed beside me.

"Thanks," I said, bumping him with my shoulder. "Do you want to listen?" I held up Max's iPod.

"You wouldn't mind?"

"No, it'll be nice to listen with a friend who understands what it means." Wrapping my arms around him, I settled down into his warmth. "Ready?"

"Go for it."

I pushed play on the iPod dock. As we lay there in Max's bed, listening to his music, I knew this was all that was left of him. I was beginning to accept that he really was gone for good, and for the first time in a long time, I didn't fall asleep crying.

By mid-November, I was hanging on by a thread. I was practically failing my senior year, and honestly, I didn't care. I was angry at the world and out of control. The only thing holding me together was the knowledge that I would be ending my day in Max's bed each night. Even though she pretended not to, my aunt knew where I was spending my nights. She didn't agree, but she kept her mouth shut. She was a very wise woman.

Deep down, I knew I would eventually have to let Max go, but I wanted to take that step on my own terms. Imagine my shock when I showed up at his house one night, only to discover a for sale sign in the front yard, and a lock box on the door.

*No.*

I immediately called Kurt, who rushed over with Harry.

"What the fuck is this?" Kurt asked, pointing to the lock box.

"It looks to me like someone's selling the house," Harry declared while bouncing up and down on the balls of his feet.

"No shit, numb nuts, but why?" Kurt responded, "And why now?"

"Uhhhhh, is that question rhetorical?"

"Who do you think is making the decision to sell?" I asked. "Could it be Malcolm or even Max?"

"I don't know," Kurt shrugged.

"Guys, I hate to break up your hopeful moment, but a bank is making the decision. The information sheet says that interested parties should call the bank's work out department. That means this house was foreclosed," Harry stated.

"So the bank just *took* the house?" *How can they do this?*

"I bet no one has made payments since they left," Kurt said.

"At least now we know how long we can go without making payments on our houses before someone actually does something about it," Harry muttered.

"Shut up, Harry," I all but yelled. Both he and Kurt jumped in surprise. "They're going to take all of Max's things away," I tearfully said. I couldn't believe this was happening. I wasn't ready. This wasn't how it was supposed to be.

"I know, El. Let's get in there, grab what we want, and get out. We don't know how long we have," Kurt suggested.

That night was the very last night I stepped foot in Max's house. At first, I just wandered around memorizing everything. When Kurt started rushing me, I grabbed Max's pillow, comforter, three T-shirts and two flannels I knew he loved. Kurt also grabbed a bunch of things, including the iPod dock. Harry stood watch on the porch in case someone showed up.

Walking away from Max's house for the last time was one of the hardest things I'd ever had to do. I could tell Kurt felt the same way. After loading my car, we stood in the front yard for half an hour staring at the house. Neither of us wanted to go. Finally, we said goodbye, and I watched Kurt and Harry drive away.

Wiping the tears from my eyes, I glanced back over my shoulder at the place that had held the most precious memories of my life and whispered into the night,

"Bye, Max."

*Five Years Later*

"I'll be at your house tomorrow morning at nine sharp for the reading of the will. Don't worry, Miss Davis, it will be very straightforward. There are no surprises," he assured.

"Thank you, Mr. Harrison. I will see you here tomorrow morning at nine."

Everything was happening so fast. The service was only two days ago, and my aunt's lawyer was already calling. I snagged my cell phone from the side table and shot both Piper and Joss a quick text to be here tomorrow morning at nine. I needed moral support.

Piper was supposed to go back to Texas in a few days, and I didn't want her to go. A part of me was afraid I'd never see her again. I knew that would never happen, but emotionally, I was all over the place. Everything was so…uncertain.

Tonight was my first night alone in the house. Piper was spending the night with a college friend and Joss was at home with Kurt. It seemed so quiet without my aunt here. Normally, she would be banging around in the house with the TV blaring *Bravo or the Food Network*. As I stood in the foyer, my mind wandered upstairs to the guest closet and a conversation we'd had while I was home for Christmas my sophomore year.

*"Are you ever going to stop sleeping with his things?"* she asked.

*"I don't know," I sighed. "I've been thinking about it."*

*"He's been gone for almost three years now, Ellison. Don't you think it's time you moved on?"*

*"I know. I have, mostly, it's just really hard."*

My aunt and I had grown closer since Max had been gone. It was as if his disappearance woke her up. Who knows, maybe she was afraid if she didn't get with the program, I would leave too.

*"Honey, it's okay to have a special place inside of you reserved just for Max, but this shrine to him that you still carry around with you worries me. It's time to stand on your own two feet. He's gone and you're still here. You have to start living again. Just think about it and know I'm here whenever you need me."*

*An empty box was sitting at the foot of my bed when I woke up the next morning. This was Aunt Elizabeth's subtle reminder.*

*I felt sick all that day. I knew what I had to do, but it was gut-wrenching. Finally, before going to sleep that night, I folded Max's comforter and carefully lowered it into the bottom of the box. I'd been sleeping with it for so long that I wasn't sure I could give it up. Next went his pillow. Before placing it on top of the comforter, I held it to my face and breathed it in, as if I could still smell him on it. God, I missed his scent. I felt a tear as it cut a path down my cheek...so much for not crying. I placed his folded T-shirts and flannels on top of the pillow and felt like I was losing him all over again. Last was the picture of us. This was by far the hardest to say goodbye to. I reverently ran my fingers over our faces, burning the image of us into my memory. As if I could ever forget. "I will love you forever, Max." I whispered. Then I carefully closed the box and carried it to the out-of- season closet in the guest room.*

Two years later and I was back here again. *Please let it be where I left it.* I sighed in relief when I discovered the box still sitting where I'd left it that day. After dragging it across the hall to my bedroom, I opened it up, and one by one, pulled Max's things out and set them on my bed.

That night, I lay in bed with my head on Max's pillow while wearing his T-shirt and wrapped in his comforter. I placed the framed picture of us on my nightstand, where I could see it, and thought back to that same Christmas break, and the last time I'd visited the quarry.

*Carrying a blanket, iPod and water, I walked from my car down the same path I'd taken with Max the summer before he disappeared. Once I settled on our rock, I stared down at the water below.*

*Are you out there, Max? If so, are you thinking about me? Do you come here when I'm not around? I wish I could let you go. I wish I could just forget. I know my life would be easier... happier. But I can't. You're with me every second of every day. I can't get you out of my head or my heart, no matter how hard I try. How long is enough, Max? Are you still alive? Are you out there somewhere living your life, or are you truly gone from this world? If so, are you watching over me, like my guardian angel? I stared for a long time up at the sky.*

Until that day at the quarry, I hadn't given voice to the possibility that Max could be dead. I'd initially thought it, when he first disappeared, but wasn't willing to admit it out loud. That day at the quarry, I finally allowed my thoughts to go there and in doing so, the realization that Max could actually be dead rooted deep inside me. I just couldn't imagine anything taking him from me, except death.

That night, I turned my iPod to repeat, and allowed Bono to drown out my memories.

When I woke the next morning, I placed his things back inside the box and the box back into the closet.

# CHAPTER THIRTEEN

"First, let me say how sorry I am for your loss. Your aunt was a wonderful woman, who will be terribly missed," Clark Harrison, my aunt's lawyer, said.

"Thank you," I replied.

"I'll make this short and sweet. Elizabeth Davis, in her last will and testament, has left all of her worldly possessions to her niece, Ellison Elizabeth Davis. This includes her home, which is fully paid for, as well as her car." I smiled when he said this. I could just picture myself cruising around town in my aunt's 1999 yellow Cadillac DeVille. *Not likely.* "Everything else, her checking and savings accounts and such, can either be liquidated or switched into your name," he added.

"The house is paid off?" This surprised me.

"Yes, ma'am. Well, you still have to pay taxes, utilities, and phone, but you will never have to make a mortgage payment. If you choose to sell, then you will receive the full price, minus the realtor fees and expenses."

*This means I can afford to come home and live here if I*

*want*. Memories of my life in this house flowed through me; my childhood, holidays, hanging out with my aunt…Max. *I can't believe she did this without telling me.* "How did I not know this?" I asked him.

"No one knew this. It's the way she wanted it. She wanted you to have a sense of home; the only home you've ever known. She didn't want you to have to worry about not having a place to return to."

"She wanted me to come home?" I was truly shocked by this.

"She hoped you would. At least, this is what she told me. She felt you'd left here a lost soul and hoped you would someday find your way back." I heard sniffles from the peanut gallery behind me and blinked back the tears.

"Lord knows this house is big enough. How many bedrooms in all, three, or is it four?" Joss asked.

"Four," I absently replied. *Aunt Elizabeth never once said she wanted me to come home.*

"I would so redo the kitchen first," Piper said.

"Ooooh, me too," Joss agreed.

"Enough, Thelma and Louise," I said glaring at them over my shoulder. "I need to think. I have a job in Greensboro, a life. I can't just drop everything I've worked so hard for and move back here, can I?"

"Sure, you can. After all, you're all alone in your apartment that you *pay* for each month, in a city where your friends and family no longer *live*," Piper stated, as if I didn't already know this.

"About the bank accounts," Mr. Harrison cut in, "as it turns out, your aunt left you a pretty sizeable amount of money. If you manage it correctly, you can hold off getting a job for quite some time."

"Good, that takes the pressure off. You can come home, live here, and apply for a job after you get settled," Piper said.

I shot her an exasperated look. "Why do you want me here? You're moving to Texas!"

"I'm only planning on staying long enough to make my parents happy. Then I plan on moving back in here…with you," she grinned.

My eyes widened in surprise. "Really?" Piper and I living together would be so much fun.

"Kurt is looking for another bartender right now," Joss jumped in. "You have more than enough experience. You could move home and work at Dragonfly, just until you find another gig. Please say yes?" She sounded so hopeful. It was too much. *Can I just drop everything and move back? What if I hate it?*

"I need to think. You're both moving way too fast, and I can't breathe," I told them. I needed air, and asked the lawyer for a five-minute break.

Piper found me on the back patio staring out at the yard. "You can't hide behind your fears and heartache forever, you know."

"I'm not. This isn't about Max anymore, at least not all of it. I left because of him, but I need to come back because of me."

"Are you going to talk to your dad before he leaves?"

"I don't know, would you?"

"I honestly don't know."

"He didn't want me, Pi."

"No, but you don't know why. No one does. Maybe it's time to find out?"

I confessed something I'd been thinking about ever since I'd seen my father. "If Max had left me pregnant, I would have kept the baby."

"Yes, but the circumstances were different. What you and Max had was once in a lifetime. Obviously, neither of your parents was ready to have kids, or they wouldn't have put you up for adoption."

"I know you're right, but that doesn't change the fact that I didn't have a father growing up."

"Look, you just lost your aunt. She's the only family you've ever known. Maybe your dad showing up now is a good thing. Maybe you should hear what he has to say before you shut that door forever."

"Maybe," I sighed. I was so damn tired. "I'm still trying to wrap my brain around my dad being here in Charlotte." *My dad. Now that's something I thought I'd never say.*

Mr. Harrison left me overwhelmed by all of the decisions I suddenly had to make. Saying goodbye to Piper was horrible, as usual. Joss and Kurt had to go work on bar renovations, so I threw on shorts and a tank. Then I laced up my running shoes and headed to the quarry. The quarry had been on my mind ever since last night and seemed the right place to go to clear my head.

I parked the car and made my way to our cliff, where I sat and stared out at the calm, blue water, and asked myself a million questions. *What do I do? Do I want to talk to my dad? Do I want to give up my job and move back here? What's the right thing to do? What will make me happy?*

As always, my thoughts drifted to Max. *I wish you were here. I miss your smile, your eyes, and your lips… God, your lips. I miss your hands on me and the way you felt as you moved inside me. If you're up there watching over me, please help me make the right decision.*

I'd dated a few guys throughout the years Max had been gone. I'd even dated one my junior year somewhat seriously. In the end, though, I was too closed off and he wasn't Max. That's when I decided to forget about dating and concentrate on my studies. *Pathetic. Maybe it was time to open that door once again? Maybe it was finally time to come home?*

I took in a cleansing breath and decided to go for it, to take that leap of faith. I was going to move back to Charlotte and get closure with my dad. Feeling a hundred times better than when I arrived, I looked up at the clear blue sky, and thought, *Thanks, babe, I love you.*

An hour later, I drove home with Imagine Dragons blaring through my speakers, my windows down, the wind in my hair, and a much lighter heart.

Bright and early the next morning, I pulled the trigger on visiting my dad. With no warning whatsoever, I drove to his hotel. As I pulled into the parking lot, I wondered if I was doing the right thing. I hadn't told anyone about my decision to move back to Charlotte just yet. I needed to get this thing with my dad out of the way before I finalized any plans. On the way up to room 405, I almost got cold feet. I knew I needed closure, but I never expected it to be this hard to do.

"Ellie," my dad said as he opened the door. By the look on his face, he was obviously surprised to see me. "I was afraid you weren't going to show."

"Samuel," I nodded. "I didn't know either, until late yesterday afternoon."

"What changed your mind? And, please, call me Sam."

"Hmmm, what changed my mind is the desire to know what would make someone walk away from their kid, and then stay away for twenty-two years, that's what," I clearly stated.

He opened the door all the way and waved his hand through the air. "Please, come in and have a seat. I'll do my best to explain."

Samuel Davis was a good-looking man. He had dark blond hair that was the exact same color as mine. His eyes, however, were darker, as well as a different shape. I placed him at a little over six feet tall. He seemed to have a no-bullshit attitude, which, I hate to admit, I respected. I didn't want to like anything about him.

"I met your mom in fifth grade," he began. "We hung out with the same group of friends through middle and most of high school. It wasn't until the summer before our senior year that we noticed each other."

"So, you started dating?" I asked.

He shook his head. "Not exactly." I could tell he was holding back.

"Look, I'm not young or naïve, so I would greatly appreciate your honesty."

"I get that, but you need to understand the circumstances surrounding your conception are not exactly the easiest thing in the world to discuss, especially not with you."

"Fair enough," I said.

"Neither your mom nor I were inexperienced. In fact, that's what drew us to each other. Uh... we both liked the same things." *Great, my parents were both nymphos.* "God," he said running his fingers through his hair, "this is harder than I thought. Okay, basically, your mom and I just hooked up for sex. We were never in love and really didn't even like each other. At least, I didn't really like her."

"Soooo, you were just friends with benefits?" I asked.

"We were two people who knew what we wanted, and it wasn't a relationship," he clarified.

"And she got pregnant."

"Yes. Just so you know, I didn't think the baby...you, were mine, so I asked her to get an abortion."

"Would you have wanted me if you had known I was yours?"

"Eventually, I did know." After an uncomfortable pause of silence, he explained. "Your aunt took you in for a paternity test when you were a few weeks old. She wanted to know if you were mine. She thought it would make me change my mind and come home."

"I see." *He really didn't want me.*

"No, I don't think you do, Ellie. I was an eighteen-year-old boy who had the rest of his life in front of him. Your mom wanted me to commit to her, when all we'd done was hook up for sex. We both knew I wasn't the only guy she was sleeping with. At the time, I had a serious girlfriend. Your mom ruined that. She told her friends she was going to catch me, as if getting pregnant was a game or something. I wanted nothing to do with it, any of it."

"Yet, you still had unprotected sex with her."

"I didn't mean to. She planned it all out. She knew there was a party that all of the varsity football players were going to. She knew we planned on getting trashed, because it was so close to graduation."

"So, let me get this straight. You're insinuating my mother intentionally got pregnant in order to trap you?"

"That's exactly what I'm saying."

"How did you learn all of this?"

"When I refused to buy into the whole scheme, her best friend let it slip."

"Wow. So why come back now?"

"I grew the fuck up. I had nothing to offer you then. Hell, I may still have nothing to offer, but I want to try. I want to get to know my daughter. I can't give you all of the years back but maybe we could have a future?" I didn't know what to say to this.

"Would you have come back if Aunt Elizabeth hadn't died?"

"I've wanted to come back for the past ten years, but your aunt wouldn't allow it."

My initial thought was, *Liar.* "Really? That's funny, she never once mentioned it."

"She said you were happy. She had custody of you and didn't want me interfering. By law, I had no ties to you. I had to stay away because she asked me to, whether I wanted it or not." *Did he really try to see me? Did he really want to know me? Why would Aunt Elizabeth keep this from me?*

"This makes no sense. She knew how not having parents affected me."

"She was protecting you. How did she know I wasn't going to show up and then bail on you again? She did the right thing, Ellie. I see that now."

"I'm not sure what to do with all of this. I mean, I know nothing about you."

"Ask me anything you want. If this is the only chance I get to talk to you, then I'm taking it."

"Where do you live?"

"In Raleigh." *So close.*

"What do you do for a living?"

"I am a book editor."

"I love books," I told him.

He smiled. "I do, too."

"Are you married?"

"I've been divorced for three years."

"Any children?"

"Only you."

"Did you want more?" I knew I was getting personal, but for some reason I needed to know.

"First, I wanted to know you, and then, yes, I wanted more children. My ex was okay with it until she couldn't conceive. Then she didn't like that I had a daughter floating around. We ended up divorcing."

"You told her about me?"

"Eventually, yes."

"I'm sorry about your divorce."

"Thanks, but I'm much happier without her. Can I ask a few questions now?"

"Sure, but I might not answer."

"That's fair. I know you went to college in Greensboro. What are you doing now?"

"I just graduated from UNCG with a degree in Business Administration. I have a job lined up in Greensboro, only…"

"Only?"

"Aunt Elizabeth left me the house, car… everything in her will."

"Ahhhh, I see. Are you happy in Greensboro?"

"I'm content."

"Do you have anything keeping you there? Like maybe a boyfriend?" I could tell he was fishing.

"No, no boyfriend," I was quick to answer.

I watched his eyebrow raise in question. "Then what's stopping you from moving back to Charlotte?"

I shrugged. "Nothing really, I just need to quit my job and move my things." *Enough with question time*. "Listen, I should probably get going."

"Ellison, for what it's worth, I'm sorry you grew up without a mom or dad. I won't apologize for letting Elizabeth raise you, though. She did a much better job than I ever could have. From what I've seen, you've grown to be a strong, down-to-earth woman, and I'm proud of you. Will you think about giving me a chance to at least be your friend, if not your dad?"

"I'll think about it, really. We can exchange numbers and go from there, okay?"

"It's better than okay," he said, smiling. I hated that he was such a good guy. I hated that I was drawn to him and wanted more time with him. I had to physically make myself leave his hotel room. I'd finally confronted my dad. I had no idea where it would go, but at least the hard part was over.

*Now, all I have left is to quit my job and move my whole life. No biggie.*

*Five years earlier*

Spring of my senior year was crazy busy. It took Max's house selling for me to realize I was going to end up in serious trouble if I didn't get myself together. I had applied and been accepted to three colleges, but if I didn't graduate from high school, I wouldn't be going anywhere, which meant I would be forever stuck with my aunt, the ghost of Max, and community college.

*Blech!*

Max wouldn't want that for me. Hell, I didn't want that for me. So, I pushed my thoughts of him to the very end of each day and frantically started playing catch-up. *One day at a time* became my mantra.

Don't get me wrong, I still called Max's voicemail every night. Hearing his voice, even if it was only a recording, felt like a direct connection to him, a life line of sorts. I'd long ago filled his voicemail with messages, but it didn't stop me from being able to hear his voice whenever I wanted. Other than what I'd taken from his house that night with Kurt, this was the one thing I had left.

I spent time with Joss and Kurt, but it was hard to be around them. They were in the beginnings of new love, and I was in the midst of love lost. I refused to go out on the weekends and felt sick to my stomach any time dating was suggested. Not knowing if Max was alive or not kept me in limbo. I was okay with this. I didn't want closure. Closure meant that he was really and truly gone, and deep down, I knew the truth was way more than I could handle.

# CHAPTER FOURTEEN

March had come and gone. The flowers were starting to bloom and warmer weather was upon us. Summer was right around the corner. I hated summer. It was a harbinger of hurt that only brought painful memories, and I dreaded it. I was mired in these thoughts as I crawled into bed one night. As usual, I pulled out my phone, snuggled down into Max's comforter, dialed his number, and waited to hear his voice.

Instead of, "This is Max. Don't waste my time and your breath by leaving a long message. Just tell me who, what, when, and where, and I'll call you back." I got, "You've reached a number that is no longer in service. Please hang up and try again later." *What in the world?* I immediately hit redial. Again I heard, *you've reached…*"Please," I whispered, as I hung up. I hit redial for a third time and prayed his voice would pick up on the other end. When I got the recording, once again, I screamed, "Fuck!" *This cannot be happening.* Immediately, I dialed Piper's number. Maybe something was wrong with my phone. *Please let it be my phone.*

"Hello?" Piper answered. Tears sprang to my eyes. After I explained what had just happened, Piper asked if I knew who Max's cell phone carrier was.

"Yes, why?" Max and I had chosen the same carrier so we could call and text each other for free. I had no idea where Piper was going with this.

"I was just thinking you could call his carrier and see if they would give you any information on his phone number. Who knows, maybe they could track it to his current location or something?"

My chest tightened with excitement. "Piper, you're a genius! Why didn't I think of that?" I gasped.

"Probably because you're too close to the situation," she replied in her matter-of-fact voice I usually hated. "Chances are they won't talk to you unless you tell them you're related to Max, though. They'll probably ask for his account password and even then, the chances are slim they'll be able to find him. All I'm saying is that I don't want you to get your hopes up, but I think, for your sake, you should at least try. You can't keep living this way, Ells." I heard her loud and clear, and in some ways even agreed with her, but until I was ready to move on...I wasn't. And, as of this moment, I wasn't.

"Scout twenty-two was his password to everything. I'll call them first thing tomorrow morning and then call you after." This was it, I just knew it! This was going to lead me to Max.

The next morning, at nine o'clock on the dot, I called the customer service department. I told them I was Max's sister and explained how he was missing. The customer service representative gave me the runaround until I told her I had his account password. Then she took me seriously. *Thank you, Piper.* I explained how my brother, Max, had been missing for months, but until last night his voicemail still worked. I told her this was the family's last hope of finding where he was.

After placing me on hold for what seemed like a year, she popped back on. "Thank you for holding, Miss McLellan. It appears this phone number hasn't been accessed by anyone since August of last year." It took a minute for her words to sink in.

"What? But, that can't be. His voicemail was still picking up until last night. Wouldn't your company have shut it off months ago, after he failed to pay his bill?" I was trying hard not to lose all composure.

"Yes, typically we allow one or two months of no payments before sending notice. However, it appears Mr. McLellan's account was in such good standing that he was given a bit longer to pay before shutting off his service."

"So someone has or has not been paying the bills?" I asked.

"Ma'am, all I can tell you is that no one has used this phone since last August for incoming or outgoing calls. It seems we didn't catch it on our end until now. I'm sorry I don't have better news for you. Is there anything else I can help you with?"

"No, no, thanks." All this time I'd been calling Max's phone - thinking, wishing, praying - he was listening on the other end... and he wasn't even there. *All for nothing.*

The last thing I wanted to do was call Piper back, but I'd promised. After a short but sweet conversation, where she attempted to console me and I tried not to cry, I hung up. I then called Kurt and Benny and told them what had happened. After that, I lay in my bed, wrapped in Max's things, and cried myself empty. This was my last hope. Max was really gone. I was done. I was emotionally empty. Never, would I ever love anyone this much again.

*Game over.*

*Present Day*

After the talk with my dad, I hung out in Charlotte for a few more days, before heading back to Greensboro to pack my things. Joss and Kurt were ecstatic I'd decided to move back home and Benny was beside himself. I think he felt as if he was getting a piece of Max back. When I asked Kurt if I could bartend for him, he was so thrilled, he wanted me to come by Dragonfly that afternoon to start training. Joss was so excited that she immediately came over to help me clean out my aunt's room.

"Now, why are we doing this now and not when you get back from Greensboro?" she asked. We were in the process of boxing up my aunt's outdated wardrobe.

"I've decided to move downstairs into the master bedroom. If I wait, I'll have to sleep upstairs while we clean down here and…well, upstairs just has too many memories," I explained.

"I get it. Kurt and I were worried the memories of Max were going to stop you from moving back home," she confided.

"They almost did, but then I realized I really want to be here, in this house, surrounded by all of my friends. I can't allow my memories of Max to control the rest of my life. At times I wonder if I'll ever truly move on. For the most part I have, but…there's still a large part of me that refuses to completely let him go."

"That's understandable. He was your first everything, Ellie. You never forget your first. In most cases, it ends up a complete mess, but every now and then you come across that couple who defies the odds. You and Max were one of those rare couples. When he disappeared, he took what might have been with him. That's what you have to learn to let go of." I knew she was right, but I wasn't convinced I could do it. Only time would tell.

On the way back from dropping the clothes off at Goodwill, we picked up my new bed and stopped off at the paint store. I told Joss if she would agree to come over the next night and help me paint my new bedroom, I would supply free booze and pizza.

After Joss left, I got ready for my first training session at Dragonfly. I hadn't been back since the bar had been renovated, and was curious to see what Kurt had done with the place. The second I opened the door, I was hit with the familiar cacophony of glasses clinking, running water, and murmuring voices. Miranda Lambert's "White Liar" poured through the speakers, and I felt as if I was home.

During my four-year stint in Greensboro, Aunt Elizabeth refused to pay for anything extra. She told me if I wanted to play, then I would have to pay. I didn't necessarily want to play; however, I did want to eat, drink, and shower... using actual soap. So one of the first things I did was get a job. Both freshman and sophomore year, I worked as a waitress at an Italian restaurant across the street from UNCG. When I turned twenty-one, I quit and got a job bartending at a popular sports bar.

I was pleased to see that Kurt had done quite a lot with the place. It looked nothing like the rundown dive bar I'd entered six months ago. A huge, rectangular shaped, cherry wood bar spanned most of the room. Sturdy but attractive high-backed stools had been stained to match the bar. The hardwood floors looked newly refinished. To the left of the bar were two steps leading up to several pool tables and dart boards. To the right of the bar stood a small stage, some booths, and some free-standing tables. Behind the bar were a couple of doors, which I assumed led to offices.

"Hello? Anyone here?" I called out.

"Can I help you?" a deep voice to my left asked.

"Shit!" I screamed. When I unlatched my claws from the ceiling, I looked around for the phantom voice, and discovered a man kneeling on the floor to the left of the bar, staring up at me. *A very nice-looking man.* His deep chuckle gave me butterflies.

"Sorry, I thought you knew I was down here."

I playfully narrowed my eyes at him. "Is this how you greet everyone who enters the bar?"

With a bark of laughter, he stood and held up a white rag. Waving it over his head, he said, "I come in peace." *Cute. No, more than cute. Try, hot.* Over six feet of blond, tattooed, silver-eyed sex appeal smiled down at me. I hadn't seen hot like this since…*Max.* Flinching in guilt, I tried to erase thoughts of Max from my brain. When Kurt walked through one of the doors behind the bar, I practically tackled him.

"Hey, babe, glad you made it," he said, hugging me tightly. "I see you've met Dragonfly's new manager, Dillon."

"More like been terrorized by him," I mumbled.

Sex God laughed at this, and said, "I wouldn't say we've formally met, yet."

"Well, in that case, let me introduce you. Dillon Whitaker, meet one of my best friends and Dragonfly's newest bartender, Ellie Davis. Ellie, meet my manager and also bartender, Dillon Whitaker." Dillon smiled, and I swear I could hear all of the vaginas in a five mile radius sigh. Yes, the man was that good-looking.

Dillon extended his hand. "Ellie, it's nice to finally put a face with a name." *Sex God would, of course, have to have an equally sexy voice,* I thought.

I shook his hand, and replied, "Nice to meet you, Dillon."

"So, what do you think?" Kurt asked.

"About?" *Surely he isn't asking what I think of Dillon.*

He arched his eyebrow at me. "The bar?" I was seriously off my game and unless I pulled it together, he was going to call me on it.

Looping my arm through his, I said, "I love it. You've done an awesome job. Show me around. I want to see everything."

After touring me around, Kurt led me back to Dillon, who was standing behind the bar. "She's all yours, man," he announced, patting me on the back. Then, noticing the panicked look on my face, said, "I have a ton of paperwork to do. Hang with Dillon for a while and let him show you the ropes. You'll be working with both him and Garrett most of the time, so you should get used to each other now. See you later, Ells. Later, man," he nodded to Dillon and escaped to the back. *Thanks a lot, Kurt.*

By the end of the hour, I'd nicknamed him Delicious Dillon because, well, the guy was yummy from head to toe. He was also really nice, funny, and super cool. We worked out a plan for the bar. Actually, it was more like he told me his thoughts and I agreed. At that moment I probably would have agreed with anything that came out of his mouth. I was in lust. Normally, it bothered me when guys got up in my space and flirted outrageously, but with Dillon it was just fun. We had undeniable chemistry, which was both exhilarating and disturbing.

I left the bar that night in a great mood. Halfway home, it dawned on me that Dillon was the reason for my good mood. For a moment I was tempted to pull the plug on moving back to Charlotte, but then I remembered what my aunt had told me long ago.

*It's okay to have a special place inside of you reserved just for Max, but this shrine to him you still carry around with you worries me. It's time to stand on your own two feet. He's gone and you're still here. You have to start living again.*

Aunt Elizabeth was right. The attraction I felt for Dillon, the chemistry, reminded me of what I'd felt with Max. But Max wasn't here now and hadn't been for a long time. Dillon was, and the possibilities... well, they just made me smile.

Joss showed up around four the next afternoon, ready and willing to paint, drink booze, and eat pizza. She informed me that, since Dragonfly was closed on Sundays, Kurt would be joining us as soon as the football game was over.

An hour later Kurt strolled in, followed by Dillon, Polly, two people I'd never seen before, and Harry. Kurt introduced everyone. "Ellie, you met Dillon yesterday. This is Elena Owens, one of my new waitresses, Garrett Lanier, also a bartender, and you already know Polly. Harry, as usual, invited himself. I brought everyone along, because I wanted us all to hang out before we start working together."

Already a few beers in and a bit loose-lipped, I announced, "Hi, everyone, welcome to my humble abode. I have all kinds of booze in the kitchen and will be ordering pizza soon. Grab a drink and help us paint, but please don't screw up my walls!" Everyone headed to the kitchen to fix their drinks, while I tried not to hyperventilate, because Delicious Dillon, which I'd shortened to DD, was in my flipping house.

Elena, who I hadn't formally met, rolled out of the kitchen first. "Hi, Ellie, I'm Elena, but please call me Lena." With a head full of long, black hair, amber eyes, and the most beautiful milk chocolate skin I'd ever seen, Lena could be a model.

"I would kill for your eyes and skin," I blurted.

"Funny, I was just thinking the same about *your* eyes and lips. I'd gotten used to getting comments about my eyes, but my lips? This was a new one."

"Careful, girlfriend, or she's gonna think you're batting for the other team," Polly teased.

"Now *that* I'd like to see," Dillon smiled and winked at me. Immediately, my mouth went dry. *This guy seriously affects me.*

"Sorry to disappoint," Lena laughed. "You're gorgeous and all, Ellie, but I love dicks…the bigger the better." She spread her hands to measure well over nine inches.

"Duly noted," I laughed with her.

In an attempt to be funny, Harry said, "I'm surprised after Max left, Ellie didn't change teams altogether." My eyes shot to his and widened in shock. *He did not just say that.*

"Harry!" Joss and Kurt both shouted from across the room.

"What?" he asked.

"Who's Max?" Polly asked.

"Help," I mouthed at Joss. I searched the room for Dillon, and found him standing in the kitchen doorway with a beer in hand and his eyes on me, of course. I didn't want to tell them about Max. This was supposed to be my starting-over paint party. Max had no place here.

I was contemplating what to say, when Garrett stepped into the room and saved the day. "Hi, Ellie. We haven't formally met yet. I'm Garrett Lanier." He held out his hand. With a stalky, muscular build, and brown shaggy hair, Garrett stood about an inch taller than me. He had a sweet boy-next-door smile, and I instantly liked him.

Taking his hand, I said, "Nice to meet you, Garrett."

"What all do you need us to do, Ellie?" Kurt asked. He threw Harry the stink eye and Harry shrugged.

I gave Kurt a smile of thanks, and said, "The master bedroom needs a few coats of paint."

"Oooooh, what color did you pick?" Lena asked.

"It's called Urbane Bronze. I wanted something dark and rich to set off the comforter set I picked out for my new bed."

Dillon waggled his eyebrows at us, and growled, "Baby, I can give you something dark and rich."

Polly, who was standing next to him laughed, and rolled her eyes. "From what I've heard, it's more like light and flaky."

"Ha! That's funny!" Harry exclaimed, eyeing Polly with interest. The room broke into laughter. *This is going to be a fun crew to work with.*

"All right, all right, people, shall we start?" Kurt called out.

Once we agreed on rock music over pop, Harry wanting Britney Spears or Ke$ha, the rest of us giving him a big "Hell, No," it went pretty fast. I was unconsciously shaking my butt while singing along to Steve Miller's "The Joker" when I felt two hands on my hips and a warm body at my back.

"You keep shaking your goods like that, and we might have a problem," Dillon's deep voice whispered in my ear. Of course, this caused an uncontrollable, but obvious, shiver to run through my body. I was about to give a flirty response when his phone rang. "Hang on a minute." His hands instantly disappeared, and I shouldn't have felt the loss…but I did. *Get a grip, Ellie.* Dillon answered his phone and said no more than three words. Then he gave the caller my address and hung up. "Dana's on her way over," he announced to the room. Joss glared at him and both Lena and Polly moaned.

"Dana?" I asked, assuming it was another of Kurt's waitresses.

Dillon opened his mouth to respond, but Joss beat him to it. "Dana is Dillon's flavor of the minute."

My heart dropped. Of course a guy who looked like that would have a *girlfriend. I'm so stupid.* I suddenly felt an overwhelming wave of guilt and shame. *The guy just had his hands on my body and was talking naughty to me when his girlfriend called. Who does that?* Just last night I'd compared him to Max. *Max would never in a million years do that.* I now had the urge to take a scalding hot shower. I felt Dillon's eyes on me, and shot him a defiant glare.

"Dana is someone I've spent some time with, but she's not my girlfriend," he lamely explained.

"Yeah, right," I mumbled. Then I turned away in disgust. When I glanced back, he was staring down at his feet with a regretful look on his face. *Good, you shouldn't have tried to play me.*

"Ellie, can you tell me if this is what you want?" Garrett asked from across the room.

Dillon's eyes met mine, and I quickly looked away. "Coming," I called out to Garrett. Without another thought, I walked away.

# CHAPTER FIFTEEN

The bedroom had a fresh coat of paint, and we'd just ordered pizza, when the doorbell rang.

"I got it!" I shouted.

Dana Harkins was nothing like I'd imagined. From the second she strutted through my front door, I knew she was trouble.

"Where's Dillon?" Were the first words out of her mouth. Not, "Hi, my name is Dana, thanks for inviting me into your beautiful home" or "Hi, my name is Dana, is Dillon around?" Nope, she strutted into my home in her six-inch heels with her plentiful ass and gargantuan breasts on full display, and a nasty disposition.

"Uh," I barely managed to get out. I was completely shocked that *this* was Delicious Dillon's girlfriend. *Maybe she pays him to say he's with her?* I thought.

"There you are," she said, flashing a blindingly white smile at something over my shoulder.

I glanced back and watched Dillon approach us. As he stepped up, I held my breath and waited for some grand show of affection. When he stopped a mere arm's length away, and said, "I see you've met Ellie," I was both relieved and disappointed.

"Yes, I was just telling her how much I liked her cute little house," she announced with a straight-face. I tried not to choke on my tongue. A part of me wanted him to lay one right on her so I would forever be cured of my fascination with him. Another part of me wanted to cheer because he didn't.

"Come," he said, grabbing both of our arms, "Let's eat."

We were halfway through dinner before Dana acknowledged that anyone other than Dillon was in the house, much less sitting at the table with her. "So, Ellie, Dillon tells me you recently graduated with a degree in Home Ec. or was it PE?" she asked.

"Um, my degree is in Business," I corrected, and couldn't help but wonder what Dillon had told her.

"My degree is in Physical Education," Lena said, holding up her hand, "Elementary Physical Education, to be exact."

Dana continued talking as if Lena hadn't spoken. "Are you planning on going into marketing or owning your own business?"

Channeling my inner Piper, I looked over at Dillon, flashed my sexiest smile, and batted my lashes. "Nope, I'm going to be bartending at Dragonfly…with Dillon." I knew I was totally poking the bear but couldn't resist. The woman was rude. Dana narrowed her eyes at me and I smiled. "Oh, and I can't forget adorable Garrett, can I?" Unlike the fake smile I'd tossed Dillon's way, I genuinely smiled at Garrett. The knowing smirk on his face almost made me laugh.

Dana's beady eyes narrowed possessively on Dillon. She reminded me of a coiled snake; toxic and always ready to strike. "Dillon, darling," she drawled, "you failed to mention Ellie was going to be behind the bar with you."

"Well, being that I'm not the owner, Dana, I really had no say in the decision," he snapped. I tried not to let his tone hurt my feelings.

She swung her head back in my direction, and I almost ducked for cover. "Well, *if* you decide that bartending isn't…stimulating enough, I'm sure I could find you a marketing position with my company."

"Oh, yes, Ellie," Lena sneered sarcastically, "in case she hasn't already told you, Dana is the number one personal shopper at Neiman Marcus, in the nation." She held up her beer in mock congratulations to Dana.

"So, *Lena*," Dana all but snarled. "Are you still shacking up with that model guy, you know, the one of…mixed descent?" She emphasized the word 'mixed' as if everyone at the table was hard of hearing, and a spark of white-hot anger ignited in the pit of my stomach. *Who in the hell is this woman?*

"I'm not shacking up with Brent, *Dina*. We just fuck when we get the urge, kind of like Dillon's doing with you right now, except he doesn't look very…excited about it. Oh, and for your information, Brent is one hundred percent African American and has the junk to prove it, trust me." I wanted to stand up and cheer.

"*Dana*," she snarled.

"Pardon?"

"My *name* is Dana."

I was shocked by her hateful tone of voice, not to mention the horrible things she was saying. My gosh, did Dillon not see how mean his girlfriend was? All kinds of scenarios raced through my head. *Is she blackmailing him? Maybe his mother passed away, and her dying wish was for Dillon to be with her best friend's daughter? Could she secretly be a prostitute whom he pays to treat him like utter crap? Maybe this is a secret fetish or something.* A picture of Dana in a witch's hat, dressed in black leather, wielding a riding crop and screaming hateful things flashed through my head.

Kurt asked, "Hey, El, do you have the hot tub heated?"

Happy to be distracted from my disturbing thoughts, I answered, "Why, yes, I do, Kurt. Are you interested in a soak?"

For years, I'd tried to get my aunt to put a pool in the back yard. Lord knows it's big enough. Instead, she appeased me the Christmas of my junior year in college, by having a six-man hot tub installed on our back patio. I have to admit it's pretty amazing, but I still want a pool. *Maybe I can afford to put one in now?*

Dillon's silver eyes lit on me. "You have a hot tub?" *Please stop looking at me like you want to devour me.*

"Ellie has the best damn hot tub in town," bragged Polly. "Her aunt used to let me come over and soak after working doubles at my old gig. It worked wonders on my back and tootsies." She wiggled her toes in the air.

"If you need a foot rub, just say the word. I love women's feet," Harry groaned. He eyed Polly's feet as if they were covered in hot fudge.

"Ewwww!" Joss and I both squealed before breaking into laughter.

"Ugh," Dana huffed. "Speak English much?" Someone behind me sucked in a sharp breath and Dillon physically cringed. A hurt look appeared on Polly's face, and I shot Dillon a dirty look.

"What did you say?" Joss quietly asked.

Dana waved her hand in the air. "Oh, nothing. I just assumed we'd all been taught proper grammar by now."

Garrett arched an eyebrow at Dana. "Why you *be* such a bitch? Is that proper enough for you?" he challenged.

Not willing to let an opportunity to tweak Dana pass her by, Lena rode in on Garrett's grammatically incorrect coattails. "She *be* a bitch, because she done got to pay her man for sex."

Trying not to laugh, I held up my hands. "Okay, you two, do I need to sit you in the corner?"

"Dana," Dillon sighed, "we talked about this the other night. This is my boss and these are my co-workers you're insulting."

"What? I didn't mean to insult anyone. I was just trying to be helpful." She innocently batted her eyelashes at him, "And for your information," she directed at Garrett, "I would never, in a million years, pay for sex."

"That's enough," Dillon warned.

"Sure, honey." A smile lit up her face, before she leaned over and kissed him right on his beautiful mouth.

Disgusted, and in need of a breather, I said, "You guys go ahead. I'm going to grab some towels, make some margaritas, and will meet you back here in a few. Ladies, there are some extra suits in the bathroom closet. I can't guarantee they will fit, but I'll let you figure out the details. Sorry, boys, but you're on your own."

"I'll help you in the kitchen," Garrett offered.

"Me, too!" Polly called out.

"Hurry back, P. I'll be saving a place on my bench just for you," Harry purred.

Garrett and Polly helped me make up a batch of my special margaritas. Garrett didn't say much. Then again, it's hard to get a word in with Polly around. He did manage to tell me he was from a small town somewhere in Kentucky.

I was about to ask him where when Polly bumped me with her elbow. "Saw you watching Dillon earlier, girl. Lord, that boy really heats my motor."

"Revs my engine," Garrett corrected.

"You, too? And I had you pegged as a straight man." The look of horror on Garrett's face made me laugh.

Before Polly could terrorize him any further, I stated my opinion on the matter. "While he certainly isn't hard on the eyes, I have absolutely zero respect for him after meeting Dana. By the way, what is up with you and Harry?"

"Who knows?" she smiled mischievously, "I might let him rub my feet or…something else a little later." I tried not to gag. Harry looked exactly like a long-haired Dana Carvey when I'd first met him. The last five years had not been very kind to him. He now looked more like a blond Jack Black circa *Tropic Thunder*.

Garrett, still looking traumatized, shook his head at us before heading out to the hot tub with the pitcher of margaritas.

I was right on his heels when Polly stopped me. "I didn't want to say this in front of Garrett, because I really don't know the guy, but don't write Dillon off yet. He's a beautiful man who has no faith that he can land an equally beautiful woman. He settles for a lot less than he deserves."

"Why her?" I couldn't help but ask. "She's hateful."

"We've been asking him that for the past six months. I think he's beginning to see the light, especially now that you're in the picture." Polly grabbed the glasses off the counter and was halfway out the door when she looked back, and said, "Please, don't write him off just yet. He's a great guy who simply needs the right woman to make him believe it." She disappeared out the door and I slunk against the counter. I was exhausted. Taking a deep breath, I grabbed the towels, and followed after. *This is going to be a long night.*

As I approached the hot tub, I spotted Dillon's naked chest peeking from the water and stutter stepped. I placed the towels on the bench, and sighed in utter defeat. The man was an absolute work of art. *Why, why, why does he have to look so good?* Not only did he have an extremely impressive upper-body, but he also had the most amazing tattoo of some sort of fish spread across his left peck. *Thank Jesus, most of the man's body is below sea level right now.*

The sliding glass door opened and all eyes shot to Dana. She'd somehow managed to squeeze her butt and boobs into my favorite bikini…from ninth grade. Dillon's eyes followed Dana across the patio and, like that, my Dillon bubble burst into a thousand tiny molecules. There were no words to properly describe how obscene she looked. *Blech!*

"I know! Let's play a drinking game!" Joss screamed. Submerged in bubbles, she, too, was in one of my bikinis…from last summer. Kurt and all of the guys had opted to wear their boxer briefs while Lena and I remained fully clothed. Plunking my rear end on the edge of the tub, I dangled one foot near Garrett, the other near Harry. I wasn't much of an exhibitionist and never had been. If I was going in, I would be wearing one of my more modest suits. For now, I was just happy playing waitress.

"Oh, I love games," Polly clapped.

"No!" Kurt and I both yelled. The last time Joss made us play one of her stupid drinking games, Kurt and I spent the next day in traction.

"Oh, come on," Joss coaxed, trying hard not to laugh, "I promise it won't be as bad as last time." Kurt threw me a bullshit look and I laughed.

"What did you have in mind?" Garrett asked.

"How about something simple, like Truth or Dare?" She smiled sweetly. Everybody groaned at this.

"No way," Dillon said. "I stopped playing drinking games back in college, and for a damn good reason."

"Really, I mean how immature can you be?" Dana chimed in. The hurt look on Joss's face made me want to slap Dana.

"Why don't I make us some munchies and put on some music? Ellie, do the speakers work out here?" Lena asked.

"Sure. Do you want help?" I offered.

"I'll help her," Polly said, hoisting her almost naked body out of the tub. She had on one of my skimpier suits, but at least it was from my college days and marginally less obscene than the one Dana was wearing. Polly's looked about two sizes too small, whereas Dana might as well have slapped on some pasties and a G-string. Joss barely missed taking out Kurt's nose as she slapped both hands over his eyes.

"Awwww, come on," he complained.

"Oh, sweet Jesus," Harry sighed. "I think my boner just got a boner."

With her hands still covering Kurt's eyes, Joss leaned over and dramatically squinted down at Harry's lap. "Is that what that is? For a minute there I thought it was Kurt's big toe."

"Ha, ha!" Harry sarcastically replied.

Joss narrowed her eyes on me, "Girl, you need to stop being Sally Server and get in."

"I might in a minute," I lied.

Kurt held up his glass. "These are damn good margaritas, Ellie. Is this the same recipe you used last year?"

I tapped my glass to his. "Yep, I obviously spent way too much time in college experimenting with mixed drinks and drowning my sorrows."

"I can't imagine what a girl like you has to be sad about," Dillon said.

"You'd be surprised," I replied. Dana was shooting daggers at me, and I fought the urge to stick my tongue out at her.

"Seriously, these are great margaritas, Ellie," Dillon said, completely ignoring Dana, who was getting angrier by the second. "Hey, Kurt, Thursday margaritas at Dragonfly sounds good, doesn't it? Especially if we have Ellie serving these babies…."

Dana cut him off before he could finish his sentence. "The ones at Cantina Fifty-Three are better." *Nice.*

I suddenly noticed the margarita pitcher was almost empty. This was my excuse to get away from Miss Merry Sunshine before I strangled her. Polly and Lena passed me with a tray of food as I made my way to the kitchen. While looking for limes in the refrigerator, I heard the door open. Thinking it was Polly or Lena, I shouted, "I'm hurrying!"

"Don't hurry on my account." *Crap! What is Dillon doing in here?* Ignoring him, I grabbed two limes, closed the refrigerator, and continued with what I was doing. "Ellie," his deep voice called out.

"Hmmmm?" I was squeezing the limes to death, but didn't want to stop and look at him. I'd already seen enough.

"Would you please look at me?" *Crap!* Slowly, I placed the decimated limes on the cutting board. Then I took a deep breath, lifted my head, and looked him directly in the eyes. *Thank Jesus, he's wearing a towel,* was the first thought that popped into my head. I could see the concern in his eyes. "I want to apologize," he told me. *This should be good.*

I quirked my brow at him. "For?"

"For the way Dana's been acting tonight."

"She should be apologizing, not you, Dillon." I couldn't keep the anger out of my voice. I mean, really? How was it his fault that his girlfriend was a total and complete hag?

"She just…"

I held up my hand to stop him. "Unless you're going to say she has a rare disease that makes her rude and completely unlikable, I don't want to hear it. I can't pretend to understand you or your choices, but as long as you're happy dating someone like…*that*, then more power to you. I will have to say, after spending such a lovely evening getting to know her, I will have to rescind her invitation into my house."

He smiled when I said this. "She's not a vampire, Ellie."

I arched my eyebrow at him. "Oh, she's something, all right. I just haven't figured out what it is, yet."

He tried again. "She's just…"

And again I cut him off. "Mean Dillon, she's mean, and

164

you're…not. You deserve better, and I hope someday you find it." I squeezed his arm. Then I grabbed the pitcher and made my way back out to the hot tub.

When Dillon appeared five minutes later, Dana was out of the hot tub, dressed, and steaming mad. Wisely, he decided it was time they went home.

Shortly after they left, everyone else decided to call it a night. Garrett spent some time looking for his missing flip-flop and was the last to go. "Make sure to arm your alarm as soon as I'm out the door," he commanded.

"Uh, thanks, but I don't have one." His brow shot up in surprise, and I felt the need to explain. "This neighborhood is super safe. It always has been."

"Yes, but, you're a beautiful woman who is living alone. Anything can happen." My heart squeezed at his kind words.

"All right, Dad," I teased. "I'll make sure I lock the dead bolt tonight, just for you."

"Good girl," he smiled. "If you decide you want to install an alarm system, I have a friend who will cut you a deal."

"So that's what this is about? You're pimping alarm systems for your friend?"

He raised both hands in the air. "Guilty as charged."

After Garrett left, I bolted the door. Then I grabbed some blankets from the hall closet and made a bed out of the downstairs sofa. That night I fell asleep with a huge smile on my face.

# CHAPTER SIXTEEN

Early the next morning, Joss and I stopped by Benny's to borrow one of his trucks before heading to Greensboro. Kurt had scheduled my second and final training session at Dragonfly for Friday night, and I wasn't about to miss it. That gave me only two days to pack up my things, quit my job, and settle the rent with my not so happy landlord.

Our second night in Greensboro, I took Joss to the Cue Ball, a really cool bar I'd spent time in during my last two years in college. Two beers in - and Zac Brown singing about toes, asses, and sand - Joss asked, "So, what do you think of Dillon?"

"I'm surprised it took you so long to ask," I smirked.

"Well?"

"He's gorgeous but obviously has horrible taste in women."

"He thinks you're pretty," she teased.

"I meant Dana."

"According to Kurt, Dana chased him for about a year before he bit."

I couldn't help but comment. "And now she has her fangs in

so deep that he doesn't know which end is up."

"Aw, cut the man some slack. He's just killing time with her."

This made me snort. "I don't know, Joss, maybe he's some kind of masochist or something?"

She stared at me for a minute and then shrugged. "Maybe. Dana *is* definitely a first rate bitch."

"Can I ask you something personal?"

"Shoot," she said, and held up two fingers at the waitress.

"After all these years, are you and Kurt happy?"

"Very, why?"

I shrugged. "Just wondering."

She shot me a knowing look. "Kurt still thinks about him too, Ellie. He wonders what things would be like if Max hadn't disappeared."

"So...he talks about him with you?" Kurt and I had stopped talking about Max shortly after Max's cell phone went silent. That was pretty much the last straw for both of us.

"Max's name still comes up, but not as often as it used to."

I took a sip of my drink. "Do you think you and Kurt will get married?"

"God, I hope so," she sighed.

The dreamy expression on her face made me smile. "I hope so too." I changed the subject and told her all about my encounter with Garrett the other night. For some reason his over-protectiveness bothered me. Joss agreed it seemed odd, but thought that he was just being a nice guy. I wasn't so sure.

We made it home the next day with just enough time for me to get showered before heading to Dragonfly. I was both excited and nervous, because, well, it's not every day that a girl gives up a well-paid marketing job to bartend. My aunt was probably rolling over in her grave right now.

The entire drive to Dragonfly, I thought about my future and what I wanted. I wasn't sure this was it, but I was willing to give it a try. Taking a deep breath, I opened the door and stepped inside.

On arrival, I found Kurt standing in front of the bar talking to Dillon. He smiled when he saw me. "Just in time," he said, and pulled me in for a hug.

"Can I have one of those?" Dillon asked. The suggestive tone in his voice made my heart skip a few thousand beats. Awkwardly, I leaned over and gave him a shorter version of the one I'd just given Kurt. Of course, he took this as an opportunity to yank me in tight. "Your hair smells good," he whispered in my ear. "Mmmmm vanilla and… citrus?"

I attempted to extricate myself from his clutches. When he failed to release me, I tried not to do something rash, like bite him. Lowering my voice so Kurt wouldn't hear, I said, "Enough, Dillon," and, just in case he didn't take me seriously, I reached for the sensitive skin under his arm and pinched.

He reared back and rubbed the spot under his arm. Then he gave me a wicked smile. "Oh, Ellie, this is just the beginning," he growled.

*So hot.*

Kurt, who'd been watching the whole thing, scowled at Dillon. "Hey, douche, don't run her off before she even starts working here, okay?" Turning to me, he asked, "When do you think you'll want to work? Weeknights, weekends, both…?"

"I can work whenever you need me. I don't want to dip into my aunt's money if I don't have to."

"Now that we have you and Garrett on staff, Kurt wants to lighten his load," Dillon informed me, "so, that means you and me, Ellie D." *Hot and corny.*

I scrunched my nose at this, which only made him laugh. Ignoring Dillon, I turned to Kurt, and asked, "Why do you want to work less?"

"Uh, you know, plans and things," he vaguely replied.

Not in the least appeased by this, I tried again. "Whatcha planning?" As far as I knew, Kurt and I didn't have any secrets. Well, except for my secret lust for Dillon, but that didn't really count, because it was all in my head.

Dillon dramatically started humming the bridal march.

Thinking he was a marble short of the whole collection, I glanced over at Kurt, who looked guilty, and it hit me. "Shut up!" I yelled.

Dillon laughed. "By George, I think she's got it."

I stuck my tongue out at him and, squealing at the top of my lungs, launched myself into Kurt's arms. "This is so awesome! When?"

He gave me a stern look. "El, I need you to keep this on the QT for about a week, okay? Joss cannot find out."

"I swear, I won't say a word, and I'll work whenever and help you with whatever and Iamsofreakingexcitedfor you!!!!!"

"Breathe, babe," Dillon said through his laughter. It's amazing how two simple words could cause such anguish. When I was with Max and something made me laugh really hard, which happened often, he would say those words to me.

*Breathe, babe.*

Closing my eyes, I let the memory wash over me. Slowly, I opened them back up and pretended that it never happened.

Kurt, who could read me like a book, folded me into his arms and sighed, "Oh, Ellie."

I smiled up at him through my tears and said, "I'm okay, really."

Dillon looked confused. "Ellie Belly, did I say something wrong?"

"Naw," I assured him, "It's all good." Eagar to change the subject, I turned back to Kurt. "Can I throw an engagement party here at Dragonfly for you and Joss? I'll plan the whole thing."

He smiled. "Sure, Joss will love that. Now, how about we

do this thing? The sooner D or I sign off, the sooner we have you working." For the next two hours, I worked with the boys behind the bar and had…a…blast.

After two more days of training with Dillon and Kurt, they deemed me fit to work. While I'd been busy training, my dad had left a couple of messages on my voicemail. I had just enough time to call him back before I needed to get ready for my first night of work.

"Hello?" he answered.

"Hi, Samuel, it's Ellie. Sorry I haven't called you back. I was out of town and then training for work."

"That's okay. I know this is a busy time for you." He sounded off.

"Is everything okay?"

"Yes. Well, actually, no. I wanted you to know I'm having some surgery this coming Monday."

"Oh?" This was the last thing I expected him to say. "Is it serious? Are you okay?"

"It seems I have a gall bladder infection they can't clear up with medicine, so they need to go in and remove it." *Oh no.*

The summer between ninth and tenth grade, Aunt Elizabeth had an emergency appendectomy. She was down for weeks. If I hadn't been there to help, who knew what she would have done.

"Do you have someone to take care of you?"

"The doctor assured me it wouldn't be that bad. I just wanted you to know, you know, just in case."

My pulse shot to the ceiling. *In case of what? There's no way he can do this alone. What the hell kind of doctor does he have?* I glanced at the clock. Crap! I needed to get in the shower like ten minutes ago. Before I hung up, I made sure Samuel knew I was bothered by the prospect of him dealing with the recovery all alone and we would be discussing it further. Then I raced for the shower.

Dillon was at the bar when I arrived.

"Ellie Belly, you're finally here!" he yelled over incredibly loud music.

Garrett rolled in from the back. "Hey, Ellie, you ready for your first shift?"

"As ready as I'll ever be. What in the world is this music?" It was loud, screechy and a definite headache producer.

Dillon grinned devilishly. "This is Iron Maiden and that -" he pointed over to the wall - "is our new IntelliTunes Jukebox that was delivered yesterday. Isn't she a beauty?"

"Does *she* have a mute button?" I sweetly asked.

He laughed. "I take it you're not a fan of metal?"

"Is that what you call it? I was thinking more like mind meld or migraine maker. It's a bit too… raw for me."

"But that's what makes it so good!" Garrett shook his head.

"Do *you* like it?" I asked him.

"Hell, no. He's alone on this one."

I glanced over at the wall and then back at Dillon. "So what's this Intelli thingy you wanted me to see?"

"That," he cooed, "is Sheila." He pronounced Sheila with an accent, so it sounded more like Shayla.

I found this both funny and endearing. "You gave it an Australian name? How…sweet." He rolled his eyes and sighed dramatically. I looked over at Garrett, and asked, "Did he just roll his eyes at me?"

He smiled. "Yep, just like a teenage girl."

Before I could get another dig in, Dillon hurdled over the bar, grabbed my hand, and pulled me over to the jukebox. "Look, we load music from our iPod's in here," he pointed to a slot on the machine. "This way we'll be able to hear a decent range of music. Garrett and I already loaded ours earlier. And here -"he pointed to another button - "all you have to do is scroll until you find the song you want and hit play, which is located here. If we make a playlist of songs to cycle through at the beginning of each night, we can lock it up so no one else can use it."

"Cooooool."

"I know, isn't it?" He grinned like a proud papa.

"How much of the screechy music do you have loaded?" I skeptically asked.

"You'll seeeee," he sang.

"I'm getting my iPod from my car." Fifteen minutes later my music was loaded into the machine.

"We'll wait to hit play until our first customer walks through the door," he told us.

*This is going to be fun.*

Approximately twelve minutes later, the door opened with the first customer and Train's "50 Ways to Say Goodbye" kicked off the night.

"Really?" Dillon asked, scrunching up his face. This made me laugh. I wasn't about to tell him it wasn't my song. Anything that irritated him was fair play.

*Game on.*

I was happy to see both Polly and Lena on the floor that night. I hadn't seen either of them since hot-tubbing. By nine, the bar was slammed.

"Is it normally this crazy on a Thursday night?" I shouted to Polly while filling her order.

"Honey, it's crazy here every night, plus, word got out that Kurt hired a pretty new *female* bartender. That's why we have more men than usual."

My jaw dropped when she said this. "Seriously?"

"Yep." She shifted her eyes down the bar to Dillon. "Hey, D!" she screamed, "What is this shit music?"

"Why, Polly, it's "Locust" by Machine Head," he gleefully replied.

Shaking her head, she grabbed her tray of drinks and shouted,

"Later, tater!"

Fifteen minutes later, I noticed a group coming through the front door. Kurt, Joss, Harry, and some guy I didn't recognize were heading toward the bar.

"Hey, El," Kurt said, as he sat on the stool in front of me. "I see Dillon has already filled the IntelliTunes with his awful music." This was like the third song of Dillon's in a row, and my head was starting to hurt.

"We all loaded songs on it. I hope you don't mind?"

Joss made her way over to us and, seeing that there were no empty seats, plopped down on Kurt's lap. "Don't mind what?" she asked.

"That they loaded their music already," he told her. Turning back to me, he said, "It should make the night interesting as long as it doesn't scare off the customers."

As soon as the two guys next to Kurt took off, Harry and his friend plopped down on the empty stools. "Elllllllieeeeee," Harry trilled, "I want you to meet Jordan." Jordan had dirty-blond hair and green eyes. I noticed that both his left eyebrow and nose were pierced. He also had sleeves of tattoos on both arms and the back of his neck. I smiled at him. "Welcome to Dragonfly, Jordan, I'm Ellie."

"Nice to meet you, Ellie." He smiled shyly at me. I couldn't help but notice Dillon scowling at us from the other side of the bar. *What's his problem?*

Joss stood on the bar rail across from me and pulled me in for a big hug. "I didn't say hello. How's your first night going?"

Dillon stepped up beside me and answered, "It's awesome, isn't it, Ellie?" He knocked me with his elbow. "Especially the part about getting to work with me," he teased as he slapped me on the ass with his bar towel.

"We are raking it in brotha," Garrett said, pushing Dillon out of the way so he could high-five Kurt. Joss and I rolled our eyes at each other.

"Ellie, Jordan here was good friends with Max, way back, before…you know!" Harry yelled across the bar. He was loud enough that everyone and their mother probably heard him.

Closing my eyes, I took a deep breath and counted to five. Then I let it out and stared him dead in the eyes. "Harry, you've got to let it go." Not only was I surprised those words came out of my mouth, but that I actually meant them.

*It's time we all just let it go.*

Dillon stopped glaring at Jordan long enough to ask, "Who's this Max character Harry keeps mentioning?" Kurt cut his eyes to me, and I shook my head at him.

"Who sings this?" Garrett asked. Once again, the guy was saving me from having to answer Dillon. Funny, he seemed to be rescuing me a lot lately.

"This, my dear," I smiled gratefully at him, "is Mumford and Sons."

"Ooooo," said Lena, as she passed by us, "I love this song!"

"Ugh," Dillon complained.

"You don't like Mumford and Sons?" I gasped. "The Cave" was one of my all-time favorite songs.

He shrugged. "They're okay."

Jordan, who'd been quietly watching us, said, "You look familiar. Do you by chance play down at Whisky's?"

"Who? Me?" I asked, clearly confused.

"Naw, man, you must have me confused with someone else," Dillon told him.

"Play what?" I asked, looking at Jordan.

"Let it go," Dillon murmured in my ear. All kinds of lustful thoughts flashed through my head, as well as other parts of my body, when I felt his hot breath caress across my neck and ear.

Before I could comment, Jordan held up his hand and, like a kid in kindergarten, asked, "Can I have one of your margaritas, please?" I swear I heard Dillon mumble something like giant tool and wondered if he knew Jordan from somewhere.

"I want a margarita, too!" Joss shouted. She ground her ass into Kurt's crotch while she danced to some Ke$ha song. The pained expression on Kurt's face made me laugh.

"Why don't you go ahead and make a round for us all, El?" Kurt asked. With a smile on my face, I made four of my famous margaritas and proudly watched my friends guzzle them down.

# CHAPTER SEVENTEEN

"So, how did you hear about my margaritas?" I asked Jordan. Finally, I had a moment where I could actually hear myself think.

"That's all Harry has talked about all week. That, and some chick named Polly's body. Oh, and something about a mean girl and hot tubs or something like that," he said, shrugging. The lack of inflection in his voice was seriously funny. It reminded me of Arnold Schwarzenegger in the Terminator movies. I glanced over at Joss, and could tell by the look on her face she was thinking the exact same thing. We both burst into laughter. "What's so funny?" Jordan blandly asked. Of course, this only made us laugh harder.

"Quit playing around and start serving, Ellie," Dillon growled. *What's his problem?* I glanced over at Joss and she shrugged.

The music changed again to another of Dillon's mind-melding songs. If I didn't know any better, I'd think he rigged the thing to play mostly his songs. "What's the name of this one?" I shouted over the screeching.

"I'm pretty sure it's Avenged Sevenfold!" Jordan answered.

Harry looked hilarious as he sat on his stool holding his hands over his ears. When he saw us staring at him, he took his hands off of his ears and shouted, "Dillon's music is about as bad as his taste in women!" This caused Joss to spew her margarita all over the bar, Kurt to hysterically laugh, and Dillon to scowl. "Speaking of women," Harry continued shouting, "where's Darla tonight? I expected her to be sitting here glaring at Ellie." He placed his hand across his chest. "Dillon," he mimicked in a high-pitched voice that was supposed to be Dana, "you didn't tell me you were going to be working with a fe-male bartender."

"Very funny," Dillon smirked. "Dana went with her best friend, Jenny, to Virginia for the weekend."

"So," Joss chimed in, "you're seriously still seeing her?"

"I'm not sure I'd call it that," he hedged.

"What would you call it then?" Lena inquired, as she waited for me to fill her order. All eyes were on Dillon, probably wondering how he was going to wiggle his way out of the hole he was digging. At least I was.

He shrugged. "We just hang out every now and then. I don't see what the big deal is. When I have an itch, she's available to scratch it, that's all."

*Did he really just say that out loud?* His words reminded me of what Max once said about his relationship with Jennifer Tilson. *I can't tell you I didn't go there, because I did. I also can't lie and tell you it was all bad, because it wasn't. What I will say is that, like all the others, she was a distraction, it's over and you have nothing to be jealous of.* Dana was apparently Dillon's distraction.

"Hey, P!" Harry called out to Polly, "come down here and keep me company." He patted his lap.

"I love this song!" Polly shouted, ignoring Harry. "Is this one of yours, Ellie?"

Finally, one of my songs was playing. "Yay! My song!" I

shouted.

"Who is it?" Dillon asked, wrinkling his nose as if he smelled something rancid.

"Why, it's Pink's "Blow Me One Last Kiss," I cheerfully said and blew him a kiss. His eyes instantly heated. *Uh oh.*

Word about my margaritas had spread through the bar, and by the end of the night, I was a margarita-making machine.

Around one, things finally began to wind down. I was busy cleaning glasses when Dillon slapped Kurt on the back, and said, "Kurt man, we've made a mint tonight. Between Ellie's beautiful looks and margarita-making abilities, we might need to add more staff."

Kurt smiled at me. "What do you think, Ells? Does Thursday margarita night sound good to you?"

Joss cut in before I could answer. "Oh, oh…me, add me. I want to bartend with Ellie!"

Kurt shot her a skeptical look. "Seriously?"

"Pleeeeease?" she begged.

"Okay, baby, you can bartend with Ellie if you want." He touched his mouth to hers and my heart sighed. Two of my very best friends in the whole-wide-world were getting hitched.

Pearl Jam's "Alive" started playing as Kurt screamed out "Last Call!"

"Ha!" I yelled down the bar at Dillon and Garrett. "Look who gets the last song of the night?"

"Ellie Belly, I'll have to give you this one. Eddie Vedder is definitely the man," Dillon said. Garrett nodded his head in agreement.

Kurt, Joss, Harry, and Jordan were the last to leave the bar. Polly ran out the door before getting waylaid by Harry, Lena was meeting up with Brent, and Garrett wasn't on closing duty, but offered to stay and help anyway. Dillon told him to go home. That left me and Dillon to close up the bar.

As soon as we were alone, he pounced. "Look, Ellie," he paused for a long moment, and I could tell he was having a hard time putting his thoughts into words. I almost felt sorry for him…almost. "I- I want you to know that things between me and Dana are just casual."

"And you're telling me this because?"

"I don't want you to get the wrong impression and think it's something it's not, that's all," he shrugged.

"Oh, I think it's pretty clear what it is, Dillon. And, for the record, you don't have to explain your relationship to me." He let out a frustrated huff. Maybe I was being too harsh. "Hey," I said, hoping to soothe whatever was bugging him, "talk to me."

He nervously ran his fingers through his hair, and sighed. "I don't do relationships, Ellie. Trust me when I say I have my reasons. I know what you all think about Dana, and for the most part, you're right. I don't love her. Hell, half the time I don't even like her, but that's the way I like it, the way I wanted it… until now."

A million thoughts bounced through my head. *What does he mean by until now? What happened to make him feel this way?* Of course, I didn't ask. His secrets were his and mine were mine. *And they need to stay that way.* I slowly rubbed my hand up and down his arm. "If it makes you feel any better, I'm not looking for a relationship either."

He pierced me with his silver-eyed stare. "What if I told you I could be into you? Like seriously into you." *First, Max, and now Dillon.* I was beginning to feel like a magnet for super, sexy commitment-phobes.

"I'm flattered, really, but I'm not sure I'm looking for a relationship right now," I repeated. Even if I was, I wasn't sure it would be Dillon Whitaker, at least not until he dealt with his issues… the main one being Dana.

"Is it because of Max?" he asked.

"Max?" I repeated, pretending not to know who he was referring to.

"You know, Max, the guy everyone keeps bringing up in conversation. The same one you're avoiding talking about." I tried not to tense at the mention of Max's name. There was no way I was discussing Max with Dillon. Not now, and not ever.

"I don't know what you're talking about," I lied.

"Really, then why are you getting flustered?"

"I'm not. Look, tonight was fun. How about we just leave it at that? I've got to run but will see you Saturday night. I'm really looking forward to hearing the band." I could tell by his expression, he wasn't buying anything I was selling. *Please don't push,* I thought.

"Mmmmhmmm, sure thing, Ellie B, catch you Saturday," he said with a knowing smirk.

With a sigh of relief, I walked across the bar to the front door. Once I was outside where he could no longer see me, I bolted for my car.

Dillon Whitaker was a very dangerous man.

Mass Seduction was a cover band Kurt had hired to play at Dragonfly on Saturday nights. Joss had been raving about them for weeks, so I was super pumped to finally hear them play. What I didn't know, but quickly found out, was that Garrett had a family emergency in Kentucky, Kurt had a meeting he couldn't get out of, and we were two men down on the busiest night of the week. At the last minute, Dillon decided to have Joss fill in. There was just one problem. Joss hadn't been trained, yet. *Bad decision.*

Joss royally sucked at bartending.

Mass Seduction started their first set with an old Blues Traveler song called "Gina". Joss was supposed to be pouring beer for Dillon, but was too busy dancing behind the bar and singing along to the music, to actually work.

"I'm so naming my first born Gina," she announced, once the song was over.

I couldn't help but smile. "You name your child Gina, and I'll learn how to play the harmonica." We grinned at each other. *So never gonna happen.*

An hour later, the band was covering One Republic's "Good Life" when Dana walked through the door. I opened my mouth to warn Joss and clamped it shut when I noticed who was with her. *Jennifer Tilson.*

"Shiiiiit," I breathed. The last time I'd laid eyes on Jennnifer Tilson was the night she tried to trick me into thinking she and Max were together – *when Max was with me.*

"What has a sweet girl like you cursing like a sailor?" Dillon asked. Of course, he would have to be the one standing beside me.

"Your girlfriend is heading this way and she has someone with her whom I really dislike."

His eyes landed on Dana and Jennifer. "Who, Jenny?" he asked.

My eyes shot to his face. "You know her?"

"Sure, she's Dana's best friend."

"Of course she is," I muttered under my breath.

He laughed. "That bitch is harmless."

"Not to me, she's not."

"Why? What did she do to you?" His protective tone was... sweet.

"It doesn't matter. It happened a long time ago. Hopefully by now she's grown up and moved on." I tried not to choke on my words. I heard Joss gasp from behind us.

"Bullshit," Dillon muttered.

"Oh my God, did you see who just walked in?" Joss exclaimed.

"Yep," I nodded. Dillon glared at us both.

"What?" Joss asked. As usual, she didn't wait for an answer. "Good to know some things never change – she's still as trashy as ever - and, is it just me or has she added on some after-market parts?" She kept her voice low enough that only Dillon and I could hear. Jennifer had definitely had a breast augmentation. Her boobs now rivaled Dana's, and I didn't remember her lips being that big, either.

Dillon looked back-and-forth between the two of us, before asking, "What the fuck aren't you two telling me?"

"Nothing," we both said. When he looked away, Joss bugged her eyes and mouthed the word, "Fuck." Then she held up her finger, telling me to hold on a minute. I watched her disappear into the back offices. *What's she up to?* I turned back to the bar right as Dana and Jennifer were sliding onto the stools in front of me. Dana shot me an academy award winning fake smile.

"Well, look who we have here? It's Ellie with the famous hot tub and margaritas," Dana crooned.

The only thing I could think to say was, "Have fun in Virginia?" She cut her eyes at Dillon and threw him a nasty look. *Oops.* Jennifer just sat there and silently glared at me. *I see someone holds a monumentally long grudge.*

Deciding to finally answer my question, Dana said, "Virginia was fine."

"Can Dillon serve us instead of her?" Jennifer asked. I wondered who she was talking to when Joss stepped up beside me.

"I'd be happy to serve you," she told them. *Ouch.* "Don't worry," she whispered in my ear, "help is on the way." I shot her a questioning look, but she just grinned maniacally.

"So, Ellie, have you run into Max lately?" Jennifer sweetly

asked.

"Max, who?" Dillon asked, smiling over at me. *Crap! I didn't see him standing there.*

"Max McLellan, the guy Ellie tried to steal from me. How many months were you two together before he took off? One?" She turned to Dana and said, "Two at the most. Then he got sick of little-miss-perfect, and left her high.... and.... dry." She elbowed Dana when she said this, and they broke into a fit of annoyingly girly giggles. *Double ouch.* I could feel Dillon's eyes burning a hole through me, but I refused to look at him.

"Like birds of a feather, bitches flock together," Joss declared loud enough for everyone to hear.

Jennifer narrowed her eyes at Joss. "You know, I can get your fat ass fired for speaking to me that way."

Joss laughed. "Really? The last time I looked, the name on the lease was not yours." An evil smile suddenly appeared on Jennifer's face. She leaned forward, and I instinctively jerked back.

"Trust me, I know good and well who owns this bar," she snarled. "I know him good...and...well, if you catch my drift." Pain flashed through Joss's pretty blue eyes and I wanted to wring Jennifer's neck.

"Liar," I hissed. I cut my eyes from Jennifer to Joss, and said, "Don't you dare believe one word that comes out of her mouth. She's a liar and always has been. You, of all people, know this." I felt like vomiting. *Please tell me Kurt didn't touch her. Max was bad enough but Kurt, too?*

Joss glared at Jennifer. "Don't worry, Ellie, I don't believe her for a second. I know my man, and I know he wouldn't give her skank ass the time of day, even if she paid him." I was proud of Joss for standing her ground.

Jennifer's smile widened. "Ask him if you don't believe me." I seriously wanted to slap her silly.

Dillon, having heard enough, finally stepped in. "That's enough. Jennifer, don't make me track down Kurt, because if I do, I'm going to make sure he bans you permanently from Dragonfly."

"Why are you sticking up for them?" Dana challenged. "It's us who are being attacked here. We just wanted to come visit you and get a drink."

Dillon glared down at her. "You started this the night you showed up at Ellie's, Dana. Now you're bringing it to my place of employment. Not cool," he admonished. She glared defiantly at him, and I shook my head. It looked as if Dana was on borrowed time.

"I'll be back in a minute," Joss quietly said. I could hear the tears in her voice, which made me fighting mad. I wanted to tell her Kurt was going to marry her, but I couldn't. As I watched her head for the offices, I worried that this was somehow going to hurt their relationship.

"Well looky here, Lena, Darla's at the bar!" I heard Polly shout as she and Lena made their way over to us. *Help had finally arrived. If only it was ten minutes earlier.*

Jennifer looked over at Dana and whispered, "Who's Darla?"

As I turned to hide my laughter, I smacked into Dillon, who happened to be standing directly behind me. "Oops, sorry," I giggled, and placed both hands on his chest to steady myself.

"Ellie B, one day you're going to tell me all about this Max character," he softly stated.

"Your girlfriend is glaring at us," I informed him.

"And I told you, she's not my girlfriend."

"Evidently, she didn't get the memo." I stared right into his beautiful silver eyes, and thought, *Why do you have to be so enticing?*

He smiled. "I think you're jealous and *that* makes me very happy."

I patted him on the arm. "Keep telling yourself that, boyo." I could hear him laughing as I made my way back over to Polly and Lena. A few minutes later, Joss returned from the back with red puffy splotches on her face. She'd obviously been crying, which infuriated me.

"Oh, Elllllieeeeee," Jennifer called out. I rolled my eyes at Joss before looking to see what the shrew wanted. When she had my full attention, she said, "Did you know Max came to visit me at USC after he left you." Joss let out a gasp.

"What did you say?" I quietly asked.

"You all thought something horrible happened to him. When, in all reality, he simply wanted to get away from here." I stood there staring at her with my mouth hanging open.

Suddenly, Joss launched herself over the bar. "You bitch!" she shrieked, and grabbed a hunk of Jennifer's bleach-blonde hair. "That's complete bullshit, and you know it!"

"Ouch, you bitch!" Jennifer screeched as she jerked out of Joss's clutches. "It's true! Max spent the entire weekend in bed with me. And baby," she preened, "I gave it to him gooooood."

My pulse raced. In my head I knew she was lying, but in my heart? Well, that was a different story. *Could the Max I knew betray me like this? Would he? Did he? After all, the Max I knew, the one who would never leave me, did just that.*

Dillon watched me with a concerned look on his face. Dana watched him jealously. Polly and Lena appeared to be gearing for a brawl. Suddenly, it was all too much, and I couldn't catch my breath.

"I knew you were bitter about getting dumped, but this is low even for you, Jennifer." Joss growled.

"What's wrong, Josselyn? Can't handle the truth? 'Cause I have plenty more where that came from."

Dana started laughing. "This is priceless," she crowed, patting Jennifer on the back. "You just killed two bitches with one stone."

"That's it!" Dillon roared. "Both of you out, now!" The bar went completely silent.

"B-but…Dillon," Dana cried as she tried to act all innocent.

"What in the hell is going on here?" Kurt shouted. I hadn't seen him come in, but was glad he was finally here.

Jennifer immediately shifted from raging bitch to seductress. "Heeeey, Kurt," she drawled. Joss clenched her teeth in anger.

Ignoring her pouty lips and fluttering lashes, Kurt said, "What the fuck, Jennifer? I heard you were telling everyone Max came to visit you *after* he disappeared. Is this true?"

"MmmmHmmm, he did," she purred. "You, of all people, know how much enjoyment I can give a man." Joss gasped, Kurt flinched, and Dana laughed. I just wanted to throw up. *Screw this. I need air.* Flinging open the bar top, I bolted for the offices.

"Ellie, wait!" I heard Dillon yell.

Stars danced before my eyes as I flung open the staff room door and threw myself onto the love seat. I felt like I was going to pass out. Lowering my head down between my knees, I took a deep breath and let the tears flow. *Breathe. Don't pass out.* Two, large hands rubbed up and down my back, and I stiffened. *Dillon.*

"Have they left yet?" I asked him.

"Kurt kicked them out."

"How's Joss?"

"About the same as you. It seems Kurt has some serious explaining to do." *That's what I'm afraid of.*

"Who's covering the bar?"

"Polly and Lena." Just the thought of this made me laugh.

"You want to talk about it?" he asked.

I shook my head. "Nope. It won't do any good and it won't bring him back."

"How long has he been gone?"

"Way too long for it to still have this hold over me," I barely managed to choke out.

"Hey, come here." He wrapped his arms around me and pulled me onto his lap. I hated to admit it, but being in his arms felt good. It had been so long since I'd been held.

I lay my head on his chest and sighed. "When am I going to get past this? It shouldn't still matter this much."

"Maybe when you meet someone else, it will fade. I don't know. Have you considered giving someone else a chance?" I reared back and glared at him. "I'm not saying me. I'm just saying someone," he quickly added.

As I relaxed back into him, he continued to rub his hand across my back. "You sound as if you know this from experience." He let out a dry laugh, which told me I'd hit the nail on the head. "Will you tell me about it?"

"Maybe...someday." His silver eyes seared through me and I felt something deep inside me stir, something I hadn't felt in a very long time. The next thing I knew, his lips were on mine. I wanted it. I won't lie. After all this time, I wanted this kiss from this man. My mouth opened in invitation, and slowly, he swept in. It felt good...so damn good. Suddenly, he yanked his head back. Before I had the chance to ask what was wrong, the door flew open and both Kurt and Joss walked in. *Crap!* Since I didn't hear anyone at the door, I didn't have time to extricate myself from Dillon's lap. From the look on Kurt's face, he wasn't too happy about this. *Good thing he didn't see us kissing.*

Kurt told me to go home. He and Dillon would close up the bar. The entire time he talked to us, Joss just stood there quietly staring down at her feet. I was worried about her but didn't want to put her on the spot, so I kept my mouth shut.

Kurt walked me out to my car. I wanted a moment to say goodbye to Dillon but decided not to push it. When I asked Kurt about Jennifer, he turned the tables and asked me about Dillon.

There was no way I was discussing Dillon with him, so I quickly changed the topic to Jennifer and Max. Like me, Kurt felt as if she was lying, but I could see the doubt I was feeling mirrored in his eyes. Neither of us was sure about anything, anymore.

I planned on driving straight home but instead found myself driving toward Max's old house. I hadn't been back since it had sold. I was surprised to discover it looking exactly as I remembered. Seeing it after all this time brought back so many memories. Life seemed so simple five years ago. *Did you visit Jennifer on your way to your so-called freedom, Max?* In the time we were together, I'd only doubted him once, and it was because of Jennifer. *Funny…all these years later and, not only is she still interfering, but we're both still spinning our wheels over the same guy…and he's not even here to witness it.*

As I sat there parked in front of Max's house, mired in my thoughts, a song came on the radio that characterized exactly what I was feeling. I had to laugh at the timing. It was as if Grace Potter had stepped inside my body and read my soul. Then she magically spun all of my thoughts and feelings into a beautiful song about losing her one and only. *Are you somewhere in the stars, Max?*

On the drive home, I thought about everything that had transpired. Questions traipsed through my head, but none of them had answers. By the time I got home, I wanted to scream. Instead, I called Piper and told her everything. She didn't have any solutions for me, but it still felt good to confide in her. Right before we hung up, she told me to trust my gut. That's exactly what I was going to do. I was going to trust my gut.

# CHAPTER EIGHTEEN

The next morning, I woke feeling clear-headed and full of purpose. First, I needed to check up on Joss, then I was going to clean my house, and last, I was going to call my dad. Joss didn't answer, so I left her a voicemail and started in on the house. After I'd finished cleaning the downstairs, I phoned my dad. He'd been on my mind since we'd last spoken.

"I'm coming for your surgery tomorrow," I told him.

"You know I don't expect you to do that."

"Also, you need to pack a bag. I'm bringing you back to Charlotte until you're better. You can start out on the sleep sofa in the office. When you're able to handle the stairs, I'll move you into one of the guest rooms."

"Honey, this really isn't necessary."

"Of course, it's necessary. You're my dad, so deal with it." The line went silent, and I wondered if he'd hung up on me. "Hello?"

"You just called me your dad," he quietly responded.

I closed my eyes and fought the urge to bang my head against the top of the desk. "Do we have a deal?" I asked.

"Yes," he answered. "I'd like that very much."

"Good, I'll be there first thing tomorrow morning to take you to the hospital."

"Thank you, Ellison."

"You're welcome, Samuel."

I hung up and immediately started cleaning the upstairs.

First thing the next morning, I headed for Raleigh. I hadn't heard from Joss, so I decided to call her again instead of spending the next three plus hours in the car worrying about her. I was relieved when she answered.

"Sorry I haven't called you back," she said.

"Are you okay?"

"Well, after a horrible fight with Kurt and sleeping in separate bedrooms, which is something we've never done before, I decided to hear him out. He told me the weekend after Max broke it off with Jennifer, he was over at Bobby's house with a bunch of people when Jennifer made a play for him. While they were kissing and fooling around, they were interrupted by a couple of her friends. He didn't gloss over it like I thought he would, Ellie. He told me he fully intended to sleep with her that night. Apparently, he went to get a beer and as he was stepping back into the room, he heard her talking about making Max jealous by sleeping with his best friend. Wanting no part of it, he claims he set down his beer and walked out the front door."

"Do you believe him?"

"Would you? You've known him as long as I have, and in some ways, better."

I didn't even have to think about it. "I believe him." Kurt was hands down the most honorable person I'd ever known. Before the incident with Jennifer, I would have placed Max at the top of that list, but I wasn't sure this was true anymore.

"I can't really get mad. I wasn't his girlfriend then. In fact, we'd only just met. For all I knew, he was nailing Piper. How can I be mad at something he did before me? You know what horn dogs those guys were back then. Kurt despises Jennifer. He has ever since the night she tried to get between you and Max. I witnessed it firsthand." I wasn't sure if she was trying to convince me or herself. As long as she was okay with it, I didn't care.

"So all is good?"

"Yes, all is great." I could hear the smile in her voice and knew everything was going to be okay. *Thank God.*

I told her all about my dad's surgery and my plans to temporarily move him back to Charlotte. "He'll be in pretty rough shape at first, but it's nothing I can't handle. I do need out of my Tuesday and Wednesday shifts, though."

"No problem, just as long as you're back for margarita night." This made me laugh.

"I wouldn't dream of missing it."

"Do you need me to drive to Raleigh and help you?" This was one of the many reasons why I loved Joss. She would give you the shirt off her back if she felt you were in need. I assured her I had it under control.

"Now, enough with the family drama, tell me what's up with you and Dillon?" I'd been waiting for her to bring this up. She too, had seen me perched on Dillon's lap the other night.

I decided to play it straight with her. "To be honest, I'm not really sure."

"You should have seen Dana's face when Dillon went chasing after you Saturday night. I thought she was going to blow a gasket. She was beyond pissed. Then we found you all cozied up on his lap when we came to check on you. Girl, I thought Kurt was going to lose his mind."

"Dillon was just being nice to me, that's all," I assured her. Something had been bothering me though, and I knew if I asked, she would tell me the truth. "Did you by chance stay until closing?"

"Yeah, I stayed so I could scream at Kurt. Why?"

"Did you see Dana anywhere? Dillon said Kurt kicked them out but…I mean… I know I left before everyone and all…. I didn't see her, but that doesn't mean she wasn't…." I was spinning my verbal wheels and getting bogged down in my own words.

"You do like him," she accused.

"No! I mean, I don't know."

"Ellie," she groaned, and before she even said it, I knew what was coming. *Dillon was with Dana after I left.* "Kurt did kick them out, but I guess she waited around or came back later, because I saw him with her outside in the parking lot after closing. Sorry." My heart somersaulted into my throat.

"Don't be. It's probably for the best anyway."

"It's complicated or, should I say, those two are complicated. They've been playing this game with each other for over a year now. Dillon acts uninterested, they fight, they fuck, he goes back to her, and the cycle starts all over again." *It figures I would be attracted to the emotionally unstable, hot guy.* "D's no good for you," she continued. "Kurt agrees with me on this. It took everything in him not to rip you out of the guy's lap and beat his ass."

"I know," I sighed, and I did. Dillon Whitaker was not good for Ellie Davis, but still…a small part of me couldn't help but wonder.

Samuel's surgery went well and I was able to move him back to Charlotte late Wednesday afternoon. I'd spoken and texted with Joss, Kurt, Piper, and even Harry, but funny, I didn't hear a word from Dillon. Just because I didn't give him my phone number didn't mean he couldn't find it. I was angry with him, but more so with myself. I knew better. Joss told me she'd worked with Dillon on both Tuesday and Wednesday night. She also informed me Dana was a no-show both nights. This shouldn't have mattered, but it did.

By Thursday, my dad was feeling better and I was starting to go stir-crazy. I was due in for work, but was worried about leaving him.

"I can cancel work tonight," I offered for probably the fiftieth time.

"Go. You need a break from me. I've got sports and hot soup, thanks to you. I'll be fine."

"Here's your pill schedule. You have my cell number, and if I don't answer, here's the number to Dragonfly."

"Go, Ellie, please."

I took extra time with my outfit, hair, and makeup that night. My eyes were smoky and my lips sexy with gloss. My hair framed my face and hung down my back in spiral curls. Wearing a form-fitting, red, short-sleeve sweater that plunged just low enough to show the tops of my breasts, my tightest Lucky jeans, and the awesome black motorcycle boots Piper had given me, I was ready to face whatever the evening had in store for me. In other words, I looked damn good. *Eat your heart out, Dillon.*

Dillon's eyes lit up in appreciation when he saw me walk through the door. "Ellie Belly, you look smokin' hot tonight."

"Dillon," I clipped. The shortness in my tone put a frown on his face.

"What's wrong?"

"You're a smart man. I'm sure you can figure it out."

"Give me a hint?"

"Nope."

"Please?"

Ignoring him, I put on my apron and began washing glasses. A few minutes later, Garrett rolled through the front door, and I inquired about Kentucky.

"It was nothing," he shrugged, obviously not wanting to talk about it. He glanced warily at Dillon before heading off to the back.

"Come on, Ellie, you can't torture me like this all night," Dillon whined.

If I didn't address it now, he was going to bug me the entire night, so I set down the dish towel, looked into his beautiful eyes, and gave it to him. "I heard you and Dana hooked up after we kissed the other night."

His eyes widened in surprise. "You heard wrong. She cornered me at my car after we closed but nothing happened. Call and ask her if you don't believe me." *As if she would tell me.*

"Look, Dillon, it was just one kiss. No harm, no foul. We can walk away as friends, and no one gets hurt."

The look on his face reminded me of a spoiled little boy who wasn't getting his way. "What if I want to be more than friends? What if I have no intention of walking away?" he challenged.

"That wouldn't be smart."

"I never said it was smart, but even you can't deny that kiss was hot. I want to see where it could lead."

I shook my head. "I don't think so."

"Before you tell me no, just think about it."

Something about this man confused me, but I couldn't seem to put my finger on exactly what it was. Good thing the arrival of Joss and Kurt saved me from having to think any more about it. It also saved me from having to give Dillon an answer. Kurt and Joss only stayed for about half an hour. Kurt was taking her out to dinner, hopefully to propose. He wouldn't give me any details, so I had to use my imagination.

Around nine or so, Dana showed up. I was relieved to see Jennifer wasn't with her. She sauntered across the bar like she owned the place and parked her butt directly in front of Dillon. Why this infuriated me, I can't say. It just did. I tried to hide my disgust, but the knowing smile on Dillon's face let me know I'd failed. Matchbox 20's "She's So Mean" came on right after Dana sat down, and I had to smile. *How appropriate.*

"Oh, Dil, I just love this song," Dana said. Her beady, black eyes beamed up at him.

"You would," I muttered under my breath. Dillon cut his eyes at me, and I smirked.

"Ellie, isn't this one of your songs?" Garrett asked, and I wanted to kick him. *I'm never listening to this song again.*

Dana shot me a nasty look, before asking, "What do you mean *one of her songs?*"

With a smile and a wink in my direction, Garrett answered, "This is one of the songs from Ellie's playlist."

"It sure beats that…noise of Dillon's we've been tortured with lately," Polly added as she stepped into the bar area and gave me a hug.

Harry and Jordan stopped by that evening and had a few drinks. Harry spent the whole time lecherously patting his crotch while trying to get Polly to sit on his lap. I talked to them when I could, which wasn't much, because the bar was slammed. It seemed like everyone and their mother had heard about margarita night.

Dana was a huge distraction. The fact that Dillon wouldn't so much as look her way unless she initiated it, made me happy but also confused me. By eleven, things started to ease off and I could hear individual conversations again.

"I'm seriously going to rip someone's hair out if this awful music isn't changed!" Polly shouted while waiting on her order. Another of Dillon's headache inducing songs was playing. He grinned at Polly like a kid in a candy store.

"Ladies, let me introduce you to Black Sabbath's "Children of the Grave"? Isn't it awesome?" he asked.

"No!" we all yelled.

"I don't care if it's called Yankee Doodle's Ding Dong! If you don't change this shit to something worth listening to, I'm going to thump you where it counts," Polly growled. This only made him laugh harder. Since I wasn't standing right in front of them, I couldn't hear exactly what was said, but it sounded like Dana told Polly to back off of her man.

Clearly unhappy about this, Dillon leaned across the bar and growled, "I'm not your man, Dana. I never have been and never will be. Go home."

Glaring daggers through him, Dana shouted, "No! You don't own me, and you certainly don't own this bar! I'm staying right here!"

Dillon threw up his hands in frustration. "You're right, I don't own this bar. Stay. Do what you want. I don't give a shit, but leave my friends alone."

With a satisfied smile on her face, Dana settled back down onto her stool, where she proceeded to watch Dillon like a hawk for the rest of the night. Poor Dillon had his hands full with that one. The words *mentally unstable* came to mind.

Two hours later, I was washing glasses with Garret when he nodded in Dana's direction. "Looks like trouble in paradise," he observed.

"If she's there, it's more like hell," I replied.

As I was loading the last drinks of the night onto Polly's tray, she pointed out a guy at the pool tables she'd been eyeing all night. I had to admit, he looked pretty good.

Dillon overheard our conversation, and, as soon as Polly took off with the tray of drinks, he leaned over and asked, "Can I see you in the lounge for a minute?"

"Nope," I answered. I was ready to cash out and get out.

"It will only take a second, really," he assured me.

I scanned the bar and noticed it was pretty much cleared out. Garrett could handle the load for a minute while I spoke with Dillon, but that was just it, I didn't want to speak with Dillon. I wanted to go home and check on my dad. Then I noticed Dana, still sitting there with her psycho eyes glued on us, and changed my mind. "Fine, but make it quick," I told him. Without another word, Dillon grabbed my hand, swung open the bar top, and pulled me toward the back.

"Dillon!" I heard Dana shout behind us.

Once we reached the lounge, he closed the door behind us. Then he whipped me around and pinned me against the wall. I opened my mouth to ask what he was doing, but before I could get the words out, his lips were on mine. At first I kissed him back, but then I remembered everything that had transpired since our last kiss, and tried to pull away. He was too strong. Finally, unable to deny the man could kiss exceptionally well, I gave in. Tonight I was seeing a totally different side of Dillon than from last Saturday. This was the take-charge, alpha Dillon, and I was in a world of trouble. If I didn't stop him now, I was afraid I wouldn't be able to.

Jerking my head to the side, I said, "Stop." We were both breathing heavily.

"No," his deep voice rasped.

"Dillon, you have to. Dana is sitting out there waiting on you. What are you thinking?"

I knew by his clenched jaw I'd hit a nerve. "Dana is not my girlfriend. How many times do I have to tell you this before you get it?"

"You may not consider her your girlfriend, but she sure does."

"That's her problem, not mine or yours." *Seriously?*

"I can't do this," I told him.

"But you want to."

"That's irrelevant."

"If I march my ass out there right now and tell Dana I'm in here with you, because it's where I want to be, will you finally give in?"

"No, yes…oh, I don't know. You're confusing me!" I closed my eyes as he stroked his fingers across my face. I couldn't help it. His hands felt good.

"Look at me," he commanded. Our eyes met, and once again, his lips were on mine. This time he was the one who broke off the kiss. "I want you. I am going crazy over you. Please believe me," he whispered. I wanted to believe him, I really did but something was holding me back.

"You said earlier you would let me think about it. Did you mean that?"

"Yes, but don't take too long." He kissed me again, and Garrett walked in.

Garrett's eyes widened in surprise before they narrowed in on Dillon. "Are you okay in here, Ellie?" he asked. Garrett had grown on me. The protective note in his voice made me like him even more.

"Yes," I assured him, "I'm good. Give me a minute and I'll be out." With a nod of his head, he turned to leave. As soon as he was out of the room, I let out a sigh of frustration. Could this get any more complicated?

"Ellie -" Dillon started to say, but I held up my hand to stop him.

"I'll help you two clean up, and then I have to go see how my dad is doing. Please, I just need some time, okay?"

With a nod of his head and one last kiss, he walked out of the room. *What have I gotten myself into?*

When I returned to the bar a few minutes later, Dillon was cleaning up, Garrett was on the phone, and Dana was gone.

# CHAPTER NINETEEN

The next night I wasn't scheduled to work. I was thankful for this, because I was worried about my dad. I'd set up a make-shift office for him in one of the upstairs guest rooms. He'd recovered enough to spend most of his day catching up on work. However, he still moved slowly and continued to be experiencing a moderate amount of pain. Of course, he never complained, but I could tell by his pinched expression each time he moved. I was conflicted about my feelings for my father. We were getting along well and I knew he was a genuinely good person. That being said, it didn't change the fact that he'd abandoned me. I felt the need to keep him at arm's length. I didn't know what role I wanted him to play in my life, but I definitely wanted him there.

Benny hadn't met my dad yet, so I decided to have him over for dinner to introduce them. I didn't know what to expect, but was surprised when they hit it off like a house on fire. They even exchanged contact information.

As I walked Benny out to his truck, he patted me on the

shoulder. "Everyone deserves a chance, Ellie girl. I would give the clothes off my back to get another chance with my family... with Max." He squeezed the back of my neck. "I know you would, too. Don't take your dad being in your life for granted. Look at it as a gift."

I hugged him and promised to think about it.

The next night, Dillon called in at the last minute and said he couldn't work his shift but didn't give a reason why. That left me working with Garrett, Kurt, and the girls. Mass Seduction was on fire. I was sad Joss wasn't there to see them, but she'd wanted to stay home and look through bridal magazines, as she was convinced Kurt was on the verge of proposing. We had a good time behind the bar. Truth be told, it was nice not having any Dillon and Dana conflict...for once.

When our shift was over, Garrett walked me out to my car and, in the nicest way possible, warned me about Dillon. He felt Dillon had some sick and twisted thing going on with Dana, and if I got in the middle of it, I would just get hurt. I thanked him for being concerned for me, and meant it. Garrett was a good guy. I felt lucky to have him looking out for me. Right before getting into my car, he pulled me into a hug and whispered, "Something better is out there for you. I just know it." I wanted to believe him, I really did.

Sunday morning, I woke with a raging fever and a throat so sore I could barely swallow. I couldn't recall the last time I'd felt this rotten. I barely managed to get myself dressed to go to the doctor. My dad, who was drinking coffee in the kitchen, took one look at me and went straight into full-blown father mode. He took me to the doctor and sat in the waiting room with me for three hours. Along with liquids and sleep, the doctor prescribed antibiotics. On the way home, Dad ran into both the grocery store and the pharmacy for me. I'd never had strep throat before. It was awful.

By Tuesday afternoon I was feeling much better. Dad and I were hanging out in the living room watching television, when the phone rang.

"Hello?" I answered.

"Ellie!" Joss screamed. "Get your ass over here, right now!"

I held the phone away from my ringing ear. "What?"

"You have to come over to our place right now!" she shrieked.

"I can't. I'm not even dressed, Joss, plus, I have strep throat."

"You're on antibiotics, for Pete's sake! It's only me and Kurt, and we sure as shit don't care what you look like!"

"Gee, thanks," I replied dryly.

She laughed. "You know what I mean. Pretty please?" she begged.

"Okay, okay. I'll be right over." As I hung up the phone, I glanced over at my dad. "Are you okay with me running over to Joss and Kurt's for a bit?"

"Ellie, you don't need to ask every time you go somewhere."
*Do I do that?*

"I wasn't aware I was doing that."

"Look, you've taken me in and nursed me, and I can't tell you how much this means to me, but I think it's probably time I get back to Raleigh and you get back to living your life, don't you?" My heart stuttered in my chest. Surely he wasn't serious?

"B-b-but you're still healing, and I'll worry about you if you leave now. You at least need one more week, don't you think?" I wasn't ready for him to go. Not yet. He saw right through me. He knew it and I knew it, yet, he was gracious enough not to call me on it.

"Maybe you're right. I do still feel a little weak. One more week and I'll be good as new," he smiled.

With a sigh of relief, I told him I'd be back in a bit. I wasn't sure I was ready to keep him, but I wasn't sure I wanted to let him go. When did life get so complicated?

Twenty minutes later, I pulled up to Joss and Kurt's place. Before I put the car in park, Joss shot out of the house like a bat out of hell being chased by a one-eyed, hairy demon. Waving her hands in the air she shrieked, "I'm getting married! I'm getting married!" *I knew it!* While we were busy jumping up and down, hugging each other and squealing like little girls, Kurt came out of the house grinning from ear to ear.

"Can we take the love fest inside before our neighbors call the cops, please?" he asked before picking me up in a bear hug. "She said yes," he whispered in my ear and my eyes welled with tears. *My best friends are getting married.*

"Well, let me see the ring!" I squealed. Joss held up her hand. Perched on her finger was a ginormous round diamond set in the most amazing diamond band I'd ever seen. "Wow," I breathed. "Kurt, my friend, you've done well. This is gorgeous."

"It is, isn't it?" Joss sighed. Kurt beamed from ear to ear.

"How did he propose?" I asked.

"You do realize I'm standing here," Kurt stated. As usual, we both ignored him.

Joss wrapped her arm around me and giggled. "Come inside, and I'll give you all the details." I followed them into the house and parked it in my usual spot on the living room sofa.

"Well, when Kurt got home last night, he was acting all tired and cranky and wanted ice cream. So I went to get some. When I got home, there were like a million candles lit all over the bedroom and bathroom. He'd run a bubble bath and had both champagne and chocolates waiting for me."

I glanced over at Kurt, who was grinning like a mad man. "Wow, I'm impressed," I told him.

Joss continued with her story. "He poured us both a glass of champagne and turned on my absolute favorite love song, you know, the one from *Titanic*, by Celine Dion? Well, wanting to properly thank him, I leaned over to bl…"

"Blast!" Kurt butted in. "Right as she was about to blast us out of the bathroom with such an incredibly *beautiful* love song, I popped the question."

She arched her eyebrow at him. "I was going to say blow out the candles. Anyway, when I said yes to his proposal, he carried me to the bed and we f…"

"Fell asleep!" he shouted. "We fell into the best sleep, ever." I was now howling with laughter. I couldn't decide who was funnier at that moment, Joss or Kurt.

Joss looked at Kurt as if he'd just sprouted four heads out of the middle of his forehead, and asked, "What in the world is your problem?"

"Awww, hell, Joss, she's like my sister."

"So?"

"I don't want my sister knowing the details of my sex life."

"For your information, I wasn't going to tell her about our sex life, but just so you know," she smiled mischievously, "your so-called *sister* knows all about the time we got hammered and you did me in the a…"

"Joss!" he shouted.

"Apartment that was vacant across the hall," she smirked. "Mind in the gutter much?" she asked him. "I also told her about the time you lubed up my….."

"Fuuuuck," he groaned.

As I rolled on the floor in hysterics, I shouted, "Stop, please! I can't breathe!" They smiled at each other, and my heart squeezed at the love in their eyes. Once I'd recovered, I asked, "So, when's the big day?"

"I'm giving Joss three months to plan it," Kurt said.

I stared open-mouthed at Joss. "Three months? Have you lost your mind? We can't plan a wedding that fast!"

"Well, you're going to have to," Kurt cut in, "because come hell or high water, I'm marrying the love of my life in exactly three months." Joss laughed at the expression of horror on my face.

"You think three months is bad? It took every trick in my bag to get that much time out of him. He wanted to go *this coming weekend* to Vegas!"

I hung out, until I noticed them making goo-goo eyes at each other, and decided that was my cue to leave. On the way home, I contemplated my life. I was truly happy for Joss and Kurt, but I also felt a twinge of sadness. *This could have been me and Max.*

As soon as I got home, I told my dad all about the proposal. This got him asking questions about my friendship with Joss and Kurt. Benny had talked a lot about Max the night before, and I knew my dad was curious about him. I wasn't ready to go there, yet. Skimming over the parts about Max, I told him about the evolution of Piper, Joss, and Kurt. It felt good to talk about my past without the pain and to laugh with him. Whether I wanted it or not, I could feel us getting closer.

I was nervous about work on Thursday night. After all, I hadn't seen or spoken to Dillon in a week. All kinds of crazy thoughts were running through my head. *Why wasn't he at work on Saturday? Was he with Dana? If he wants me so badly, then why hasn't he called or texted me? What if everyone is right about him? What if he ends up hurting me?* By the time I got to Dragonfly, I was completely frazzled. I took a few deep breaths before going in, squared my shoulders, and opened the door.

Dillon's deep voice greeted me from the bar. "Ellie D, I was wondering when you were going to get here." I couldn't help but smile. The man was way too sexy for his own good.

"Hey there, stranger, where have you been?" I asked as I slipped behind the bar.

"Stranger? I'm no stranger, or at least I hope I'm not." A shiver of lust skittered up my spine when he slid my hair off my shoulder and touched his lips to the back of my neck. "I want to know you up close and personal," he whispered as he brushed his lips against my sensitive skin. Goosebumps shot up all over my body. I dropped my head forward in invitation, and shivered when he ran his tongue across the back of my ear.

"What the hell is going on here?" Dillon and I both jumped. *Oh shit!* I turned in time to see Kurt storming toward us. The man was furious. I quickly took a step forward, and tried not to cringe when Dillon pulled me back against his chest.

"Nothing, why?" Dillon answered.

"Did I just see you kissing her neck, D? And are those your hands on her hips? It doesn't look like nothing, so I'll ask you again, what the hell is going on here?"

This time when I pulled away, Dillon let me go. Rolling my eyes at both of them, I answered, "Nothing is going on Kurt."

Dillon smirked. "Oh, something is most definitely going on," he muttered under his breath.

I gave him a dirty look and mouthed, "Stop."

"Ellie, can I see you in my office, now?" Kurt stressed.

"No, Dad, you may not," I snapped.

"What happens between Ellie and me has nothing to do with you," Dillon calmly told him. "Now it's time to open the doors."

Kurt scowled. "The hell it doesn't. You have no idea who she is or what she's been through, D."

"Who, who is?" Lena asked, coming through the door.

Not wanting anybody else in my private business, I said,

"Kurt, I will meet you in your office after the shift and we'll talk, okay?"

This seemed to appease him. "Fine, but *you* -"he pointed at Dillon - "keep your hands to yourself."

Dillon saluted him with his middle finger. "Aye, aye, captain," he sarcastically replied.

*Great.*

Before Kurt could punch him, Lena cut in, and asked, "D, did you finally get caught playing with yourself behind the bar?"

"It's about time he got caught," Polly smirked as she played along. "I was getting tired of cleaning up his mess."

Crudely grabbing his crotch, Dillon grinned maniacally. "Well, when you've got one this big, ladies, he has to be handled regularly."

"I'll be sure and ask Dana about that the next time I see her," Garrett said, winking at me. Everyone laughed at this, except for me...and Dillon.

Kurt shouted from the back of the bar, "Okay, people, Joss is running late, so it looks like I'll be filling in until she gets here! Tonight is margarita night, so all hands need to be on deck and not on each other! Am I clear?" He looked straight at Dillon, who just smiled and flipped him another bird. The sound of the bar phone ringing broke the tension.

Being closest to it, I answered "Dragonfly."

"Ellie, let me speak to Kurt," Joss said.

"Hey, Joss. Is everything okay?"

"I need you to get Kurt," she snapped.

"Bite my head off, why don't you?" I snapped back, and before she could chew my ass, again, I thrust the phone at Kurt. *What's her problem?*

"Kurt here," he said. He listened for a few seconds, and then whispered, "What did you just say?" Apparently, whatever Joss told him was a doozy. Of course, my mind went to the worst possible place. *Someone died.* A minute or so later, he said, "I'll be right there," and hung up. I waited for what seemed like forever for him to say something, but he just stood there staring at me.

Finally, not able to stand the silence any longer, I asked, "Kurt, what's wrong? Has something happened to Joss?"

He shook his head back and forth a few times, as if trying to break out of a trance. "Uuuh...no. It's nothing," he finally answered, but I could tell he was lying.

"It sure didn't sound like nothing to me," Lena quietly replied.

"I'm sorry. I have to go."

"Kurt," I called out.

He looked confusedly around the bar, before focusing back in on us. "Uhhhh...Joss dropped me off here earlier. I need a ride. Dillon, since you're managing tonight, you need to stay here. Ellie needs to stay and make the margaritas. Garrett, can you give me a lift?"

"Sure, man," Garrett answered.

"D, can you, Ellie, and the girls handle it here until Garrett returns?"

*What did he mean he had to go?* He wasn't going anywhere until he explained. If something was happening with my two best friends, then I needed to be there for them. "I'll take you," I told him.

Without acknowledging I'd spoken, he looked at Garrett and said, "Let's go."

*What in the world is going on?*

"Kurt!" I yelled.

"We'll talk later!" he shouted over his shoulder as they disappeared out the door.

I grabbed Dillon's arm and squeezed. "Oh, God. Something is seriously wrong. Maybe I should follow them?" I felt his hand on the back of my neck, and glanced up into his silver eyes.

Concern was written across his face as he squatted down until he was eye level with me.

"Ellie Belly, if he wanted you to go with him he would have said so. Let him deal with it. He'll talk to you about it later. Plus, we have a bar to run, and I really need your help, okay?" he gently said.

I closed my eyes and prayed that everything was okay. "Okay," I finally agreed.

He kissed the top of my head, and whispered, "That's my girl."

The night ended up being crazy busy. Kurt and Garrett never came back to the bar and no one called to tell us what was happening. By closing, I was sick with worry. We were in the middle of wiping everything down when I realized Dana hadn't stopped by to terrorize us. This got me thinking, and I turned to Dillon and asked, "Where were you last week?"

"Huh?" He gave me a strange look.

"Sorry, I know that was completely out of the blue, but you cancelled work last Saturday and Joss said you were gone for most of the week. I forgot to ask if everything was okay."

A sad smile appeared on his face. "It's fine now. I had to go home for my aunt's funeral."

"Oh my God, Dillon! I'm so sorry!"

"It's okay, really. She's had cancer for a long time, so we knew it was coming. Still, it sucks when it finally happens." I wanted to hug him but, with Polly and Lena still around, didn't want to deal with the aftermath.

As if reading my mind, Dillon shouted for the girls to go home. I still had to take the aprons and bar towels to the laundry room before I could leave, so I headed in that direction. I'd just turned on the washing machine, when I heard the door click shut behind me. I glanced over my shoulder, and my breath caught in my throat. Dillon was standing there, his silver eyes feasting on me as if he wanted to swallow me whole. Slowly, as if he was some sort of sexy jungle cat, he advanced. My heart was beating out of my chest, and for a split second, I felt hunted. *What will he do when he catches me?* Before my fight or flight instinct had a chance to kick in, his mouth was on mine and I was being lifted up and placed on top of the dryer. As he stepped between my legs, he grasped my upper thighs and yanked me forward. Every inch of his lower body was now touching mine. Just the feel of his hard body pressed against mine made me yearn for things I hadn't had, or wanted, in a very long time.

His head lowered, and right as he was about to kiss me, he whispered, "I want you Ellie. I want to make you moan for me and then I want to hear you scream out my name when I'm deep inside you. Tell me you want that, too."

"I do…but-"

Placing his finger to my lips, he said, "Shhhhh. That's all I need to hear. I want you all night long…in my bed." He touched his lips to mine. "Come home with me?"

I reared back in surprise. "Now?"

"Right now," he confirmed. It was too soon. Something was going on with Joss and Kurt, and my dad was still staying at my house. I needed more time. A part of me wanted to go with him, but a bigger part of me wasn't completely sure. As if reading my mind, he asked, "If not tonight, then what about tomorrow night? Did Kurt schedule you to work? He mentioned something about it earlier, but then he had to go."

"I'm off," I confirmed.

"Why don't you meet me here sometime before closing? That way you can either leave your car here or follow me back to my place. I'll leave the logistics up to you." He pulled me in close, and I gasped when I felt how hard he was for me. I wanted him, so why shouldn't I have him?

"Okay," I breathed, "tomorrow night."

He jerked back in surprise. "Really?"

"Yes," I said through my laughter.

After we finished cleaning up, he walked me out to my car and kissed me goodnight before letting me go. If I hadn't been so worried about Joss and Kurt, I would have floated home on cloud nine. Instead, I debated whether or not to drive over to their place and check in on them. At the last minute, I decided against it. Dillon was right. If they wanted me to know what was up, they would tell me. Still, I couldn't deny that it stung.

# CHAPTER TWENTY

Friday morning I woke with a sick feeling in the pit of my stomach. I'd called and left Joss, Kurt, and Garrett messages before going to bed, but none of them had bothered to call me back. My thoughts kept going back to the haunted look on Kurt's face right before he took off last night. Something bad had happened, and no one was talking. My dad was busy with a deadline and holed up in his office. Looking at magazines wasn't helping, so I decided to call Piper.

"Hey girl," she answered. "I was going to call you this afternoon."

"You sound tired. Are you okay?"

"Not really."

Something about her tone worried me. "Are you sick? Is your family okay? Talk to me."

After a long, silent pause, she said, "I need something from you, and I need you to not ask any questions."

"Piper, you know I would do anything for you. Just name it."

"I'm...I'm in trouble, but I can't talk about it, and I really need to get out of Texas. The only place I want to be right now is in Charlotte with you."

Needing clarification, I asked, "You can't or you won't talk about it?"

"Both, I guess. I miss you." Her voice trembled with emotion, and I could tell she was on the verge of tears. *What has she gotten herself into?* "I miss North Carolina. I need to come home. I want to be there through the wedding planning for Joss. I don't know what's happening in your lives anymore. I feel so disconnected from everything." The more she talked, the more worried I became. *What isn't she telling me?*

"Whatever it is, we will deal with it. And, yes, you can always stay with me," I told her.

"Can I?" She sounded like a lost little girl instead of my strong-willed best friend.

"Of course you can. My dad is in my old room and is presently using the front guest room as his office, but the back room is all yours."

"Oh, Ellie," she sighed, "things are so messed up." A million questions danced on the tip of my tongue, but I knew she didn't need me pressuring her. What she needed was to get out of Texas, and safely to Charlotte. Then I would get my answers.

"When will you be here?"

"Soon."

"I don't like this at all, Piper. Will you eventually tell me what this is about?"

"I swear, if I talk to anyone about it, it will be you. I can't right now. Just trust me."

"Fine, but for the record, I don't like it."

"I hear you," she responded.

After we hung up, I realized I'd completely forgotten to tell her about last night, and Dillon.

By the time seven o'clock rolled around, I was done. Joss and Kurt were missing in action, and not a single person had returned my phone calls…all day. Dillon wasn't expecting me until closer to closing, but I was sick and tired of waiting around and twiddling my thumbs, so I decided to head to Dragonfly early. Maybe someone would be there who could give me some answers.

Both excited and nervous about what was about to transpire, I decided to wear my sexy new black lace bra under a sheer black long-sleeve tee, and my tightest, most flattering pair of Levi's. With my hair blown out, my eyes done up, and my lips glossed, I felt pretty damn good about myself. I told my dad I would be out for the night and to call my cell if he needed anything. He gave me a stern look but didn't say a word. *Smart man.*

After I pulled on my boots, I grabbed my purse and overnight bag, and headed for the door. "See you later!" I called out.

As usual, Dillon's awful music accosted me as I walked into Dragonfly. Instead of making me cringe like it normally did, it made me smile. *Vintage Dillon.* I spotted him standing behind the bar and headed his way. As I got closer, I could see that he was bent over talking to someone, but I couldn't tell who it was from this far away. However, I could see the familiar 'I want to swallow you whole' look on his face. This was the exact same look he'd given me last night, only now he wasn't directing it at me. Who was he giving that look to? The person just-so-happened to turn their head, and my heart froze. I felt as if I'd been punched in the gut.

*Dana.*

The closer I got, the more damning it looked. When he reached over and touched his hand to her face, I saw red. Slowly, I approached. Clearly he had no clue I was in Dragonfly, much less standing there watching him.

*When will I learn? Apparently, the answer is never.*

214

Right as I turned to make my escape, Polly saw me. "Hey, Ellie Belly!" she shouted.

*Crap!*

Dillon's head shot up. His eyes landed on me and rounded in surprise. I wasn't sure if I should laugh or cry at the guilty expression on his face. His eyes darted from me to Dana, and, as if he'd been burned, he yanked his hand out of her grasp.

"What's wrong?" I heard her ask. Following his stare, she swiveled around in her chair. When she saw me standing there, her eyes narrowed into tiny, little slits. "Oh, it's only you," she huffed. Then, as if I wasn't there, she swiveled back around, and said, "Keep telling me about what you're going to do to me later tonight, baby." I bit my tongue to keep from gasping out loud.

*Stupid, stupid, Ellie.*

"Shut up, Dana," Dillon warned.

Enough was enough. I stepped up to the bar, leaned forward, and asked, "Do you even have an aunt, or was that also a lie?"

Before he could answer, Garrett spotted me from the opposite end of the bar and shouted, "Hey, Ellie! Dillon said you weren't coming in until later tonight." I shot Dillon a look of disgust.

"Of course he did," I bitterly responded. With a shake of my head, I dismissed Dillon, and headed to the opposite end of the bar to where Garrett was standing. With a disgusted sigh, I plopped my behind on the stool directly in front of him, and shouted, "Hit me with a shot!"

He stared at me as if weighing his options, and then asked, "Do you think that's a good idea?"

"What are you, my mother?" Before he could reply, I answered for him. "Nope, you can't be my mother, because she's dead. You're not my father because he's back at my house convalescing, and since I have no siblings, you can't be them. So what does that make you? Oh, yes, that makes you the bar-ten-der," I spelled out, "and I...want...a...shot!" He chuckled and pulled out two shot glasses. Then he grabbed the bottle of tequila and slammed it down on the bar between us.

"Hell, I think the word convalescing alone should get you two." We both burst out laughing and, like that, the tension was broken.

My smile quickly faded when Joss and Kurt appeared from the back. I waited patiently for Joss to step behind the bar before blasting her. "I want to know where in the hell you two have been? You haven't answered my calls, and I've been worried sick. You, of all people, know how cruel that is." Joss paled, and a look of pain flitted across her face. *What the hell?*

"Ellie," Garrett warned, and I held up my hand to stop him from speaking.

"You didn't call me back either, so...don't."

Polly handed me a shot from her tray as she passed by, and before anyone could stop me, I quickly downed it. Joss didn't notice because she was busy whispering sweet nothings in Garrett's ear. It seemed everyone had secrets these days, including me. I could feel Dillon staring at me from his end of the bar. I wanted to poke both of his beautiful eyes out. *Give me a couple more shots and I might just try.*

I spotted Lena heading my way with a tray of shots. A guy stopped her as she passed by, and while she was distracted, I slid from my chair, snagged a shot from her tray, and sucked it down. When I returned to my stool, Dillon was standing in front of me.

"It's not what you think." he said, and I wanted to scream. How many times had he said those words to me? *Too damn many.*

"No? Then by all means, slick, tell me how it is?"

His brow shot up. "Slick?"

I looked him up and down, and replied, "Yep, definitely slick." This seemed to piss him off. *Good.*

"Another?" He raised my empty shot glass in the air.

"Nope, I'll take a Shiner, though."

As he reached into the fridge to pull out the bottle, I felt my resolve start to crumble. After opening it, he plunked it down in front of me, and asked, "Can we talk?"

I took a sip from my beer, and shook my head. "Nope."

"Are we still on for later tonight?" My jaw literally hit the bar.

"Are you for real?"

"I told you it's not what you think," he growled.

"You are unbelievable," I hissed. Then I chugged the entire beer, slammed the bottle down on the bar top, and yelled, "Another please!"

Lena stepped up beside me. After giving Dillon a dirty look, she said, "Hey, girl, you might want to slow down on those drinks. I don't want to clean up a mess in the bathroom later on, even if it is yours."

I threw my arm around her waist and gave her a tight squeeze. "Lena, babe, I'm going to get hammered tonight!"

Polly scooted in on my other side, and shouted, "I wanna get hammered! Why do I always have to be working when all the good stuff happens?"

Three beers later, I felt a tap on my shoulder. I turned to blast whoever was rudely interrupting my drinking binge, and froze.

*Hot guy alert.*

Over six feet of mouth-watering yumminess stood before me. His short, sandy-blond hair highlighted the bluest eyes I'd ever seen. Normally, I didn't go for facial hair, however, on this guy it was definitely a plus.

"Hi, I'm Gage. Are you by chance Ellie Davis?" His voice was deep and had an edge to it. What was it about deep-voiced alpha men that got me every time?

I summoned my sexiest smile and hoped Dillon was watching. "I sure am. Do I know you?" Before he could reply, I said, "Who cares, you'll do. Do you want to dance?'"

"Uhhh, I'm not much of a dancer, but wouldn't mind going somewhere to talk."

"Ellie," I heard Dillon warn. At this point, the guy could be a serial killer, and I wouldn't care. That's how disgusted I was.

"Sure thing, *Gage*," I said, stressing his name. "By all means, let's go *talk*."

His eyebrow rose in question, and he tilted his head toward Dillon. "He bugging you?"

With a sexy lash flutter, I snagged Gage's hand, and couldn't help but laugh at the furious look on Dillon's face. "Yep, and now I'm going to use you on the dance floor, or wherever, to bug him back." This made him chuckle. "You don't have to actually dance since you don't like it…just stand there looking pretty, and I'll do all the moving," I instructed.

Gage shook his head. "She said you were funny. I can see she wasn't lying," he muttered.

"Who?" I asked. Sounds of a fight drifted from the offices, and suddenly Joss was in my face.

She glared at Gage, before addressing me. "Ellie, you need to stop drinking right now."

"Why? I'm not hurting anyone. Am I? No, that's what you and Kurt do, not me."

"Ellie," she whispered, "I wanted to talk to you, but I couldn't."

"I don't know what that means, Josssss. Tell me what that means," I half-slurred.

"I can't." The pain in her voice made me want to comfort her, but I wanted to kick her ass more, so I held back.

"What are you not telling me? 'Cause, if it has something to do with Piper, I already know." At the mention of Piper's name, Gage stepped forward.

"What's wrong with Piper?" Joss asked.

"Ha! So this isn't about Piper? Good to know."

Joss threw up her hands, and shouted, "I can't tell you right now, Ellie. I just can't!"

With a loud huff, I rolled my eyes at her. "Well then, meet my new friend, Garage," I flung my arm in his direction.

"Gage," he corrected.

Suddenly, it dawned on me that Dillon was no longer standing behind the bar. I scanned the room, but didn't see him anywhere. "Where is he?" I asked.

Joss looked around the bar and then back at me, before asking, "Who?"

"Dillon. Where's Dillon?"

"I don't know. He said something about walking Dana out so she could catch a ride home."

I turned to Gage, who was still patiently waiting to talk to me, and shook my head. "This night just keeps gets better and better."

"Ellie, is there something going on between you and Dillon? Because if there is-" Joss started to say.

"Stop," I told her. I was officially sick of hearing how wrong Dillon was for me. I was the one living it. Instead of listening to Joss tell me something I already knew, I decided to march outside and confront him.

"Ellie, wait up!" Joss shouted, but I was already halfway across the bar.

Sure enough, Joss was right. Dillon was outside, and he was with Dana. Was he putting her in a cab? No. They were locking lips behind some parked cars, like two teenage kids afraid of getting caught by their parents.

Anger, hurt, and humiliation raged through me, but somehow I managed to keep my mouth shut until I was practically on top of them. "You know, for someone who claims there's nothing going on, you sure have a funny way of showing it," I loudly announced. They both jumped, and Dana shrieked in surprise. *Good, hopefully she just pissed her pants.*

"Ellie, we were just-" Dillon started to say.

I held up my hand, and surprisingly, he shut his mouth. "For your information, *Dillon*, I have eyes. I saw what you were *just* doing." Right as I opened my mouth to blast them both, a car pulled up beside us. And just as I thought my night couldn't get any worse, it did.

*Jennifer Tilson.*

Jennifer stepped from the driver's side of the car with an evil grin on her face. "Well, well, well, what do we have here?" she sneered.

Dana opened her mouth to answer, but Dillon cut her off. "We have Dana getting in your car and going home or wherever, that's what." Dismissing them both, he turned to me, and said, "Ellie, we need to talk."

I'd been so caught up in the Dillon, Dana drama, that I'd failed to pay attention to what was happening around me. When I saw at least half the damn bar outside watching us, I took a step back. *When did they get here?*

"You'd better watch out, Ellie," Jennifer sniggered, "Dillon is a love'em and leave'em kind of guy, just…like…Max was. She clicked her tongue. "So sad…you just can't seem to hold onto your men, can you? Now, why is that, do you think?"

"Fuck you, Jennifer!" Dillon roared.

For a second, I felt like we were back in high school, where Jennifer dished out a heavy helping of humiliation and cruelty, and I just took it. I felt like that lonely pathetic girl again, and then I remembered where I was…who I was, and let her have it.

"Jennifer, Jennifer, Jennifer," I mocked. "I seem to remember Max's friends talking about how you and Megan Malloy got drunk one night and were passed around by the whole football team. Hell, they didn't even have to pay for your services, those lucky dogs." I clapped my hands together in fake glee. "In fact, the only reason they wanted anything to do with you was because nothing was off limits with you, and I mean no-thing. Two words come to mind right now, and they are self-respect. Apparently, you have no clue what that means, but I do. I had it five years ago with Max and I still do. That's something you will never be able to say." I looked over at Dana and added, "You either."

I heard someone cough, and then Joss's loud mouth shout, "That's my girl! Push her far enough and she will re-ta-li-ate!"

Jennifer, of course, had to get in the last word. "Really? If Max loved you so much, then why was he mine for our entire senior year, and not yours?"

I placed my finger next to my mouth, as if seriously contemplating her question. "Gee, let me think. That's a hard one. Ummmm…maybe because he was a guy, and you were a girl with no morals?" I shrugged, and muttered, "Just a wild guess."

An evil glint appeared in her eyes, and I mentally braced for the onslaught. "You know what I heard? I heard Max went after you on a *bet*. As a matter-of-fact, it was a cherry-popping bet." She laughed, and I tried not to flinch. "He and his boys were supposed to go after a virgin, lure her in, and pop her cherry." She made a vulgar popping noise. *Ouch.*

"I call bullshit!" Joss shouted. I jerked my head in the direction of her voice, and found her surrounded by familiar faces. Joss curled her lip at Jennifer, before addressing me. "Kurt was Max's best friend and one of his so-called 'boys' and, to this day, there has never been anything said about a bet. Don't you dare believe her, Ellie." Her protectiveness made me smile. I may be mad at Joss for hiding things from me, but I knew that no matter what, she always had my back.

"Don't worry about me Josselyn, I'm pretty much done here,"

I told her. Now, officially feeling the effects of the alcohol, and really needing to pee, I turned to head back into the bar.

"That's it? You're going to just walk away?" Jennifer challenged. "See? You know I'm right."

My aunt used to taunt me when she wanted a fight and I wouldn't give her one. It drove me crazy. I threw my hand out to the crowd. "The only one here who thinks Max gave a shit about you, Jennifer…is you." I cut my eyes to Dana. "And maybe her, but we all know she's a couple of cards short of a full deck."

"Oh yeah?" she yelled. I could hear her desperation, and once again, I braced. At least, I tried to, but it felt like more of a sway. "Tell me, if Max was so in love with you, then why did he show up at my dorm after leaving you, and spend two weeks in my bed?"

I sighed. "Who knows? But *if* Max ended up at your place, and we both know that's a big if, it certainly wasn't because he loved you." Surprisingly, she had no come back.

Dana, however, decided this was the time to put her two cents worth in. "For your information, Ellie, I have a big deck in my backyard, and Dillon is mine. He always has been and always will be." A couple of people snickered when she said this. I didn't care anymore. I didn't care what she said or he did. She could have him. After tonight, there would never be anything between us.

I shook my head in disgust, then turned and headed for the door. "You can have him!" I shouted over my shoulder. Not watching where I was going, I smacked into a very broad chest, and let out a squeak of surprise when two hands shot out to steady me.

I opened my mouth to apologize, when a voice I hadn't heard in five years growled, "Before we get out of here, I want to set the record straight." My lungs seized and my ears started ringing. "In no way shape or form did I ever pay a visit to Jennifer. In fact, I haven't set eyes on the bitch since she tried to break us up…five years ago." It took me a few seconds to realize he was speaking directly to me. I closed my eyes and did my best not to hyperventilate. He started to move away, but I panicked and grabbed for his arm. As if sensing my freak out, he pulled me protectively back to his side. "How about you tell the truth for once, Jen?" he quietly asked. No one said a word, but I could tell they were still there. Jennifer's silence made him angry. "Tell her!" he shouted. I turned to bolt but he tightened his hold on me. The familiar scent of leather and spice filled my head, and I swayed on my feet.

*This is not happening.*

"Max?" Jennifer gasped, and he tensed beside me.

"Go away Jen. Haven't you caused enough trouble? Just get in your car, drive the fuck away, and don't come back." His body shifted, and I knew I was now the focus of his attention. "Ellison, look at me," he quietly said. I shook my head and clenched my eyes together. I was afraid if I opened them, I would find this was only a dream. "Babe, you need to look at me," he repeated more forcefully. With a deep breath, I tilted my head up and opened my eyes. There, looking down at me was my beautiful, missing Max.

# CHAPTER TWENTY-ONE

I glanced over at Joss for confirmation that this was really happening and could see the tears running down her face. Hell, even Kurt looked a little teary-eyed.

"Okay people!" Kurt shouted. "We're closing early tonight! Time for everyone to head home! Be right back," he said to us, and disappeared inside the building.

I couldn't stop staring at Max. His hair was a little longer than I'd remembered. It looked great on him. He was the same, but older, taller and more beautiful, if that was even possible. He'd filled out in all the right places and obviously had been taking care of himself. *Five years. I haven't looked at this face for five years,* played over and over in my head. Suddenly, the reality of the situation started to seep in, and I took a step back from him. Max was here. *He didn't die. He wasn't an angel in the heavens looking down on me and protecting me.* He was alive, and from the looks of it, doing quite well. This meant one thing...*he left me.* Staring down at his hand on my arm, I said, "Let go."

The entire time I'd been having my mental freak out, he'd

been watching me like a hawk. From the look on his face, he knew exactly what was running through my head. "Ellison," he whispered. I shook my head. Then I took another step back, and wrenched my arm from his grasp. Slowly, as if dealing with a frightened animal, he took a step toward me. "Ells, baby-"

"No," I repeated, cutting him off. "No, no, no!" I took another step back and slammed into something hard.

"What the fuck?" Dillon asked in my ear.

A wave of nausea rolled over me, and I turned and ran for the bushes, where I dropped to my knees and spewed up most of the alcohol in my system. I sat back on my haunches and saw both Max and Dillon heading for me. "Don't," I said, holding up my hand. "You-" I pointed to Dillon - "don't get near me and you-" I pointed to Max- "aren't really here."

"Ellison, baby," Max spoke, as if addressing a small child, "I'm here, standing right in front of you. Let me get you cleaned up, and then we can talk." I stood up on shaky legs, and Dillon moved closer to me. Max clenched his hands into fists, and growled, "She said get the fuck away from her. Who the hell are you anyway?"

Suddenly, the bar door opened and Joss and Kurt reappeared. I glanced at the parking lot, and noticed Jennifer and Dana were no longer there. I hadn't heard them leave. Then again, I hadn't heard anyone leave. My eyes flew back to Joss and Kurt. "You knew. You both knew he was here and you didn't tell me?" I accused.

"Ellie," Kurt implored.

I was beyond hurt. "You were there. You went through that hell with me. And you," I directed at Joss, "I thought you were my best friend. Best friends wouldn't keep something like this from each other." She let out a sob, and as sad as that made me, it changed nothing. I stared at Max, soaked him in, and then stiffened my spine. "I have mourned you for five long, miserable years, and it was all…for…nothing."

His face filled with pain, and he took another step toward me. "God, Ellison, please let me explain."

I didn't want to hear his explanation. As far as I was convinced, they were all liars. Without another word, I turned on my heels and took off for the door.

Right as I got to my purse, a hand snagged me from behind. "Let me take you home," Dillon said, pulling me tightly to his chest. "You can talk to me."

Out of breath from running, I panted, "No talk."

"Ellie, please," he practically begged.

"Nope," I said, and shook my head at him.

Max, Kurt and, Joss were suddenly all three standing there. "Who the fuck is this guy and what did he do to her?" Max asked. I closed my eyes and soaked in the sound of his voice. I was still having a hard time believing he was actually here.

"That's our manager and one of our bartenders, Dillon Whitaker, and they are…uh… friends," Kurt lamely replied.

"I thought you said she wasn't seeing anyone?" Max growled.

"She isn't. I mean, wasn't," Joss answered. "At least, not that I was aware of!"

I don't know why I found this funny. Maybe it was because there were four people talking around me and over me but none of them were talking *to* me. Maybe it was because I was simply overwhelmed. Whatever, it didn't matter, because it was funny – funny and pathetically sad. Before I came anymore unglued, I dug inside my purse for my phone. When I had it in my grasp, I quickly punched in my dad's cell number. The second I heard his voice, something inside me snapped and the laughter turned to tears.

*Five years.*

"Ellie?" I heard my dad say. "Is that you? What's wrong?"

"D-D-Dad, I need for you to come get me." At this point, I

was crying so hard I couldn't talk, so Joss grabbed the phone and gave my dad directions to the bar.

"Ells, don't go," Max pleaded. "There's so much I have to say, please?" All I could do was cry.

Joss stepped between us and grabbed his arm. "Let her go, Max. There will be plenty of time to talk later. Let's give her some space right now."

"Fuck space!" he shouted. His beautiful, blue eyes seared through me. "Don't you think we've had enough of that already? I've been forced to live with nothing but space for five fucking years. I'm here! I'm right fucking here! Please, let me explain," he begged. I wanted to go to him, to be with him, to touch him, but...I couldn't.

Dillon leaned in, and spoke into my ear. "This is far from over between us, Ellie. I know you've had a shock tonight, but nothing is how it seems, and I want the opportunity to explain, okay?"

I'd completely forgotten about Dillon. God, I was so confused. I couldn't seem to stop the tears from flowing. I realized the only way I was going to get rid of him was to hear him out, so I nodded my head yes.

"Fuck!" Max shouted. "You'll listen to this creep, but you won't let me explain why I had to go? How is that fair, Ellison? Huh? Tell me!"

Right then my dad pulled up. Without a backward glance, or even a goodbye, I got in the car, closed the door, and started sobbing uncontrollably. "Get me out of here," I barely managed to get out.

I cried the entire way home. Thankfully, my dad didn't ask any questions. He did, however, offer me comfort by slipping his warm hand into mine. Hand in hand, we walked silently into the house. I felt numb. I'd spent so many years crying and worrying about Max, and here he was, alive and healthy. *And more beautiful than ever.*

After making us tea, which gave me time to pull myself together, Dad joined me on the sofa. "You don't have to talk if you don't want to, but I want you to know I will always listen." He really was a good man, so why was I still fighting so hard to push him away? I needed someone to talk to. He was here.

"I wish I'd grown up with you as my dad," I blurted. I could tell from his surprised expression that this was not what he expected to hear.

His concerned expression broke into a wistful smile. "Me, too. I should have fought to see you. I shouldn't have let Elizabeth scare me into walking away. I want you to know I will regret that for the rest of my life."

His words made me both happy and sad. As I fanned the tears away, I said, "No mushy stuff, Dad. I've already cried enough tonight." His chuckle made me smile. "I'm glad you think my tears are funny," I huffed. This made him laugh harder.

"You do realize that's the third time you've slipped and called me Dad. It makes me feel old, but I really like hearing it."

I scrunched my nose, and hesitantly admitted, "It just keeps slipping out."

He winked. "I think we might be growing on each other." My mind drifted back to Max and my smile slipped. I couldn't even begin to wrap my brain around it all. "Ellie?" my father called out, interrupting my thoughts. "Do you trust me?"

"More and more every day," I told him and honestly meant it.

"Then you need to talk about what is eating you up inside, baby girl." Calling me his baby girl did the trick, and before I knew it, I found myself spilling the whole story. It took most of the night to get it all out.

"Wow, that's some story," he commented, once I'd reached the end. "Okay, for what it's worth, here's what I think. You can take it or leave it, but know that no matter what I'm on your side and yours only, okay?" I nodded. "Max has a story. He left you and his friends here for a reason, and by the sound of it, he didn't want to go. I'm not sure you will be able to move forward, either with or without him, until you hear what he has to say. Either way, you need closure. You need the opportunity to forgive him or to forget him. Believe me, I sympathize with you. It took me years to forgive your mother."

His confession surprised me. "You forgave her?"

"How could I not? I'm here with you. You are a part of both of us, and I'm lucky to have this chance with you." My eyes welled with tears. "Okay," he waved his hand back-and-forth through the air. "No tears. Now, let's move on to Joss and Kurt. Did they really betray you? It sounds to me like they were trying to protect you. Could they have handled it better? Sure, but from where I'm sitting, it looks as if they were simply trying to figure out how to ease the shock of Max's return."

As I brushed the tears away, I realized he was probably right. "I said some horrible things to them."

"Give yourself a break, kiddo. You were hit with a couple of big whammies and were drunk to boot. No one would have handled that well, even sober. As for Dillon, it sounds to me like that boy needs to screw his head on tighter and keep his dick in his pants for a while."

I couldn't help but laugh. "I can't believe you just said that."

"Well, from what you've told me, he's been on and off with this Darla girl for quite some time now."

"Dana," I corrected through another fit of giggles.

"Darla, Dana, whatever her name is, she's obviously got the boy's nuts in a stranglehold, and from the looks of it, she ain't gonna let go without a fight. You have to decide if you want him badly enough to have this girl constantly at your throat." I didn't even have to think about it before shaking my head no. The last thing I wanted was another second, much less a lifetime, of having to deal with a head case like Dana. "I didn't think so."

"Dillon wants to talk to me, though."

"Are you afraid to listen?"

"No, but…he says things aren't what they appear to be, but I know what I saw."

"So maybe the truth lies somewhere in-between."

"See, this is where it gets all messed up in my head. Black and white, I can handle. Gray? Not so much."

"Let me ask you this. If you were to find out Max had a valid reason for leaving you, never stopped loving you, and wanted a future with you in it, would you give him a chance?"

My eyes instantly filled with tears, and I shrugged. "I don't know."

"Okay, well how about this. Do you feel for Dillon the way you felt for Max?"

"Not even close. I don't think I'll ever feel that way about anyone again."

He reached over and squeezed my hand. "I think you have your answer, baby girl. As for Piper, she can have my room. It's bigger, and I've more than worn out my welcome."

My heart plummeted. "You can't leave."

"Ellie," he protested.

"Not now. Not when all of this is happening. Please stay… please?"

He pulled me in and wrapped his arms around me. "Tell you what. I'll stay until I know you're going to be okay."

"Promise?" I buried my face in his chest and held my breath. When he said the words, I let it back out. He was going to stay… for now.

We talked through the night about our lives. He told me where he'd been and what he'd seen and I filled him in on what he'd missed. Around five that morning, I brewed a pot of coffee. On the way to the patio, I grabbed two mugs and a blanket. With the blanket wrapped snugly around us, we drank our coffee and watched the sun rise. Talking to my dad was cathartic. It was the first time I'd told anyone the entire story of what happened with Max. Even though I was still confused, I felt as if a huge weight had been lifted from my shoulders.

After sitting outside for a couple of hours, I started to drift off. Dad told me to go crawl into bed.

"Before I crash, can I ask a favor of you?"

He smiled. "You can ask me anything." After last night, I believed him.

"I need space from all of this...stuff. Would you mind if I unplug and hide in the house for a few days?"

"How about this, I'll personally tackle anyone who tries to get through the front door."

"Thanks, Dad."

"Are you sure this is what you need?"

I rubbed the spot on my head that was starting to ache, and sighed. "Truthfully, I'm not really sure what I need anymore."

"Take all the time you need. You'll figure it out," he assured me. Something told me it wasn't going to be that easy.

The second my head hit the pillow, I thought of Max and how long it had been since I'd last heard his voice. The memory of the day he disappeared washed over me, and I thought about everything we did to find him, the last time I was in his house, his phone - So many memories.

*I've spent five years pining for the Max of my youth. What if he hasn't been doing the same? What if he's married? If so, does he have children? What kind of person just walks away like that? Not one who really loves me.*

This was the crux of it all. If Max loved me as much as I loved him, he would never have left. The Max I loved would have fought Heaven and Earth to get back to me. Only...he didn't. I drifted off to sleep wishing he'd stayed away.

I slept off and on for most of that day and night. The following day, I woke feeling disoriented. After moping around the house for hours, I went in search of comfort, and found myself standing in the guest closet staring down at the box of Max's things. My first inclination was to burn it all. But then I remembered that, without these things, I probably wouldn't have made it through the toughest time in my life. They'd been my lifeline for a very long time. Did I really want to destroy that? *Maybe. No. I don't know*. After staring at the box for an indeterminate amount of time, I dragged it downstairs to my bedroom, pulled everything out, and laid it on top of my bed. Then I asked myself, *What do I want?* I realized I couldn't answer this question until I talked to Max. My decision hinged on the outcome of that conversation. It didn't seem fair, but when was life ever fair? As I crawled onto the bed filled with his things, I made my decision. Tomorrow, we would talk.

That night I had pizza with my dad on the back patio. He told me he had to unplug the home phone because it wouldn't stop ringing. I told him about my decision to talk to Max. He suggested I take the time to talk to Joss, Kurt, and Dillon as well. It looked as if tomorrow was going to be a very busy day.

# CHAPTER TWENTY-TWO

The next morning, I woke to someone crawling into bed with me.

"Ellie," Joss softly said, "are you awake?"

"I was," I groggily mumbled, "how did you get past my dad?"

"The back door was unlocked, and I walked right in." *So much for guarding the door.* I felt her hand stroke across my back. "Ells, I'm so sorry," she said. I could hear tears in her voice and felt horrible.

I rolled over and gave her a hug. "Don't cry, Joss, I'm not mad anymore. I would have done the same thing. I was drunk and mad at Dillon, and then Max showed up...and I took it out on you and Kurt. It was all just too much. Don't cry, please?"

She raised her head and glared at me. "Speaking of Dillon, What in the hell is up with *that*? I didn't even know you were interested in him? If I'd known, I would have never let Max ambush you that way."

I adjusted the pillow under my head and groaned. "You were right. I should have stayed away from him, but he was so yummy to look at. I wasn't seriously interested, but he just kept at me and then he kissed me. Then he really kissed me and…I know he has a history with Dana, but he kept telling me it meant nothing. I wanted to believe him, and then I saw them together and suddenly it was in my face and I just couldn't ignore it any longer. I feel like such a fool, and the worst part is I *let* him do that to me."

"It's not just you, honey. Dillon has been with Dana on and off for the past year. She's like a bad wart. The second you burn her off, she just comes back bigger, spreads farther, and is much harder to get rid of the next time. She's basically stalking him, you know. Kurt and I told him we think she's pathological and probably dangerous, but he's taken no real initiative to permanently end things with her."

"He swears it's not what it looks like, if that makes sense."

Her eyebrow shot to the ceiling. "Do you believe him?"

"I don't know," I sighed. "I walked into the bar Friday night so happy. I was ready to *be* with him. I didn't expect to be slapped with an eyeful of them together. Then, to top that, he was kissing her in the parking lot. I actually believed him before all of this, but now…"

"Now, Max is back," she finished for me. Before I could ask, she launched straight in. "He showed up late Thursday afternoon. I was shocked, but after hearing some of his story, I knew I needed to call Kurt."

"Was that when you phoned the bar?"

"Yes, and I am sorry for being a bitch, but all I could think about was protecting both you and Kurt."

"What did Kurt end up doing?"

"After punching Max in the face and yelling at him for the hell he put you through, Kurt ended up hearing him out."

"What about the hell Max put Kurt through? I wasn't the only one who suffered his loss."

"Trust me Max got an earful before I even thought about calling Kurt. Listen, El, I really think you should hear him out."

"I'm going to. But please know that no matter what he says, it won't change that he left. Nothing will."

"I know that, and I made sure he knows it, too. I would be hurt and angry, too, but I think you'll understand once you hear what he has to say."

"Can't you just save us some time and tell me?" I asked.

Placing her hand on mine, she squeezed. "You know I can't. He's the only one who can make sense of it all, and he will, I promise. Now, not to change the subject or anything, but Kurt really wants to come over and see you. I made him hold off until we talked. Is it okay if I call him?"

I narrowed my eyes at her. "Is Max staying with you?"

She laughed. "You're thinking about the time Jennifer tried to break you two up and I ambushed you with Max, aren't you?"

"Yes."

"I promise that's not the case this time. Max will stay put until you say otherwise."

While I threw on some sweats and put my hair in a ponytail, Joss called Kurt. By the time we'd moved into the living room and had a pot of coffee brewing, Kurt had arrived. The first thing he did was hug me.

"Please don't be mad at me, Ellie. I tried to keep him in the back of the bar, but he just *had* to see you."

"Why didn't you want him to see me?"

He sat across from me on the leather sofa, and took a sip of his coffee. "I wanted to talk to you first, but then he saw Dillon serving you shots followed by that guy asking you to dance. By the time he heard you were outside with a third guy, it was all over."

"Gee, you make me sound so wholesome and pure," I dryly commented. With a bark of laughter, Kurt snagged Joss by the waist and pulled her down onto his lap. His reference to dancing stirred my memory. "Oh! I forgot about Gage."

"Who?" they both asked.

"The guy I was attempting to dance with when you so rudely interrupted," I directed at Joss.

A confused look appeared on her face. "I thought you said his name was Garage?" My face heated in embarrassment and Kurt laughed.

"With a name like that, he would definitely be memorable." Kurt mused, and then added, "I thought Max was going to take apart the office when he saw you walk off with him."

"Is that the noise I heard in the back? I thought someone had gotten into a fight."

Joss motioned her hand for me to continue with my Gage story. "So…who was he?"

"He said his name was Gage, and he apparently knew me, but I didn't have a clue as to who he was. He also said something about someone telling him I was funny. I thought it was an odd thing to say, but I was halfway drunk and mad at Dillon. I have to say, the guy was flipping hot. When you told me about Dillon, I ran out before he got the chance to talk to me."

Joss smiled, "Hmmm, he was cute, wasn't he?"

This got her a pinch from Kurt, who asked, "Did you see him outside later with everyone?"

"I didn't, but that doesn't mean he wasn't there. I lost sight of everything else in the parking lot the second I saw Dillon kissing Dana."

"Listen, Ellie," Kurt started to say.

I cut him off. "I know what you're going to say, and the answer is yes. I plan on talking to Max sometime today or tomorrow. I'm not sure it will change anything, though."

After a long, silent pause, Kurt asked, "Are you into Dillon now? You know you can tell us."

"I went to Dragonfly Friday night, thinking it was the beginning of something, but now, I'm not so sure."

"Do me a favor?" he asked.

I hesitated for a second, before answering, "It depends."

"Hold off on anything with D until you hear what Max has to say."

"Sure," I shrugged. "Like I said, I don't know if I have anything more to say to Dillon. After what happened Friday night, I don't think I can trust him." Kurt looked relieved.

"Not to change the subject or anything, but there's something I've been meaning to ask you," Joss chimed in. "I was distracted by Max showing up, so before I get sidetracked again...here goes. Will you be my maid of honor?" I watched her suck in a lungful of air and hold it while nervously waiting for my answer. *As if I would say no.*

"Oh my gosh, Yes!" I shrieked. I sprung from my chair, bounded over to the sofa, and threw my arms around them both.

"What in God's name are you three doing?" My dad asked. He was standing at the bottom of the stairs staring at us with a strange look on his face. I laughed at the confused look on his face and explained how I was going to be in their wedding.

His shoulders slumped with relief. "Phew, I thought I was walking in on the beginnings of a threesome."

"Daaaad!" I screamed. Kurt and Joss burst into hysterics.

My father laughed at my obvious discomfort. "Not to interrupt your fun, but do you want to start on the third bedroom today?" he asked.

"Oh, that reminds me! Piper called and said she's moving back to Charlotte," I told Joss and Kurt. "I meant to tell you last night, but with everything that happened, I forgot."

"Did she say when?" Kurt asked.

"Soon, I think. That's why we're cleaning out the third bedroom. She's planning on staying here."

"After I have a cup of coffee I'm going to get started on it," my dad informed us. "You stay down here and hang out for a while." He nodded to Kurt and Joss. "Good seeing you both." Then he winked at me. "Glad they're here with you, honey."

"Your dad is hot," Joss mouthed.

Kurt shot her a dirty look, and asked, "Why is Piper moving back now? The last time Joss talked to her, she said she loved living in Texas." I settled back into the chair and told them about our phone conversation.

"Wasn't she seeing some biker guy? She was crazy about him, but would never really give any details about him," Joss said.

"All I know about him is he rides a motorcycle, and a little over a month ago she told me he might be the one for her. I'm worried something bad happened."

We all three agreed we should watch Piper closely when she arrived in Charlotte. Joss wanted her to be a bridesmaid, which would hopefully help cheer her up.

Before Joss and Kurt took off, they told me they were going to have to change the wedding date due to Joss's parents' travel schedule. They were still letting me have the engagement party at the bar, though, so I was happy. I promised I would call Max by tomorrow at the latest. In the meantime, I needed to get the room ready for Piper's arrival.

After working on the upstairs bedroom, I decided mine could also use a good cleaning. It was a good way to stay busy and keep my mind off of Dragonfly. Dillon, Joss, Kurt, Polly, Lena, and I assumed Max, would all be there tonight. *And I wouldn't.*

Around four that afternoon, my dad came downstairs carrying my cell phone and a set of keys. "Are you feeling better?" he asked.

"I will be, once I finish cleaning the downstairs. Where are you off to?"

"Do you mind if I borrow the extra car for the night to drive to Raleigh? I need to see my boss tomorrow and pick up more clothes from my place. I'll be back late tomorrow afternoon. Oh, that reminds me." He held my phone up. "I thought you might want this back."

With all of my emotional crap, I hadn't even considered he might want his own car. "Do you want me to drive you there, so you can pick up your car?"

He jingled my aunt's keys, and smiled. "Believe it or not, your aunt drove a nicer car than I have, so I'm good. That is, if you're okay with me using it?" The image of my dad in the Caddy made me giggle.

"You can drive it as long as you want. Hell, if you pay the taxes on it, you can have it."

"I might just take you up on that." With a chuckle, he turned to leave.

"Promise you'll be back tomorrow?" I called after him.

This stopped him in his tracks. He turned, and in three strides, was standing in front of me. Framing my face between his hands, he looked into my eyes, and calmly said, "Everyone has left you, haven't they? Your whole life, all you've *known* is that people leave. I want you to know I will not leave you again, Ellie. Okay? I promise you I'm here to stay."

Tears stung the backs of my eyes. "Okay," I whispered.

Using his thumbs, he wiped the tears away and hugged me tight. Then he said goodbye and was out the door.

After he left, I finished cleaning the downstairs. After that, I watched some television, and read part of a book. Finally, sick of sitting around, I made myself a BLT and ate it in the kitchen. I tried to call Piper a couple of times but just got her voicemail. She would flip out about Max being back. I couldn't wait to tell her. Wondering whether it was too early for bed, I glanced at the clock. Nine p.m. *Everyone is at the bar.*

As I stared at my reflection in the patio doors, I thought of the hot tub, and how I could use a good soak. I opened a bottle of red wine and poured myself a glass. Then I thought, *Screw it,* and snagged the bottle from the counter. With my dad gone and everyone at the bar, I had no qualms about naked hot-tubbing. Carefully, I set the glass and bottle down where I could reach them, stripped off my clothes, and slipped down into the mind-numbing heat.

*I so need this right now.*

It was strange not having my dad around. I'd gotten used to him being here. As much as I hated to admit it, the man was under my skin.

*I actually miss the old fart.*

My second glass of wine went down better than the first, and I was feeling good. However, something was missing. *Music.* Hoisting my rear out of the tub, I padded bare-assed through the house to my bedroom to retrieve my iPod. I chose a semi-mellow playlist, and plugged it into the dock. As soon as I heard Big Head Todd and the Monster's "Bittersweet" start playing on the outside speakers, I headed toward the kitchen. Max had introduced me to some great music. Big Head Todd was just one of the many bands that had stuck with me through the years. *Don't think about Max, Ellie.*

Before heading back out to the hot tub, I snagged a second bottle of wine and the opener. *Why make another trip if I don't have to?* With my hands full, I managed to nudge the door open with my foot. Right as I stepped onto the patio I saw him. The bottle wobbled in my hand, but I managed to save it before it crashed to the ground. My heart flip-flopped in my chest. Sitting with his back to me, in my hot tub, was the last person I expected to see tonight.

*Max.*

With his hair pulled back, I had an unobstructed view of his bare shoulders.

"Great song," he drawled. "I especially like this version."

My breath hitched at the sound of his voice. "What are you doing here, Max?"

"What does it look like I am doing, Ellison? You've been avoiding me since Friday night, so I felt it was time to pay you a visit." I couldn't see his face, but I could hear the smile in his voice. *He thinks this is funny. If he were standing up, I would kick him right now.*

"Well, it sure looks to me like you're breaking and entering." His arm lifted, and I spotted my wine glass in his hand...right before he took a sip. *The nerve.* "And you've stolen my glass of wine! Yep, definitely breaking and entering." The sound of his laughter gutted me. At the same time it infuriated me.

His head turned and he pierced me with his gorgeous blue eyes. "Whatcha gonna do about it?" he challenged. *God, why did you have to make him so damned irresistible?* As his eyes feasted on my naked body, I fought the urge to squirm.

Trying not to be too obvious, I placed a hand over my chest and moved the bottle in front of my crotch. "Couldn't you have called first or something?" I breathily asked.

"And I thought you were beautiful five years ago," he softly replied.

I closed my eyes and inhaled deeply. I could feel my resolve crumbling. I knew if I didn't break away from his blue-eyed stare, I was likely to do something really stupid. So I dropped both hands, bolted like a bat-out-of-hell across the patio, and flung myself into the hot tub. At the last second, I managed to save the bottle of wine, but dunked both myself and Max with my acrobatics. I came up for air both spluttering and laughing. "I didn't really think that through," I coughed. His bark of laughter sent flutters through my body. The sound of his laughter was so sweet. I'd forgotten how much I'd missed it.

The pain on my face must have registered, because he immediately stopped laughing, and stated, "You know we have to talk."

I nodded my head in agreement. "I know, but it's nice being here with you like this. Can't we just sit, drink, and enjoy…just for a minute?"

A look of anguish skittered across his face. "Baby, you're killing me here. I can feel your pain. Give me the chance to take it away, please?"

Ignoring his plea, I took the empty glass from his hand and set it off to the side. I then opened the second bottle of wine and handed him the half-empty bottle. "Cheers," I said, and tapped my bottle against his. I could tell he was less than thrilled, but nevertheless, he went along with it, and drank. After we drained both bottles, I was back to feeling good. In fact, I was feeling great. We sat there for what seemed like forever, just staring at each other. Finally, not being able to stand it any longer, I broke the silence. "You were the hottest boy I'd ever laid eyes on back then. I didn't think you could get any hotter, but—" I fanned my hand across the hot tub— "here you sit. Time has definitely treated you well, Max." His beautiful eyes danced with humor, and I wanted to eat him up. I also wanted to punch him.

"See, baby doll, I was just thinking the very same thing about you."

"You were thinking about how hot you were…are…were?" I giggled. The wine was starting to go to my head.

Openly laughing at me, he said, "You're an absolute goddess. I thought you were the most beautiful girl I'd ever seen then, but now…you steal my breath." Trying not to let him see how much his words affected me, I focused on my toes floating in the bubbles as I sang the words to "Stubborn Love".

"I've never heard this song. Then again, I haven't had a lot of time to listen to much music lately," Max confessed.

"I want to ask you why, but I can't...not yet." I giggled, now really feeling the effects of the wine.

His eyebrow rose in question. "Why not?"

"Because I like pretending."

"What exactly are you pretending, Ellison, or do I really want to know?"

"I'm pretending you never left me and I haven't spent the past five years broken." With a loud gasp, I threw my hand over my mouth. "I'm sorry. I can't believe I actually said that out loud," I mumbled through my fingers.

"Jesus, Ellison." Before I could apologize again, Max glided over to me. He grasped the back of my neck with one hand and my chin with the other. Once he had my eyes, he started talking. "Please believe me when I tell you that I would never have left you in a million years if I didn't have to."

Once again, I found myself trapped in all that was Max. I'd spent five years starving for him. But now that he was sitting here - right in front of me - all I felt was...overwhelmed. His eyes, lips, body, and smell were all-consuming. If I'd been standing instead of sitting down, the raw emotion would have taken me to my knees. Completely caught in the moment, I leaned up and pressed my lips to his.

Instead of kissing me back, like I wanted, he pulled back and searched my eyes. "We need to talk."

I placed my fingers over his lips, and shushed him. Then I reached down into the steaming hot water and found him. I was surprised he was wearing underwear. Nevertheless, he was hard. Once I had him, literally, in the palm of my hand, I looked up into his eyes. "I need this, Max, please?" We were so close that I could feel every hard inch of him pressing up against me. His eyes heated in surprise, and his hand flexed on the back of my neck. One by one, I wrapped my fingers around him, and began stroking. Groaning in pleasure, he closed his eyes and dropped his head back onto the patio. After a minute or so, he grabbed my hand. Out of my head with lust, I touched his face and asked the only question that would stop me from being with him. "Are you married?"

His head jerked up and his eyes widened in shock. "What?"

"I asked if you're married? Do you have a wife, family, children, girlfriend…boyfriend?"

His eyes narrowed in obvious anger. "What the hell kind of question is that, Ellison?" he growled.

Before he could lay into me, I yanked his head back down and pressed my lips firmly to his. I slowly ran my tongue over his bottom lip, as if daring him to open up and give me more. As soon as he complied, I swept in to taste him. Framing his beautiful face with my hands, I pulled my body in closer and pressed my breasts against his chest. Wanting, no, needing more, I spread my legs to straddle his hips, and groaned when I felt his hardness right at my entrance. I wanted to absorb him, to suck him deep inside me and never let him go.

Right as I was about to sink down on top of him, he jerked back. "Not a good idea, babe," he warned. "I'm not wearing any protection."

"I'm covered," I panted. All I could think about was what I wanted to do to him right at that moment.

Before he could get the "No" out of his mouth, I slammed down and filled myself with something I never imagined I would have again.

"Fuuuuck," he loudly moaned, his hands tightly gripping my hips. I couldn't stop. I was frenzied with years of pent-up lust and love for this man.

*It was only ever you,* I thought, as I lifted up onto my knees and drove back down again. By the third time he took over, and it was as wild and magical as it had always been between us, if not better. I gasped when he gripped me by my hips, lifted me bodily out of the hot tub, and laid me down on the patio. My ankles and feet still dangled in the water. Kneeling on the top step of the hot tub, he seized my knees, spread them apart, and slowly licked me from top to bottom. He taunted me by gently sucking on my clit while running his fingers lightly back and forth over my entrance. When I was beyond wild with desire, he crawled up my body and slammed himself back into me. I was caged between his forearms; every inch of our bodies was touching as we moved in unison, a perfect cadence. All I could think about was how right he felt inside me and how much I'd missed this.

"You're really here," I whispered.

With a tilt of his head, he looked down into my eyes, and said, "I have thought about you every day for five years." The second the words left his lips, I was there. Screaming out his name, I took him over with me.

We both lay panting until, slowly, he rolled off of me. Before giving him a chance to overanalyze the situation, I grabbed both of his hands in mine. I hoisted myself up off the patio, pulled him up with me, and led him toward my bedroom.

As we hit the living room, he pulled back. "Ellison, wait."

"No, Max, I have waited for five freaking years, and right now, I'm done waiting." I continued steering him to my room. Finally, we made it to the foot of my bed. "Sit," I commanded. He just stood there glaring at me. "Fine, have it your way." Before he knew what was happening, I shoved him down, climbed on top of him, and kissed him silly.

Turning his head to the side, he protested once again, "Ells, baby, hold up a minute."

This made me mad. Here I was, straddling the love of my life, who I hadn't laid eyes on for five years, and all he wanted to do was chat. "Look, if you don't want me, then you're free to go." I pointed to the door. His eyes narrowed into tiny slits and I knew he was about to toss my ass across the room, finishing this between us once and for all.

Without warning, he flipped me onto my back. As he hovered over me, he lowered his head an inch away from mine, and growled, "Before this goes any further, you have to promise me we'll talk first thing tomorrow morning." My mouth went completely dry. With his flashing blue eyes and his rock hard body, he was magnificent.

"I promise," I breathily replied.

In a flash, his fingers were on me, and then inside me. "You feel like heaven, just like I remember," he murmured, all signs of anger gone.

"Don't stop," I gasped.

He chuckled. "Don't worry, darlin,' stopping never even entered my mind." He flipped me to my stomach and pulled me up onto my knees. "Grab on to the top of the headboard and don't let go," he commanded. I grasped the headboard. "Wider," he said against my ear. I shivered as I spread my legs wider apart. We both groaned as he entered me from behind. After a few shallow pumps, he shifted both of his knees to the outside of mine, and squeezed. In doing this, he forced my thighs closer together, and restricted all movement. "Are you holding on?" I could hear the strain in his voice, and knew he was on the edge.

"Yes," I panted.

"Good girl."

I wanted to ask him how this was going to work when, slowly, he started moving inside me. I felt his hands as they skimmed down my stomach, his fingers finding my center, and as he picked up speed, I realized why he wanted my legs together - the friction. I was tightly gripping every inch of him. My inner thighs were pressed together and rubbing him as he pulled out and pushed back in. The friction was mind-blowing. This combined with his hand slowly strumming me was driving me insane. I hummed in pleasure, and he picked up the pace, surging in and out of me, faster and harder. We were both on fire.

"I'm there, baby," he panted. "Need you with me." I screamed as he made me soar. Seconds later, he shouted out my name as he spilled himself inside me. Tears coursed down my face. For a moment in time, I had him back. Nothing in the world could ever compare to Max McClellan, and I was seriously screwed.

# CHAPTER TWENTY-THREE

The sound of a phone ringing woke us up. Max was curled tightly around me, and my head was resting on the inside of his arm.

"It's yours," I moaned. "Mine doesn't sound like a dead goose."

With a grunt, he reached down, and snagged his phone from the pocket of his jeans. "Yo," he groggily answered. In order to give him some privacy, I decided to head to the bathroom. Halfway there, I heard him mutter, "No fucking way." He sounded surprised. "Thank God, it's finally over," he said, as I made my way back to the bedroom. With another grunt, which I assumed meant goodbye, he tossed his phone onto the foot of the bed. When he sat up and swung his feet to the floor. My jaw dropped in complete awe. *How in the hell did I miss seeing this last night?* Spread across Max's lower back was a stunningly beautiful tattoo of a hawk.

"Oooooo," I murmured, as I crawled across the bed and settled in behind him. "It's beautiful." I ran my fingers over it.

He glanced back at me and smiled. "You like?"

"I like," I whispered as I reverently traced my fingers over it.

"Look closely at the left wing."

I leaned down and turned my head sideways to read what was written on the left wing. It took me a minute to see it. My eyes shot to his. "It says *Ellison*," I gasped.

"Now look at the right wing." Tears sprang to my eyes when I saw the word *Always.*

"You had *Ellison Always* permanently inked on your skin? But, why?"

"That's what I wanted to talk to you about last night. Unfortunately, it's going to have to wait a while longer." My heart dropped.

"Why? Did something happen?"

"Yes, something has happened, and I have to go take care of it. Look, it's complicated. I wasn't supposed to come to Charlotte...to see you, but I couldn't stay away." His fingers caressed the side of my face and I wanted to melt into them... into him. "I've been waiting for this day for five years. It's the reason I had to leave you in the first place. The whole story will take too long to tell you right now, but I promise I will, just as soon as I return. Right now, I have to go." Too shocked to speak, I sat there with my mouth hanging open. Was he kidding? He clasped my hand in his and threaded our fingers together. "I will take care of this as quickly as I can and will be back before you know it, okay?"

"No," I shook my head. "We're supposed to talk. I promised you. You made me promise. So...talk."

"Look at me," he commanded. I tried to hold back the tears but they had a mind of their own. He was leaving me again.

"Please don't leave me again, Max," I begged.

He stroked his hand across my cheek. "I'm coming back, babe. There is nothing that could or would keep me away from you ever again."

"I want to believe you but...I can't."

"I understand," he patiently replied. "How about I text you every day and call you every night while I'm away? Will that make you feel better?" The knot in my throat was too big to talk around, so I nodded my consent. "Oh, Ellison," he sighed. As he pulled me onto his lap, he held me tight and gently kissed the tears away. Then, moving down, he kissed the tip of my nose. When he reached my mouth, he slipped his tongue in and slowly stroked it against mine. Not able to control it any longer, the damn broke and the heartache came pouring out. "Please don't cry. I'm not leaving you, I swear." His voice hitched, and I could tell he was having a hard time keeping it together. "Hopefully, this will only take a week. I swear - on everything I hold dear - that I will come back to you. You have to believe me. Please, believe me." He buried his head in my neck and broke down. As we clung to each other, we cried for all of the years we'd lost.

A little while later, as I watched him get dressed, I couldn't help but wonder if this would be the last time I would ever see him.

"We'll talk as soon I get back?" he asked. Worry was written all over his face. I gave him a nod and a shrug. "Can you do something for me?" I nodded, again. This time, because I was trying not to cry. "Wait for our talk before doing anything rash or deciding anything life- altering?"

I rolled my eyes at him. "You don't ask for much, do you?"

His eyes pleaded with me. "Please?"

"Fine. But you better call and text every day."

He gave me a smile. Then he kissed me one last time, and was out the door.

After Max left, I moped around the house all day. By the time my dad showed up, I was a basket case of mixed emotions, which randomly alternated between love, sadness, anger, and elation. As soon as I spotted the Caddy rolling into the driveway, I was out the door. "Are you sure you want me here?" he joked as I helped him lug in three of his suitcases.

"I don't think I've ever needed a dad more than I do right now," I replied.

This stopped him in his tracks. "Hey, what's happened, pretty girl? What did I miss?"

Once we made it to the living room, I plopped down in my favorite chair, curled my legs under me, and began talking. "Well, last night I decided I needed a soak in the hot tub. So I poured myself a glass of wine and hopped in. Then I decided that more wine and music were a must. When I got back out to the tub, guess who had his gorgeous rear parked in it?"

He smirked. "Either Dillon or Max."

"Max...in all his naked glory."

"Did you kick him out?"

I looked into his stern fatherly face and squirmed. "Uh, not exactly."

"Did you happen to be in all your glory, too?"

This made me flinch. "Kind of."

"Please, tell me you did not sleep with the man who left you heartbroken for the past five years. The man who, without the courtesy of a word, note, or sign to the supposed 'love of his life' disappeared off of the face of the damned planet. Tell me you were smarter than that." *Wow, he's really riled up about this...*

His words made me wince. "Well, gee, when you put it *that* way, it sounds really bad, doesn't it?"

"Jesus, honey, what am I going to do with you?"

"He was my first everything, Dad," I quietly replied. "He's all I've dreamt about for five years."

"And now?"

I shrugged. I wasn't sure about anything, anymore.

"Well, at least tell me you were smart enough to use protection." My eyes bugged in shock when he said this. Having the sex talk with Aunt Elizabeth was bad enough, but as a twenty-three-year old woman with her *dad*? *Hell, no.* Taking my silence to mean I'd had unprotected sex infuriated him. "Are you shitting me, Ellie?" he shouted. I'd never seen him mad before. I had to admit, it was kind of scary. He scanned the room. "Where's Max now? Why isn't he here with you? This is not completely on you. It's on him too. So where is he?"

Before he blew a gasket, I grabbed his hand, and said, "Relax, Dad. No need to call the sex police. I'm on the pill."

"That's beside the point, Ellie. Are you one hundred percent sure that Max is clean? Just because you haven't slept around doesn't mean he hasn't. Did he show you his test results? And where the hell is he now?"

Of course, none of this ever occurred to me. "He had to go," I faintly replied. "He said he would explain everything to me when he returned. He's supposed to call and text each day he's away." I was starting to fidget under his scrutiny.

"Do you believe him?"

"I want to. I really, really want to."

"What about Dillon?"

I rolled my eyes. "Who knows? Maybe I'll decide after I have unprotected sex with him, too."

He laughed. "Okay, Sarcastic Sally, point taken. I just don't want you hurt...or accidentally pregnant."

"Well, after last night, even if Max and I don't work out....I wouldn't turn to Dillon." His eyebrows shot to the top of his forehead and the serious look on his face made me laugh. "Is it strange that we are talking like this?" I asked. "I mean, I don't really know exactly how daughters are supposed to talk to their fathers."

He smiled and touched his chest. "I think we can't go wrong if we do what feels right, in here. But I do think you owe Dillon the courtesy of telling him you're not interested. Don't string him along, especially if you already know he's not the guy for you."

"I won't. In fact, I already texted him this morning and told him I wanted to talk for a minute after our Thursday shift."

Joss came over later that afternoon to talk about wedding plans, parties, and time frames. I didn't want her to know about last night. It was mine, and I wasn't ready to share. In the middle of deciding what color the bridesmaids' dresses should be, I got a text from Max. I opened it up and read while trying to play it casual in front of Joss.

*Gorgeous, can't stop thinking about you, last night AND this morning. Will get back to you as soon as I can, promise. -Max*

I quickly texted him back. *Joss is here going over wedding details. I can text more when she leaves. I've been thinking about last night, too. ~ E*

"Who's texting you?" Joss practically sang.

Hitting the mute button, I dropped my phone into my lap, and answered, "No one."

"Liar. I bet it's Max."

"Oh, what makes you say that?"

"Hmmm, maybe because he disappeared last night and called Kurt this morning and asked him to keep an eye on you while he is away."

"Why would he feel the need to do that?" I wondered if I should feel flattered or angry by this.

"Maybe because he's worried about someone named Dillon?"

I shook my head. "No way."

"Yes way," she mocked, nodding her head.

This surprised me, especially after last night. "What does he think is going to happen with Dillon?"

"It's not you he's worried about Ellie. It's D."

"Why, though? What aren't you telling me?" I asked, smacking her on the shoulder.

"Well, apparently, D talked to Kurt and told him you texted him and wanted to hang out after work on Thursday. Dillon is super pumped, because he plans on finally getting you where he's wanted you for months...in his bed." I gasped and she nodded her head. "Yep, he told Kurt what he was planning, and Kurt freaked. Anyway, Max called Kurt on his way to the trial and told Kurt to watch out for you. Kurt told Max about D's intentions toward you, and Max is majorly pissed now, as is Kurt. Kurt wants you to take the week off, Ellie."

I held up my hand to stop her dissertation. "Hold right there, blabber butt. Let's go in order here. First of all, I told Dillon I wanted to 'talk' after work on Thursday, not 'hang out.' Second, he actually told Kurt he wanted to get me in his bed? That's just...crass. Third, what trial?"

"What, what?" Joss innocently asked.

"You said Max was on his way to 'the trial.' What did you mean by that?"

"Uhhh." I could see the wheels turning.

"Cut the innocent crap. You've already let the cat out of the bag. Now, before I threaten you with bodily harm, explain."

"Max needs to tell you about it, Ellie, not me," she whined.

"I would be happy to let him tell me. However, since he's not here and you are, I want to know what... *trial*."

Sighing dramatically, she said, "Okay, I'll tell you, but you have to promise not to tell that I told you first."

I motioned for her to get on with it. "Yes, yes, whatever."

"Something happened to Max, Sarah, and Malcolm five years ago. That something forced them to leave Charlotte. That something is just now being resolved, and Max has to be in court to make sure it's really over."

*Oh my God.*

"He said he *had* to go, but I didn't think he literally meant he *was forced* to go. I didn't let him tell me what happened, Joss. He wanted to, but I wouldn't let him. I didn't even ask about his dad or Sarah."

Joss clapped her hands together. "I knew it!" she squealed. "I knew Max was over here last night!" I must have looked like a deer caught in the headlights, because she doubled over with laughter. "You are so fucking busted, girlfriend. Spill it! Especially after you made me tell you about the trial!"

"Every bit of this conversation stays between us, yes?"

"Totally," she agreed. "The last thing I need is both Kurt and Max mad at me."

After I shared every last detail about my night and morning with Max, she asked, "Was it everything you'd hoped for?"

"Yes, but I still don't know what happened to him. I didn't know he was leaving again, or I wouldn't have jumped him. I thought we would have time today to talk about everything."

She pulled me in for a hug. "I know you're worried about him not coming back, but Garrett assured us that the chances of Max having to run again are zilch."

This confused me. "Wait, what does Garrett have to do... with Max?"

She flinched. "Shit."

"Tell me," I warned.

"You're the one who was all sassy sexpot last night, and here I am just trying to do the right thing and not tell you things you should already know. Look, Ellie, can we talk about the wedding, please? I'm about to get myself into some serious trouble, and I promised someone who I love more than my next breath that I wouldn't talk to you about it, because it's *not mine to tell.*"

The last thing I wanted was to get her in trouble with Kurt, so I let her off the hook. I also agreed to take the week off, but that was it. If Max wasn't back by next Thursday, then too bad, because I wasn't missing anymore work for him.

For the rest of the afternoon, we made plans for the engagement party at the bar and talked about dresses. I was worried about talking to Dillon. Apparently, he'd read something into my text that wasn't there. As screwed up as he and Dana were, I genuinely liked him as a person and hoped we could be friends, but first I had to tell him about Max.

After Joss left, I cooked dinner and allowed myself to open up to a feeling I hadn't felt in a very long time...hope.

After dinner, I was in the process of introducing my dad to *Sons of Anarchy*, when my phone rang. "Keep watching, Dad. I swear it only takes one episode to get hooked.

"If that's Max, tell him I have a bone to pick with him when he gets back," Dad called out.

"Will do," I replied. *Not.*

Max and I talked for at least an hour. I wanted to ask about the trial but had promised Joss I wouldn't say anything. He kept making references to Dillon, but because I wasn't sure where I stood with him, I tried to avoid that topic. By the end of our conversation, I was exhausted. There was so much we should be talking about, but weren't. We ended the call with a promise to talk and text the next day.

# CHAPTER TWENTY–FOUR

A week later, and Max still wasn't back. He had, however, kept his promise about staying in touch. My heart soared every time my phone pinged with his text or rang with his call. He mentioned his businesses in a text and later that night told me about the chain of garages he'd opened all over the south. I was sad I'd missed out on his happiness but proud of his success. We talked about college, my aunt dying, me moving back to Charlotte and reconnecting with my dad. I could tell he was skeptical of my dad and didn't blame him for being protective. When we were together, my dad was known as that schmuck who'd abandoned me, and now, he was...my dad. The only thing we didn't talk about was his disappearance, and it was starting to wear on me. *Why, why, why didn't I let him talk to me?*

Max's silence, combined with the stress of talking to Dillon, put me in a bad mood. I'd managed to avoid thinking about the situation with Dillon for the better part of the week, but knew I would finally have to face him and his expectations when I walked into Dragonfly later that night. I also knew I would be dealing with an overprotective Kurt.

*Maybe I should just call in sick...*

As if reading my mind, Joss sent me a text an hour before I was due in, asking if I was sure I didn't want to take another week off. *Such a great friend.*

The moment I stepped foot into Dragonfly, I sensed the tension between Dillon and Kurt.

Pasting a happy smile on my face, I asked, "Hey, you two, what's up?"

"Nothing," they replied at the same time.

"Ellie B," Dillon said, as he pulled me in for a tight hug. "I've missed you, sugar." He kissed my forehead. Then he scanned my face. "How are you doing? I'm sorry you weren't feeling well last week." *So that's what they told him.*

As I stared into his beautiful silver eyes, I realized he was still Dillon and I was still...me. Being with Max hadn't changed the fact that I genuinely liked this guy and could see something special in him. What it did do, however, was solidify in my mind *why* he wasn't right for me. Not only was he *not* Max, he was entirely too wishy-washy. My life with him would be full of indecision. Suddenly, I felt relieved. Taking a deep breath, I said, "I'm good, thanks, but I need to talk to you before you leave tonight."

A huge smile appeared on his face. "When Joss told me you were working tonight, I made plans for the two of us."

"Dillon," Kurt warned.

"Kurt," Dillon growled. I could see the shift was starting off in a bad way.

I cut my eyes over to Kurt, who was apparently waiting on my reply. "Uh, Dillon, I never said we were doing anything *but* talking tonight."

"Gotcha," he winked again.

*No, I don't think you do, but you will when I'm through telling you about Max,* I thought.

Kurt looked ready to maim, so I decided to go find Joss before the two Neanderthals started pounding on each other. "Where's Joss?" I asked.

"In the office," Kurt said. He rescued me from Dillon's clutches and steered me in that direction. "Why don't you go and see what the girls are doing back there? D and I will take care of the bar prep."

"You know, you're about as subtle as a flying brick," I told him.

As I strolled into the office, Polly exclaimed, "You can't discriminate here, Joss! Lena and I should be able to download music, too."

"Okay, okay, keep your panties on," Joss mumbled. When she spotted me standing in the doorway, she asked, "Do you have a problem with adding Country and whatever Lena likes to the mix tonight?"

Before I could answer, Polly explained. "We're sick of Dillon ruling the tune thingy with his vomit-rock music. It's only fair we level the playing field a bit. You have to admit it's rigged, and I don't know about you, but I'm sick of leaving here with a headache every night."

I glanced over at a frowning Joss. "She does have a point."

"Yes, but she wants to download a bunch of Country music. I *hate* Country music," she whined.

This was coming from someone whose favorite love song was from the movie *Titanic.* "I say, let her. It beats hearing Dillon's crap over and over again."

She huffed at Polly. "Fine, you win, but you better make it good."

Polly gave us a victorious smile, clapped her hands in glee, and gave Joss the middle finger.

Rolling her eyes, Joss said, "Bring me your iPods, and I'll

load your playlists while you prep your tables."

An hour later, the bar opened on a high note with a live version of U2's "Bad" and sailed into an even higher one with Alicia Key's "Girl on Fire".

I was busy mixing a batch of margaritas while dancing to a song about pontoons when something caught my eye. I glanced up to see what it was and almost dropped the pitcher. Coming through the door was Gage from last weekend. Better yet, he was followed by five incredibly hot men. The amount of beauty that was heading my way was life-affirming.

I was pulled from my stupor when they landed on the stools in front of me and Gage said, "Ellie from the other night. You okay after all that shit that went down?"

"Which shit?" I asked. With all the shit in my life at the moment, I was not sure which particular shit he was referring to.

Dillon rudely butted in. "What can I get you boys?"

"Ellie's got it," Gage said, ignoring the scowl on Dillon's face. "The shit that went down with you-" he nodded toward Dillon - "him, and that other guy," he clarified.

Not wanting to get into it, I simply answered, "It's all good." He arched a brow in disbelief. "You sure?"

"Yep, I'm sure. Uh…did you…uh… happen to be outside with everyone that night?" I hoped he hadn't witnessed me puking in the bushes. *How embarrassing!*

"Nope, just heard about it. Listen, I'll give you my cell number before we leave tonight. Call if you need anything."

Not wanting to offend him, I said, "Okay." Then, remembering where I was and what I was supposed to be doing, I asked, "What can I get you boys to drink?"

"Beer!" they unanimously shouted.

Right as I set down their beers, Joss and Kurt appeared. Beyoncé was singing her song about putting a ring on it. By the way Lena and Polly were wildly shaking their goods, I was pretty sure it was one of their song choices, but for all I knew, it could be Garrett's.

Joss shot me a knowing smile when she saw the guys sitting in front of me. "I see you've made some new friends."

I nodded my head toward Gage. "Joss, this is *Gage* and... sorry, boys, but I don't know your names."

"Sorry, Ellie," Gage said. "This right next to me is Sledge. If you follow down the line, you have Ax, Zippo, Rider, and Buck"

Joss shot me a *got it* look, and laughed. "There have to be stories behind those names. Care to share?"

The one named Zippo said. "Sledge likes to beat shit, including himself."

Sledge scowled at him. "Fuck you, man. At least I didn't get my name from collecting stupid trinkets."

"Zippo collects Zippo lighters," Gage clarified. "He has like...how many now Zip?"

"Over five thousand," Zippo muttered.

I bugged my eyes at him. "Five thousand?" He nodded shyly. *Wow. That's a lot of lighters.*

"Do you have a story behind your name, Gage?" Joss asked.

"Gage got his name because of the way he looks at things," Rider explained. "He can't just be normal like the rest of us. He has to analyze everything...gauge it."

These guys were interesting and entertaining, not to mention good looking. I looked up from the bar, and Gage was staring at me. "What's your real name?" I asked him.

"No one knows," Sledge mumbled. Joss and I found this highly amusing.

"Shania, do you think we're funny?" Gage teased.

"Shania?" I laughed. "Who's Shania?"

Zippo snapped his fingers. "That's who she looks like, a blonde Shania Twain! I've been wracking my brain trying to think of who she reminds me of. Thanks, man. I mean, I'm not really a fan of country music, but if Shania Twain is singing, then you can definitely count me in. That girl is gorgeous." *Awww, how sweet.*

"Thanks, I think?" *Note to self – Google Shania Twain after tonight's shift.*

"Ax is really Alex," Buck said. "When we were in high school, he got into a fight and had to have his mouth wired shut. When he said his name, all he could get out was Ax, and it stuck. He's been Ax ever since."

"How did you get a name like Buck?" Joss asked.

"He's a wild ride in bed, likes to try and *buck* 'em off," Zippo answered. Our eyes shot to Buck, and Zippo started howling with laughter. Apparently, he was the joker of the group.

"My parents," Buck said, glaring over at Zippo. "Why? You don't like it?" he directed at Joss.

"Easy, killer," Joss laughed. "I was just asking."

"Rider here hated his name, so he changed it sometime before he met up with us," Ax added.

Joss smirked. "What is your real name? George?"

"Melvin," he mumbled, and we all laughed.

"Well, with a name like Melvin, I would have done the same," she agreed.

I slapped my hand over her mouth. "I can't believe you just said that." Changing the subject, before she got her butt kicked by some huge biker dude named Melvin, I asked, "Are you all members of a motorcycle club or something?"

They found this amusing. After the laughter calmed down, Gage answered, "Naw, we're just visiting from Texas and like to ride and rally when we're not working."

Joss elbowed me as if I wasn't standing right there listening. "So, you guys are visiting from Texas? Well, we have a friend who's on her way here from Texas right now. You would like her. She apparently has a thing for motorcycles."

"Yeah? This friend have a name?" Gage asked.

"Piper O'Connell. Do you know her?"

Ax's eyes bugged. "Gage, isn't that -?"

I watched Gage's not so subtle hand motion telling Ax to shut it, and narrowed my eyes at him. "*Do* you know Piper?"

Conveniently, Rider interrupted before he could answer. "We're heading to a rally in Myrtle Beach tomorrow. You ladies want to come along for the ride?"

"Can't, sorry." I replied.

"Sorry boys," Joss said, flashing her big ass engagement ring. "My fiancé might get upset if I take off on the back of some guy's motorcycle."

Buck grinned, "We won't tell, promise."

I was about to ask where in Texas they were from when I heard someone shout my name.

"Dillon's summoning you. Go see what he wants. I'll cover for you here," Joss said.

"Thanks," I muttered under my breath. Then, smiling at Gage and his friends, said, "Be right back, boys. Don't get into any trouble while I'm away."

"Sure thing, Shania!" Zippo shouted after me.

I made my way down the bar to Dillon. When I reached him, I asked, "Whatcha need?"

He glared over my shoulder at Gage's group. "Can we talk for a minute?"

"Sure, what's up?"

"Kurt, Ellie and I are taking a break for a minute!" Dillon yelled at Kurt, who had just entered the bar area. "You and Joss good without us for a few?"

Beckoning me with his finger, Kurt asked, "El, can I have a minute?" I started toward him but was cut short when Dillon pulled me back. As soon as he did this, Kurt's face tensed and Gage stood up.

"It's fine," I told them. "I need to talk to him anyway."

Before I had a chance to say anything else, Dillon grabbed my hand and pulled me to the break room. When we got there, he yanked me in, locked the door, and immediately started in. "If some girl walked out of my life and five years later came waltzing back in, I sure as hell would have some serious reservations about her. From where I'm standing, it looks like you didn't even blink before jumping back in the sack with the guy. I gotta say, Ellie, I don't get it." I didn't know what to say to this. In some respect, he was right. I wanted to explain, but I didn't want to hurt him. Moving closer, he said, "You were into me, Ellie Belly. I felt it." His thumb brushed across my cheek, and I took a step back.

I swallowed hard. I was so not good at this. However, I knew it was time to deal with Dillon once and for all. Delicately choosing my words, I said, "After Max disappeared, my life was complete hell. I couldn't eat or sleep, much less date. I'm not saying I didn't try, because I did. I just felt...nothing. Then I met you, and for the first time in five years, I'd found someone who I wanted to take a chance with. You kept throwing up red flags, though. Dana is a bitter pill for anyone to swallow, but especially someone who has commitment issues, like me."

"You don't have commitment issues, sugar...abandonment issues maybe, but definitely not commitment issues. And, for the record, just because Max is back doesn't mean you have to be with him."

"Look, I'm not trying to hurt you, Dillon. You're truly an awesome guy. That's why the thing with Dana didn't make me run from square one. I need you to understand. I have to see this thing through with Max to the end, and even if you don't see it, you have stuff to deal with, too. We can be friends and work here together. I don't want to lose all of this. But after five years, I owe it to myself to see where this - whatever *this* is - goes. I am sorry. In a million years, I never expected any of this to happen."

He studied me for a minute as if trying to find some loophole in my argument. "Let me explain about Dana."

"You do not have to explain Dana to me. The girl is clearly not stable, and I know you know this. I do worry, though. I worry about what she's capable of doing to you, or anyone you may end up with, in the future."

He sighed as if the weight of the world was sitting on his shoulders. "I've been trying to shake her off for a while now, but until you, I wasn't really serious about it. As far as who I end up with, well...I'd really hoped it was going to be you." He held up his hand. "Before you spout some bullshit about Max and years and chances, I need you to know that *you* are everything *I* have ever wanted. You're funny, sweet, cool as shit, and so unbelievably gorgeous." I stood there listening to him with such mixed emotions. *Why am I feeling guilty? He's the one that had the girlfriend the whole time he was hitting on me, yet here I stand feeling like crap.* When I let out a groan of frustration, he pulled me into his arms and pressed his lips to the side of my head. "I don't want to make this easy for you. In fact, if you are going for Max, I want to make it as hard as possible. He's not good enough, and he sure as hell doesn't deserve someone as special as you." I pulled back in attempt to put some physical distance between us.

"Look, maybe you're right and maybe you're wrong, but either way, I've waited *five years* for this, Dillon. The love of my life disappeared, and not one day has gone by that I haven't wondered where he was, how he was doing, or whether he was even alive. Not...One...Day. I owe it to myself to follow this to the end. I have to get closure one way or the other, or all of this will have been for nothing, and I simply cannot live with that. Do you understand? I need to make you understand. I want your friendship, because you mean something to me."

With a bitter laugh, he released me and took a step back. "Just not enough to drop him and take a chance on me."

"This isn't just about you and me. This is about me and my past. This is so much bigger than the two of us. I saw you in the bar and then again outside with Dana, and I realized the two of have history together. We-" I motioned between the two of us - "were only at the beginning. We didn't even know each other. Max and I were…" I threw up my hands. "There really are no words for what we were, Dillon. I can't even begin to explain it to you. I wish I could, but I can't. All I can say is that it was so much more than history between us." I was getting worked up trying to find the words to explain my feelings.

He pulled me back into his arms. "Shhh. Say no more. I get it, but I don't like it. I will, however, say this-" he tilted my chin with his finger- "and I want you to hear me loud and clear. If he fucks up- and I won't lie- I hope he does. I will be here. Do you get me?" Before I could answer, he kissed me. It was gentle and sweet and made me feel…sad. If I wasn't sure before, I knew now I'd made the right decision. From the look on his face, he finally understood he had no chance. "Let's get back out there, before Kurt comes in with guns blazing." He turned and started toward the door. As I followed behind, I felt relieved. When he got to the door, he paused. "Are you sure this is what you want?"

I grabbed his hand and squeezed, before answering, "I'm sure."

With a nod of his head, he turned back, pulled open the door, and stopped short. "Figures," he muttered. I stepped up beside him and tried not to wince. There, leaning against the wall with his arms crossed, stood a very angry-looking Max. *Well, crap!*

He glared at Dillon, before asking, "You two done here?"

"Max—"

"I *asked* if you were done… *here*?" Yes, Max was definitely not happy.

"For now," Dillon snapped.

He shot off the wall and got in Dillon's face. "What the hell is that supposed to mean?"

"Guys, stop," I said as I attempted to pull them apart.

In a chilling tone I'd never heard him use before, Dillon said, "I cannot wait until you fuck this all up. When you do, which you will, I'll be here, and nothing on this earth will ever make me leave her."

Max growled at him. Then he turned to me, and held out his hand. "Get your purse, babe, we're out of here."

"But I'm not finished with my shift."

"You are now." Before I could give him my hand, he reached out and snagged it. He walked me over to the bar and silently watched me retrieve my purse and say goodbye to everyone. Then, lacing his fingers through mine, he led me out to my car.

"Meet you at your place?" he asked as he opened my car door for me.

"That depends. Are you going to yell at me?"

He scowled. "Why would I do that?"

"Uh…because you look really mad at me right now," I dryly replied.

"Ellison, why would I yell at you for cutting him loose?"

"I don't know. You just seemed really angry back there, Max."

"Was I happy to find my girl alone in a room with some guy who had less than good intentions? Hell, no. Was I happy my girl had to do something that made her sad? No, I wasn't. Now, do you want me to meet you at your place?"

His words made my heart soar, and I couldn't help but smile. "Yes." He squatted down in front of me. Once he was eye level with me, he softly touched my face. The vulnerable look in his eyes made my heart hurt. "Is everything okay, Max?"

In a voice that was slightly above a whisper, he said, "I swear

I will not fuck this all up. Nothing on this earth will ever make me leave you again." He brushed his fingers across my face, again. Then he stood up, closed my door, and headed toward his truck. I was left with my mouth hanging open.

# CHAPTER TWENTY-FIVE

When we arrived home, Max pulled me out of my car, and asked, "Have you eaten, yet?"

"No, have you?"

"No. Is your dad here?"

"He's upstairs asleep. Why don't I load some food on a tray? We can eat it in the living room and -"

"The bedroom," he interrupted.

"Huh?"

"Let's take it to the bedroom. There's a lot I have to say, and we might as well be comfortable for it."

I loaded up a tray with cheese, bread, and ham. Then I tossed in some grapes and strawberries for good measure. Snagging two beers from the fridge, I carried it all to my bedroom. My breath stuck in my throat when I saw Max stretched out on the bed, waiting for me. *God sure didn't leave anything out when he made this man.*

After kicking off my shoes, I crawled onto the bed beside him, and settled the tray between us. We ate for a few minutes before he began telling his story. "That last night we were together, before everything happened, was the best night of my life. I knew without a doubt I'd found the girl I was going to spend my forever with." He grabbed a pillow and shifted it under his head, before continuing. "I was seriously pissed off that I had to go to work the next morning, because I wanted to spend the day in bed showing you all the ways you were mine."

"I wanted that, too. I remember feeling so sad when you drove away."

He smiled and squeezed my leg. "I planned on getting off work early that day, so I could surprise you at the café. Around eleven that morning, my phone rang. Normally, I wouldn't have answered, but the caller ID said it was Sarah. She was crying so hard I couldn't understand what she was saying. All I could make out was something about there being a man and guns and something about our dad. I knew she was in trouble and left the garage thinking that, once again, my dad had done something really stupid. Not only was I going to have to take care of my sister, but I was also going to have to clean up his mess. When I got to the house, Sarah was sitting on the front porch crying. She looked scared out of her mind. It wasn't until I got out of my truck that I noticed the two men with her."

"Did you know them?"

"No. I'd never laid eyes on them before. I figured by the way they were dressed they were probably law enforcement. When I called Sarah over to talk to me, one of them asked if I was her brother. She answered him, and he nodded as if giving her permission to speak to me. I remember how pissed off that made me. She was crying hard and babbling shit I couldn't begin to understand, so I knew something bad had happened. The men gave us a minute to talk before introducing themselves." Pausing, he looked up at me. "They were FBI agents, Ells."

"What did your father do, Max? It had to be really bad to call in the FBI, right?"

"Oh, yeah, it was bad, alright. Agent Marshall and Agent Caldwell informed me that my dear old dad was involved in a drug ring. Apparently, the local police arrested him in a raid six months earlier and he agreed to become an informant in order to avoid jail time and a possible prison sentence. He was supposed to help get evidence on the head of the organization, a real winner of a guy named Rocky Ponterelli."

Tears sprang to my eyes, but I swallowed them back. "Benny swore it was something to do with your dad, but I never dreamed it was *this*. By the way, does Benny know you're back?"

"I stopped by to see him on my way out of town. I'll tell you about that later."

I waved my hand in the air. "Okay, sorry to interrupt. Please continue."

He grasped my hand in his, and continued. "In addition to dealing drugs in North Carolina, Rocky was also dealing in South Carolina, Georgia, and Virginia. Because he went across state lines, the local police brought in the FBI. The plan was for my dad to arrange a drug buy. The FBI was going to swoop in and bust them all. Since our house was their usual meeting place, it made sense for it to be the location of the sting. It was supposed to be a cut and dry operation."

A horrible thought hit me, and I gasped out loud. "Please tell me your dad was smart enough to get Sarah out of the house?"

"Not quite. Something went wrong with the plan. At the last minute, everything went to shit. Sarah came home early from her friend's house, and somehow Rocky was tipped off that the meeting was a sting. He sent three of his guys to our house hours before the designated time. When my dad saw them pull up, he knew something was wrong and told Sarah to get into her closet and not to come out. Rocky's guys came in, found my dad in the living room, and shot him in the back."

"Dead?" I whispered. He nodded, and I clapped my hands over my mouth, and gasped, "Oh God, that's what the stain on the floor was? Blood?" He stared at me quizzically, and I explained. "Kurt and I knew that the stain on the floor hadn't been there when we were last at your house. We thought it was coffee or something like it but never considered blood." The thought made me sick.

"When were you at the house?"

"Joss and I drove by the day after you didn't show up at the café. Both your truck and your dad's car were sitting in the drive. I knew how you felt about your dad and didn't want you to be mad at me, so we didn't stop. A couple of days later, Kurt knocked on your door but got no answer. Your cars were there the whole time." I swallowed back the tears. "We knew something wasn't right. When we couldn't take it any longer, Benny helped us break into your house to see what we could find. We found some of your things gone and thought you might have headed to school early. We checked in at ASU, but you weren't there either. The school said you hadn't finished your enrollment and they hadn't seen you." Max ran his fingers through his hair. He was clearly agitated. I wanted to comfort him, but also wanted to hear the rest of the story.

"God, Ells, it was all so damn complicated."

"Go on," I encouraged. I needed to hear the rest. "What happened after they killed your dad?"

He exhaled loudly, and continued. "Sarah sat in her closet for several hours before the FBI decided the coast was clear."

"How do you know all of this?"

"Because the FBI had our house bugged and had been listening in for quite some time."

My pulse spiked and I could feel my face turning red. "Please tell me your room wasn't bugged?"

His blue eyes twinkled with humor. "I think the whole house

was, why?" My eyes widened in surprise. *Holy hell, the FBI has tapes of us doing who knows what.* Max grinned wickedly. As if reading my mind, he said, "I told them I would pay my entire inheritance to have those tapes of us."

"You did not!" I screeched.

He burst out laughing. "Naw, I just wanted to see your face when I said that."

I rolled my eyes at him. "Did they really tape us?"

"No, they skipped over mine and Sarah's bedrooms. Anyway, the FBI knew when Rocky's guys showed up early the bust had gone south. They waited for over an hour after seeing the guys leave before approaching the house. They had to make sure the coast was clear. They didn't go in when they heard the initial gunshots, because they didn't want to compromise the case. They failed to get Rocky, but thanks to my dad, they now had two of his guys on their radar. They were pretty sure Sarah had been killed. When they got inside, they found her huddled in a ball in the closet and scared out of her mind. That's when she called me, crying hysterically. When I got there, FBI agents told us to grab only what we could carry. They'd discovered several recording devices in our house which didn't belong to them. This meant one thing. Rocky also had eyes on my dad. He saw everything. He knew his guys screwed up and missed an important factor when they took out my dad."

"They missed your sister," I filled in. "Did Sarah actually see them?"

"Yes, which meant she was a target. If she could point out the guys in a lineup, the trail would lead them straight back to Rocky. There was no way he was going to let a thirteen-year-old girl take him down, so they had to immediately relocate us. They gave us ten minutes to pack. Since I already had a duffle packed for school, I just grabbed it and helped Sarah pack hers. Another set of agents came by, picked us up, and drove us to a safe house in Kentucky."

"Wait a minute, were the local police ever involved, or was it only the FBI?"

"The local police were involved until they realized Rocky's tentacles reached beyond North Carolina. Then they were forced to turn it over to the FBI. Why?"

"Because when Kurt and I first went to the police, Detective Copeland seemed interested in everything we had to say. He kept us waiting for a week. When he finally got back to me, he basically told me you'd moved on without me and I should get on with my life."

"I'm sorry, babe. They were probably pissed because the FBI took over their case and no longer required their assistance. I bet this happened sometime between the time you first spoke to Copeland and the time he got back in touch with you. I'm sorry you had to go through that." He pulled me into his lap and wrapped his arms around me.

I nestled into the warmth of his arms and, sighed. I was tired, but wanted to hear more. "So they took you to Kentucky?"

"They relocated us to Danville, Kentucky, where I became Jack Barnett and Sarah became Amanda Barnett. They put us in a two-bedroom house and set me up with a job at the local garage down the street."

I stared up into his beautiful eyes, and still couldn't believe he was actually here. "You just disappeared. You were there for the best months of my life, and then you were gone. I can't even tell you what that felt like, what it did to me." I tried to stop the tears from falling but couldn't.

"I begged them to let me call and tell you goodbye, but they told me Rocky may already have eyes on you and if I called you or came to see you, I would put you in danger. I couldn't risk your life, Ellison. I just couldn't. I had to let you go. I had to walk away." We both had lost so much.

"I called you every night. At first I left messages, but in the end, I just wanted to hear your voice."

"I know, babe, believe me, it's the only thing that got me through those months."

I jerked in his arms. "Wait, you listened to them?" I didn't know whether to be hurt, angry, or relieved.

"Hell, yes, I listened. At the end of every night, right before going to sleep, I hit play and listened to your messages. I heard every last one of them." I tried to grasp what he was telling me.

"But, the AT&T operator said that no one had used your phone for months."

"The FBI can do anything, Ells, including tamper with phone bills."

"So you knew I listened to your iPod and went with Kurt and Joss to ASU to look for you? You knew I was sleeping in your bed just to feel close to you? You heard me pour my heart out over and over in all of those voicemails. Yet you couldn't manage to get a note to me or something, telling me you were alive and well?" Years of pent up emotion was bubbling to the surface and I wasn't sure I could stop it from boiling over. I wasn't sure I wanted to.

The intensity of his stare was a little frightening. "I couldn't call you, Ellison. Fuck! I couldn't write to you. Hell, for months I wasn't even allowed to shit by myself!" He growled in frustration. "Don't you think it killed me? All I thought about for most of that first year was, at the end of my day, I was going to hear your sweet voice again. I couldn't wait to get Sarah to bed each night so I could push play and hear about whatever it was you were doing. Night after night I went over scenarios in my head, trying to figure out of how I could safely contact you. Yes, I knew you were sleeping in my bed, and you know what? I wanted you there. Hell, I imagined I was there with you. I knew the FBI was watching over you, but so was Rocky! I knew you were safe as long as I stayed away. I was protecting the only person, besides my sister, I'd ever let myself love. Don't you get that?"

"Why did you get rid of your voicemail, Max? One day it suddenly didn't work. If you missed me so much, then why did you take that away from me? It almost killed me not to be able to hear your voice anymore." I swiped at my tears, angry that I was shedding them like a weak little girl.

He pulled me in closer. "It almost killed me, too, babe. You have to believe me. Unknowingly, Sarah told one of the agents I spent every night on my cell phone. I wasn't supposed to have a cell phone anymore. When they discovered I'd been paying Max McLellan's cell phone bills in North Carolina, they freaked. The agents in charge of us were sure it was going to lead Rocky straight to us, but I convinced them otherwise. The only way they would let us stay in Kentucky, and not relocate us to somewhere off the grid was if I got rid of the phone and the account. It was one of the hardest things I'd ever had to do. Please believe me," he choked out.

"Did you even *go* to college? Do you really own garages?" My voice cracked with emotion. Who was this man?

He wiped his eyes with the bottom of his shirt, before replying. "I used some of the money my mom left me to attend Centre College in Danville, where I graduated with a degree in business. Right before I graduated, my boss at the garage decided to retire. I used the rest of that money to buy him out. Slowly, I built the business, and now I have MMG's all over the south. In fact, I just bought Benny's. I was thinking this might be my final expansion and maybe I would settle down here and grow some roots."

"MMG?"

"It stands for Max McLellan's Garage. For the past five years, I've had to hide behind a fake name. When I purchased my first garage, I named it MMG, in honor of the guy I used to be. Seeing that sign above that garage every day helped me remember who I was and where I wanted to be."

"What made you come back here now?"

He frowned. "Do you even have to ask that?" When I failed to answer, he shook his head. "Sarah and I were told we couldn't step foot back in North Carolina until they had Rocky and all of his guys in custody. They eventually got his guys, but Rocky always slipped the noose. Finally, last month, they told us they were close."

Something he said reminded me of my earlier conversation with Joss. "Do you by chance know Garrett Lanier?" He blinked and then glanced away. *I knew it!*

"Oh my God, is he an agent?" I gasped.

"What? No. Garrett does not work for the FBI," he assured me.

"He was never my friend, was he?" I tried to keep the hurt from my voice.

The contemplative look on his face told me all I needed to know. "Garrett Lanier and I go way back and, no, he wasn't supposed to be your friend."

"Oh." I was surprised by how much this bothered me.

"As soon as they told me they'd found Rocky, I sent Garrett here to keep an eye on you and Kurt."

"So, who is he...really?"

"He owns a contract security company in Kentucky. We've been friends since college."

"Wow... so you paid him to watch me?"

"In a sense. We trade favors, and he owed me one." He paused, but I waved my hand and told him to continue. After eyeing me speculatively for a moment, he continued with the story. "I had to leave you last week to go testify. Rocky is locked up for life, and we've officially been released from the Witness

Protection Program." He grabbed a strand of my hair and twirled it around his finger. "Nothing in this world could have stopped me from coming back to you," he murmured. His sexy blue eyes devoured me. Realizing I had put distance between us, he reached over and pulled me back onto his lap.

"How did you know I wasn't married?" I asked. "For all you knew, I could have been married and had six kids by now."

"Let's just say I became really good friends with the agents who have been watching over you for the past five years."

My eyes narrowed when he said this. "How good of friends?"

He laughed. "Relax, babe, there was only one female agent, and she was married with two kids."

"So you spied on me?"

"I wouldn't exactly call it spying. I did, however, make some deals. If they kept me informed as to how you were doing, I would service all of their personal vehicles for free."

I laughed. "Oh, you bribed them then?"

"If that's how you want to see it, then, yes. They made me walk away from the love of my life, and if that wasn't bad enough, they made sure I couldn't communicate with her for five fucking years. All because they couldn't do their jobs and catch the fucker who killed my dad and wanted my little sister. The least they could do was tell me how you were doing. It's how I survived. Hearing about you and what you were doing was the only thing that kept me going." He shrugged unapologetically.

I never thought I would hear these things from him. I never imagined in my wildest dreams he would actually come back to me. "I have so many questions running through my head, like how you built your business. Where did you start? How did you expand? I want to hear all about Sarah. How is she? Where is she? What is she doing?"

"Sarah is great. Once she finished high school, we decided the safest place for her to be was out of the country. So we researched and got her into Napier University in Edinburgh."

My eyes widened in surprise. "Scotland? Cool. I've always wanted to travel to Scotland."

"Not without me, you won't," he seductively whispered. This sent chills coursing through my body. After giving me a knowing look, he began telling me about his business. "After I bought the garage I worked night and day until it could basically run itself. After that, I focused on a business plan to quickly expand. I had the money to open a second shop, but didn't want it in Kentucky. I talked the agency into letting me open another MMG in Tennessee. The location was close enough that I could travel back and forth by car or motorcycle. They agreed as long as I was willing to alter my looks. Fifteen pounds of muscle, a beard, much longer hair, and I was ready to go. I bought a Harley and made sure I was in tight with the locals in the area. By that time, Sarah was forming her own life. She didn't need me as much anymore, at least not like she did when she was a kid. Still, I didn't want to be too far away from her. It took me a few months to have the Tennessee garage up and running. After that, I scouted and found one in Mississippi, then Louisiana and last, Texas. My plan was to buy garages that didn't need too much work done for as little money as possible. I needed to find someone to manage each garage, so I didn't have to be there every day. This is how I met my manager, Nolen. Originally, he worked with Garrett, but Garrett wasn't looking to expand out of Kentucky at that time. Nolen's degree was business management and, since Garrett ran his own business, Nolan was pretty much twiddling his thumbs and wasting his time."

"So…you hired him?" I asked.

"So I hired him. He helps screen and hire dependable people for all of the garages. My goal was always to return to Charlotte, to you. You asked how I knew you weren't married. I didn't. It was something I thought about all the time. I knew there was a chance you would eventually move on without me, but something inside me just couldn't give up on the dream of us. My deal with our protection detail and their weekly reports were the only thing that kept me sane."

"Gee, my own personal stalkers," I dryly replied. I wanted to hear more but was tired. We'd been talking for hours.

As if reading my mind, Max said, "You're wiped. It's been a long, crazy week. We've got the rest of our lives to play catch-up. For now, I just want to hold you. Sit up and let me get these clothes off you." I leaned forward while he stripped off my shirt and jeans. This left me in my pretty black lace bra and matching panties. "God, I dreamt about this body," he hummed as he unclasped my bra. Leaning his head down, he gently took my nipple into his mouth and I moaned in pleasure. He crawled off the bed and quickly shed his clothing.

Just the sight of him made my mouth water. His chest was twice as broad as I'd remembered and his stomach muscles looked like they came straight out of a hot guy magazine. I reached out to touch him. "Hmmm, I see you still don't like to wear underwear."

"Not yet," he whispered as he pulled back from my reach. Cupping my face in his hands, he leaned down and gently kissed my lips. His fingers reverently stroked a path of pleasure down my neck and over my breasts, where they paused for a minute so he could play with my nipples. Chills of lust shot straight to my core. He left my breasts wanting and continued his path down to my stomach, and then to my waist, where I felt a sharp tug, and my panties break free. His hands felt like magic. They always had.

"Please, Max," I whimpered.

"Just a minute more," he huskily replied.

I groaned in frustration when he took his hands away, only to sigh as he replaced them with his mouth. In no time at all, he had me shouting my orgasm.

I smiled when he crawled back up my body and straddled my waist. "Now, before we go any further," he admonished, "I need you to know I'm clean. In fact, my last test was just a couple of months ago. If you want to see it, you can."

This threw me. *Do I want to see it? Has he been with other women? Do I even want to know?* I really didn't want to ruin the moment with talk of past relationships. Like he said, we had a lifetime to play catch-up. "I believe you," I breathily told him.

He flashed a sexy grin. "Good. Now, since you're so tired, I promise to be quick."

I scrunched up my face and mumbled, "Don't rush on my account." He laughed, and before I could tell him where to stick it, he slid down my body and planted a hot, hard kiss on my mouth.

"I've missed this mouth," he whispered against my lips, and my heart melted. Then he moved to my neck. "And this neck." Lowering his head, he kissed my left breast and then my right. "God knows how much I've missed these." I could feel his smile against my skin and couldn't help but return it. I gasped when he hit my stomach. "I missed the smell of your skin," he murmured. *Oh My.* I held my breath as I waited for him to move down that final notch. Instead, he started back up, causing me to whimper in distress. When he reached my mouth, he gently touched his tongue to my lips.

Not able to stand it any longer, I ignited. As I opened up, our tongues clashed, and I dug my hands into his hair and yanked. "I need you now, Max," I groaned. That was all it took. Like a huge wave, he slammed into me and took...me...down. The last thought I had before passing out was that I would have waited a whole lifetime to have this man back.

# CHAPTER TWENTY-SIX

A loud banging noise in the kitchen woke me. I rolled over and moaned. My mouth was dry and my eyes felt like sandpaper. Wondering how long I'd slept, I glanced over at the clock. *Two hours. No wonder I feel like roadkill.* I took a deep breath and froze. I smelled traces of Max on my pillow. *Where's Max?* My stomach dipped. The side of the bed where he'd slept was cold, which let me know he'd been gone for a while. As I flung the covers back, I heard the deep timbre of his voice from the kitchen. *Thank God,* I thought, and wondered if there would come a day when I wasn't afraid of losing him. I padded to the bathroom and smiled at the pleasant soreness between my thighs. I hadn't felt this way since… Max left. *The things we take for granted.*

With a smile on my face, I threw on a long-sleeve thermal and a pair of flannel pajama pants. Then I slipped on my fuzzy slippers and was out the door in search of a cup of coffee. I hit the kitchen and stopped short when I spotted Max standing next to the refrigerator mixing something in a bowl. He was talking to Piper, who was parked on a barstool next to…my dad. I'd completely forgotten about my dad.

When Piper saw me, she slowly rose from her stool, and started in my direction. "I can't believe you didn't tell me that Max had come home," she scolded. I let her words wash over me. *Max is home.* Then, I noticed her face. *What the hell?*

"Piper," I whispered as I met her halfway. "What happened? Who did this to you?" I pulled her into my arms, and she flinched in pain. Rearing back, I yelled, "Oh my God! Where else are you hurt?"

Smiling warily, she said, "I'm okay, Ells. This is actually good compared to what it was." My eyes bugged in horror, and I glanced over at a concerned-looking Max. Before I could say anything else, she stopped me. "Look, your dad and Max have already given me the third degree. Can we give it a rest for now?"

Not able to resist the pleading in her voice and eyes, I sighed. "Fine, I'll drop it for now."

Gently squeezing my arms, she pulled me in, and whispered, "I'm so glad he's back." Then she let me go, and gingerly sat back down. *Oh Piper, who has done this to you?*

During breakfast, the story of the morning unfolded. Apparently my dad woke up at his regular five a.m., and headed downstairs to make the first pot of coffee. When he hit the bottom step he caught movement from the sofa.

"I contemplated going back upstairs to get my gun, but thought it wouldn't look good if I accidentally shot one of your friends, so I thought better."

"You have a gun...in my house?" I squeaked. *Who is this man?*

"I own three but only have one of them here with me in Charlotte." He then went on to explain how he crept up to the sofa and...

"Scared the living shit out of me," Piper huffed. "I was lying there minding my own business, and suddenly Rambo here is leaning over the sofa in my face. I opened my mouth to scream, and he slapped his big paw over it."

Looking contrite, Dad said, "Now, Piper, I thought we were past this already."

She gave him a smirk. "We are, Sammy. I just got riled up in the re-tell." I felt like I was following a bouncing ball as their conversation pinged back and forth between the two of them. *Who are these people?* "Anyway," Piper continued, "I knew Sam was staying here, so I introduced myself and helped him make coffee." Turning to me, she said, "Ells, I forgot your dad is a total DILF!" Max exploded into laughter. At my confused look, she explained, "DILF, you know, opposite of MILF. Dad I'd Like To…"

"Don't you dare finish that sentence Piper O'Connell," I scolded. "You're talking about my *dad* here."

He chuckled. "Would it be wrong to say I'm flattered?"

The look of horror on my face made everyone join in the hilarity. I however, was not humored. Changing the subject, I asked Piper how she managed to get into the locked house in the middle of the night. She shot an evil glare at Max.

"Max already grilled me. Everyone knows you keep a key under the ugly clay frog in back by the hot tub, Ellie."

"Who's everyone?" I asked, eyeing her skeptically.

"Don't you remember the night Joss and I talked you into going to Joey Edgerton's party? It was the end of our senior year, and I was home for spring break."

"Ugh, how could I forget? I spent days trying to get the taste of Fireball and Goldschlager out of my mouth and nose." I cringed and crinkled my nose at the memory.

"Nose?" Max asked, his eyes dancing with humor.

"Ellie sat at the beer pong table all night pissing off all of the guys because they couldn't beat her."

"But doesn't that mean she didn't have to drink?" My dad

asked. I arched my eyebrow at him, and he grinned. "Honey, I practically invented the words 'drinking game.'"

"Anywaaaay," Piper continued, "Lance Lawson didn't like losing, so he made up new rules in order to beat Ellie. Every few points they alternated taking shots."

I screwed up my face at the memory. Just thinking about it made me want to vomit. "How was I supposed to know he made up the rules? Before that night I'd only had a few beers." Both Dad and Max scowled at this.

"How did the damn key play in?" Max growled.

"Oh, that's the best part," Piper smirked. "On the way out the door, your girl here announced to the party that anyone who wanted to come over and play beer pong in the future had an open invitation, just use the key under froggers in the backyard."

My dad almost spewed his coffee across the table he was laughing so hard. "Froggers?"

I shot Piper a dirty look. "I don't remember saying that!"

She gave me a toothy grin. "Thank goodness she was slurring and nobody knew what she was talking about. It could've been ugly."

"So you got sick?" Dad asked, wiping tears of laughter from his eyes.

"Yep," Piper answered, "all over the side of Lance's car, Joss's front and back yard, and finally, the toilet."

I tried not to wince at Max's angry expression. "In all fairness, I thought it was Piper's car," I lamely replied.

"I see my girl was busy while I was gone," Max muttered.

Not wanting to go there with him, I quickly changed the subject. "What time did you get up this morning?"

"Early," he clipped. Obviously it was going to take him more than a minute to get past the fact that I'd had a life while he was gone. "I heard a commotion in the front room and came to check it out."

"And?" I encouraged.

"Saw a man and what looked like Piper. I asked if everything was okay and got pulled into introductions and coffee."

Piper sighed heavily. "Well, now that we have this all settled, I'm going to go shower and crash. Wake me only if the house is on fire."

After giving her an *I will so be talking to you later* look, I asked, "Hey, where are your things?"

"Uh…coming some time in the future. I didn't want to overwhelm you with my shit all at once. I'll catch you all at dinner, okay?" I could tell she was evading my question but wondered why. "How about I cook dinner for everyone tonight? Let's say, six-thirty." She waved at us over her shoulder as she shuffled up the stairs. The sick feeling in the pit of my stomach almost overwhelmed me. *Someone hurt my best friend, and I can't do anything about it because she won't talk to me.*

While Max and my dad talked out on the back patio, I cleaned up the dishes. I had a pretty strong suspicion they were discussing Piper. Right as I'd loaded the last plate into the dishwasher they strolled back in the house looking like best friends. Max made a beeline straight for me. When he got within arm's-length he tagged the back of my neck, folded me into his chest and kissed the top of my head.

My dad poured another cup of coffee and asked, "When are you planning on heading back to Kentucky?"

"Soon. I need to deal with some things here before I head back, though." My heart did a free fall into my fuzzy slippers. *He's going back to Kentucky!*

"You're going back?" I asked. I felt his wonderful pancakes inching back up my throat. I don't know what I expected but this definitely wasn't it.

"Yeah," he replied. As if sensing something wrong, he asked, "Hey, you okay?"

I nodded, yes, as I blinked back the tears.

"Sweet thing, when your beautiful body stiffens up and you go all cold on me? That's a strong indicator you're not okay. Plus, you're a shit liar. Want to tell me what crazy thing is going through that head of yours so I can make it better?"

Not ready to discuss him leaving me again, I said, "Nope." We stood there staring at each other, the silence a huge gulf between us, until his phone rang. Relief washed over me. I didn't want to explain my abandonment issues to him. He hadn't been back long enough to handle my emotional baggage. *Maybe, in a couple of years I'll introduce him to it.*

I'd just escaped to the other room to call and invite Benny, Joss, and Kurt over for dinner when Max informed me he had to go check on the garage and would see me at dinner. My dad had editing to do, so I made my calls and sat down with a cup of hot chocolate to listen to my music. Soon, I was back to thinking about Max and Kentucky.

Piper came downstairs while I was prepping the burgers for dinner. She looked better but still not herself. The bruising on her face was awful.

"Tell me who hurt you," I implored.

"Let's just say I've had an extraordinarily bad month and leave it at that."

"Can I at least say I'm worried about you?"

"You can, but I still can't talk about it."

I set down the knife I'd been chopping onions with, and stared at her. "Can't or won't?"

She shrugged and then winced from the pain. "Both, I suppose."

"Look at me," I demanded. She raised her eyes to mine, and I gave it to her. "Someone hurt my best friend, and I'm not okay with that. If the tables were turned, you wouldn't be either. I understand that, for some unfathomable reason, you think you can't talk about it, but eventually, Piper, you will need to. Promise me when that day comes, if it's not me you choose to tell, it will be someone who can help you through it."

"I promise", she said, with tears in her eyes.

The question of whether it involved her ex-boyfriend was on the tip of my tongue when Max came through the door. His eyes immediately found me, and I went liquid inside. *God, I've missed this*. I couldn't take my eyes off of him as he made his way over to me.

"You better?" he asked. I was so tied up in his presence that all I could manage was a nod and a smile. He leaned down to kiss me, but instead, whispered seductively in my ear, "Good, I missed you today and can't wait until later tonight." I could feel my face getting hot. He let out a knowing chuckle, and turned toward the bedroom. About halfway across the room, he looked back and shouted, "Want to join me in the shower?"

"Max!" I scolded. "There are people who can hear you." I cut my eyes to Piper, who was busy watching Charlie Hunnam strut across the television screen.

He grinned wickedly. "Don't want to shower with her. I just want you, gorgeous." I gave him a *don't mess with me* look and heard him laughing all the way to the bedroom. As soon as he was gone, I smiled to myself and continued making dinner.

Kurt and Joss flipped when they got a look at Piper's face. Max, my dad, and I all backed off while she talked to them. Joss, like me, was unhappy about Piper's decision not to talk, but what could we do?

During dinner, my dad asked Max about his plans for MMG Charlotte. I could have kissed him for asking. There was no way

Max would have given me the depth of information he gave to Benny, Dad, and Kurt. Ever since Max told me he was going back to Kentucky, I'd been worried. What did this mean? Was he planning on staying there, or was it just a visit?

Max explained how he'd purchased the garage from Benny the moment he was told Rocky had been found. It hurt that Benny kept it from me. Max and Benny finalized the sale while Max was staying with Kurt and Joss. This was before he'd even seen me. The construction to add three more bays, a waiting room, and finish out the upstairs with four functional bedrooms had already started. My ears perked up when he mentioned bedrooms. *Is he planning on living there?*

The guys talked about his plans for the new shop throughout dinner. He wanted Benny to help him run the bays. I thought this was a great idea. Before dinner was over, he asked Kurt if I could take off from work until their engagement party, which was Thursday night. He wanted to spend time with me. Of course, Kurt said yes.

Once everyone had gone home, I left Max and Piper in the living room watching television. After having only three hours of sleep the night before, I was running on fumes. Instead of my usual T-shirt and shorts, I slipped on a nightie. I was standing in front of the sink brushing my teeth when I heard the bedroom door open and close. I watched through the mirror as Max entered the bathroom and leaned against the wall behind me.

"Everything okay?" I asked as I put my toothbrush away.

"Piper's in the living room watching TV," he stated.

"Yeeees." I had a pretty solid idea where this was going.

"Your dad is upstairs."

"He is."

"With this many people in the house, I don't like that we have to be so quiet." His soft, husky voice made the back of my neck tingle. *Oh...My.* His blue gaze held me captive. "You wearing any panties under that?"

"No," I hungrily replied.

I could see every move he made in the mirror. My breath hitched as he stepped to me and pressed his full length against my back. Fingering the bottom of my nightie, he whispered in my ear. "I'm going to lift this up around your waist. Then I'm going to take you hard and fast." A spear of red-hot lust shot through me, and chill bumps erupted all over my body. I felt my nightie slowly creeping up to my waist. His fingers skimmed around my belly button and then down between my legs. I purred down low in my throat.

"You like that?"

"Yes," I breathily replied. As his fingers began working me, I dropped my head back on his shoulder. He had me almost there, when he suddenly pulled away. Gasping in dismay, I jerked my eyes to the mirror and watched him unzip his pants.

"Hold on to the edge of the sink and spread your legs for me." I'd barely had time to grab the sink when he yanked my nightie up further and thrust deep inside me. One hand slid up my stomach to my breast while the other traveled down between my legs. "I've been thinking about this all day. Jesus, just the smell of you makes me want to come." He slid out and thrust back in. "So fucking perfect." His voice was tight and laced with need. "Want you with me, baby." That's all he had to say, and I was there.

"I'm there Max," I loudly gasped. My eyes drifted from his hand on my breast back into the mirror. The second our eyes met, he sped up his thrusts.

"So fucking beautiful," he ground out.

"Baby," I whimpered.

"Now, he commanded, and I flew apart. A second later, he followed.

I woke the next morning with Max's fingers trickling down my back. I forced open one eye and was surprised to see him sitting next to me already dressed in jeans and a black long-sleeve tee. I couldn't stop my eyes from flaring in appreciation.

"Hey," I sleepily said.

"I could get used to this." The rasp of his voice made my nipples pebble.

"To what?"

"To falling asleep every night with you wrapped around me after I've been deep inside you and waking with you the next morning, all sleepy and sexy-like."

I felt his words right between my legs. "Max," I softly said as I ran my hand over his damp hair.

"I look at you and…there's so much I missed. Just hearing about you being at a party where some dickhead named *Lance* could take advantage of you? It makes me sick to my stomach." *My man has been doing some thinking.*

I tugged his hair. "Hey, don't do that to yourself."

"I wasn't here to protect you. All I can think about is how that never would have happened if I'd been here."

"I wish you'd been here, too, but you weren't." I squeezed his arm and forced him to look at me. "You're here now, though. I'm so glad you told me why you left, but I think we need to talk about what happened in the past five years while you were gone. Don't you? I'm not very good with surprises and, judging by your reaction to Piper's story yesterday, neither are you."

He leaned down and touched his lips to mine. "We'll talk, but first I have to go check on the garage. You need to get up, eat breakfast, and shower. I've got plans for us this afternoon. Clear your schedule."

"Whatcha planning?"

"You'll see. Pick you up at noon." He laid one last kiss on me and was out the door.

I ate breakfast with a very quiet Piper. My dad was holed up in the office working on a big project. Shortly after breakfast, Joss stopped by and helped finalize the plans for Thursday night's party. While I was waiting on Max to get home, I showed Piper my vast collection of movies, books and magazines. Her eyes bugged at the magnitude of my stash. *Yes, Piper, this is what five years of heartache will get you.*

# CHAPTER TWENTY-SEVEN

When Max told me to make sure to dress warmly, I had a good idea we were heading to the quarry. He ushered me up into his huge black truck, and off we went. As soon as we hit the countryside, he rolled down the windows and turned on the stereo. I jumped when incredibly loud music blasted from the speakers. He patted the dash, grinned, and revved the engine. "This is one of the reasons I bought this baby!" he shouted over the music.

"The music or the engine?" I yelled. My fingers itched to reach up and turn it down.

"Both!" He grabbed my hand and placed it on his leg. He then proceeded to give me a teeth- rattling, ear-bleeding ride to the quarry, while being serenaded by a guy singing a song about Bruce Springsteen.

Like long ago, we held hands as we walked up the path to our spot. I waited until we'd settled ourselves onto the blankets and were enjoying a thermos of coffee before telling Max about my visits to the quarry over the years. "You probably already know all of this. You had an advantage. I didn't get to spy on you for the past five years." I couldn't help but pout.

"That's not necessarily true. I knew you weren't married but had no idea if you were seeing someone or not."

This surprised me. "What? Your spies didn't tell you whether or not I had guys coming in and out of my house?" His scowl made me laugh.

"No, and trust me, I asked. Plus, they backed off when you moved to Greensboro for college. They felt you weren't in any danger as long as you weren't in Charlotte."

I let out a sarcastic snort. "That must have chapped your ass."

He arched an eyebrow at me. "Was there?"

I played dumb. "Was there what?"

"Someone special in your life?"

"No Max, there wasn't anyone special." *There wasn't anyone at all.*

"*Ever?*" Clearly this surprised him.

"Why do you seem so surprised?"

"Babe, I watched every move you made for almost three years, and trust me, when I finally got the chance, I took it and was not disappointed. It's seriously hard to believe that the second I lost that chance, someone wasn't there to pick it up."

This made me angry. "You think I would just jump into someone's bed the second I realized you weren't coming back? That's insulting."

He gave me a tight squeeze, and in a pain-filled voice, said, "I left you, Ellison. I took your virginity, gave you promises I fully intended to keep, and then had to walk away. I'm just saying it wouldn't surprise me if you had."

"Well, I didn't. Instead of trying to find someone to replace you, I did everything I could to find you. I didn't want another guy. I wanted you. I wanted to know why you left. I wanted answers or some form of closure that only you could give." I could feel the back of my nose stinging and knew it was a matter of seconds before the tears arrived. *Will I ever stop crying over this man?*

"What about you, Max?"

He rested his head on my shoulder. "What about me?"

"Was there someone special for you?" I wasn't sure I wanted to know the answer.

"No."

I tilted my head up in order to see his face. "Never?"

"Never. You were it for me." His beautiful eyes stared right through me, and I shivered at their intensity. I had to admit, I was surprised.

"So you haven't slept with anyone...in over five years?"

The sparkle in his eyes went flat. "Don't ask questions you don't want answers to," he warned. "You notice I asked if you had anyone special, *not* if you had anyone at all. There's a big difference. If you want to go there, we can, but why dig up something that's better left buried?" *Good point. I don't want to tell him about the guys I slept with either.* His stern expression melted into a smile. "Now, tell me what I missed out on."

I regaled him with stories about my aunt and Benny. This led to funny stories about Joss, Kurt, and Piper. He wanted to know everything he'd missed and I was happy to indulge him. However, it did not slip past me that I was the one doing most of the sharing.

We were packing up our things when Max asked me about Dillon.

"I thought we were leaving the past in the past?"

"We are, but Dillon isn't the past, yet."

As I gazed into his eyes, I prayed he could see the truth in mine. "He is to me."

We were halfway back to the car when he zinged me with another question. "Did you sleep with him, Ellison?"

"Does it really matter, Max?" I sped up, hoping to outrun the conversation.

He stopped me outside the truck. "Baby, I'm not stupid. I knew when I showed up at Dragonfly and saw you two together that I was about to step in the middle of something. Now, I'm asking you what that something is." I inwardly cringed. Why did he have to be so flipping perceptive?

"Look, it's over and done with, now. I'm with you, am I not?"

"Yes, but Dillon pulls no punches about not wanting me in your life. I assume that's because he wants you for himself. I need to know what I stepped in the middle of." I understood what he was saying, but didn't see how it mattered. "Ellie," he warned.

I threw my hands up in exasperation. "Okay! No, we did not sleep together, happy now?"

"Yes, but like I said before, I know there was *something* between you, and if so, I need you to tell me what that something is. Baby, no guy is going to get *that* pissed off unless he's already been there and is either staking his claim, or has been given the green light and is afraid of losing his chance. So, if you haven't slept with him, I assume it's the latter of the two."

I could tell by his tone he was losing patience. "Oh, all right," I hissed, now sick of the whole conversation. "I kissed him a few times and considered doing more."

"How much more?" he asked in a chillingly quiet voice.

Before answering, I searched his face, hoping he wasn't as serious as he sounded. "You aren't going to let this go, are you?"

His eyes bored through me. "No."

Grabbing onto every bit of patience I could muster, I told him what he so desperately wanted to know. "The night you showed up at Dragonfly, I was supposed to go over to Dillon's place after his shift. However, I changed my mind when I walked in and saw him at the bar in a huddle with his ex."

"And just like that, you were done?" He sounded as if he didn't believe me.

"Just like that," I confirmed.

"The black-haired bitch with Jennifer is his ex?" He scrunched his nose up as if he smelled something rancid.

Trying not to smile at his obvious dislike for Dana, I answered, "Yep."

"Who was the guy you were dancing with?"

"Oh, that was just Gage."

"Gage, who?"

"I'm not really sure. Blackwell, I think? He was just some guy that I was using to piss off Dillon. It was all stupid and childish." I quickly dismissed it with a wave of my hand. In the scheme of things, it held no relevance. Max, however, didn't see it this way.

"Why were you trying to make him jealous, Ellison?"

"Well, for one, I'd just caught him with Dana. So I thought I'd give him a taste of his own medicine. That's why I said yes to Gage's invitation to dance. If that wasn't bad enough, I found out he was outside with Dana while we were on the dance floor. When I got out there, they were kissing. I knew right then I could never be with him. After everything was said and done, I could never trust him."

"Fuck me," he muttered.

"Max!" I chastised.

"So, you're telling me this guy is pissed because he was seconds away from having you and fucked it all up...with *her*?" *Well, when you put it that way.* "Then I came along and he knew he'd never get that chance again. Hell, I can't say I really blame him." My jaw dropped, and he smiled. "Baby, he screwed up and before he got the chance to make it right, I showed up and you permanently shut him down. Can't say I blame him for being pissed off. What I can say is I'm glad nothing happened, because now I don't have to kill him."

I shook my head and rolled my eyes. "Are we done here?"

"Yep," he chuckled, "we sure are."

The next morning, Max got an early call that took him to the garage for the day. When I asked him about it, he said something vague about construction and personnel. My dad had to drive to South Carolina to visit an unhappy author, so that left me and Piper to fend for ourselves.

Around noon, Joss, Polly and, Lena came over to work on party plans for Thursday night. Hanging out with the girls was refreshing, not to mention good for Piper. I was doing everything in my power to pull her back out of the shell she was hiding under.

Polly and Lena took off at four. They were both working at Dragonfly that night and needed to get ready.

"Since Max is with Kurt in Tennessee, why don't you both come hang out at the bar tonight?" Joss asked.

Assuming I'd heard her wrong, I asked, "Did you just say Max is in Tennessee?" Out of the corner of my eye I saw Piper shake her head at Joss, and I threw her a dirty look.

I could see Joss mentally scrambling. "Uh…maybe I heard Kurt wrong this morning."

"No backpedaling," I warned. "Max told me he had to be at the garage, and obviously I now know he's not. Spill, Josselyn. Why is Max in Tennessee, and why didn't he tell me he was going?"

"Uhhh, I'm not sure," she hedged. After a minute of me staring her down, she broke. "I swear. I need to learn to keep my damn mouth shut around you! Max called Kurt early this morning and said there was something up at MMG in Tennessee and he needed Kurt for backup."

"Did he say what for?" Piper asked.

"That's all I know…really. Kurt just threw on clothes, kissed me, and told me to man the bar with Dillon tonight until he returned."

Shock and hurt seared through me. "I can't believe Max would lie to me. Should I call him? I should, shouldn't I?"

Piper snorted. "All guys lie, Ellie." Joss shot her a scathing look.

"Not all guys lie, Piper. Kurt doesn't and neither did Max. He probably just didn't want to worry you, Ellie."

"Yeah…right." Piper huffed. Her condescending tone wasn't helping matters.

Joss shot me a *what the hell is wrong with her* look, and I answered with a shrug. "Why don't you both come by the bar tonight, and when Max shows up later, you can just ask him about it?" she suggested. I shook my head. I was both hurt and mad. This was a really bad combination for me.

"Nope, I'm calling him."

"Ellie," Piper warned, "you've got that bullheaded look on your face right now, you know, the one where you go off half-cocked and get into trouble? I *really* think you should listen to Joss and wait until you see Max later. I'll even join you for a while at the bar." As tempting as it was to get Piper out of the house for a few hours, I just couldn't let it go. Grabbing my phone, I punched in the number Max had given me and waited for him to answer.

"Max here," he abruptly answered. *I know he sees it's me calling because he has Caller ID.*

"Hi," I shyly murmured.

"Yeah?" he clipped, as if I were interrupting. *Maybe this wasn't such a good idea.*

"Uh… I was thinking I would come by the garage and bring you dinner tonight," I blurted. "But I didn't know how many guys I needed to cook for," I quickly added. "So I was calling to find out," I finished. Max was right, I was a terrible liar. I watched Piper roll her eyes at Joss and stuck my tongue out at both of them.

"Probably not a good idea tonight," he told me. His cold tone bothered me.

"Why? Is everything okay?"

"I'm tied up here right now and don't know when I can get away. No need for you to walk into this mess. Maybe some other night, okay?"

I tried again. "Want to talk about it? Maybe I can help?"

"I haven't had a mother in years, babe. I sure as hell don't need one now. Catch up with you later." Before I could reply, I heard a click on the other end. I double checked the display on the phone to make sure that it didn't just drop the call. *Nope. The A-hole just hung up on me!*

I turned to Piper and Joss, and held up the phone. "He just told me he didn't need a mother and hung up on me. If this is the new Max, I've just decided I don't really like him!" I was hurt and angry and there was no way in hell I was going to sit home all night waiting for him to grace me with his lying presence. "Why are you two just standing there? Come help me pick out a hot outfit! And, for the love of God, don't even think about saying I told you so."

We decided I should wear my short black skirt, because it fit like a glove through my hips and flared at my thighs. It moved with my body when I danced, and I planned on doing a lot of dancing. *Maybe Gage would be there.* I debated whether or not to go sans panties until flashes of big gusts of cold wind, slipping on spilled beer, or having to go to the ER for some odd reason rolled through my head. So, panties it was, but I made sure they were on the skimpier side. Piper always had the best T-shirts, so when I asked if I could borrow one, she told me to grab one out of her suitcase. I found a really cool gray and black vintage-looking tee with the word *Dooley's* written across the front. I threw it on and headed downstairs. Piper was standing in the kitchen when I hit the bottom step. Her eyes drifted to the shirt, and her smile wavered.

"Is this one okay? If not, let me know. I love the vintage look of it. Where did you get it?"

"I don't remember," she replied with a shrug. I could tell she was lying but was afraid if I pushed too hard, she would either bail for the night or change the subject back to Max. After Joss and Piper helped me with my wardrobe selection, we both helped Piper cover the bruises on her face. Joss ran home to get dressed, while Piper and I finished getting ready. Then we hopped in the car, and headed for Dragonfly.

I could tell Piper was worried about me but wasn't in the mood to pacify her. *Max is lying to me* played like a broken record over and over through my head. It was sitting in my gut like a lead weight, right along with a large dose of hurt and anger. Both were driving me to do something I would probably end up regretting.

*Doesn't it always?*

I was surprised to see how packed the bar was, especially for a weeknight. Then I remembered Kurt had just hired a new guy to play on Tuesday nights.

"Oh my, who is that fine piece of man flesh behind the bar?" Piper asked, as we threaded our way through the crowd.

I knew who she was referring to without even looking. "That's Dillon," I told her.

She yanked my sleeve and halted our progress. "Ellie, you were definitely holding out on me. He is super-hot, like...*super-duper* hot," she stressed.

"Yep," I replied, not wanting to get into it. Boy, did *I know* how hot Dillon was. *He's nowhere near the hotness of Max, but after today....*Deep down I knew this was just my hurt and anger talking, but still...*Max lied to me.*

Dillon's silver eyes hit on me right as we reached the bar, and I couldn't help but smile when he mouthed, "Hey, Ellie Belly."

"He likes you," Piper sang in my ear.

"He *did* like me." I made sure to stress it was in the past.

"No, he really *likes* you. His eyes are practically eating you up. Surely, you can see that?" I didn't know what to say to this. I'd made my decision, which if I was being honest, really wasn't much of a decision, and I wasn't going to change my mind. *Even if I'm being lied to, I still choose Max and always will.* Still, it didn't hurt my ego to see the look of appreciation in Dillon's eyes.

"Scoot down two stools, guys," I heard him say to the two men sitting right in front of him.

"See, I told you!" Piper blurted, as we neared the two stools, "He *still* really likes you."

Slowly enunciating each word, I said, "Piper, we...are... friends. Now, let it go."

"Okay, okay!" she huffed as we sat down.

"Hey Dillon, this is my best bud, Piper O'Connell. Piper, meet Dillon Whitaker."

My stomach somersaulted when he flashed his vintage Dillon-Sex-God grin and asked, "How's it going?"

"It's getting better by the second," Piper beamed.

I scowled at her. I may not want Dillon, but I knew if Piper got her claws in him, she would eat him up and spit him out. That's the last thing he needed, especially after Dana.

As we watched him saunter to the end of the bar to fill a tray for Polly, I turned and gave her a concerned look. "I thought you said you were done with guys? Remember...the reason you came back to Charlotte and all? The thing you refuse to talk to me about?" Dillon laughed at something Polly said, before heading back in our direction.

"Oh shut it! You're just pissed at Max and taking it out on the world," Piper hissed.

"I am not," I argued.

Dillon shot me a look, before asking, "I thought you were taking time off to spend with Max? Did he fuck up already? I knew it was going to happen, but damn, I gave him at least a month."

Ignoring both of them, I slapped my hands on the bar. "I don't know about you two, but I sure could use a shot. I feel like getting drunk tonight!"

"Demanding, isn't she?" Dillon asked Piper.

She shot him one of her ear-splitting grins. "She always has been."

Directing his sexy smile back my way, his voice deepened when he asked, "It makes me wonder if she's like this... everywhere?" Now, thoroughly embarrassed, I searched the room for signs of Joss. I needed someone on my side, and it obviously wasn't Piper. "Well, okay then," he sighed, when he realized I wasn't going to bite. "Shots it is!" He pulled down three different bottles and, with a shake here and a shake there, voila`. "Drink up!" he said, slamming a shot down in front of me while gently handing Piper hers.

We tapped our glasses together and Piper shouted, "Here's to getting rid of lying a-holes!" Before I could tell Dillon his shot tasted like vomit, Piper flew off of her stool. "Harry!" she shouted as she threw her arms around him. Out of the corner of my eye I saw Polly watching them, and she didn't look happy. *Hmmm, looks like Harry may be getting to Polly after all.*

I was so busy focusing on Polly that I'd failed to see who Harry had walked in with. That is until I heard a familiar "Hey, Ellie."

*Garrett.*

"Well, well, well, look who the cat dragged in? It's Garrett the protector. I figured you'd be long gone now that your job is over, or did Max send you here tonight to spy on me?" I knew I was being harsh, but I was hurt and mad and needed an outlet.

His eyes widened and his nose flared. "Max said you were angry. I figured you would've realized by now that I was just keeping you safe and gotten past it."

"I don't like being lied to, Garrett. I thought you were my friend."

"First of all, I had a job to do, Ellie. After that, I could play it any way I wanted, and that's exactly what I did. Being your friend wasn't a lie. In fact, I'm still your friend."

I narrowed my eyes at him. "Why are you still here? Why aren't you back in Kentucky?"

"I'm expanding my business to Charlotte, so I'm scouting locations."

Before he could say anything else, we were interrupted by the obnoxiously loud squeal of the amplifier.

Piper plopped a full beer in front of me, and said, "Harry says this guy is great. Let's find a closer spot so we can dance." From the way she was bouncing around, it was obvious she was feeling no pain. This was definitely not a good sign.

"Piper, how many pain killers did you take tonight?" She stuck her tongue out at me, and giggled. *Great.*

I followed Piper through the crowd. Once we reached the high top table where Harry and Garrett were sitting, we set down our beers. As the main attraction walked out onto the dark stage, we cheered with the rest of the crowd. The guy was carrying a bar stool and had a guitar strapped around his front, but the stage was too dark to see much more than that. Suddenly, Joss's voice boomed through the speakers. "I'm sorry to say that Ben had a last-minute family emergency tonight and can't be here." The crowd started booing. "Hey, hey now, none of that," she continued. I asked a friend of mine for a huge favor, and here he is now. Please give it up for Dragonfly's own Dillon Whitaker!"

The stage suddenly lit up, and there sat Dillon. *How did I not know this?*

My eyes instantly shot to Piper. Her shocked expression mirrored my surprise. "Holy shit, Ellie, you didn't tell me he was a musician!" she squealed. *I didn't know.*

Dillon's deep voice echoed through the bar. "Hi, in case you don't know, I'm Dillon Whitaker. I help Kurt manage this place, and every now and then, if you catch me on a good night, I might be willing to play a few tunes for you."

"Oh...My," Piper panted in my ear. I had to agree.

"Sorry Ben couldn't be here tonight, because he's really good. I'll try not to disappoint." Piper and I looked at each other and sighed. He really was quite dreamy. He started strumming his guitar, and it took me a second to recognize the song. When he began singing "Hey There Delilah" by the Plain White T's, the crowd went nuts. I had to admit, Dillon's version was pretty damn impressive.

We were dancing to his mind-blowing rendition of "Blister in the Sun" when I spotted Dana and Jennifer down in front of the stage. *Figures.*

"After what happened, I'm shocked that ho bitch has the nerve to show her face around here," Piper snarled. Not overly excited about getting in another altercation, I was contemplating going home when Harry and Garrett showed up toting a bucket of beer. I'd barely taken a sip when Dillon broke into his amazing version of "Lola". I couldn't decide which was more comical, Harry, who danced like he was on a pogo stick, or Garrett who was doubled over in hysterics laughing at him. We were all gearing up to get 'down on our knees' when I felt Piper's body jerk as if she'd been slapped.

"Hey!" I yelled, grabbing her arm. "You okay?"

"I've got to go," she clipped. Her eyes looked haunted and her face was super pale. I wondered when the painkillers and booze would catch up with her. I guess I had my answer. "Give me your keys, Ellie. I have to get out of here, now." The panicked look in her eyes instantly sobered me.

"Okay. We'll go," I assured her.

"No, you stay and have fun."

She was starting to scare me. "Honey, if you're feeling sick, I'll come home and take care of you. I don't mind."

"That's not it. I'm fine, really. I just need some air and have stayed way longer than I planned. Please give me the keys," she begged.

"I'm heading home, Piper. I'll drop you off at Ellie's," Garrett offered.

"Thanks, Garrett, that would be great," she said. Relief poured off of her, and I couldn't help but wonder what I was missing. She turned to me and pulled me into a tight hug. "See you at home," she whispered in my ear, and bolted for the front door.

*What the hell just happened here?*

# CHAPTER TWENTY-EIGHT

After Piper's hasty departure, Harry and I resumed drinking and dancing. The more alcohol I consumed, the funnier he got. I was laughing at him swaying to Dillon's hot as hell version of Matchbox Twenty's "3 AM" when I felt hands on my hips and large body flush against my back.

Startled, I turned my head to see who it was when a familiar sexy voice started singing in my ear. Max was back, and I was totally unprepared. Before I could give him a piece of my mind, I spotted Gage and the boys heading our way.

"Shania!" Zippo shouted. He stepped up to hug me and I felt Max's body stiffen behind me. Thank goodness, Zippo noticed and decided to give me an arm-squeeze instead.

I glared over my shoulder at Max, and mouthed, "Be nice."

He wound his fingers through my hair and lowered his lips to my ear. "Don't know these guys and even if I did, I wouldn't want them putting their hands on you." I hated to admit it, but it kind of made sense, and the possessive thing was a huge turn-on, so I just nodded my head.

When I felt his body tense a second time, I wondered, *what now*? Then I noticed Gage walking toward us with a sexy-as-hell smile on his face. I could see by the scowl on his face that Max was less than impressed. The vindictive side of me - the one that didn't appreciate being lied to - cheered Gage on.

"Hey, babe, long time no see," Gage said when he reached us. I inwardly smiled when Max let out a growl of disapproval. *Seriously thinking I want to be a biker chick about... right... now.*

"Hey Gage. How was the rally?" I asked.

Max snorted, and I tried to scowl at him, but he had me in a vice lock and I couldn't turn around. Testing his hold, I tried to wiggle free, but it only caused him to tighten his grip. "Ellison," he warned in his *don't mess with me* voice. I sighed and relaxed back into him.

Gage, who had been watching our struggle, answered. "The rally was good."

Ignoring Max's Neanderthal-ass antics, I asked, "When did you get back?"

"I've been sitting at the bar for a little over half an hour. The blonde haired waitress with the big rack said you and your friend Piper were somewhere over here." The music had stopped, so I assumed Dillon was taking a break.

Harry, who was standing next to Zippo, cleared his throat. When everyone stopped and looked at him, he said, "Hi, I'm Harry Greenfield."

"Oh, I'm sorry!" I exclaimed in embarrassment. Normally, I wasn't this rude, but Max had me flustered. "Harry and Max, meet Gage, Zippo, Rider, Ax, Sledge, and Buck. Guys, this is Max and Harry."

After they all shook hands, Max's voice rumbled behind me. "Hey, man, you got a cousin named Skeeter?"

Gage grinned. "I thought you looked familiar, except I swear

I heard Skeeter call you Jack." I tensed when he said this and Max squeezed my hips.

"It's a long story. Call me Max."

Gage nodded. "Been keeping busy since Texas?" *Texas?*

"Somethin' like that," Max answered.

"Hey, I remember you now, you were there with that bl —" Ax chimed in, before Max cut him off.

"Nolen. I was with my manager, *Nolen*." Gage and Ax cut their eyes at each other, and I wondered if I'd missed something.

I tilted my head up, and asked Max, "Who's Skeeter? And when were you in Texas?"

"Skeeter works for me at my garage in Texas," Max said. "Nolen and I drove down there four or five months ago to check on a property, and Skeeter took us over to a...party. Gage was there."

"Hey, Shania, where'd you get the T-shirt?" Sledge interrupted.

"Her name is Ellison," Max informed.

"Yeah, but she looks exactly like a blonde Shania Twain," Zippo explained, "except with better eyes and..."

Max growled, "Don't even think about finishing that sentence."

Ignoring Max's caveman act, I asked, "T- shirt?"

Sledge nodded at the shirt I had on. "Yeah, do you know Dooley?" Max's hand twitched on my stomach.

I glanced down at Piper's shirt, and laughed. "I'd completely forgotten I had this on. Piper let me borrow it. Isn't it cool? I love the vintage look."

"Gage, is she talking about-?" Ryder interrupted.

"Nope," Gage clipped, and shook his head. I was totally lost, but could sense something was up. I just didn't have a clue as to what that something was.

"Where's Piper?" Max asked.

"She wasn't feeling well, so Garrett took her home," Harry chimed in.

"You two together?" Zippo nodded at Max's hands on my waist.

"Yes," Max said.

"Max and I are...old friends," I explained. I knew this would make him angry, but I just couldn't resist.

"Babe," Max growled. Then he turned me around to face him. He searched my eyes and I guess didn't like what he saw, because suddenly he was in my face. "What the fuck, Ellison?"

I leaned in to where only he could hear and said, "I know you lied to me."

His eyes darkened. "I'm not sure I like the attitude you're throwing right now."

"Really? Well, I don't really like being lied to, *babe*. So I guess we're even," I shot back in the same challenging tone.

Max tensed, and I fought the urge to take a step back. His head lowered and he put his mouth to my ear. "I'm thinking we need to head back to your place and clear the air." His quiet chilling tone made me want to run.

Instead, I stepped out of his arms and glared up at him. "Nope, I'm breathing just fine right...here. In fact, I think it's probably a good idea if you stay with Joss and Kurt tonight." As soon as the words left my mouth, I knew I'd pushed him too far. Before he could reply, I whipped around and started for the dance floor. Five steps in, and I felt his arm tag my waist. "Max!" I hissed.

"It was good seeing you guys," he casually said to Gage and the boys, as he reeled me back in. Then he asked, "You staying in town for a while?"

"Probably," Gage answered. I ignored the amused look on his face.

"Come by MMG. I'm there every day. We'll talk," Max said. Then he dismissed them and began pulling me toward the bar.

"Max, what are you doing?" I tried to jerk away from his grasp, but it only made him tighten his grip.

"What does it look like?" he snapped.

"Stop manhandling me!"

The second the words left my lips, he stopped dead in his tracks. I thought he was going to let me go, but instead, he twirled me around like we were dancing and hoisted me bodily up over his shoulder. *Oh. My. God.*

"Keys!" he shouted at Kurt as we passed by the bar. I heard the jingle of keys and the clink as they landed in Max's hand.

"Max McLellan, you put me down now!" I growled.

"Not gonna happen," he growled back. I heard the key in the door and felt the whoosh of the air as it swung open. Max set me down in the middle of the floor. Then he walked back over to the door, kicked it shut, and flipped the lock.

I placed my hands on my hips and stood there, determined to give him *nothing.*

He crossed his arms. Then, placing one ankle over the other, he leaned back against the door and made himself comfortable.

His nonchalance infuriated me. "You lied to me."

His eyebrow arched, and I wanted to rip it off of his face. "Just what is it that I lied to you about, Ellison?"

I threw up my hands. "Seriously? Where were you today, Max?"

"What's the point in answering if you already know?"

"What I can't figure out is why? Why would you lie to me?" I dropped my eyes to my feet, and fought back the tears.

"I didn't lie to you. I was going to the garage today. I got a call on the way there and had to change plans."

I narrowed my eyes at him. "And... since I'm not your mother or apparently anyone who *matters* to you, you owe me no explanation. I get it, Max, loud and clear. Now, if that's all, I think I'll take off now." I was done.

He let out an explosive sigh. "If that's *all*?" I could see the tick of anger in his jaw, but I was too far gone to care what it indicated.

I stepped forward, leaned in, and slowly enunciated, "I... Am...Done."

He shot off the wall, and before I could blink, he was in my face. "Yeah? Tell me, Ellison, are you done because I didn't end up where I said I was going? Are you done because I failed to call home when you deemed it was the appropriate time? Or are you done because I failed to *explain* myself to you?" His words sliced through me.

"No, *Max*. I'm done because the past five years have been One. Huge. Fucking. Lie. And, when I finally get you back, the first thing you do is lie to me, again! That's why I'm done!" I shouted.

Pain sliced through his eyes. "It wasn't like that, baby."

"Yeah, well, I wouldn't know what it was *like,* because you don't feel the need to explain!" I threw my hands up in frustration. He took a step forward, and I stepped back. "Don't," I held up my hand to stop him from coming any closer. I knew if he touched me, I would give in.

"It wasn't like that," he repeated in a half whisper. Then, acting as if it wasn't there, he pushed past my hand, pulled me into his body, and wrapped himself around me. He placed his lips on the top of my head, and started to explain, "I got a call this morning while I was driving to the garage. Nolen told me he was on his way to Tennessee to deal with the manager of the garage, Tim. Tim has been skimming money for months now, and Nolen finally figured out how he was doing it. I couldn't just ignore it, so I grabbed Benny and Kurt and headed to Tennessee." He tightened his hold. "You called right in the middle of Tim explaining how he'd screwed me over, and I handled it poorly. I didn't think about my tone, or what I'd said until we were heading back to Charlotte and Kurt lit into me. I didn't call to tell you what was going on, because I had nothing to tell. I was mad at Tim and took it out on you. I'm sorry for how I spoke to you, but I didn't lie. I would have told you about it tonight, I promise."

"You were harsh," I muttered into his chest, because he still had me in a death grip. He pulled back just far enough to look me in the eye. "But I overreacted," I admitted.

"Why did you tell Gage and his boys we were just friends?"

"Because I was mad, and truly Max, I have no idea what we are. For all I know, you're here simply to set up MMG Charlotte, and then you're heading back home to Kentucky."

His eyes narrowed. "I spent five years away from you. Five years where all I could think about was making my way back to you." He wove his hands through my hair, and cupped the back of my head. "You are everything to me, Ellison." With the slightest pressure, he tilted my head back. Then, oh so gently, he touched his mouth to mine. "You are my end game. When I'm with you, wherever it may be, I'm home, because you, Ellison, are my home." He kissed me again with more force, and I couldn't hold out any longer. God, this man was my kryptonite, my weakness. He always had been and always would be. I opened my mouth, and let him in. Tongue against tongue, we ate each other up. He broke away long enough to say, "Wrap your legs around my waist." I did as he said, and he lifted me up. We resumed kissing as he walked over to Kurt's desk, and lowered me down. My pulse shot sky high when he stepped between my legs. *I am so thanking Joss later for picking out this skirt.* Max smiled down at me. I didn't want to talk anymore. I wanted to be naughty - very naughty. As I slid my hands behind his neck, I pulled his lips down to mine, and poured myself into him. Right as we were about to ignite, his phone rang.

"Don't answer," I panted into his mouth. I was seconds away

from discovering what desk sex with Max would feel like.

He pulled back and gave me a look of apology. "I have to, babe. I've got too many balls in the air right now." Punching the talk button, he answered, "Max McLellan." By the irritated tone of his voice and facial expression, I could tell I would not be getting desk sex with Max tonight. *Damn!*

"The garage?" I asked, once he'd ended the call.

"Yep."

"The one here or somewhere else?" I wanted to make sure I didn't make the same mistake twice.

"Here," he sighed.

"Go." I pushed him back, and started to scoot off of the desk, but he stopped me.

"Look at me babe." I looked up into his beautiful worried eyes. "Are we good here?"

"We're good," I told him.

"Can you drive home?" I nodded yes. "I don't know how long this will take. If it's too late, I won't wake you. I can see from what happened today you are unsure about us. I can see I haven't done a good job of explaining myself. I'm going to fix this tomorrow, okay?"

Relief washed through me. "Okay, Max."

He snagged my hand in his, and said, "I'll walk you out to your car." When we got to my car, he gave me a long, lingering kiss and made me promise to text when I got home.

My dad's car was in the driveway when I pulled in. I was glad to see he was home. After making sure that both he and Piper were asleep, I texted Max to let him know I was home safe. A little while later, I crawled into bed and turned out the light. I was out before my head even hit the pillow.

Sometime in the night, I felt Max pressed against my back. When I woke the next morning, however, he wasn't there. I threw on my robe and shuffled out to the kitchen in search of him and coffee, but all I found was my dad.

"Morning, darlin'."

"Morning Dad. Where is everyone?"

"Piper's hasn't come down yet, and Max had to go to the garage to check on things. He mentioned taking the afternoon off."

I was disappointed he wasn't there and a little worried. With the blowout at the bar, I couldn't help but wonder if he was really okay with everything. "Did he say why he was taking the afternoon off?"

"Nope, he said just to tell you he'd be back before lunchtime. Listen, sweetheart, while we have some privacy, can we talk?" My heart dropped at the sound of his voice.

"Sure, what's up?"

"First, I want to hear how things are going with you and Max."

"Good." I made sure my voice sounded cheery. *There's no way I'm telling him about yesterday.*

"Are you happy?"

I nodded my head. "I am."

"Is there a reason why you aren't being honest with me?" *He's good.*

"For the most part I am being honest," I sighed. "I am happier than I've been in a really long time, but at the same time, I'm frustrated, confused and...well, frustrated," I shrugged.

"I can see that. Do you want to talk about it?"

"Not really, at least, not until I talk more with Max. We're just figuring each other out and it's..."

He smiled. "Frustrating? Well, if you need to talk, I'm always here."

"Thanks, Dad."

"Listen, I've been doing some thinking, and I wanted your opinion." I wasn't sure I liked the sound of this.

"About?"

"I'm thinking about selling my place in Raleigh."

Excitement whipped through me. "You're moving here?"

"I was thinking about it." He smiled, and added, "That is, if that's okay with you?"

"That would be awesome!" I shouted, and threw my arms around him. "When?"

"Well, that's what I wanted to show you." He handed me a set of papers. They looked like pictures of condominiums.

"What are these?"

"Condos for sale."

"But I thought you would just move in here with me?"

"Ellie, as much as I love being here with you, and I do, I'm a single man in my early forties who is currently living with his twenty-three-year-old daughter. That's just not right. I want to live close to you, so I thought I would check out the condos in the area. I've narrowed it down to these four, and want you to help me choose."

"What's wrong with living here with me?" I pouted. "I know lots of kids who live with their parents."

"Yes, but usually it is the parent taking in their kid because they have to. How many single fathers do you know who are living with their daughter, her boyfriend, and best friend?" *Hmmm, I have to think about this. I'm sure I must know someone…*

"Essentially, Ellie, what he's saying is that you are a gigantic cock-block, and as much as he loves you, he needs his personal space in order to score with the ladies. That about cover it Samuel?" Piper asked. She was standing behind the sofa with a grin on her face.

"Yes Piper. As usual, so eloquently put." I could tell he was trying not to laugh.

She winked at him. "Always glad to help, Sammy."

Piper left around eleven to go help Polly and Lena buy party decorations for tomorrow night. Since I had practically done all of the party planning, I didn't feel guilty about spending the afternoon with Max. When I hadn't heard from him by lunchtime, I contemplated giving him a call, but was feeling a little gun shy after yesterday's oh-so-happy events. I had my phone in hand when I heard his truck in the drive.

He walked in carrying a bag of groceries, looking like sex on a stick.

"Hey," I meekly said and shot him a shy smile.

His blue eyes lit up when he saw me. "You okay?"

I shrugged. Was I okay? I wasn't sure.

He placed the bag on the counter, before he walked over to me and stroked his fingers lovingly across my face. "I noticed you have a space heater on your back porch. I was thinking we could turn it on and have a picnic. Is your dad around?" *He wants to have a picnic?* This surprised me. Max didn't seem like a picnic kind of guy.

"No. He's gone to look for a condo to buy."

His eyes widened in surprise. "Here in Charlotte?"

"Yes." I couldn't help but smile.

"That's great news, my gorgeous girl." I loved when he called me this. "And Piper?"

"Gone to buy party decorations and to lunch."

His grin widened. "Even better. I realized when we were talking last night that I have assumed too much and said far too little, so today we will eat and talk." He gave me a quick peck on the lips and headed to the kitchen. "You set up the blankets and heater while I get the food ready."

*Well, okay then.*

We'd just finished eating when he broke the news. "I have to head back to Kentucky to check on things there." My stomach instantly knotted up. "I want you to come with me."

"To Kentucky?"

"I was thinking we could either leave after the party tomorrow night or early Friday morning? Kurt said he and Joss could fill in for you and you could work for him next Wednesday and Thursday."

"You asked Kurt if I could go with you to Kentucky and stay until next Wednesday?"

"We'll drive back Tuesday afternoon, so really, we'll only be gone until Tuesday evening."

My breath caught in my throat. "So…you're coming back to Charlotte with me?"

He gave me a questioning look. "What did you think I was going to do?"

"I wasn't sure," I shrugged.

In a not too happy voice, he said, "Ellison, why exactly do you think I'm here in Charlotte?"

"Because you're building the garage," I answered without hesitation.

His eyebrow shot into his hairline. "Seriously?"

I wasn't quite sure what he was looking for, so I hedged. "Uh… yes?"

Reaching over, he yanked me onto his lap. "The garage is a part of it, babe, but the reason I came back here is for you, and only you. I told you last night you're my end game, you always have been." I remembered him saying it, but there was alcohol and anger involved, so it didn't really sink in. "I realize the past five years have been all kinds of fucked up for us both, but I meant it last night when I said you're my home. Wherever you are is where I need to be. I told you that summer at the quarry that I would always come back for you, and I meant it. When I left, not a day went by that I didn't think about that promise. You've always been my end game, Ellison." He pressed his fingers under my chin, and I lifted my eyes to his. "Are you getting me? Am I making myself clear? I want you to come to

Kentucky with me. I want to show you where I've lived and what I've been doing for the past five years. I need to clean things up at the garage, and then I need to pack some things up to bring back with us." My heart soared. *He's really coming back with me.*

"Where are you going to stay?" I asked. *Please say here with me.*

"Here with you, if that's all right. If you find you need space, I have my own space above the garage. In fact, I checked this morning, and the rooms are ready to go. All they need is a coat of paint and some furniture, which won't be in until sometime next week. I don't want to pressure you, though."

"I would rather you stay here with me," I said, biting my lip. *You, too, are my end game. I'm just afraid that the second I tell you, you'll leave me again. How screwed up is that?*

His eyes dropped to my mouth, and he made a sexy sound, "Me, too."

I wanted his lips on mine, but I also wanted to make sure this was what he really wanted, so I flipped around and straddled his lap. As I wrapped my arms around his neck, I slid my fingers through his hair, looked him straight in the eyes, and asked, "Do you really want to stay here with me? I don't want to pressure you either, Max."

His face split into a seductive smile, and the entire lower half of my body tightened. "I've never wanted anything more," he said, and I could tell by the look in his eyes, not to mention the bulge in his pants, he meant every word. When he kissed me, any doubts I had flew out the door. We kissed for a while longer, and when things started heating up and we were ready to take it to the bedroom, Piper and the girls showed up. *Talk about a cock-block.*

# CHAPTER TWENTY-NINE

The morning of Kurt and Joss's engagement party, Max received a disturbing phone call from Nolen. Someone had tried to break into the garage in Kentucky. When they couldn't get in, they tried to burn it down. The police told Max that the security alarm scared them away. Very little damage was done, but the police were tagging it as an attempted burglary and arson, and therefore needed to speak with the owner in person. Being that I was the one hosting the engagement party, I couldn't go with him. We were both terribly disappointed, but there was nothing we could do about it. Before leaving for Kentucky, Max promised he would do everything in his power to cut the trip short. Hopefully, this meant he would be back in a few days.

Joss and Kurt's engagement party was a blast. We closed Dragonfly down to the public. Ben, who was back in Charlotte, played all of their favorite songs, and Lena's Aunt Rachel catered the food. Had I known Dillon was such an amazing musician, I would have asked him to play. Instead, he and Lena worked the bar. Because Max wasn't there to monitor me, I got rip-roaring drunk with Piper. We danced and sang along to all the songs.

The only surprise of the evening was Polly getting mad at Harry, who was dancing with anything that moved. In a very drunken moment, she disclosed to Piper, Joss, and I that she and Harry had been hooking up since the hot tub night at my house. After hearing, in vivid detail, about Harry's sexual prowess, I seriously doubted I would be able to look at him the same way ever again.

*Blech!*

Garrett and I made up somewhere between shot number five and beer number three. In fact, he was nice enough to give Piper and me a ride home as well as put up with us serenading him the entire way there. I was aware that Max probably put him up to it, but I really didn't care.

Piper and I both stumbled into the kitchen around the same time the next morning, and according to my dad, we both looked like death warmed over. I certainly felt like it. It took me until well after lunch to shrug off the effects of the night before.

At this point, I'd spoken to Max three times, and all three times he'd seemed distracted and in a foul mood. I guess someone trying to ruin your business would do that to you, but still...I missed him. I wanted him here with me. We were both tense and moody, not to mention sexually frustrated.

Night four of Max being gone, Piper ordered pizza for dinner. Afterwards, my dad shut himself in his office, where he seemed to spend most of his time these days. This gave us the perfect opportunity to chat. We settled in the living room with a glass of wine, and before she could turn on the television and drown me out, I asked, "What happened the other night at Dragonfly, Piper? You were fine and then you weren't. Did the alcohol and painkillers finally catch up to you, or was it something else?"

She stared blankly out the French doors, and just when I thought I'd lost her, she started talking. "Look," she whispered, as if someone was in the room with us and possibly listening in. When she scooted closer to me on the sofa, my pulse quickened, and the hair on the back of my neck stood up. "I can't tell you everything, but only because you're my best friend and I would never do anything to hurt you." The whispering was really freaking me out.

"Why would I be hurt, Piper?"

"You wouldn't, you won't." She grabbed my hand and squeezed it. "Let's just say I fell hard for a guy in Texas and things turned out really badly."

Squeezing her hand, I stared into her pretty blue eyes that still showed traces of bruising and felt sick to my stomach. "Like the bruises on your face kind of bad?"

She nodded her head, and I gasped. I watched her eyes pool with unshed tears and pulled her into a hug. "He had some scary friends, Ellie. I was stupid and naïve and got caught up in it, but I got myself out," she sniffled.

"Oh Piper," I sighed.

"Don't feel bad for me. I deserved every bit of what I got."

I pulled back, so I could look her in the face when I properly scolded her stupid ass. "Why would you think that? Nobody deserves to get hurt, Piper…ever."

"I left Charlotte for boarding school and never looked back. I left you here, alone."

"Your parents made you go, and we talked on the phone all the time," I pointed out.

"I knew that you were going through hell when Max disappeared, and I bailed. I felt as if you were just being melodramatic about it all, and I blew you off," her voice cracked. "I didn't take you or your feelings seriously. I told you to get over him and move on, and I will never forgive myself for treating you that way. I didn't understand." Her grip on my hand tightened. "I had no idea what it meant to love someone, really love someone, like *I would die for you* kind of love someone. But, I now know what that feels like." I watched her fight the tears and that sick feeling in the pit of my stomach returned.

"What did he make you do, Piper?" I was having a hard time staying calm. *What did this guy do to her?*

"He didn't make me do anything. I did it all on my own. I want you to know I'm sorry Ellie, truly sorry, and I'm so happy for you that Max is back." She stood up. "I have to get to bed now. I have a couple of job interviews first thing in the morning. This conversation is over, okay? I'm moving on and won't be talking about it with you again…ever. Please, just allow me to forget," she begged.

I wanted to tell her she would never be able to forget. That is, if she loved this guy the way I loved Max. I wanted to track him down and hurt him the way he'd hurt her. I wanted to shout the house down, because some monster had broken something deep inside of my beautiful best friend. But, of course, I did none of these things. Instead, I let her go to bed and said goodnight to my dad. After getting myself ready for bed, I curled up with a new romance novel, and fell asleep before finishing the first chapter.

I was sleeping so soundly I barely registered Max moving the book off of my chest, turning off the light, and crawling in bed behind me.

"Hmmmm," I hummed as I snuggled down into his warm body.

His low husky voice roused me from my slumber. "Is my girl too tired to play?"

"Never," I answered with a sleepy smile. I glanced over my shoulder to make sure he was really there, and boy, was he. The look of complete and total lust on his face stopped my breath.

"I missed you. All I could think about was getting back to you, and now… finding you like this… I couldn't have dreamt it better. You, right here, right now, are the most beautiful thing I've ever seen." Hearing these words - from this man - was indescribable. The fact that he felt this way about me, after all this time, filled up the parts of me that were left empty when he went away. His fingers skimmed down between our bodies and halted right below my nightie. "I like this," he murmured, thumbing the material. "But I like this better," he grinned, and cupped me between my legs. Slowly, he slid his hand under my panties and dipped a finger inside. I let out a throaty sound of need.

After four days of not being with him, I was strung so tight I almost came the second he touched me. "Max," I uttered.

"Hmmmmm? What do you want Ellison? Tell me what I can do for you."

"More," I breathed. I dropped my head back against the headboard when I felt a second finger slide in. After torturing me with this for a minute or so, he withdrew and pulled away. "No," I gasped, not wanting him to stop.

His eyes danced with lust and humor. "Hang on, greedy girl. I'm just getting started here." He pulled his shirt off and tossed it on the floor. I was admiring his ripped upper body when he stripped off his jeans. *Does the man ever wear underwear?* "Do you see what you do to me?"

"I think the neighbors a block over can see what I do to you," I teased, loving every second of it.

He gave me a heated look that scorched me from the inside out. "I need you, Ellison," he seductively whispered.

Reaching up, I pulled him down on top of me. "I'm yours Max, always," I whispered against his lips. His blue eyes held me captive as he pinned me to the bed and slowly eased inside. Thrust after thrust, he took me higher and higher, his eyes never leaving mine, and I cried out as I came apart around him. Moments later, he threw back his head and moaned through his release.

He woke me early the next morning to tell me he was going to the garage. I was terribly disappointed, because we didn't get a chance to talk last night. After four days of bad moods and tense conversations, I needed some serious alone time with him.

I couldn't help but pout. "Will I ever see you again?"

"Babe, it's always hell getting a new garage off the ground, but I promise as soon as we're up and running, you'll be begging me to leave you alone."

"I doubt that," I muttered.

"I'm happy my girl wants me around." He kissed the top of my head and headed out the door.

"Will I see you tonight?" I called out after him.

"Hopefully!" he shouted back.

I pouted myself to the bathroom and then to the kitchen for coffee, where I found my dad and Piper.

My dad gave me a knowing smirk. "What's got your panties all ruffled, Ellie, dear?"

"Samuel, you are really showing all of your sixty-five years with that question," Piper teased. "In 2013, we ask *What crawled up your ass, girl?*"

He narrowed his eyes at Piper. "If you weren't my daughter's best friend, I would bend you over my knee and spank *your ass* for missing my age by twenty-two years. I won't, though, but only because I don't want to risk getting kicked out of here before my condo is ready."

"Now we're talking," she laughed. "I like a good spanking every now and then."

Scrunching my nose in disgust, I made a gagging noise. "God, would you quit flirting with each other, especially in front of me. It's gross and inappropriate." Obviously finding me highly entertaining, they both started laughing.

"As entertaining as this is, I'm off for my first interview. Wish me luck!" Piper announced. We both wished her luck. Then Dad headed upstairs to work, and I headed to my room to mope.

Max hadn't called or texted by the time I needed to leave for work that night. I figured he had a lot to do and was probably running behind because of his trip to Kentucky. He showed up at Dragonfly around ten, ordered a beer, and barely spoke a word to me. I knew something was wrong by the way he kept staring at his phone. He even ignored Dillon's taunts, which was unheard of. When I finally had time to talk to him, he told me he was tired, would see me at home, and took off before I could question him anymore. We were slammed, so I didn't have much time to process his mood. I was a little surprised and disappointed he didn't stay and follow me home. After all, he was the one who'd made a big deal about me working until all hours of the morning and leaving the bar alone.

When I got home, the lights were out and Max was already asleep. Being that it was after two in the morning, I expected this, but still, I was a little disappointed. Feeling tired but frisky, I wanted more of what he'd given me last night. After getting ready for bed, I crawled in behind him. As I pressed my body against his back, I slowly ran my tongue down his neck. Normally this would make him moan or say something enticingly sexy. Instead, he flinched and pulled away. *He flinched at my touch.* He might as well have slapped me. It would've had the same effect. I felt as if I'd been burned, and quickly withdrew. As I lay on my back and stared at the ceiling, I fought to keep the tears from spilling over. Finally, after what seemed like hours, I drifted into a restless sleep. Max was gone when I woke in the morning. Neither Piper nor my dad had seen or heard him before he left.

Piper had interviews again that morning, and Dad had to work. I, however, had an appointment with my obstetrician, Dr. Cooper. I was two months overdue for my yearly exam, and needed her to write me another script for birth control. I waited around the house for as long as I could before heading to my appointment. I thought maybe Max would show up and we could talk about what was going on. From the way he'd acted last night, I knew something was bothering him, but how could I help him if he wouldn't talk to me? By the time I arrived at the doctor's office, I was more than worried. I was scared. Max still hadn't texted or called, so I contemplated whether or not to call him. Before I could decide, they called my name.

After the usual weight check, blood pressure, and get changed routine, Dr. Cooper flitted in. We played catch-up for a few minutes, and then she launched into the same questions she asks every year.

"Are you still using the birth control pill?"

"Yes."

"Do you take it every day, as instructed?"

"Yes, in fact, I need a new script."

"When was your last period?"

"Uhhhhh...." This one stumped me. *When was my last period?*

"Do you need to see a calendar?"

"Yes, please." She handed me the calendar. After checking it several times, I said, "This can't be right." According to the calendar, I hadn't had a period this month, and should have started my period over a week ago.

Reading the look of concern on my face, she said, "There's no need to panic, Ellie. How about we start with a routine urine test."

"Okay," I squeaked out. *Please don't let me be pregnant. Please don't let me be pregnant.*

The nurse swooped in and led me to the restroom. She handed me a cup and instructed me to bring it back to room six when I was done.

*I can't be pregnant. I don't even know if Max likes kids. Hell, I don't even know if Max likes me right now.*

When I returned to the room, Dr. Cooper was waiting. She dipped something into the cup of urine and checked her watch. *I haven't told him I love him yet. How in God's name can I be pregnant?* After what seemed like forever, she lifted the object from the cup.

"Well, it looks like it's positive. Now, I want to follow up right now with a blood test just to be sure. I can have the results to you tomorrow by noon. Let's reschedule the pelvic exam. I really don't like to do them during the first trimester if I don't have to."

I was completely floored by this. In fact, I wasn't sure if I believed her. "How?" I asked.

Her eyes widened in obvious surprise. "Ummmm."

"Not how did I get pregnant," I clarified. How did I get pregnant when I'm on the pill and take it like clockwork?"

"Oh," she sighed, probably relieved that she wasn't going to have to explain the birds and the bees to an already pregnant woman. "Let's see, if you haven't missed any pills then have you been on any medication during the past month? Antibiotics are usually the culprit. Specific ones can weaken the effects of birth control pills and even sometimes render them ineffective."

I dropped my head to my hands and groaned. "I'm in so much trouble. How could I be so stupid?"

I felt Dr. Cooper's hand on my back. "Sometimes, these tests aren't one hundred percent accurate, Ellie. Let my nurse take your blood and then give me a call after lunch tomorrow. Until then, try not to worry."

*Yeah, right.*

Minutes later, I'd given blood and was free to leave.

# CHAPTER THIRTY

I didn't want to go to work that night. I wanted to stay home and wait for Max. All kinds of crazy things were running through my head, and I was making myself sick with worry. *I may have his baby growing inside me and I'm afraid to tell him. How messed up is that?*

I wanted to confess everything to Joss and Piper that night, but felt it was a bit premature. Until the blood test confirmed the pregnancy and I had spoken to Max, my hands were tied. So I did the only thing I could think to do. I got myself dressed and went to work. I left a note for Piper, telling her to come hang out. Then I texted Max and told him he could find me at work.

Dillon sensed that something was wrong the second I walked through the door. He rode me about it most of the night.

Around ten, Harry rolled in. Directly behind him were Gage, Zippo, and Ax. I was thrilled to see them and hoped they would be able to take my mind off of my worries. Ax was in the middle of telling a story about a chick with three nipples when the front door opened. Every time someone walked through the door, I expected it to be Max. This time, instead of Max, in walked one of the most beautiful women I'd ever seen. A mane of black hair fell past her shoulders and cascaded down her back. She was short, but had a perfect figure, as in just the right amount of... everything.

Of course, Dillon noticed her, as did every other man in the bar. Flashing his me-so-sexy smile he, asked, "What can I get for you, darlin'?" Up close I could see her eyes were a cobalt shade of blue.

Flashing Dillon an equally sexy smile, she answered, "I'm looking for Jack Barnett." My gut clinched when I heard the name. *What does she want with Max?*

Dillon's brow furrowed. "Who?"

"Jaaaack Barrrrnett," she repeated, slowly enunciating his name as if Dillon was a little slow in the head. Normally, I would find this incredibly funny, but since she was looking for my Max... *not so much.*

After a minute of indecision, I addressed her question. "Jack hasn't made it in tonight. Is he expecting you uh...?"

"Priscilla Newman, but my friends call me Cilla, and to answer your question, I was with Jack last night and again this afternoon. He mentioned heading this way, so I thought I would join him for a drink." Her words floored me. *What does she mean, she was with Max last night and today? Who the hell is she?*

Dillon was looking at me as if I had grown three heads. "Do you really know a Jack Barnett, or are you just fucking with her?" he muttered under his breath.

"Oh, I know Jack, all right," I told him.

While Dillon and I were quietly conferring behind the bar, Priscilla was taking stock of her surroundings. Suddenly she cried out, "Hey! I know you guys! You were at the party at that mansion in Texas, weren't you? Gage, is it? And I remember one of you was named Lighter and Hammer…or something like that." She paused, as if looking for something else to say. "Uh… are you guys here visiting Jack, too? What a coincidence. I'll have to make sure we invite you over for a cookout or something real soon." *She was in Texas with Max? And now she's planning get-togethers? What the hell?*

"Wow, gee, it sounds like you *all* had a great time in Texas. When did you say you were there again?" I cut my eyes at Gage and Zippo. Zippo flinched, and I wanted to throw up.

"Oh…maybe four, or was it five months ago?" She asked Gage. I closed my eyes and rubbed the ache that had set up residence deep within my chest. When I opened them back up, Gage was watching me with an anxious look on his face, and it clicked. *Gage knew Max was in Texas…with her. This is what they were talking about the other night. Max has been acting distant since he's been back from Kentucky, because he's been with her. I am such a fool.*

"Fuck," Gage said.

"What the hell is going on here?" Dillon asked.

Fuck was right. I had to know the truth. Is the guy I fell in love with so long ago really a cheating bastard? Looking Priscilla straight in her cobalt-blue eyes, I asked, "So, you and Jack are…together?" I could see why he would want her. She was gorgeous.

"Ellie," Gage warned.

As if completely oblivious to the destruction she was causing, Priscilla gave me an award winning smile. "Well, Jack and I have been friends for about a year now, but we started seeing each other seriously about seven or eight months ago. I saw him when he was home a few days ago, but he barely had any time for me." She puckered her lips into the perfect little pout, and I wanted to curl up and die. "He told me he was coming here to work on the new garage." She threw her hand in the air. "So here I am."

This wasn't happening. I could not be this unlucky in love, could I? Was anyone this unlucky? Placing a hand on my chest, I tried to catch my breath. *It was all a lie… every last word of it.*

"What the fuck?" I heard Dillon ask, but it sounded like he was under water.

"Hey, are you okay?" Priscilla asked. Her voice also sounded far away.

"Get her head down between her knees," Gage ordered.

Before I knew what was happening, I was lifted into someone's arms and we were moving fast. "Hang on sweetheart," I heard someone say, but wasn't sure if they were talking to me or not.

When I came to I was lying on the break room sofa with a cold cloth on my head. "I'm okay," I said.

"Ellie, what the fuck is going on here?" Dillon asked. He raised my legs, sat down, and draped them back across his lap.

Gage stepped into my line of sight. "Don't you think you're getting a little too personal with someone else's woman?" he directed at Dillon.

Dillon narrowed his eyes at Gage, and snapped, "I don't see him here? Do you?"

"Who's manning the bar?" I asked, trying to distract them.

"Zippo and Harry," they both replied.

"Don't worry about the bar, El," Dillon said.

Gage squatted down beside me and wiped the cold cloth across my face. "Sweetheart, sometimes things aren't what they seem."

My eyes filled with tears, and I couldn't help but let out a self-deprecating laugh. "And sometimes, as much as we don't want them to be, they are." He closed his eyes when I said this. When he opened them back up, they were filled with such agony I had to look away. Apparently, I wasn't the only one who'd been hurt.

"What am I missing?" Dillon asked.

I let out a tired sigh, and explained. "It appears the man I've loved for most of my life has spent the last five weeks lying to me. If that's not enough, he's also been cheating on his obviously sweet and beautiful *girlfriend,* who is currently standing out there waiting for him to show up." I glanced over at Gage. "I'd say it's exactly how it looks. What I don't get is *why*? Why would he do this to me?" I needed to get out of here before I completely lost it, but I had nowhere to go.

Dillon reared back. "Are you trying to tell me that your Max is her Jack?" He was beginning to catch on, which meant he was about to flip out. When I didn't answer, he picked up my legs, stood up, and gently set them back on the sofa. Then he stalked over to the sink, picked up the soap dish, shouted "Mother fucker!" and hurled it against the wall. Pieces of it flew everywhere. I stared at the shattered pieces on the floor, and thought, *that's exactly what my heart feels like*. Jerking his hands through his hair, he pierced me with his silver-eyed stare. "He split us up knowing that he had some snatch waiting for him back in Kentucky?" His voice was full of disbelief.

Gage scowled at him. "You're not helping here, Dillon. Don't make this about you." He pointed at the door. "We've only heard her side of the story out there, and we don't even know her. Ellie needs to talk to Max."

"Yeah, except for he won't talk to me. He's been avoiding me since yesterday, and now I know why. I don't want to see or talk to him right now, and I *certainly* can't go home, because he could be there. What do I do?"

"Here," Dillon said, handing me his keys. "You know where I live. I'll close up here and meet you back at my place. If you get hungry, eat something, and if you get tired, you can crash on the bed. I'll take the couch. Stay as long as you need."

Gage shook his head at me. "This is not a good idea."

"Why not? She needs a place to regroup. You got a better idea?" Dillon challenged.

"Call your girls when you get to Dillon's. That way, if this isn't how it looks, you won't be making it worse," Gage directed at me. He was right. There was a small chance I could be wrong.

"Okay, I'll call Piper and Joss when I get to Dillon's," I assured him.

"How 'bout this, I'll drive you over in your car and get Ax to follow. I can catch a ride home on the back of his bike."

Dillon pulled me off of the sofa. "Go out the back so you don't have to walk through the bar. I'll see you in a while, and El?" I looked up at him. "I'll do my best to help you through this, okay?"

"Don't tell Max where I am, Dillon. Promise me. If he comes looking for me, promise you won't tell him where I am, okay? You too, Gage." After they both agreed, we left for Dillon's.

*You're my end game, you always have been. You're it for me.*

"I can't believe this is happening."

I didn't realize I'd spoken out loud until Gage reached over the middle console of my car and grabbed my hand. "Hey, nothing is definite until you hear it from Max, okay?" I could feel the tears coming, and knew I wasn't going to be able to keep them contained much longer. All I did anymore was cry. I wanted to tell Gage I was possibly pregnant. I wanted someone to understand how serious the situation was, but I couldn't.

"I just got him back, Gage." Tears spilled down my cheeks, and I wiped them away with the back of my sleeve. "H-h-how could he do this to m-m-me? Wasn't it e-e-nough that he left me to begin w-w-ith?"

He squeezed my hand and spoke in a low, calming voice. "Don't know the details of your past relationship, but what I do know is that Priscilla is not who she's pretending to be. I met her five months ago in Texas, and she did not give a favorable impression."

"Evidently, he sees something in her," I sniffled.

"I wouldn't be so sure about that. After seeing him with you, there's no comparison. I think we're missing something, here. I can feel it in my gut."

"It looks pretty damning, Gage. She is so beautiful. It kills me to say it, but I totally see why he would want her."

He laughed. "There is nothing hotter than a woman who underestimates her own beauty. I know you're hurting and how it looks right now. I'm sorry. What you need to do now is pull out your phone, call your girls, and get them over here. Then you need to sleep on it. Before you walk away, though, you need to hear Max out. You owe him the chance to tell his side, okay?" I nodded. "Good, now call your girls."

Normally, I would have called him out on his bossiness, but I couldn't muster the energy. I reached down between my feet, snagged my purse off the floorboard, found my phone, and powered it on. My phone dinged, indicating I had missed messages. Ignoring them, I called Joss and Piper. Both girls swore up and down they wouldn't tell Max where I was, and both agreed to meet me at Dillon's.

We pulled up to Dillon's apartment and Gage motioned for Ax to hold on. He ushered me inside and pulled me in for a hug. I thanked him, and promised to call if I needed anything.

Joss was the first to arrive. When Piper arrived, we were sitting on Dillon's sofa sipping Sprites.

"Sheesh, your dad is a giant pain in the ass," Piper complained.

"Did you tell him where I was?" If she did, it was only a matter of time before he told Max.

"No, I told him you were upset with Max and needed some space. He wouldn't let me walk out the door until I promised to have you check in."

"Thanks." I let out a sigh of relief and shot him a quick text.

"Now, tell us what this is all about, Ellie."

I told them everything from Max's distant behavior to Gage dropping me off at Dillon's apartment. I managed not to cry until the end.

"She was in Kentucky with him," I choked out. "He was never going to be mine. I've spent five years thinking that no matter what, we belonged together. No matter where he was or what he was doing, he would always be mine. I was good with that. I'm not good with this. *This* makes me sick inside. I can't watch the man I love more than anything in this world…loving someone else. I just can't," I sobbed.

"I'm so sorry," Piper whispered, and pulled me in for a hug. Joss let out an angry snort, and we both looked up at her.

"This is bullshit." She shook her head. "Max wouldn't do this. I'm telling you, this is not right." She was gearing up for a lecture when her phone rang. She held up her hand for silence and mouthed, "Kurt."

"Please Joss," I tearfully begged, "don't tell him where I am." Thankfully, she told Kurt she was at her parents' house going over last-minute wedding details and that she hadn't seen or heard from me all night. She glared at me and asked, "Why is Max frantically trying to reach her?" After a few more minutes of clipped answers and nods she hung up, and narrowed her eyes at me. "I do not like lying to the man I'm about to spend the rest of my life with. Don't ever ask me to do it again."

"I'm sorry, Joss." I told her, and I really was. I hated putting her in that position.

She placed her hands on her hips, and said, "Riddle me this, Batman. If Max is so in love with Priscilla, then why did he practically tear apart Dragonfly tonight looking for you?"

"What?" I whispered. Surely she was kidding.

"Dillon told Max you'd left early and had no idea where you were headed. Kurt said Max went nuts. He's out of control worried, because apparently, you have your phone turned off and he can't find you. Ellie, you need to *talk* to him." *He tore apart Dragonfly looking for me?*

"It seems the man doesn't like not knowing where his girl is...at...all." *But I'm not his girl...she is. Isn't she?*

Joss had to get back to Kurt, so she didn't spend the night with us. She did, however, make sure I was still helping with inventory at Dragonfly the next morning. Piper and I found extra sheets and pillows in the hall closet and made up the fold out sofa. We crawled into bed and somehow got on the subject of Gage. Glad to have my mind off of Max, I told her everything I could remember about Gage and his friends. I was starting to put two and two together, and they were not adding up to four. Something bad had happened to her, and I wasn't sure, but I had a sick suspicion that Gage was somehow involved. *I hope not, because he's a really good guy and there are so few left in this world.*

Piper fell asleep before I did. As I lay there listening to her breathing, I thought about Max. *How did I get it all so wrong?* I rubbed my hand over my belly. *I will protect and love you, I swear.* Once again, my eyes filled with tears. Not wanting to wake Piper, I got up and made my way to Dillon's bedroom, where I curled into a ball on top of his comforter, and wept for things that would never be.

I woke sometime later to the sound of someone talking. It took me a minute to figure out where I was. When I realized I'd fallen asleep on Dillon's bed, I shot up, embarrassed he might find me there. Movement at the foot of the bed caught my eye. *Too late.* There was Dillon, standing at the foot of the bed, talking to someone on the phone. His eyes were fixed on me. *Crap!*

In a take-no-prisoners tone of voice, he clipped, "I told you when you tore apart Dragonfly that I wasn't sure where she was, Max, so what makes you think that has suddenly changed?" *Oh no! He's talking to Max.* My breath hitched, and in a blink, he had his finger pressed to my mouth. "You know what? How about instead of bugging me with this shit, you just ask your girlfriend, Priscilla? She was in Dragonfly earlier tonight and told us all about your love for each other. You wanna know why you can't find Ellie? Well, there you have it, dickhead." He hit end, turned off his phone, and tossed it across the room. I was shocked, to say the least.

"Dillon," I breathed. "Why did you do that?"

"You want to know why? Because I'm sitting here watching you hide like you're the one who has done something wrong when you haven't, Ellie. This is all on him, not you."

This was too much to handle. When I burst into tears, he wrapped his arms around me and told me everything would be okay. I wanted to believe him, I really did. I let him hold me for a few minutes. Then I made my way back to the fold-out, crawled in next to Piper, and waited for the sun to come up.

# CHAPTER THIRTY-ONE

It was kind of Dillon to let me stay at his place, but I didn't want to give him mixed messages. After inventory, I decided I would go home, and face Max. I needed answers only he could provide. *Before I do that, however, I have to confirm the pregnancy.*

Piper brought me a pair of jeans and a long-sleeve tee from the house. Since Dillon had lucked out of doing inventory, I gave him a hug, thanked him for taking care of me, and headed with Piper to her car. After dropping me by Dragonfly, she was heading home to shower and change for more interviews. We made plans to meet back at the house later.

Upon arrival, I headed to the office. When I heard voices coming from the supply room, I veered in that direction.

"Joss...Kurt..." I called out.

"In here," Joss yelled. I peeked around the corner and was relieved to find them fully clothed. "Hey, guys."

Kurt gave me a big hug. "Have you spoken with Max?" he asked.

"No. I just left Dillon's and came straight here."

He gave me a stern look. "You spent the night with Dillon?"

"And Piper," I stressed.

"So you haven't talked to Max yet?"

Joss cut in. "She said no Kurt. Are you hard of hearing?" The last thing I wanted was them fighting over me.

"I'll talk to him when I get home, okay? I know what's up, Kurt. I know all about his girlfriend."

His jaw clenched in obvious anger. "If you think that, then you don't know shit," he rasped. "He's going crazy, because he can't get to you, and here you are… all smiles after spending the night with Dillon. You haven't got a fucking clue." My eyes widened in surprise. I'd never seen Kurt this angry… at me. Too bad he had it all wrong.

"For your information, I did not spend the night with Dillon. I slept on the sofa bed with Piper, and what don't I know, Kurt? That Max's girlfriend showed up at my place of work and introduced herself to me? That they've apparently been together for months, now? By all means, please fill me in!"

"You're never going to forgive him, are you?" He blew out an angry breath. "Joss and I have to go get more bar towels and glasses at the supply store. While we're there, call Max and talk to him. We'll inventory when we get back." Why was he so mad at me when Max was the one who had the girlfriend? This made no sense. Were Kurt and Gage right? Was Max innocent in all of this? If so, I'd really screwed up…again.

Before calling Max, I phoned Dr. Cooper's office. The nurse confirmed what I already knew. I was pregnant. I wasn't sure if I was ready to tell Max just yet, but I knew I needed to talk to him about Priscilla. As I started to dial his number, I heard the chime on the door ding, and quickly set down the phone. Joss and Kurt were back, and Kurt was going to be pissed.

"I'm in the office!" I called out. The sound of heels clicking across the wood floor let me know it wasn't Joss or Kurt.

"Well, looky here. This must be my lucky day. I was hoping to find the bar owners, but this is so much better," Priscilla drawled. She stood in the doorway, smiling. Her lustrous black hair was pulled back in a high ponytail. She had barely a hint of makeup on her perfectly flawless face and was wearing a baby-blue camisole underneath a matching knee-length cardigan. Her skinny jeans fit her like a glove and were tucked into some badass leather high-heel boots. She was everything I wasn't and then some. She and Max complimented each other in looks. The injustice of it made me want to cry. It also made me want to beat her over her gorgeous head with my phone. I felt that was probably a bad idea as I didn't want to have my baby in jail.

Pasting a fake smile on my face, I asked, "Can I help you?"

Not wasting any time, she said, "I had no clue you were interested in Jack when I came into Dragonfly last night."

"Max," I corrected.

She cocked her head. "Pardon?"

"His name is Max," I clarified.

"No, his name *was* Max," she informed me as she delicately perched her ass on the chair across the desk from me. "It's now Jack." She gave me a look that made the hair on the back of my neck bristle, and I knew right then and there something wasn't right with her. "Look," she sighed dramatically, "I know you dated Jack when you were like *fifteen*, and that you had strong feelings for him. I also realize you're having an exceptionally hard time letting go of those...memories, but...Ellie? That's your name, correct?" Without waiting for an answer, she continued, "Jack and I are together and have been for some time now. Dragging him back into the past is both confusing and hurting him. For your own sake as well as his, it's time you let him go."

The longer I stared at her, the more sure I was about Max... about our love. Piper and Joss would know how to diffuse the situation. I, however, did not. I didn't know whether to challenge or placate her. My gut was screaming challenge, while my head was saying placate and get her the hell away from me. Before I could say anything, she leaned forward as if she was going to tell me a secret. Her face was so close I could smell the mint on her breath. I wanted to pull back. I wanted to run from the room screaming. Instead, I squared my shoulders and looked her in the eye.

"I don't want to hurt you, really I don't, but you should know that Jack and I are in a relationship and have been for months," she half-whispered. When I refused to respond, she continued, "Our relationship is extremely healthy, both in and out of the bedroom. Do you understand what I'm telling you?" My shoulders eased when she relaxed back into the chair and crossed her legs. "Now, I don't know about you, but hearing this would make me want to… move on." I had no idea what had transpired between Max and this woman, but one thing was for sure, she was nuttier than a fruitcake.

"I'm confused. If you were with Max the past two nights, where did you stay?" I asked.

A look of unease flickered across her face, but then she rallied. "Why, the garage, of course. The rooms are plush." I knew she was lying, because Max said the furniture wasn't due in until sometime next week. Not only that, but he was in my bed night before last, not hers.

"And the tattoo on his back doesn't bother you?" She gave me a questioning look. "You have seen the tattoo on Max's back, haven't you?"

She licked her lips, and her smile turned wicked. "Oh, I've much more than seen it."

I wanted to slap the smile from her face. Instead, I sucked in a calming breath, and proceeded with my plan of attack. "You do realize that *Ellison Always* refers to me, don't you?" A somewhat pensive look appeared on her face. Mocking her earlier movements, I leaned forward and half-whispered, "He has *Ellison Always* needled permanently onto his back, Priscilla. In case you didn't know, my first name is Ellison. Now, I don't know about you, but that sure would... bother me. "

She flipped her hand nonchalantly through the air. "Jack had that done long before he met me." It was obvious this was a game to her. It wasn't to me. It was my past, present, and future. If I was going to have a future with Max, I needed to know beyond a shadow of doubt, there was nothing going on between him and this awful woman.

"Did you say you were moving to Charlotte? I have to admit, this is a bit awkward and...unconventional, but I'm sure we can figure something out." I told her. Her brow rose in question, and I was happy to fill her in. "Max didn't tell you? He moved in with me just this week." A look of pure hatred rolled across her face. *And the real Prissy comes out to play.* Her eyes narrowed to tiny slits. She reminded me of a viper. I had a feeling that when she struck, it was going to leave a mark.

"Tell me this," she snarled. "If *Jack* loves you so much, *Ellie*," she spat out my name, "then why weren't you the one warming his bed in Kentucky last week?" I couldn't answer this. I was pretty sure it never happened, but being that I wasn't in Kentucky, and hadn't spoken to Max about his trip, I couldn't be sure. She knew she had me. "And if he loves you so much," she continued, "then why am I the one he's been pounding in his office for the past two days?" He may be living with you, but he had me twice Tuesday night and once yesterday, and it was epic!"

I had to admit, this stung. I couldn't help but think about how Max hadn't called much from Kentucky, and when he did call, he was always in a bad mood. On the flip side, there were the loving words he spoke and the gentle way he made love to me the night he returned from Kentucky. But then again, he flinched away from my touch the very next night. This was about the time Prissy claims they were together. From the satisfied look on her face, she knew I was having doubts. Even if she was right, and she and Max had been together, I refused to let her get the best of me. I had an ace up my sleeve that hopefully would give me what I desperately needed – the truth.

"Look…Priscilla. I trust Max. If he tells me I'm the one he wants, then I'm the one he wants, not you. I also trust that when he tells me he loves me, he means it." She smirked, and I wanted to claw her eyes out. "He moved in with me, not you. And when I tell him I'm carrying his child, trust me, he'll be over the moon about it." I protectively placed my hands over my stomach.

Her beautiful face contorted in anger as she shot up out of the chair, and shrieked, "You liar!" There was no doubt in my mind I would have been in a world of hurt had the desk not been between us at that moment.

Ignoring her outburst, I added, "It looks to me, *sugar*, like you're the one who needs to let him go and…move on. Now, I'm done with this conversation. If you don't want me to call the police, then I suggest you leave." I waited for her to retaliate, but instead she burst into loud, messy tears.

I was weighing what to do next, when I heard Max shout, "Ellison!" *Thank God.*

"In the office!" I shouted back.

Max stormed into the office. His eyes landed on me and moved hungrily over my face. When he seemed satisfied I was okay, he turned to where Priscilla was sitting with a pretty fake, tear-stained pout on her face. The heat of his anger was tangible. "First, you showed up in Charlotte unannounced, claiming your dad sent you," he said in a scary *I'm about to lose my shit* voice. "Then, when I called you out and told you to go home, you acted like a spoiled two-year-old. If that wasn't enough, you showed up at Dragonfly knowing good and well who Ellison was to me and fed her a load of bullshit." He clinched his fists. This was very scary Max, and he was seething mad. "What the fuck is wrong with you?"

"Now, Jack, honey-" She reached her hand out to touch him.

He flinched and took a step back. "I never led you on, Priscilla. I told you from the beginning I was in love with someone, and the first chance I got, I was making her mine. You knew this and said you were okay with it. What will it take to get it through your head? We were never going to happen. Will spending some time in jail do it for you? I'm seriously tempted to make that happen."

She gasped. "You don't mean that, Jack."

She reached for him again, and again, he took a step back. "I don't? Is that why I told you no more? Is that why I haven't touched you in months? Is that why I had to get your dad to come and get you not once, but twice from the garage?" Priscilla's eyes darted to me and narrowed into slits. *Uh oh.*

"If you don't want me, then why did you sleep with me in Kentucky? Why didn't you tell me no the past two days in your office?"

Max's brows lifted in disbelief. "Are you shitting me?" he quietly challenged.

"Ellie should know what's been happening behind her back. Sh-"

Max held up his hand, and asked, "How did you know I was in Kentucky, Cilla?" She blanched. "Holy fucking shit! It was you, wasn't it? You tried to break in to the garage, and when you couldn't, you decided to torch it. Why?"

"I have no idea what you're talking about," she defiantly replied.

His jaw hardened, and his eyes shot to me. "For the record, we were in my office all of ten minutes the first day and twenty the second. Both times, the door remained open and our conversations were recorded." He turned back to Priscilla and in a low menacing voice said, "You have no idea who you're fucking with." He reached into his back pocket, pulled out his phone, dialed a number, and began talking. "Mark, this is Max McLellan. Yeah, I was hoping it wouldn't come to this, but Priscilla Newman is back and is at Dragonfly right now. I need you to come and get her. She's the one who torched my garage in Kentucky, and now she's harassing Ellison. I want her in a cell until her dad picks her up. Before you let him take her, you need to let her know what will happen if she ever steps foot in Charlotte again."

"Jack!" Cilla shouted.

After exchanging a few words about a restraining order, he hung up. His eyes remained on me the whole time he was on the phone. After shoving his phone into his back pocket, he stalked across the room, reached across the desk to where I was sitting, and snatched my hand. "Police will be here to get you shortly," he said to Priscilla. Then he pulled me onto my feet. That's when I noticed Kurt and Joss standing in the doorway watching us. "You two good to watch her until the police show?" Max asked.

"We got it, man," Kurt assured. "Go take care of your girl." We were halfway across the bar before I began to process what had just happened.

"Do you record all of your conversations in your office?" I asked.

"All the ones with Priscilla Newman, I do. I don't trust her and never have," he replied.

"How exactly did you record her?"

"The first thing I did after purchasing the garage was have the office wired."

The drive home was painfully quiet. If I'd pushed Max to talk about his past that day at the quarry, this never would have happened, and I wouldn't be sitting here now feeling like a complete fool.

As we pulled into the driveway, I asked, "Who's Mark?"

He turned off the ignition and let out a wary sounding sigh. "Mark is Detective Copeland's first name." This surprised me.

"When did you talk to Detective Copeland?"

"Right after you told me what an ass-hat he'd been to you, and again after Cilla showed up in Charlotte."

"Oh."

Before I could stall any longer, Max was out the door and heading around to my side of the car to get me. He looked tired. Neither of us spoke a word as we entered the house. As we stepped into the bedroom, I turned to apologize, but saw his pained expression, and quickly swallowed my words. His beautiful blue eyes scanned slowly over my body, and I felt a pang of guilt. *He was really worried about me.*

"I'm okay, Max. It took a minute, but I finally realized she was one donut shy of a dozen. I-"

"I did this to you," he cut me off. I could hear the pain and regret in his voice.

"I'm okay Max, really," I assured him. A part of me wanted to let him off the hook, but before I did, I had to hear it all. I wasn't sure I was strong enough to deal with a future filled with psycho ex-girlfriends.

As Max slumped on the edge of the bed, he reached out, hooked his arm around my waist, and pulled me in for a tight hug. *I need to tell him I'm pregnant.*

"I should have told you about Cilla. I should have warned you this could happen. That's one hundred percent on me, but you running away without talking to me? I don't get that." His words stung. I disengaged from his arms, and took a step back.

The hurt and anger I'd been living with for the past few days came rushing back, and I lashed out at him. "Last night while I was working, a beautiful woman came in asking for Jack

Barnett. Imagine my surprise when she said she was with you that day and the night before - the very same night you blew me off at the bar, and flinched when I touched you in bed - the same day I called and texted you all day long, but you didn't feel the need to respond. Imagine my surprise when she recognized Gage… from your trip to Texas. The one you took *together*. And to think, that was just a mere few months before you showed up here and swept me off my feet…after five years of being gone from my life. How was I supposed to act, Max?"

"Are you finished?"

"What?" I asked, surprised by his harsh tone.

"Are. You. Finished?" Before I could answer, he said, "I thought you knew me. I see I was wrong." His calm, angry tone made my stomach knot. "'Cause if you knew me at all, you would know that never, in a million…fucking…years, would I intentionally hurt you. But, since you obviously don't know me, I'm going to clue you in, babe. Cilla's dad brought his truck in to the garage to be serviced about a year ago. Cilla picked it up when it was done and was not hard to look at." My heart squeezed. "She saw me and decided she wanted me." *I do not want to hear this,* I thought. "Look at me!" Max growled, and my eyes shot to his. He was really, really angry. "I did not want her, but she wouldn't let it go," he continued. "Four months later, I was at a bar with my crew from MMG. We'd been doing shots all night and were pretty shit-faced, when Cilla and some of her friends came in. The next thing I knew, we were back at her place doing more shots. One thing led to another and I slept with her." Jealous anger pulsed through me. I knew he wasn't with me then, but that didn't mean he wasn't mine. In my mind he'd always been mine. When he pulled me onto his lap, I didn't even attempt to stop the tears. "I laid it out to her from square one, Ells. She knew she was nothing but a good time to me. She never slept at my place, and I sure as hell didn't sleep at hers."

This hurt to hear, but I needed the closure in order to move on. "If you knew you were coming back to me, why did you take her to Texas?" I tearfully asked.

His brow wrinkled in confusion. "I didn't take her to Texas. Is that what she told you?" he shook his head, and muttered, "Stupid, lying bitch. Her dad was the reason for the trip. I was wrapping things up with the Witness Protection Program and preparing to make my move to get back here to you when an associate of mine offloaded five trucks at MMG in Texas. Next thing I knew, Cilla's dad had me on the phone. He needed some trucks for his crew and offered me a load of money to facilitate the purchase and move the trucks for him. I didn't have time for that shit. The deal was that he, Nolen, and I would go to Texas to finalize the details. I had to charter a private plane so I could be home the next day. When we got to the plane, Cilla was there instead of Ted. That's how she ended up in Texas with me."

"So you weren't together?"

He pulled back and looked into my eyes. "We were never together, Ellison. I only slept with her a handful of times. In fact, by the time Texas happened, I hadn't been with her in months."

"She said you two have been a couple for the past eight months."

"She lied. Look at me, baby." When he had my eyes, he continued. "At first I thought Cilla was a sweet girl. I thought she wanted me, because I presented a challenge for her. She'd clearly never been turned down before. As time went by, she kept at it. Believe me, she was persistent. Then I made the mistake of sleeping with her. It was the biggest mistake I ever made."

I rolled my eyes at him. "But yet you kept doing it."

"I did for a while. I needed a release. She was there, and that was it."

His words disgusted me. "That's crude, Max."

"You wanted the truth, Ellison. You can't be mad at me for

giving it to you."

"Why did you flinch when I touched you the other night? Why did you ignore my calls and texts?"

"I didn't realize I flinched, and I wasn't avoiding you. Cilla showed up at MMG Tuesday evening. I was far from happy to see her and made that very clear. She gave me some bullshit story about how her dad had sent her there to talk business because he was too busy. I told her I couldn't talk to her right then, but I had some time first thing the next morning. As soon as she left, I called Nolen and asked him to find out the real story. Then I came to Dragonfly to see you. While I was with you Nolen sent me a text. Ted had no idea Cilla was in Charlotte. This worried me. I knew she would try to fuck things up between us. You were crazy busy tending bar and I needed to think, so I left early. If I flinched, it was probably because I was worried and all in my head about Priscilla being in town. The next day, I wanted to get in to MMG early to prepare for my meeting with her. When I got to the garage, I realized my phone was dead, so I put it on the charger in my office and completely forgot about it."

"Were you ever going to tell me about her?"

"No."

"Really?"

"There was nothing to tell. She meant nothing to me. Why risk upsetting you over nothing?"

"Did she know about me?"

"The first time I was with Cilla, I told her that unfortunate circumstances split me from the girl I was going to spend the rest of my life with. I made sure she understood that when I got the chance, I would move heaven and earth to get that girl back. She knew she would never be anything to me but a distraction, and it didn't take long for me to get tired of that distraction. When I told her it was over, she threw the mother of all fits. I spent time I didn't have calming her down and making sure she was okay. A week or so later, she was at it again. I wasn't as nice the second time. In fact, she pissed me off to the point I had to call her dad and tell him to come and get her."

"Let me get this straight. You called her dad to tell him his daughter was freaking out because you informed her you would no longer service her sexual needs?" I tried not to laugh at the visual in my head.

"When you put it like that, it sounds ridiculous. Hell, it was ridiculous. She has a major screw loose, and I didn't realize how loose it was until I tried to get out. I was hoping her dad would help."

"Did he?"

"He did. In fact, he told me this wasn't the first time Cilla had 'fixated' on something."

"Oh, wow."

"Yeah. Her dad said she wouldn't bother me again, but then she showed up here in Charlotte claiming she's on an errand for him." He shook his head. "I told her if she didn't want me calling her dad, she'd better march her ass straight out of my office and back to Kentucky. I didn't want to see her ever again."

"But instead, she came straight over to Dragonfly," I grumbled.

"When I showed up at Dragonfly, Gage and the boys were sitting at the bar. The icy reception I received tipped me off that something was wrong. Dillon said you'd left early, but wouldn't tell me anything else. I powered up my phone, saw that I had several missed messages, and started to panic. I called your dad, who told me you weren't there. When Joss and Piper wouldn't tell me anything, I lost it."

"I heard."

He gave me a guilty smile. "Your turn."

I explained what happened from the time I woke up Wednesday morning to now, minus the doctor visit.

"Can't say I'm happy you turned to Dillon, but seeing as Piper and Joss were both there, I'll learn to deal with it.

I smiled back at him. "That's big of you."

"One more thing, Ellison, and then we're moving on." I could tell by his tone of voice that I wasn't going to like what he was about to say. "I want to know why it's so damn hard for you to believe you're the *only* one I want? This is going to be a problem for us unless I can get to the root of it." He brushed his fingers down my face. When he got to my chin, he tipped it up, looked deep into my eyes, and said, "Talk to me."

Placing my hands on either side of his face, I tenderly kissed him. "I love you, Max McLellan. You are everything to me and you always have been." I could feel the tears well. "There will never be another for me, and Lord knows, I've learned this the hard way. I got scared and overreacted. You, too, are my end game." His breath caught, but before he could take over, I had one last thing to say. "The day before yesterday, I went to the doctor for my yearly exam. While I was there, we discovered that my period was late by almost two weeks." His eyes widened in shock, and his jaw dropped, but he didn't say anything, so I kept going. "Apparently, taking an antibiotic while on the pill renders it ineffective, and I had been taking one for seven days the first night we slept together."

He grabbed my face between his hands and asked, "You're having my baby?"

"Yes," I nodded.

He pulled back, shifted his hands to my belly, and blew out a huge breath. "Holy shit."

I couldn't tell if this was a happy or unhappy 'holy shit,' so I explained. "I was upset because five seconds after I found out I was pregnant, Priscilla showed up claiming to be your girlfriend."

"We're done with that," he muttered. "Let's go back to you

having my baby." He glanced up from my belly, and gave me a heart-stopping smile.

"You're happy about this?" I needed to make sure he was on board.

"Hell, yes! I've been in love with you since I was eighteen, Ellison. I've dreamt about you having my babies. Of course, I planned on marrying you first, but I'm not complaining. You becoming my wife and having my babies is all I've thought about for the past five years. I told you that you were my end game, and I should spank your ass for not believing me." He smiled wolfishly. "That'll have to wait until you're no longer carrying my baby." I rolled my eyes, and he burst out laughing.

# CHAPTER THIRTY-TWO

We were in the mood to celebrate, so we invited my dad, Piper and Benny all out for Thai food. Piper squealed and launched herself into my arms, Benny patted Max on the back, and my sweet dad got a little teary-eyed when we told them the news. It's not every day you find out you're going to be a grandpa. *Looks as if we all get a second chance.*

On the way home we stopped by Dragonfly for a celebratory drink. *And for Max to gloat in front of Dillon about knocking me up.*

Finally we made it home. We'd barely made it through the door before Max had me stripped and on my back. He took care of me first with his mouth. Needing more, I pulled him up, rolled him onto his back, and started riding him. "I need to go faster, harder," I panted. Max had his hands on my hips. He stared down at my belly as he controlled my every move. I tried to speed up, but he kept me at a leisurely pace. *Seriously?* I was starting to get frustrated. "If I'd known you were going to go all grampy on me, I would have held off on telling you about the baby," I complained. I was about to whip out my vibrator, when he flipped me onto my back, wrapped my legs around his waist, and carefully sunk back in. I grabbed his face and forced him to look at me. "You're killing me here," I told him as I tried not to give in. The look of desire shining from his eyes and the rocking of his hips was mind-melting, but I needed for him to understand he wasn't going to hurt me or the baby. I also needed some good, toe-curling sex. "I really need this, Max, and only you can give it to me. So, please, please give…it…to…me."

"I don't want to hurt you or the baby," he ground out. I could tell he was holding on by a thread.

"You won't. I promise." He ran his tongue over my lips and slightly deepened his thrust. There was no way in hell I was going to put up with this for eight more months. I slid my hands up his back and tightly gripped the tops of his shoulders. Then I brushed my sensitive nipples against his muscular chest while at the same time pulling up into his downward thrust. His head tipped down and his eyes locked on mine. "Again," I gasped and let out a throaty moan. He closed his eyes, cursed under his breath, and I knew I had him. He gave it to me again, except this time, it was hard and deep and exactly what I needed. Suddenly, I was there. "I'm there, Max." Three thrusts later, he buried his face in my neck, let out a long guttural moan, and poured himself into me. I gave myself a silent pat on the back.

As we lay in bed, I watched Max rub his hand up and down my belly and couldn't help but smile. I ran my fingers through his hair and quietly confessed what was on my mind. "Priscilla got to me when she said you'd had sex with her at MMG. I know I shouldn't have believed her, yet I started thinking about our lack of communication and how I hadn't even seen the garage, and I let what she said get to me."

His eyes slid from my belly up to my face, and I glanced away. "Look at me," he softly demanded. I shifted my gaze back to him. "I would never have done that to you, but I get why you doubted me. This is all new to us both. I forgot that. I should have been more open and more cautious in dealing with her. That's on me, and I promise it's a mistake I won't repeat. Kurt watched her leave, and I filed an application for a restraining order against her. It's over. I promise. As for the garage," he shrugged, "I didn't want you to see it until it was finished."

I arched my eyebrow at him, and asked, "Are there anymore scary, psychotic women from your past I should be aware of?"

He smiled and touched his mouth to mine. I took that as a no.

Max and I spent the next few days helping my dad move into his new condo. Max was worried about me bartending while pregnant, and since Piper still didn't have a job and Max didn't have a manager for MMG Charlotte, he came up with a plan. He proposed that I help him run MMG until the baby was born and Piper take my place bartending at Dragonfly. Apparently, this plan suited Piper, because not even three seconds after Max had presented it, she was on the phone with Kurt setting up bartending lessons.

Joss picked teal green as the color of her bridesmaids' dresses. Now that I had put on some pregnancy weight, mine was a little snug. A month ago, it fit perfectly and barely accentuated my chest. Now, it looked obscene. Max loved it, of course. He couldn't keep his hands off of me, and every time he talked about how much he wanted to tag me in it, he earned himself an eye roll.

Max in a tuxedo was a sight to see. I almost cried when he came home with his hair cut short, but he quickly got me over it. He was a gorgeously sexy badass in his dinner jacket, sporting his new haircut, and a five o'clock shadow. *And he's all mine.*

The wedding went off without a hitch. Joss looked stunning in her dress and was the happiest I'd ever seen her. Kurt? Well, Kurt, like Max, was just hot.

After the ceremony, while waiting for the photographer to finish up, I watched how seamlessly Max fit back in with everyone. He was even getting along with Dillon. I'm sure my being pregnant and madly in love with him had a little something to do with it. Finally, we followed the bride and groom up a flight of stairs to the reception.

The table decorations and flowers were amazing, but what made the night, other than two of my best friends getting hitched, was the music. Ben Edwards, Dillon Whitaker, and Mass Seduction were all three playing together, and it was brilliant.

I was on the dance floor with Polly and Lena when I glanced outside and spotted Piper and Gage on the balcony. From their body language it looked like they were arguing, but when I glanced back a minute later, they were gone. *I knew there was something up with those two.* Gage was a good guy. I couldn't imagine him ever hurting Piper. Before I could further investigate, the music paused for the cutting of the cake. While Joss and Kurt were shoving cake into each other's faces, I scanned the room for Max. Dillon, Lena, and Polly were laughing at something Dillon had said, while Harry and Garrett were conversing at the bar, and my dad was trying to cheer up a glowering Piper. Max was nowhere to be seen. Just then, the lead singer of Mass Seduction started strumming his guitar. When I recognized the song, my heart flip-flopped in my chest and my breath caught in my throat.

"All I Want Is You".

The words to this song were permanently etched into my heart. Every time I heard it, I thought about the night we danced, before Max disappeared. Suddenly, he was standing in front of me. Our eyes met, and he held out his hand. My pulse spiked. *God, I love this man.*

"Did you plan this?" I asked as he swept me onto the dance floor.

"Mmmmm - maybe."

"I can't believe I am here…dancing with you…to this song." I barely managed to get out.

"Shhh," he whispered as he pulled me close and quietly sang the words to the song in my ear while dancing us around the floor. Feeling him pressed firmly against me with his hands on my body while singing this song made my heart ache. I wanted him here with me…like this…forever.

"Oh, Max," I sighed and planted my face in his chest. He tipped his head down to look at me. I swallowed deeply as I looked up into his beautiful eyes, and allowed him to see the power he held over my heart.

His eyes moved over my face. "You believe it now, don't you?" he quietly asked.

"Believe what?"

"That you're my end game."

"I believe it Max," I barely managed to say through my tears.

Placing his hands on either side of my face, he leaned in, and slowly touched his lips to mine. "You…are…mine," he whispered against my lips. "Let me hear you say it."

"I am yours."

He stepped back and placed his hands on my belly. "This… is…mine," he declared. "Say it, Ellison."

I put my hands on top of his. "This is yours."

"Come," he said, and held out his hand. I took it and was whisked from the dance floor, and into a quiet side room. "I told

Kurt that I wouldn't do this until the time was right."

My breath hitched. "Do what?"

"I've been waiting a long time for you to get that you're mine, babe. I've always known this, but somewhere along the way, you forgot. I knew from the moment I saw you in Dragonfly's parking lot that it was going to take some work to make you remember. I've gotta say, my gorgeous girl, you have made me work for it." *What?*

I opened my mouth to protest, but was silenced by a kiss. "I am crazy in love with you, Ellison Elizabeth Davis, and have been for as long as I can remember." *Oh, God.* I blinked back the tears. "I've told you time and again that you're my end game. When we danced, just now, you showed me you finally fucking get it. I love you. I want to take care of you. I will never leave you. I will protect you and our children," he paused, cut his eyes to my belly, and continued, "for as long as I breathe. Tell me you get this." The love in his eyes for me was staggering.

"I get it Max," I whispered through my tears. *I so get it.*

"About fucking time," he muttered. Before I could get a word in, he reached down into his pants pocket and dropped to his knee. *OhGodohGodohGod.* "I want our forever, Ellison. Will you give it to me?"

"Yes," I sobbed, "I will give you our forever, Max."

He stood back up and took my hand in his. "This was my mom's. My dad gave it to her when he wanted a forever with her. This ring represents the good before the bad. I want you to wear it, because, other than the brief time my mom was alive, you are the best thing that has ever happened to me. We've already had our bad, so now begins our good." The ring was an exquisite round diamond surrounded by sapphires. He slid it onto my finger. Then he leaned down and gave me a soul scorching kiss. My heart belonged to this man.

"From the bottom of my soul, I love you, Max McLellan."

He smiled. "I would have followed you to the ends of the Earth, if that's what it took to make you mine. Promise you'll love me always?"

I touched my mouth to his and smiled. "I promise I will love you always."

The End

# ACKNOWLEDGEMENTS

Getting married, giving birth, and writing this book are among my biggest accomplishments....so far.

Susannah and Sarah ~ Thank you for being with Ellie and Max from conception to birth, and for loving them as much as I do. Thank you for your incredible feedback, patience and generosity with your time.

My Beta Babes ~ Susannah, Sarah, Laura, KC, and Elizabeth – There aren't enough words to express my thanks to you all for taking time out of your busy lives for Max and Ellie. I am forever grateful to you all for your invaluable input.

Lisa Capps ~ Thank you for being my cover model, and for allowing me to photograph you a million times. You make a hot Ellie!

My husband and editor ~You may have blown past three deadlines, but you Got. The. Job. Done! There are no words to express how grateful I am. You never doubted me for a second and proved, once again, we make a great team. I love you to pieces.

Stay tuned for Piper and Gage's story!

# OTHER BOOKS BY RB HILLIARD

Not Letting Go
One More Time
Right Side Up
Keep It Simple
The Last Call
Utterly Forgettable
Fractured Beat
Broken Lyric
Shattered Rhythm

www.ingramcontent.com/pod-product-compliance
Lightning Source LLC
Chambersburg PA
CBHW060156260626
47160CB00001B/293